"A sweet yarn about magic gone awry and a young noble's coming-of-age through adversity.... Swiftly paced, with likable characters." —*Publishers Weekly*

"Watt-Evans brings new life to his popular Ethshar series with a tale of wizardry and witticisms that belongs in most fantasy collections." —*Library Journal*

"Fine ideas and fascinating developments."
—*Kirkus Reviews*

"This fast-paced novel, full of magical people and mysterious forces, goes beyond pure entertainment to confront many real issues. The characters grapple with prejudice, fear, and the ideas of personal and societal responsibilities." —*VOYA*

"A lighter, but fascinating fantasy . . . this tale is quite fun."
—*Philadelphia's Weekly Press*

"The Estshar series is fairly loosely connected, and thus any of the books can be read as a standalone. This one—a well-crafted, entertainingly told story—would be a fine place to start." —*Asimov's*

Tor Books by Lawrence Watt-Evans

Night of Madness
Dragon Weather
Touched by the Gods

Split Heirs (with Esther Friesner)

Night of
MADNESS

Lawrence Watt-Evans

A TOM DOHERTY ASSOCIATES BOOK
NEW YORK

This is a work of fiction. All the characters and events portrayed in this book are either products of the author's imagination or are used fictitiously.

NIGHT OF MADNESS

Copyright © 2000 by Lawrence Watt-Evans

A Tor Book
Published by Tom Doherty Associates, LLC
175 Fifth Avenue
New York, NY 10010

www.tor.com

Tor® is a registered trademark of Tom Doherty Associates, LLC.

ISBN: 0-812-57794-9
Library of Congress Catalog Card Number: 00-031681

First edition: November 2000
First mass market edition: January 2002

Printed in the United States of America

0 9 8 7 6 5 4 3 2 1

Dedicated to my daughter,
Kiri Evans,
who is an endless source of delight

Chapter One

Lord Hanner was panting slightly as he hurried across the plaza toward the red stone bridge that led into the Palace. He'd had a long, busy day and had been moving at a constant fast walk for over a mile, his bones carrying more weight than they should, so it was no surprise that his breathing was a bit heavy as he trotted across the brick pavement.

Perhaps that was why the stench of decay rising from the Grand Canal, which he had scarcely noticed when he set out that morning, hit him so strongly. That the tide was now out, so that the water level in the sea-fed canal was a foot or two lower than it had been when he left, might also have contributed.

Whatever the cause, his steps slowed, and he swallowed hard. The reek of dead fish and rotting vegetation was overpowering—and hardly appropriate for the immediate environs of the seat of the city's government and the official residence of the overlord of Ethshar of the Spices. The golden marble of the palace walls glowed beautifully in the light of the setting sun; the dark red brick of the plaza complemented it nicely; the sky above was a lovely blue streaked with pink and white wisps of cloud—and the whole scene stank like an ill-kept fishmarket. The city's usual smells of smoke, spices, and people were completely smothered.

The guards on the bridge and the well-dressed strollers in the square did not appear troubled by the smell, but there were not quite as many strollers as Hanner would have expected at this hour on a beautiful summer day.

This lovely afternoon was the fourth day of Summerheat;

so far this year the month had not lived up to its name, and the weather was mild. Hanner was sweating, his tunic sticking to his back, but from exertion, not the day's heat.

Hanner waved a hand in front of his nose, trying unsuccessfully to dispel the odor, as he kept walking, more slowly now, toward the bridge. "Confound it," he muttered to himself. "Someone's not doing his job here."

He tried to remember who was in charge of seeing that the canal was cleaned regularly; wouldn't that be the responsibility of Clurim, Lord of the Household—and, not incidentally, one of the overlord's younger brothers? Or was there some other, lesser official whose job description specifically included handling such things as seeing that the canal was cleaned?

Hanner couldn't remember. He was a resident of the Palace and a hereditary noble, so he was acquainted with most of the city's officials and functionaries, but right now he could not think who was responsible for the regular purification of the Grand Canal.

Uncle Faran would know, of course; the simplest thing for Hanner to do would be to mention it to him. In fact, the chances were good that Lord Faran had already noticed the stench, and that the magicians who would perform the purification spells were already on their way. After all, Faran's windows, like all the windows in the Palace, overlooked the canal.

That did assume, of course, that Lord Faran hadn't allowed himself to be so distracted by other matters that he was ignoring his surroundings and leaving such minor mundane details unattended. Hanner certainly *hoped* his uncle wasn't shirking his duties while he once again pursued his obsession—or rather while he waited for Hanner to pursue it.

Ethshar could ill afford to have Lord Faran, chief advisor to Lord Azrad the Sedentary, neglecting his duties, since the overlord had long since turned most of the city's day-to-day administration over to his chief advisor.

Hanner picked up his pace again, trotting across the

bridge without a glance at the stonework, barely nodding at the guards on either side.

"Who comes . . ." one began, lifting his ceremonial spear; then he recognized Lord Hanner and let the spear fall back into place.

In the palace entryway Hanner had to stop and wait impatiently while the additional guards there went through their rigmarole of signs and countersigns before opening the door. The captain watched his men, but remarked, "A pleasure to see you, Lord Hanner."

Hanner did not deign to reply, though he did wave an acknowledgment. He had spent the entire day roaming the city and talking to strangers, at his uncle's orders, and he really did not want to talk to anyone else just now—not that the captain, a man named Vengar, was another stranger; he was the commander of the guard detachment inside the Palace, and Hanner had known him slightly when Vengar was still a lieutenant, since before Hanner himself was old enough for breeches.

At last the soldiers inside acknowledged that the person requesting admission wasn't an invader and swung open the heavy, iron-bound doors. "Thank you," Hanner said as he hurried past them into the central hallway.

That passage was twenty feet wide and twenty-five feet high, floored with tessellated marble and hung with rich tapestries, and it led directly to the ornately worked golden doors of the overlord's main audience chamber. Hanner barely even glanced at that display of grandeur; instead he immediately turned right and stepped through a small wooden door into one of Lord Clurim's offices. There he merely waved to the clerk at the desk before proceeding on through, emerging into a narrow corridor and heading for his own family's quarters.

Had Lord Clurim been present Hanner would have mentioned the smell, but he knew from unhappy experience that telling the clerk would result not in a prompt cleaning, but in assorted messages wandering about the building, accomplishing nothing but the annoyance of other clerks.

Hanner wound his way through a maze of passages and antechambers and two flights of stairs before arriving, finally, at Lord Faran's apartments—the apartments Hanner and his two sisters had shared with their uncle since their mother's death two years before. He paused at the door to catch his breath, then straightened his silk-trimmed tunic, opened the door, and stepped into Lord Faran's sitting room.

His uncle was standing there, resplendent in a fine cloak of dark green velvet that hardly seemed appropriate to the season, while Hanner's sister Lady Alris, wearing a faded blue tunic and dark-patterned skirt, sat in the window seat, ignoring the beautiful weather beyond the glass as she glowered at Hanner and Faran. Their other sister, Lady Nerra, was not in sight.

Lord Faran's cloak was clearly for appearance, not warmth. Faran was, as always, elegant and graceful; and as always, Hanner was reminded of his own shorter stature and heavier build. He was not, he frequently told himself, actually *fat*, but he was definitely well rounded—quite unlike his trim, handsome uncle. Hanner had taken after his long-vanished father's side of the family.

Lord Faran spoke before Hanner could. "Ah, Hanner," he said. "I have a dinner engagement, so I can't spare more than a moment just now, but I must know if you learned anything important."

"I noticed that the canal stinks," Hanner blurted.

Faran smiled wryly. "I'll see to it before I leave," he said. "Anything else?"

"Not really," Hanner admitted. "I interviewed almost a dozen magicians, and none of them reported any threats or abuse from the Wizards' Guild."

"You asked Mother Perréa?"

"I spoke to her and her partner," Hanner said. "She insisted that it was her own decision to limit herself to witchcraft and not accept her father's post as magistrate. The Guild's rules had nothing to do with it."

"Either that or she was sufficiently terrified that even now she won't speak of it," Faran said, frowning.

"She didn't appear at all nervous," Hanner said.

"You'll have to tell me more later," Faran said. "If I'm to chastise Lord Clurim for the state of the canal and still reach my destination in time, I can't spare another second here."

"What's her name?" Hanner asked, smiling as he stepped aside.

"Isia, I think," Faran replied, his frown vanishing. Then he swirled past Hanner and was gone.

Hanner listened to the footsteps retreating down the hallway for a moment before closing the door. Then he turned to Alris.

"He's off again," Alris said before Hanner could speak. "As usual. He spends more nights away than he does here."

Hanner knew that was, at most, only a slight exaggeration. "It's not our business if he does," he said.

"You can say that because he's never dragged you along," Alris said. "He insists I have to *meet* people."

"He sends me out to meet them on my own, instead," Hanner said. "I don't see that as much better."

"You don't have to stand there looking innocent while the great man seduces some poor woman who's dazzled by his title." She picked at a loose thread on her skirt and said, "I don't *want* to meet people."

"Have you ever told Uncle Faran that?"

"Of course I have! But he doesn't pay any attention." She looked up from the thread. "You'll get to meet his latest conquest."

"I will?"

"He told me this one wants to see the inside of the Palace, so he'll probably be bringing her up here."

"And he'll probably want us to stay out of the way," Hanner said. "She won't be coming to meet *us*."

"Which is a good thing. She's probably stupid. Most of them are."

Hanner did not want to argue about their uncle's taste in

women, so he attempted to change the subject. "Where's Nerra?" he asked.

Alris gestured toward the passage to their bedchambers. "In there somewhere," she said. "She and Mavi were talking about clothes again, and I got bored."

"Mavi's here?" Hanner tried not to sound too pleased. While he generally didn't think much of his sisters' friends, Mavi of Newmarket was an exception. Nerra had met her while shopping for fabrics in the Old Merchants' Quarter, and the two had quickly become close; Hanner admired Mavi's generosity of spirit and lively interest in almost everything. And her fine features, charming smile, shapely figure, and long lustrous hair didn't lower Hanner's opinion a bit.

Alris nodded. "She's boring," she said. "Like Nerra."

Hanner grimaced. Alris was thirteen and thought everything was boring.

Or almost everything; like Uncle Faran, she was fascinated with magic. She had tried for months to convince Faran to apprentice her to a magician, but he had refused, on the grounds that she might well inherit or marry into an important position in the government of the Hegemony of the Three Ethshars—but that she could not take such a position if she were a magician.

Hanner suspected that Uncle Faran might well intend to marry Alris off to some important politician, as much for his own advancement as hers; as Alris said, she and Nerra were often taken along on Faran's travels, while Hanner never was.

Any such intention got no support from Alris herself. She had argued that she didn't *want* a government position or a prestigious marriage, but as usual their uncle had prevailed, and now that she was six weeks past her thirteenth birthday she was too old to be properly apprenticed to anyone, magician or otherwise.

So now she spent her time moping around the Palace, being bored and disagreeable.

"You were talking to magicians all day, weren't you?" Alris demanded.

"Most of it, yes," Hanner agreed. "Three witches, a theurgist, two sorcerers, and four different wizards."

"Did any of them show you any magic?"

"Not really," Hanner lied. One sorcerer and two of the wizards had shown him a number of spells and talismans, and one of the witches had read his mind and offered to heal some of the discomfort in his soul.

Hanner did not have any discomfort he wanted cured, so he had refused the offer. He suspected that whatever he might have cluttering up his soul was the result of his dissatisfaction with his own actions, and he wanted that left intact, to give him incentive to do better in the future.

"I'll bet they did," Alris said enviously. "You just aren't admitting it."

Before Hanner could reply he heard footsteps; he turned to see Nerra and Mavi emerging from Nerra's bedchamber.

Nerra was five years younger than Hanner's twenty-three years, five years older than Alris, and like her siblings a little shorter than average. While not as stocky as Hanner, she was definitely heavier than Alris.

Mavi, on the other hand, was an inch or so taller than Hanner, and shaped very nicely indeed, in Hanner's opinion—though of course he would never dare tell her so.

"I thought I heard your voice," Nerra said. "Has Uncle Faran gone?"

"He just left," Hanner replied.

"Does he still think the Wizards' Guild is plotting to take over the World?"

Hanner sighed. "Something like that," he admitted.

"*Are* they plotting to take over the World?" Mavi asked with a sly smile. "Have you found any evidence of their dire schemes?"

"They're enforcing their rules, just as they always have," Hanner said wearily. "No mixing different sorts of magic. No mixing magic and government."

"It's stupid," Alris said from the window. "Why should they care?"

"They don't want anyone getting too powerful," Hanner explained, as he had several times before—but never in Mavi's hearing, which was why he continued. "After all, some wizards live for centuries—if the overlord were to live that long, who knows what he might do?"

Mavi and Nerra looked at each other, then burst out laughing. Hanner blushed. "Not *our* overlord," he said. "I don't think Lord Azrad the Sedentary would ever get much done no matter *how* long he lived. But imagine if the *first* Lord Azrad were still alive, and had had two hundred years . . ."

"What if he had?" Alris demanded. "What business is it of the Guild's? *I* wouldn't mind if old Azrad the Great were still running things!"

"Uncle Faran would mind," Nerra said. "He couldn't order everyone around the way he does if Azrad the Great were the overlord."

"Who cares?" Alris said. "The overlord is sixty-seven. Someday he's going to choke to death on a fishbone or something, and then Azrad the Younger will be Azrad VII, and he'll probably throw Uncle Faran out anyway. They don't like each other very much."

"And suppose that the overlord had some sort of magic that would let him live for hundreds of years—what would Azrad the Younger do?" Hanner asked. "Just *wait*?"

"He might just find another job," Mavi suggested.

"Or he might hire a wizard or a demonologist to assassinate his father."

"Lord Azrad wouldn't do that," Nerra protested.

"He can't," Alris said. "The Wizards' Guild would kill any magician who agreed to assassinate a government official."

"But we're assuming the Guild isn't enforcing their rules anymore," Hanner said.

"It's stupid," Alris said. "It's a stupid assumption, because they *are* enforcing their stupid rules, and Uncle Faran can't make them change that."

"And this is a stupid argument," Nerra said. "I'm hungry—is the overlord dining in state tonight?"

"I don't think so," Hanner said.

"Then let's go down to the kitchens and get ourselves some supper. I don't want to eat here, and besides, Uncle Faran would probably rather we aren't here when he brings his current woman in."

"True enough," Hanner agreed. He looked longingly at the couch by the wall—his feet hurt, and he would have liked to rest them briefly—but turned and led the way to the door. He was as hungry as Nerra, and he could rest his feet when they got to the kitchens—three flights down and a hundred yards to the west, beneath the great hall.

The vast and cavernous kitchens were swarming with servants and courtiers, preparing, transporting, and consuming a variety of fine foods. One table was roped off, with a guard standing nearby—that was where the master chef was making the overlord's dinner.

The overlord was traditionally expected to dine in the great audience hall, with his family and courtiers gathered about him, but Azrad VI had never wanted to put that much effort into his meals; he preferred to eat in his apartments with a few close advisors—usually his brothers and Lord Faran, if Faran was around. That left the other occupants of the Palace free to make their own arrangements.

Lord Faran often dined elsewhere, in the mansions of various important figures or the homes of various women, but Hanner's sisters were only rarely invited, and Hanner himself even less often. Helping themselves from the stocks of food in the kitchens had become commonplace.

The party of four collected a roasted hen, a bottle of Aldagmor wine, and a plateful of vegetables and sweet rolls, then found themselves a quiet corner and settled cross-legged on the floor. There they ate, chatted, and watched the bustle around them. Hanner noticed buckets of offal being dumped out a window into the canal and remarked, "There's one reason the water stinks."

"It certainly does stink, doesn't it?" Mavi said. "I think the last cleaning spell didn't work properly."

"You can't trust magic," Nerra said. "It's unreliable. At least, Uncle Faran says it is."

Alris snorted derisively.

"Maybe that's another reason the Wizards' Guild wants to keep magic and government separate," Mavi said.

Hanner shook his head. "I don't think that's it," he said. "Wizardry isn't any less reliable than anything else, really."

"That's wizardry," Nerra said. "What about the other magicks? Uncle Faran is obsessed with *all* of them, even if it's the wizards who particularly annoy him."

"The Guild doesn't want *any* magicks combined," Alris said.

"But *is* wizardry less reliable?" Mavi asked. "I hadn't heard that."

Hanner turned up a palm. "I think it depends what you want to do," he said. "The theurgists certainly don't claim to be infallible, and plenty of prayers go unanswered, but they always seem to be able to get certain things done. I never saw anyone die of a fever in a theurgist's care."

A sudden brief silence fell, and Hanner realized what he had just said. Nerra and Alris stared at him in silent shock, but Mavi asked, "How many people have you seen die of fevers anywhere?"

"Our *mother*," Nerra said angrily, shoving her plate aside. "He saw our mother waste away with a fever. And the magicians wouldn't help because she was Lady Illira, Lord Faran's sister. They would have used their spells for a shopkeeper or a sailor or even some stinking beggar from the Hundred-Foot Field, but anyone with a hereditary title or ties to the overlord, no—the wizards wouldn't allow it." She glanced at Alris, who looked down at her own supper and picked at a chicken bone.

"That's another reason Uncle Faran's obsessed with magic," Hanner said quietly.

"I'm done eating," Nerra said, getting to her feet. "I'm going."

"I'll come with you," Alris said, putting her own plate on the floor.

"But *I'm* not finished!" Mavi protested.

Nerra didn't answer; she stomped off, with Alris close behind, leaving Hanner and Mavi seated on the flagstones.

"I'm sorry," Hanner said. "I wasn't thinking. I should have known better than to remind them about Mother."

"Well, it didn't bother *me*," Mavi said. "My mother's alive and well. But it *was* a bit . . ."

"Tactless?"

"Something like that . . ."

"Insensitive?"

"Maybe . . ."

"Unbelievably stupid?"

"I think that describes it, yes," Mavi said, smiling.

"I'm good at that," Hanner said. "I never know what to say, or when to keep my mouth shut. That's one reason I'm still my uncle's errand boy, instead of holding a post in my own right."

"You could do worse than be an assistant to the over-lord's chief advisor."

Hanner grimaced. "And as that advisor's nearest surviv-ing kin, I ought to be able to do better. Uncle Faran always knows what to say."

"Your uncle's had twenty years of experience in govern-ment."

Hanner had no good reply to that. He picked up his re-maining piece of chicken.

The two of them finished their meal in companionable silence. When both had eaten their fill and wiped or licked away the last of the grease, Hanner frowned.

"I don't know whether Nerra would want to see you again yet," he said.

"I should be getting home in any case," Mavi said.

"I don't think Nerra will want to see me, either, and I'd

enjoy a walk," Hanner found himself saying, even though his feet were still slightly sore from the day's excursions. "May I escort you home?"

"I'd be honored," Mavi said.

Chapter Two

Hanner and Mavi were in no hurry as they made their way out of the Palace, across the plaza, and up Arena Street into the New City. The torches and lanterns in the gateways and intersections provided plenty of light, but the daytime crowds had thinned to almost nothing; the dust of the streets had settled and the night breezes, blowing south from the sea, were salty and pleasantly cool—though the Grand Canal still stank. Once they had gone a few blocks that smell faded, and they slowed even more.

They paused in front of one of the larger mansions and admired the fountains and statuary visible through the wrought-iron fence. Hanner found himself holding Mavi's hand and seriously considering kissing her.

But then she pulled away to point out a particular piece of sculpture, the marble figure of a sleeping cat, and the opportunity had passed.

"Do you think that might have been a real cat once?" she asked.

"Why would anyone petrify a cat?" Hanner asked.

"For practice, maybe?" Mavi suggested. "Or for revenge against the cat's owner? If you're asking that, then why would anyone carve an image of a cat?"

"To put in his yard, like that," Hanner said, gesturing at the little statue.

"*I* think some magician did it for practice before setting out to avenge some slight by turning a *human* to stone."

"If it was just for practice, wouldn't the wizard have broken the spell afterward?" Hanner asked.

"Are petrifaction spells reversible?"

"Some are, some aren't," Hanner admitted. "Wizards usually call the reversible spells 'superior,' and the irreversible ones 'irreversible,' so I think they prefer the ones that aren't necessarily permanent."

"I suppose," Mavi admitted, her head tilted thoughtfully as she studied the cat. "But maybe this particular wizard didn't know the superior ones. Or his vengeance failed and his enemy killed him before he could undo it." She frowned. "Would the magician have to be a wizard?"

"I *think* so," Hanner said. "A theurgist wouldn't do something like that, and I never heard of witches doing anything that unnatural. I suppose there might be some way for a sorcerer or demonologist to do it, but I never heard of such a thing."

Mavi turned and looked at him curiously. "Why do you know so much about magic? I thought you said your family wasn't allowed to study it!"

"We aren't allowed to *use* it," Hanner corrected her. "The lords of Ethshar are not permitted to learn magic, nor to use magic for our personal benefit—though of course we're free to hire magicians if it's for the *city's* benefit, or else the whole government would fall apart. But we can learn *about* magic all we please, and that's what I do, ever since my mother died—I talk to magicians for my uncle. He's obsessed with magic, and whenever he's not actively working on the overlord's business or chasing women, he's out trying to learn everything he can about it." He sighed. "And when he *is* busy with his women or the overlord's business, I go out and try to learn about magic *for* him."

"It sounds exciting."

"It isn't, really."

"Oh," Mavi said. "Is it at least interesting, then?"

"Sometimes," Hanner said. He was not entirely comfortable with the subject. He gave the stone cat a final glance, then stepped away from the fence and said, "Come on."

They moved on down the block and turned left onto East Street, leaving the fine houses and spacious yards of the New City for the ancient, cramped buildings of the Old. Neither of them was inclined to linger in the Old City nor to speak openly there, but a mere fifth of a mile brought them to the massive stone levee at the upper end of the Old Canal, and beyond that they were in Fishertown.

"Now, why doesn't that canal smell as bad as the other?" Hanner asked when they were safely clear of the forbidding streets of the Old City and surrounded by the ordinary homes and shops of Fishertown.

"Better drainage, perhaps?" Mavi suggested. "And the odor's none too sweet, at that."

"Hmph." It annoyed Hanner that the Old Canal, which divided Fishertown from the Old City, somehow contrived to not stink anywhere near as strongly as the Grand Canal that surrounded the overlord's palace and connected it to the sea.

The two ambled on through Fishertown and into New-market, where they turned onto Carpenter Street and found Mavi's home, a narrow three-story stone house wedged tightly between two other similar structures.

Despite the address her father was not a carpenter at all, but a dealer in tools and weapons who, among other things, provided the city guard with their spears. Mavi's mother worked as bookkeeper in the family business, and Mavi managed the household. Nerra had explained all this to Hanner when she first realized her brother's interest in the subject.

Hanner had not been here before, though. He stopped in the middle of the street when Mavi pointed out her home. He had been holding her hand again; now he released it and said, "Well, there you are," as he looked up at the house.

The stone was weathered, but had been finely polished once. The broad window lintels were carved with floral designs that might once have been brightly painted, though it was hard to be sure in the dim light from the torches at the corner. An oil lamp shone from one front window, but the walls were thick enough, the window deeply set enough, that little of that light reached the lintels. Brackets that had once held heavy shutters now supported pairs of copper chimes instead, chimes that occasionally rang a soft note in the gentle sea breeze.

Two broad stone steps led up to the front door, which was painted dark green and trimmed with black iron. A small niche beside the door had probably held a shrine once, but was now decorated with a pot of flowers.

All in all, Hanner thought it was a fine example of a traditional Ethsharitic home, but one that had changed with the times rather than being carefully preserved.

"Thank you for walking me home," Mavi said. Then, to Hanner's pleased surprise, she kissed him before turning and hurrying to her parents' door.

Hanner stood in the street for a moment after Mavi had vanished into the house, savoring the memory of that kiss.

He had been kissed before, but not by Mavi. He had not been entirely sure until this moment that she reciprocated his interest in her.

It wasn't unreasonable, he told himself. After all, Mavi came from a family of tradespeople, comfortable but far from truly rich; a match with a lord, even one so unimportant as himself, would surely be seen as a step up the social ladder. And he wasn't actively repulsive, even if he didn't have one-twelfth his uncle's charm.

And maybe she really liked him.

He felt considerably younger than his twenty-three years as he stood there staring at the closed green door of Mavi's home. He hadn't been seriously shy around women since he was sixteen or seventeen, but somehow Mavi brought back the uncertainties of adolescence.

Did this mean he was falling in love, perhaps?

That seemed silly, but he had to admit the possibility.

He also had to admit that his feet were hurting badly. It was time to limp home to bed. The sun had set hours ago, the streets were almost deserted, and Uncle Faran had undoubtedly had his way with Isia, or whatever her name was, by now.

He looked up at the sky. Wisps of cloud obscured most of the stars and turned the black of night to a dull dark gray, making it impossible to judge the exact time. The lesser moon was low in the east, but Hanner could not remember when it was due to rise and set.

A shooting star burned its way across the heavens, from southwest to northeast, as he watched—an extraordinarily big, bright one, he thought. He wondered whether it was natural or the result of some fiery spell; perhaps it was no star at all, but a wizard flying somewhere.

Whatever it was, it was not his concern. He sighed, turned, and began trudging back toward the Palace.

He had just reached the corner where he turned from Carpenter Street onto Newmarket Street when he stumbled and gasped. He did not know *why* he had stumbled; he felt as if something had struck him, but nothing had. He had a momentary sensation of heat and smothering, but it passed— and he had no time to think about it, really, before the screaming began.

He straightened up, his eyes wide. Several voices were screaming somewhere in the distance—at least four or five, perhaps more. They had all begun simultaneously, at the exact instant he had gasped.

Something crashed somewhere far off; he heard glass breaking and heavy things falling.

Mostly, though, he heard the screaming.

Then, as he tried to determine which direction the screams were coming from, they stopped, one by one—and as they did he realized they had come from several different directions.

Half a dozen voices scattered all over Fishertown and Newmarket had begun screaming simultaneously. No single natural shock could have caused that.

"Magic," Hanner said. He remembered the shooting star he had seen moments before and wondered whether there was a connection. He frowned. He hoped that this wasn't the beginning of trouble.

He couldn't think of any particular spells that would have caused it, but magic—especially wizardry and demonology—could be unpredictable.

He looked up at the sky, but there were no more shooting stars. He did see several dark shapes moving in the distance—large night birds, perhaps, or wizards flying on some errand. He couldn't judge their size well in the darkness.

And it was then he heard the shattering of glass, much closer at hand than before, and renewed screaming, from somewhere ahead and to the right. He broke into a trot, despite his sore feet, and steered toward the sound.

Someone might need his help.

Chapter Three

Lord Faran sat bolt upright in his bed, gasping for air, eyes wide and staring into the dark; he fought down an urge to scream, and instead found himself coughing uncontrollably.

The woman beside him rolled over and raised herself up on her elbows. "Fari?" she asked. "Are you all right?"

He tried to wave her away, but he was coughing too hard to complete the gesture; nonetheless she rolled away again, and in fact tumbled out of bed onto the floor.

The braided rug provided little cushioning, and the bedroom floor was stone. "Ow!" she exclaimed.

Faran had no time to worry about the woman's clumsiness—he barely remembered her name. (Isia, a part of his mind reminded him, and she hadn't been at all clumsy an hour or two ago.) He stared at the window, where the glow of the city, the stars, and the lesser moon filtered dimly through the lace curtains, and tried to calm himself.

The coughing tapered off.

The dream that had awakened him had been *important*—he knew that, he had *felt* it, unmistakably. It had been not merely important, but *urgent*, as no natural dream could be. It must have been magic.

Faran had experienced magical dreams before, when wizards had used one version or another of the Spell of Invaded Dreams to send him messages, and he had always remembered the gist of them after awakening—it was, he had assumed, part of the spell, since they wouldn't be much use as a means of communication otherwise. This time, though, his memory was vague and confused, as it might be after an ordinary nightmare.

He remembered that he had been falling, and something had been burning him, there had been fire and rushing air, and then all motion had stopped and he had been trapped somehow, and throughout there had been pain and terror . . . but it was all a jumble. The images he could recall were all distorted. He could not bring back any faces, nor even any totems—all he could remember seeing were flames and clouds and stone.

He knew that whoever had sent the dream wanted him, Lord Faran, to *do* something, to go somewhere and do something as soon as possible—but he had no idea where, or what he should do, or who had sent it.

If this was the Spell of Invaded Dreams, it had gone wrong somewhere.

He wondered whether perhaps this was some other sort of magic entirely, one of the less reliable sorts—witchcraft or sorcery, perhaps, or even herbalism or one of the really minor schools like science or spiritism or ritual dance. He couldn't see how it could be theurgy—if a god sent him a dream, he was fairly certain he would know it. The gods might be whimsical and subtle, but this didn't seem to be their style.

Demonology, perhaps—could demons send dreams? If

they could, they might well produce a tangled, ambiguous mess like this.

"That wasn't very nice," Isia said, climbing back into the bed.

"What wasn't?" Faran asked, startled from his thoughts.

"Shoving me out of bed like that," Isia replied. "You could have just waved me away, and I wouldn't have bothered you."

"Shoving you?" Faran looked at her, astonished but not allowing it to show on his face. "Did I shove you?"

"Oh, no, why, of *course* not! I just dove out of bed onto hard stone and bruised my shoulder on a whim." She glared at him, then whirled and reached for the shift she had left draped on a nearby chair.

"My dear, my dear, I *am* sorry," he said—not that he was actually sorry, but a man in his position should not make enemies, no matter how trivial, unnecessarily. "I was caught up in the dream that awakened me."

"A dream? What kind of dream?" She paused, the shift in her hand, eyeing him suspiciously, her mouth drawn into a tight line.

He allowed himself a puzzled smile. "Do you know, I can't remember!" he said. "A nightmare, I think—I believe it was trying to scream that started me coughing. And I really didn't mean to shove you, Isia—I hadn't even realized I had done it." In fact, he was quite sure he had not touched her—yet she was clearly convinced he had pushed her out of the bed. He watched for any sign of a softening in her anger, and when he saw her thinned lips relax slightly he leaned over and kissed her lightly on her bare shoulder— he couldn't reach her cheek without stretching, and that would not have the properly casual air.

She accepted the kiss with a small sigh, and put down her shift, draping it on the side of the bed. Still sitting up naked in the bed, she turned and smiled at him. "I should go," she said.

"Well, not to please *me*, certainly," he said. "But is there some other reason?"

"My parents," she said. "I shouldn't stay the night; they'll think we're betrothed."

"I wish we were," Faran said, "but as I told you before, there are family considerations." That was a lie—one he told all his women. His position was mostly his own achievement, and his bloodline, while technically noble, was not particularly notable; his surviving family, comprised of two nieces and a nephew, didn't care who, if, or when he married.

"I know," Isia said with another sigh. "You've been very sweet, Fari—except for pushing me out of bed just now."

"And I'm very sorry about that. Blame whatever ghost or demon sent me that nightmare, and forgive me, please."

She bent over and kissed him on the forehead. "Of course," she said. Then she reached for her shift, and this time pulled it over her head.

Faran took a moment to light a bedside lamp—he kept a sorcerous sparker handy, far easier than an ordinary tinderbox and quicker than calling a servant. The wick caught quickly, and he turned it up, filling the room with the yellow glow of burning oil. Then he turned back to Isia. He watched her dress, pretending his attention was entirely on her beauty and his affection for her.

Now, why did she think he had shoved her? He hadn't touched her; he was quite sure of it. He had been leaning on one elbow, and his other hand at his throat, trying to control his coughing; he could not possibly have shoved her.

A kick would have been physically possible, but a look at the bedclothes convinced him that he had not unconsciously kicked her; his feet were still tucked neatly under the snug coverlet.

Isia was not clumsy, though—at least, he had never seen her do anything else clumsy in the four days he had known her, nor had she seemed inclined to fancies or delusions. On general principles he avoided bedding women whose grasp on reality seemed less than solid, and Isia had shown none of the warning signs he had learned to recognize.

So perhaps *something* had shoved her out of bed. He had

already concluded his rapidly fading nightmare had been magical in origin; might there have been other magic at work? A ghost, a demon, a sprite of some kind?

There had been no other manifestation, though.

Once Isia had her shift in place she crossed the room to the bench where she had draped her skirt.

Faran tried to remember exactly what had been happening when Isia found herself propelled from her place. She had been lying on her belly, propped up on her elbows; he had been on his back, on one elbow, his right hand at his throat. He had tried to wave her away with his left hand, as he had not wanted her touching him . . .

He remembered his desire to keep her away, and the helplessness of the coughing fit, and the strange images of the dream, and then he remembered something else.

He had done something, drawn something from the dream. He could recall the sensation, though he could not find words to describe it.

He looked at Isia as she tugged her skirt into place, and he tried to recapture that sensation while somehow reaching out for the hem of her skirt. He felt the space between them, perceiving it in a way he never had before, saw the nature of the skirt's shape, and tried to alter it . . .

The silk suddenly hitched up over her left knee, exposing a shapely calf. She brushed it back down apparently without noticing anything out of the ordinary.

Faran tried again, this time lifting the back of the skirt slowly—from across the room, a good ten feet away. He let it drop before she noticed.

Was it something about Isia, then? He concentrated his attention on one of his own shoes, cast aside in a corner.

It slid out into the room, then rose into the air. He lifted it to a height of four feet or so, then slowly lowered it back to the floor.

Isia, struggling into her satin tunic, didn't see a thing.

A moment later Isia blew him a kiss and slipped out of the room, closing the door gently behind her.

Lord Faran lay in the bed, but did not put out the lamp

or go back to sleep. Instead he mostly stared at the ceiling thinking, his thoughts interrupted only by brief experiments with his newfound ability.

He could lift or slide anything he could see, he discovered, though only up to roughly the size and weight of a grown man—the wardrobe against the far wall did not budge. He could see the shape of the space between himself and the wardrobe, but could not force it to change as he could with smaller objects. He could also, he found, control the size, brightness, and temperature of the lamp's flame.

This was magic, beyond question.

But what *kind* of magic? And how had he acquired it?

It wasn't anything he immediately recognized, and he had been studying magic for years. It bore a resemblance to witchcraft, in that witches could also move small objects without touching them, but it somehow didn't *feel* like the witchcraft he had observed in the past.

The Wizards' Guild forbade any use of wizardry by any nobleman and frowned upon the idea of *any* sort of magic in the hands of nobles—or for that matter, any part of the city government of Ethshar of the Spices or any other government. No ruler or administrator or magistrate, hereditary or otherwise, was permitted to learn magic, and no one who had served an apprenticeship in magic was permitted to hold any governmental position of authority. Magicians hired as magicians were allowed, such as the wizards who purified the canals or the theurgists who made certain that witnesses told the truth in criminal proceedings, but not magicians who made decisions about the city's workings. The Wizards' Guild was quite unreasonably insistent on these rules. People who defied the edicts of the Wizards' Guild had a tendency to die suddenly and horribly. Even if they acquiesced quickly, they suffered lesser, though still unpleasant, fates.

But what about *this* magic? Azrad VI, overlord of Ethshar of the Spices and triumvir of the Hegemony of Ethshar, had named Lord Faran as his senior counselor, and as such Faran was forbidden to work any magic himself, and instead hired magicians as he might need them in the course of his duties—but now Faran seemed to have come into possession of a mysterious magical power through no act of his own. How would the Wizards' Guild react to *that*? Surely, they could not blame him for this accident!

It was so very appropriate that *he* had received this, after all the years of studying magic he was forbidden to use. He had looked for loopholes in the Guild's rules, and now a loophole had found *him*. The Guild *couldn't* blame him for that!

Then he frowned. No, they wouldn't blame him. They would acknowledge he hadn't done anything to cause it.

But they might well kill him anyway.

The Wizards' Guild had never shown any great interest in fairness, after all—they wanted their edicts obeyed, and they really weren't especially interested in equity or justice or motivation, just obedience. Faran knew that well. He had his own theories about what the Wizards' Guild *did* want, but he was quite certain it wasn't justice.

He would keep his abilities secret, then. That would make it more difficult to learn exactly what they were or where they came from . . .

Faran had gotten that far in his thoughts when the noises from beyond his window finally penetrated his consciousness—shouting, screaming, thumpings, and bangings.

It was the middle of the night, he thought; what was going on out there beyond the canal? Curious, he rose and crossed to the window, opened the curtains, and looked out.

"Gods and demons," he muttered as he took in the scene.

His room was on the third floor of the overlord's Palace, at the east end, with a view across the East Branch of the Grand Canal into the tangled streets of the Old City. Since most of the structures in that ancient warren were only one or two stories, and some were half-sunken into the mud, he could look out across the entire Old City into Fishertown.

Now, as he looked out at that panorama, he could see a dozen buildings ablaze, scattered across the city. He could see figures in the streets, standing, running—and flying, and the airborne figures were not wearing wizards' robes, nor carrying any visible magical apparatus, not even the traditional wizard's dagger.

Most of the flying shapes seemed to be moving northward, high and very fast, out across the Gulf of the East, but others were down near street level and were going in various directions about the city.

He could see other things floating or flying as well— wagons, silver plate, gold coins. Broken glass was strewn all over the streets of the Old City.

And he was fairly certain he saw at least one corpse lying in the street amid the glass.

This was unquestionably serious trouble. He would be needed soon in his official capacity; reports would be reaching the Palace. The city guards would want instructions; the overlord would probably be awakened and want an explanation. He had to get downstairs at once.

And why, he asked himself as he hurried to his dressing room, had he ever thought *only he* had received this mysterious magical power?

Chapter Four

At the same instant that Lord Hanner stumbled on the streets of Newmarket, and the same instant that Lord Faran sat up in bed and began coughing, Varrin the Weaver awoke suddenly in his third-floor bedchamber atop his workshop-home in the Seacorner district of Ethshar of the Spices. He awoke gasping for air. He had dreamed he was wrapped in his own cloth, buried in thick, heavy wool, trapped under tons of material after falling through a hundred miles of impossibly fine lace that had shredded as he fell through it, shredded and burned around him.

He awoke in darkness as complete and black as in his dream and he pushed out in all directions, with arms and legs—and with something that had never been there before, something that let him see and feel the walls of his little garret despite the darkness, something that let him push at those walls . . .

And burst them outward, snapping oaken beams like sticks of kindling, shattering plaster into white powder. Its support removed, the roof fell in on him and his wife.

And he caught it, before it reached his upraised hands, caught it and held it.

Then he froze, finally awake enough to realize what was happening. He could feel the night air blowing in where the walls had been; he could hear the distant rattle of wreckage and broken furniture bouncing from the awnings and overhangs and falling to the street. He could hear distant screams. He could feel the mass of the roof, pressing down harmlessly on something he couldn't describe, and even over the screams and falling debris he could hear his wife's ragged breathing. She was awake, beside him in the darkness, not moving.

"Annis?" he said.

"Varrin?" she replied. "What's happening?"

"I don't know," he said. "I had a dream that I was being crushed, and . . . and the walls are gone, and I'm holding up the roof, but I don't know *how*."

"*You're* holding it?" Annis rolled out of the bed and fell to the floor, then got to her knees and stared at Varrin. He couldn't see her clearly in the dark—even with the walls gone, the dim glow of the lesser moon and the city's fires didn't provide much light—but he could sense her, just as he could sense the roof hanging over him, pressing into his awareness.

She was terrified, and part of that terror was directed at *him*.

"Go downstairs," he told her. "Then I can put this down and make a light and see what's going on."

"Yes," she said, scurrying away from the bed, snatching

her robe from the hook on the bedpost. She got to her feet, keeping her head lowered, and ran for the bedroom door.

The door was gone. The entire *wall* was gone. She almost fell down the open stairwell before catching herself on the remaining fragment of railing. She half ran, half tumbled down, out of Varrin's sight—and out of his strange new awareness of his surroundings, as well.

Once he was sure she was safe, he looked up at the ruins of the roof and ceiling. Huge cracks ran through the remaining plaster, and chunks had fallen away, exposing the wooden beams. He studied it and saw that he was holding it together as well as holding it up.

Keeping the space above him unavailable to the wreckage, he let it go.

The roof split into two large pieces and a thousand small ones, falling down on either side of the bed. The crash shook the entire house and echoed from the upper stories of the surrounding buildings, and as some of the smaller fragments skittered down the walls to the street Varrin found himself gazing up at the cloudy night sky.

Dark shapes flew swiftly across his field of vision, headed northward, but before he could recognize what they were, they were gone.

He sat up and looked around at a landscape that no longer made sense. He was still in his bed, his familiar feather pillow at the head, the quilt Annis had made from factory scraps bunched at the foot—but his bedroom was gone, reduced to a pile of rubble lying all around the bed, atop the still-solid lower floors. The broad rooftop that had extended out behind the bedroom was intact, though the ruins of the back wall were strewn across it; the clothesline where Annis hung their laundry was undamaged, the last batch of washing still swaying gently in the breeze.

The houses on either side still stood; the one to the south, on the other side of the tiny alley between street and courtyard, was untouched, while Kelder the Felter's roof, to the north, was now strewn with broken planking and bits of shattered roofing tile.

That view to the north was oddly fascinating; he stared at it for a moment before tearing his gaze away and looking at his own house again.

Only the one room and its adjoining hallway, the little wooden addition he had built atop the original structure so that more room below could be used to store fabrics, had been damaged—but that one room had been not just damaged, but obliterated.

"Gods," he said. "What *happened*?"

No one answered.

He swung his feet over the side of the bed, kicking aside a chunk of ceiling, and stood up—and realized he was naked. He looked for the wardrobe, but it had plunged into the alley.

He had clothes on the line, though. He pushed himself upward, thinking he would climb across the wreckage.

Instead he found himself floating *above* the wreckage.

"Gods!" he said again.

This was magic, of course—but what kind of magic? Who was doing it? Had he managed to offend a wizard or sorcerer without knowing it?

He moved himself eastward over the broken roof and fetched girdle, tunic, and breeches from the line. He dressed hastily and looked out over the city to the west.

A building was on fire somewhere—he could see leaping flames and a bright orange glow. The screaming had stopped, but there were voices in the street, shouting at one another.

Who was up at this hour? Had the destruction of his home woken the whole neighborhood?

He made his way to the stairwell and hurried downstairs.

He found Annis in the front showroom on the ground floor; she was staring out the front window at the street.

"What's happened?" he asked her.

She whirled and stared at him. "Don't *you* know?" she asked.

"No," he said, puzzled. "It's some sort of magic that

smashed our room, obviously, but I don't know why or who did it."

"*You* did it, somehow!"

"But . . ." Varrin stopped, remembering.

Yes, he *had* done it. He didn't know how or exactly why—something to do with a nightmare of being smothered—but yes, he had done it.

And he had held up the roof, which must have weighed hundreds or thousands of pounds, and he had flown across the wreckage like a wizard with a levitation spell.

"How did you do that?" Annis demanded.

"I don't know," Varrin said. "You mean you can't? I assumed that whatever it was happened to *both* of us."

She waved that idea away. "It's just *you*," she said. "At least, in here. There are others out there." She pointed at the window.

"There are?" Varrin glanced at the window.

"Yes," Annis said. "I saw them."

"Maybe I had better go talk to them," Varrin said. "They might know what's happening."

"Yes," she said, stepping backward, away from him. "You do that."

"Annis, don't be frightened," he said as the firelight from outside spilled across her face and let him see her eyes. "Especially don't be frightened of *me*."

"But I'm not sure it *is* you!" she wailed. "What if you're some demon that took my husband's form?"

"Annis, I'm me. I'm Varrin." He stepped toward her. "We've been married for thirty-one years—you know me!"

She squealed and backed away again. "Go away!" she said. "If you're really Varrin, go find out what happened to you!"

He stopped, baffled.

"All right," he said at last. "I'll go see what I can find out." He turned away.

A moment later he was out on the street, looking around in confusion.

Something in him wanted to go north, but that was absurd; he lived and worked just three blocks from the beaches along the eastern shoals and four blocks from the city's eastern wall. Almost the entirety of the city of Ethshar lay south and west of Seacorner.

He could hear voices shouting to the south; he turned and headed toward them, and found his feet leaving the ground. At first he fought it, but then he turned up a palm, lifted his feet, and flew.

At the same time as the others, Kirsha the Younger dreamed of fire and falling and then entombment somewhere deep beneath the earth, dreamed she was fighting her way upward through unyielding soil, and then awoke to find herself floating a foot or so above her bed. She stared up at the too-close canopy of her bed in astonishment, awash in unreasoning panic.

Then the panic popped like a soap bubble, and she smiled as understanding dawned.

"I'm still dreaming," she said.

She rolled over in mid-air and pushed herself toward the bedroom window.

It worked, just like in so many other dreams—she could fly, swim through the air like a fish through water. She didn't even have to wriggle like a fish; thought alone was enough to propel her.

Kirsha felt the cool night air on her bare skin as her bedsheet slipped free and fell away, could hear voices in the street outside—and some of them were screaming.

She wondered why, but then dismissed the question. This was a *dream*; it didn't need to make sense.

It was the oddest flying dream she had ever had, though, starting with a vague nightmare like that and then turning so intensely real. Still, she was enjoying it.

She reached the window and fumbled with the latch, then opened the shutters—or rather she made the shutters fling themselves open, she didn't use her hands. She looked out at the night.

People were flying, dozens of them. Kirsha smiled happily at the thought of sharing her newfound talent. She swung open the casement, planning to fly out into the street.

Then she realized she was still naked.

It probably didn't matter in a dream, but still, she hated dreams where she went outside naked and could feel people staring at her. She flew quickly across the room to a chest of drawers and found a tunic and skirt.

A moment later she was soaring above the streets, watching people running below and flying above. She didn't see anyone she knew, and did not want to talk to strangers, even in a dream—at least, not yet—so she did not rise up to join the other flyers.

They were all going the same direction, anyway, and she didn't want to go that way. She wanted to look at the shops on Dyer Street and see what pretty colors the cloth there had in this wonderful dream. They were lovely in real life, as she had seen when she and her mother went over there just two days ago, but her mother had refused to buy her any of the best fabrics for a new tunic.

And there was that jeweler around the corner, where her parents had refused to even set foot inside the door.

Her parents weren't even in this dream, though, as far as Kirsha could tell, so she could do anything she pleased.

She would smash out the shop windows and take the things she liked best, she decided, and then fly away, like a big brightly colored bird. She would fly to the lesser moon and see why it was pink, and she would find a handsome prince from the Small Kingdoms or a Sardironese baron there, and . . .

She was getting ahead of herself, she decided. First she should see whether Dyer Street was even there in this dreamworld.

People below her were screaming, but she paid no attention. She swooped around the corner, laughing.

*   *   *

Someone was bellowing, and Kennan of the Crooked Smile woke up, annoyed at the interruption of his sleep.

The noise faded away quickly—whoever was bellowing was moving away very fast. Something about it bothered him though, so Kennan did not immediately go back to sleep.

And then he heard running footsteps in the corridor, and then his son's wife Sanda shouting, and he climbed out of bed and grabbed a robe.

"What is it?" he demanded as he stumbled out into the dark hallway. "What's happening?"

No one answered; he hurried to the door of his son's bedroom and found it standing open. He stepped inside warily—he didn't want to intrude. Aken and Sanda were sensitive about their privacy.

Aken was nowhere to be seen; instead, Sanda was standing at the open casement, leaning out and calling, "Come back! Bring him back!"

"What's happening?" Kennan asked again.

Sanda turned, and even in the dim light from the open window Kennan could see the tears gleaming on her cheeks.

"He's gone," she said. "They took him!"

"*Who's* gone?" Kennan asked, confused.

"Aken," Sanda said. "I was downstairs, closing the shutters, and I heard him shouting, so I ran up to see what was wrong, and I got here and the window was open—look at the latch!"

Kennan looked. The iron latch had been twisted into an unrecognizable lump.

Kennan still didn't understand. He didn't understand where Aken was or what had happened to the latch. It looked as if someone very, very strong had crushed it in his fist.

Aken was a strong young man, but he wasn't *that* strong.

"Where is he?" Kennan asked.

"Gone!" Sanda shrieked, pointing out the window. "I saw him flying away! They *took* him!"

"*Who* took him?" Kennan was beginning to comprehend,

though he didn't want to. "What do you mean, flying?"

"*Flying!* Through the air! By magic! The magicians took him!"

"Sanda, that's crazy—why would magicians take Aken? What magicians?"

"Those magicians, out in the street," she said, pointing. "They're flying around smashing things. And they took your son, I saw it."

Kennan, not really wanting to look, tiptoed across the room and looked past Sanda, out the window.

It was as she had said—there were people flying through the streets and up above the rooftops, most of them heading north, toward the docks, and there were things flying with some of them—clothes and jewels and furniture. It was all madness.

And there was no sign of Aken.

Like so many others, Zarek the Homeless awoke from a nightmare, screaming—and was astonished to hear perhaps a dozen other scattered voices screaming as well. He sat up, still wrapped in his moth-eaten blanket, and looked out at his surroundings.

He lay in the middle of the Hundred-Foot Field, not far from where Sway Street met Wall Street, in the Westwark district of Ethshar of the Spices. Around him were the blankets, tents, and crude huts of scores of the city's other destitute—and several of them were screaming, though the number of voices seemed to be declining rapidly.

A lantern flared up nearby, and voices chattered excitedly inside little Pelirrin's tent.

"Shut up and let me sleep!" someone called as the last two or three voices continued to scream.

One voice dropped to a low moan; another fell silent. Finally only one woman's voice still screamed, a thin, breathy wailing that sounded almost like a night wind—but the air was still.

"Blasted magicians," someone said.

"Is that what it was?" another voice asked.

"What else could it be? People waking up screaming all at once—if that's not magic, I'm Azrad the Great."

Zarek could hardly argue with that; he wondered idly what *kind* of magic it was, and why it had affected *him*. It clearly hadn't struck everyone, or there would have been *hundreds* screaming, rather than a dozen or so, but it had struck *him*, all right. His throat was sore from screaming— though his throat was often sore anyway, from bad water and worse food or the various contagions found in the Field.

He tried to remember *why* he had been screaming, and could only remember a feeling of suffocation and entrapment.

He mused about the significance of this. It might be important, he supposed.

In the morning he would go make a few inquiries—talk to the guards at Westgate, maybe, or see if anyone in the Wizards' Quarter would answer a few questions. Perhaps there was some way he could capitalize on being included in this misdirected magic—he thought he might get a decent meal out of it, anyway. Maybe some curious wizard would pay him for a report on what had happened.

In fact, he thought, maybe he shouldn't wait until morning. That woman was still screaming, and he wasn't going to get back to sleep right away, and if he waited someone else might collect whatever payment the magicians might be willing to make. He kicked aside his blanket and got to his feet.

A moment later the woman finally stopped screaming, but Zarek had already headed eastward into the city streets.

Throughout the city, dozens of others tried to figure out what had happened, or rolled over and went back to sleep, or panicked and ran or flew out into the streets. Hundreds walked or ran or flew northward.

And in Ethshar of the Sands, forty leagues to the west, the same scenes were repeated, on the same scale.

In Ethshar of the Rocks, far to the northwest, again the

same events played out, though fewer people were affected there than in the more southerly cities.

In farms and villages beyond the walls of the cities, throughout the Hegemony of the Three Ethshars, people awoke choking or screaming, and a few of those who had been awake all along felt the touch of a strange new power. In the Baronies of Sardiron, in the war-torn land of Tintallion, in the many tiny nations of the Small Kingdoms, magic flashed across the World and drove unsuspecting people from their beds.

Everywhere, those touched by the magic and those who saw them wondered what had happened, what this unfamiliar magic was, what would happen next.

And nowhere were there immediate answers to any of these questions.

Chapter Five

Lord Hanner ducked down in the doorway of a potter's shop, hands over his head, as a nightgowned woman flew past shrieking at the top of her lungs, surrounded by a cloud of kitchen knives, broken glass, and miscellaneous debris. When she had passed he straightened up and looked after her.

Despite her screams, he could see no sign that she was injured or in pain; presumably she had simply panicked when . . . when whatever it was that happened had happened. She appeared unhurt and seemed to be controlling her magically propelled movements and the movements of her accompanying objects.

Anyone who wasn't quick enough getting out of her way was likely to be hurt, though.

As the wind of her passage died away Hanner wondered

what he should do. He was a lord, one of the overlord's servants, responsible for keeping order in Ethshar, and whatever wild magic had broken loose moments earlier, it was definitely not orderly. That flying woman hadn't been the first manifestation of out-of-control magic he had encountered in the quarter hour since the screaming and other commotion started—nor the second, nor the fifth. Something magical was definitely loose in the city, and definitely causing trouble.

So far he had been unable to make sense of it; the people he had encountered who were caught up in the magic, whatever it was, had shown no interest in talking to him. They didn't seem to want any help, either, not even the ones who were still screaming. Instead they tended to fly about wildly, and some of them seemed willing to smash anything that got in their way.

"Is she gone?" a voice behind him asked. Hanner started.

"I think so," he said, turning to find that a plain woman of uncertain age had opened the door of the shop. She peered about cautiously, then stepped out beside Hanner.

"Why was she screaming?"

"I don't know," Hanner said.

"Is she a wizard? She was flying, wasn't she?"

"She was flying," Hanner agreed, "but I don't think she's a wizard. There's some kind of magic causing trouble. She might be hurt—maybe we should follow her, see if we can help . . ."

The woman snorted. "*I'm* not going after anyone who can fly! If you want to deal with magic, find a magician. I'm just a potter." She looked back and forth along Newmarket Street. "Are there any more?"

"There were other people screaming earlier, but I don't—"

Hanner's sentence was interrupted by the sound of breaking glass.

"I think there are more," he concluded.

"Then I'm staying inside," the potter said. "And *you* should go somewhere else." She pushed Hanner out of the doorway into the street, then stepped back inside her shop and slammed the door shut.

Hanner looked around.

"Go somewhere else," the potter had told him—but where? He could just go home—while it was his responsibility in general to keep order, no one could fault him for not getting involved with some mysterious magical mess that was none of his doing.

But *he* would fault himself. He and his uncle were the closest thing the overlord had to experts on magic, and it was his duty to find out what was going on.

"If you want to deal with magic, find a magician." That was obvious advice—and obviously *good* advice. And the best place to find a magician in Ethshar of the Spices was the Wizards' Quarter.

Presumably the wizards and the rest would already know what was happening, but it wouldn't hurt to make sure and see whether he could be helpful. If he went on down Newmarket to East Street, then turned left on Fishertown Street . . .

He began jogging, despite his tired feet.

The route wasn't quite as simple as he had hoped, as Fishertown did not go through to Arena Street, but twenty minutes later he was crossing Games Street into the Wizards' Quarter.

Along the way he saw at least a dozen more instances of the strange magic running amok—looted shops, people or objects flying, doors and windows shattered, and a distressing number of buildings aflame. Although the streets were largely deserted, even more so than usual at this hour, the few people Hanner *did* see either seemed to be using the magical power, fleeing it, or caught in it. Several people ran and hid at Hanner's approach.

For his own part Hanner refused to be cowed—he was a public servant, a city official, and was determined to act like one, within reason. He marched on, facing the out-of-control magicians he encountered.

In one case a woman was walking along with a man held

screaming in the air over her head—eight or nine feet over her head. Hanner hesitated, considered intervening—but then she took off as well, flying away with the man in tow.

Whatever had happened had clearly not been limited to Newmarket and Fishertown; Hanner saw people and things flying about in the Old City, the New City, Allston, and the Arena district. He wondered just how widespread the mysterious effect really was—did it extend outside the city walls of Ethshar of the Spices? Were the other two great cities of the Hegemony affected? Or the Small Kingdoms, or the lands to the north and west of Ethshar?

But that was absurd. Who would unleash a spell powerful enough to cover so great an area as that?

Of course, the broader the affected area, the less likely the effects would be permanent—perhaps the spell, whatever it was and whoever was responsible, would fade away soon, and his trip halfway across the city in the middle of the night would have been for nothing.

He was here now, though—and he was not the only one. He could hear voices ahead, angry voices.

He hoped the madness had not affected any wizards or other magicians—that could be *really* dangerous. He forced himself to trot faster.

At the corner of Wizard Street he turned and found himself facing a crowd.

It was perhaps less than an hour before midnight, but unlike anywhere else he had been, the street was full of people. Torches and lanterns, ordinarily extinguished by this hour of the night, were brightly ablaze; doors and windows stood open, and dozens, perhaps hundreds, of people were milling about, talking excitedly. Some wore ordinary tunics, skirts, and breeches; others wore the formal robes of magicians; and some had clearly come directly from their beds and were dressed in nightshirts or hastily donned household robes. Most of them looked scared or at least nervous.

No one seemed to be in charge; instead the crowd was gathered into small groups, a few voices in each arguing loudly, while people around the periphery would drift from one bunch to the next. Hanner guessed that these were people at least as confused and frightened by the night's events as he was, come, as he had, to seek the help of the city's magicians.

And judging by the snatches of conversation and debate he overheard, no one was getting very satisfactory answers.

He hurried down the block, listening, but heard nothing that hinted at an understanding of what was happening.

These were apparently all wizards here, though, and Hanner thought other kinds of magicians might know more. He turned left at the end of the block, then right, and trotted into Witch Alley.

This area was quieter—witchcraft was generally a quieter sort of magic than wizardry, and its practitioners and purchasers followed suit. Still, there were two or three dozen people clustered in the street and in doorways, talking. Here, too, they wore the same assorted clothing; he even saw one man in the yellow tunic and red kilt of the city guard.

Hanner spotted a familiar face, one he had hoped to see, and called, "Mother Perréa!"

The old woman at the center of one of the smaller groups turned. "Lord Hanner," she said. She beckoned to him, and ignoring the aching of his feet he ran up to join the handful of people gathered about her.

He paused there, struggling to catch his breath, and the witch asked him, "Did the overlord send you, my lord, or your uncle?"

Hanner shook his head. "Neither," he said. "I came on my own."

"And have you come to ask questions or answer them?"

"Ask them, I'm afraid," he said. "Though I'll answer any I can."

"Then let me answer the most obvious and say that we do not know who or what is responsible for this outbreak of magical madness."

Hanner's face fell. He had told himself, after seeing the situation on Wizard Street, that this was the most likely answer, but he had still hoped. "Do you know *anything* about it, then? Is it a wizard's spell gone wrong, perhaps, like the legendary Tower of Flame?"

Perréa turned up an empty palm. "We don't know what it is—but we know a few things it isn't."

"That would be better than nothing," Hanner said.

"It isn't wizardry at all," she told him. "I don't know whether the wizards themselves have determined that yet, but I can assure you, it's not wizardry. The feel of it is entirely different."

That astonished Hanner; he had not thought anything but wizardry could be so powerfully chaotic. "Is it witchcraft, then?"

"It's more like witchcraft than wizardry, but no, it's not witchcraft. A witch could not have the strength to do some of what we've seen. Nor is it sorcery, nor theurgy—the priests have consulted Unniel and Aibem, and there is no question."

"Demonology?" Hanner couldn't think of any other possibilities that remained. It was unimaginable that any of the lesser magicks he was familiar with, such as herbalism, could be responsible for something like this.

"We have not yet ruled that out, but neither have we found any evidence to support it," Perréa said. She pointed at a black-robed man a few yards away. "That's Abden the Black, an excellent demonologist, and as trustworthy as any I have dealt with—"

"Which is not a strong endorsement, is it?" Hanner interrupted.

Perréa smiled. "No, I'm afraid it's not—but he assures me that this is no sort of demonology he knows, and he seems quite sincere. My craft can read truth and falsehood in most people, and although it's not completely reliable on demonologists, I believe him."

Before Hanner could ask another question, one of the others in the group interrupted.

"You came from the overlord's Palace?" she asked him.

Hanner had given the others present very little attention, but now he looked at the questioner and felt himself flush.

She was a slender woman of slightly below average height, heavily made up. She wore a bright red tunic embroidered in red and gold, cut very low, and a darker red skirt that was slit up one side almost to her hip. Her long, full hair was fiery red as well—an extremely unusual color, though Hanner had heard it was more common in distant places like Tintallion and Meroa.

Her occupation was obvious, and Hanner was not sufficiently worldly to avoid reacting to it. He was not accustomed to encountering streetwalkers in the Wizards' Quarter, or anywhere else he went regularly, for that matter. They tended to stay near the gates or docks or in Camptown, none of which he generally frequented.

"More or less," he said hastily, trying to cover his embarrassment. "I was in Newmarket, actually, when the trouble started, and I came directly here."

"It's happening in Newmarket, too?" asked a man in gray homespun.

"In Newmarket and the Old City and Arena—everywhere I've looked," Hanner replied.

"But you don't know what's happening at the Palace?" the streetwalker persisted.

"Not firsthand, no," Hanner admitted.

"We thought it was just Camptown at first," the man in homespun said. "But then we discovered it was here, too."

"We thought it might be some sort of attack on the soldiers," the redhead added. "Several of them apparently vanished right out of the camp, flying away, and it didn't seem as if they *wanted* to. I wondered whether anything had happened to the overlord."

That possibility had not occurred to Hanner. "I don't know," he said unhappily. "People were breaking into houses and shops in Newmarket, flying about screaming, and I thought that . . . well, someone said to deal with magic, find a magician, which made good sense, so I came here."

"So did we," the streetwalker said.

"Rudhira is a regular customer of mine," Perréa added.

"She suggested we ask Mother Perréa what we should do," the man in homespun said. "So about half a dozen of us came here together."

Hanner did not see the half dozen described in this particular group; the conversation included only himself, Mother Perréa, the woman in red, the man in homespun, and two young men who had not yet spoken. Perréa, apparently reading his face, said, "When I couldn't help, the others moved on."

"Yorn came with me," Rudhira said, pointing to the guardsman who was now standing by himself, looking lost. "And that man there; he said his name was Elken." She pointed at a person in ill-fitting rags who was sitting against the wall of a shop, looking dazed; his hair and beard were so tangled and matted that they obscured most of his face, making it hard for Hanner to judge his age.

Hanner frowned, trying to think what he should do, what questions he should ask. The soldier's yellow tunic caught his eye. "That guardsman," Hanner said. "He's in uniform. He was on duty when it began? Did he desert his post to come here or was he sent?"

"I think he came on his own," Rudhira said.

"He should have waited for orders from his captain. The guard should be trying to restore order."

"I guess he panicked," the man in homespun said.

"Guards aren't supposed to panic," Hanner replied.

"Guards aren't supposed to be able to fly, either," Rudhira retorted.

Hanner turned, startled. "He . . . what?"

"Well, not literally fly, in his case," Perréa said. "At least, I haven't seen him do it."

"All right, not Yorn," Rudhira said. "But some of the soldiers *did* fly; most of the ones who could flew off and didn't come back. That didn't happen to Yorn, but that's why he came here with me—he has the magic, too, but not very strong. He thought it might be a curse or a trap, so he came here for advice."

"But he didn't go mad?"

Rudhira put her hands on her hips. "Neither did I," she said.

Hanner's mouth opened, then snapped shut.

"Look," Rudhira said. She raised her arms and floated gently upward, a foot or so into the air, then sank back to the ground. "Why did you *think* I came?"

"Uh . . . to find out what was happening," Hanner said, confused.

"Yes, exactly," Rudhira agreed. "But why would I care, if it wasn't happening to *me*?"

Hanner said, "I thought maybe you were robbed or attacked by one of these madmen."

"I'd probably be dead if that had happened," Rudhira said. "I passed at least two corpses on the way here."

Hanner closed his eyes and swallowed. He suspected that he had passed at least one himself, but had refused to look closely enough to be sure.

Then Rudhira's words registered. "*Can* you fight back?" he asked.

"Of course," she answered. "I can . . . well, *feel* it, and make it stop . . ." She frowned. "I don't have a good way to describe it."

"Of course," Hanner said. "You never did it before. You aren't a magician."

"Well, she wasn't one until tonight," Perréa said. "Now I'm not so sure."

"You think this might be *permanent*?" Hanner asked. That thought was just as astonishing as the discovery that not all the people affected had turned into rampaging monsters.

"It might be," Perréa said. "I told you we don't know much about it. We're just guessing. It seems a little bit like descriptions I've heard of something witches used to do sometimes for emergencies during the Great War, where several witches would lock their magic into a single person for some special job—*that* sort of magic did eventually get used up, and some of the contributing witches could die of exhaustion without ever getting out of their chairs if the war-locked person burned away too much of it, but the person *using* the magic could keep on going without getting tired or feeling any strain right up until the last contributing witch died."

"So do you think someone somewhere is supplying the magical power for *this* war-locking?" Hanner asked. "Will it end when that source dies?"

Perréa turned up an empty palm. "Who knows? I told you, I'm guessing."

"And while we're guessing, people are dying," Hanner said. "Things are being smashed and stolen and burned all over the city. We need to *do* something." He looked at Rudhira. "Get Yorn, and anyone else who came with you who can use this magic. To deal with magic, find a magician, she said; well, it would seem the ordinary magicians can't deal with this, but maybe *you* can." He took a deep breath, then said, "As a representative of Azrad, overlord of Ethshar of the Spices, I hereby require you to accompany me and obey me, and I pledge that service will be rewarded."

Even as he spoke, Hanner had second thoughts. He always said the wrong thing, he had told Mavi as much a few hours ago. Had he just done it again?

But somebody did have to do something!

Rudhira looked at the embroidered silk on Hanner's shoulders and the bay-leaf sigil on his breast. "He can do that?" she asked Perréa.

"He's a lord of the city, so he has the authority, yes," Perréa said, looking somewhat bemused. "I'd never have expected this of *Lord Hanner*, though. He's taking a risk. If he misuses this power he can be beheaded for it—but that's up to the overlord to decide, not you. For now, the law says you have to obey him."

Hanner shuddered at the reminder of the possible consequences—but he was sure now he was doing the right thing, and that his uncle and old Azrad would approve. "Get Yorn and the others," he told Rudhira. Then he raised his voice and announced to the entire street, "Any of you who can use this new magic, I hereby require you to accompany me and obey me, in the overlord's name!"

The hum of conversation stopped, and half a hundred faces turned to look at him.

"Your services will be rewarded," he said. "And disobedience will be punished."

Though just how he would enforce that if these people could fly and throw things around without touching them, he had no idea.

Chapter Six

Throughout the World, as people discovered their new talents, sudden dramas played themselves out. Most of these were quick and ended badly.

In the Small Kingdoms His Majesty Agravan III, King of Tirissa, was very drunk as he made his way up the stairs to his apartments, so drunk that one of his bodyguards had to support him. The evening had begun as a celebration of the arrival of the new ambassador from Trafoa, but had quickly turned into simply another night of swilling ale with the gentlemen of the court.

Queen Rulura, until recently a princess of the more strait-laced neighboring kingdom of Hollendon, had, as usual, gotten disgusted with her husband and gone up to bed early. She had married King Agravan for dynastic reasons, and while they generally got along well enough despite the twelve-year difference in their ages, she never pretended to love everything about him. Excessive drinking usually meant a few days of frosty silence between them.

It was a surprise, therefore, when Agravan found the door of her bedchamber ajar and two lamps burning therein. He signaled to his bodyguards and stumbled over for a closer look.

"Rulura?" he asked, leaning into the room.

"Agri!" she called happily, turning to smile at him. She was sitting at her writing desk. "Come in!"

He took a cautious step into the room. "What are you doing?" he asked.

"Look what I can do!" She gestured, and a quill pen floated in midair before her outstretched hand.

Agravan frowned at it, puzzled—but much less drunk than he had been a moment before.

"How?" he asked.

"I don't know," she said cheerfully. "I just discovered that I could do it."

"It's magic?"

"I think it must be, yes."

"Rulura, you're a queen," Agravan said quietly. "You don't do magic."

"I do now!" she said proudly. "Oh, Agri, think how useful it could be! I can pass things to you where no one can see them, pick things up . . . I could even be an assassin!" She giggled. "I could go up to someone with empty hands, and then stab him in the back."

"You could," Agravan said slowly.

"We could use this, Agri, I know we could. It might not be much of anything, but I'm still learning. If there are other things I can do, this might make Tirissa the most powerful of all the Small Kingdoms!"

"Ruli," Agravan said gently, "the Wizards' Guild forbids kings and queens to use magic."

Rulura hesitated. "I thought that was just for wars."

"No, the agreement not to fight wars with magic is just good sense, that's not the Guild's doing."

"Well, I didn't go out and *learn* this," the queen protested. "It just happened."

Agravan nodded. "I'm sure it did," he said. "Maybe it will go away again. Good night, Ruli." He stepped back and closed the door.

Then he beckoned to one of his bodyguards and told him quietly, "Tonight, when she's asleep, kill her." He no longer sounded drunk at all.

"Kill the *queen*?" the guard asked, startled.

"Yes," Agravan said. "Kill the queen." He glanced back at the door, hoping this mysterious magic hadn't given Rulura the ability to hear through a closed door.

"It'll mean war with Hollendon, Your Majesty," the bodyguard warned him. "Are you sure you shouldn't wait until you're sober to decide such a thing?"

"I'm sure," Agravan said. "We can't afford to wait. You heard what she said about putting a knife in someone's back. She might well put one in *my* back, if she thinks she can use her magic to get away with it. There's a *reason* the Wizards' Guild won't allow anyone of royal blood to learn magic."

"She's just levitating pens," the guard protested.

"*So far* it's just pens. I'm not going to risk waiting. You have your orders."

The bodyguard sighed. "Yes, Your Majesty," he said.

An hour later the only member of any royal family in the Small Kingdoms to have become a warlock became a corpse, eliminating any possible threat to the Guild's prohibitions on mixing magic and government.

In one small village in Aldagmor, easternmost and most mountainous of the Baronies of Sardiron, an old woman named Kara had hidden in her wardrobe when the screaming and other noises began. Now that everything had been quiet for a time she finally emerged, looking around cautiously by the dim moonlight.

Everything appeared normal. She lit a lamp and saw that her bedroom was undamaged.

The village was quiet.

The village was, she thought, *too* quiet. After all the commotion before she would have expected her neighbors to be gossiping in the road, but she couldn't hear any voices through her open window. She threw on a shawl—even in midsummer the night breeze could be cool on the slopes of the mountains—and hurried through the other room of her cottage, out into the center of the village.

It was utterly deserted.

She looked around at the other houses. Some were intact, untouched and dark.

Others were just as dark, but far from intact. The greenhouse at the east end of the cottage where Imirin the Herbalist lived had been smashed to bits. Half the roof was gone from her brother Karn's house. And Elner's house was gone completely.

"Hai!" she called. "What happened?"

No one answered. The only sound was the gentle sighing of the night wind in the trees.

Frightened, Kara began searching the village house by house, looking for some sign of life, someone who could tell her what had happened.

She found no one. Doors were unlocked, many standing open, even in the intact houses, so she was able to investigate thoroughly. Every remaining bed was empty; no one replied to her cries.

Finally, she stood in the center of the village again, certain she was the only person left there, alive or dead.

She had found footprints leading southeast. She had noticed that the open doors, broken walls, missing roofs, and so on were all on the east or south. She looked in that direction, into the darkness of the night, and saw nothing.

For a moment she thought of following, of walking southeast in search of her missing friends and family. The urge grew, huge and irrational, and she took a step.

Then she caught herself. She hadn't survived seventy-three northern winters by acting on impulse or following blindly after other people. Something had *drawn* the villagers in that direction, and now it was belatedly trying to draw *her*, and she wasn't going.

She turned and began marching determinedly northwest. She chose that direction simply because it was the opposite of the direction everyone else had taken, but she knew it was also taking her the first few steps toward Sardiron of the Waters, thirty leagues away, where the Council of Barons met. If nothing intervened, she intended to walk the entire way and ask the Council for succor.

It would take at least a sixnight to walk that far, but after all, she had no further obligations here.

And in Ethshar of the Rocks, the smallest, westernmost, and most northerly of the three great cities of the Hegemony of the Three Ethshars, a man named Shemder Parl's son stood at the window of his rented room, watching the lunatics in the street below.

He had awakened from a nightmare, sweating and shaking, and when he reached for the pitcher beside his bed he discovered that he had somehow acquired magical abilities, that he could move things without touching them. He heard the commotion in the streets and went to the window to see what was happening.

He stood there, watching and listening and thinking, for some time.

There were others who had received the same magic, and they were out there running wild, stealing things and smashing windows and setting fires, shouting about the end of the World, many of them flying off to the east.

Shemder thought they were fools.

This wasn't the end of the World. The faint sensation in his head urging him to go east was a feeble annoyance, at most. Smashing and stealing was too loud, too obvious, too blatant. Sooner or later the overlord's guards or the established magicians would organize, recover, and deal harshly with those idiots. The magic would surely pass—the spell would wear off, or some damnable high-ranking wizard would find a way to remove it—and then those rampaging morons would be rounded up and flogged or hanged. They would have wasted the opportunity of a lifetime.

Shemder was not about to waste his one unexpected chance at revenge.

He had been planning it all out, step by step. He would start with his landlady. He wouldn't touch her, but she would fall down the cellar stairs and crack her skull on the stone steps.

The magic would ensure that.

And then his brother Neran, who had gone from a childhood of bullying to an adulthood of rubbing Shemder's nose in Neran's success as a woodcarver and Shemder's own failure to ever be anything more than a stevedore at the Bywater docks, poor Neran would fall on one of his own knives.

That witch Détha of Hillside who had refused to accept Shemder as an apprentice all those years ago, and who kept telling him he needed to find his own path—*she* would find her own path, right off the cliffs at the end of Fortress Street, onto the rocks at low tide.

Falissa and Kirris and Lura and all the other women who had refused him over the years—some hearts would burst, some women would mysteriously choke to death.

The magistrate who had sentenced Shemder to three lashes for stealing that statuette from the Tintallionese ship last year—*he* was on the list, along with the ship captain who noticed the loss in the first place.

Shemder doubted the magic would last long enough to finish the list. It was a *long* list.

And, he decided, he had spent enough time just thinking about it. It was time to start doing it, to see just how far down the list he could get before the magic stopped.

The idea that *he* might be stopped before the magic was didn't occur to him; he wasn't a fool like those people running in the streets.

He was going to use his gift *right*, he told himself as he opened the door and called for the landlady.

Who could stop him?

Chapter Seven

Lord Hanner marched up the broad dimness of Arena Street with a mismatched dozen of the "war-locked" walking behind him, and three more flying overhead. The rest of the crowd in Witch Alley—the man in homespun who had been speaking to Mother Perréa, the old man in rags who had followed Rudhira from Camptown, and most of the others—had either denied being "war-locked" or had quietly slipped away rather than obey Hanner's orders.

But this group had accepted his authority. They were, he had told them, on their way to the Palace to volunteer their services to the overlord, and along the way they would confront any other war-locked magicians they found and stop them from doing any more damage.

"Do you see anyone?" he called up to the airborne trio.

"No, my lord," Rudhira called down in reply. Hanner quickly turned his gaze to avoid looking up her skirt as it flapped in the breeze.

"How can she fly like that?" the guardsman to Hanner's left muttered. "I can barely lift myself a foot off the ground, and there she is, swooping along as if it were nothing!"

"And I can't get off the ground at all," Hanner replied. "Obviously, this thing affected people differently."

"Well, it didn't affect *you* at *all*, my lord," the soldier said. "I can move things, as she can—but I can't *fly*."

"So she got more of this . . . this warlockry than you did," Hanner said.

"But why?"

"My guess would be random chance."

"My lord!" One of the flyers, an older man in a fancy linen tunic, was calling.

Hanner looked up and realized he ought to know the man's name, but didn't. "What is it?"

"There's someone flying," the man called down. "Off to the right, on Circus Street."

"I'll take a look," Rudhira said.

"Go ahead," Hanner said as the woman veered sideways and swooped up Circus Street. He broke into a run, into the intersection and around the corner.

The other warlocks hesitated, looking at one another, unsure what to do. "Stay together," Hanner called back over his shoulder as he peered into the darkness. There were no shops along this stretch of Circus Street, no lanterns, and all the windows in the half-timbered little houses were dark; only the torches at the corner gave any light.

He saw Rudhira's target now—a boy, scarcely old enough for breeches, hovering in midair above the center of the street.

"Stay back!" the boy called. He held up an arm warningly, but none too steadily.

Rudhira stopped suddenly and hung motionless in midair where she was. Hanner did not think she had done so deliberately; the boy had stopped her somehow.

"Oh, you think so?" she said, and the boy abruptly dropped to the street, landing on his back on the hard-packed dirt with the wind knocked out of him. Rudhira swept down and landed beside him. She didn't touch him, but Hanner could see the boy struggling unsuccessfully to sit up.

"Don't you try to push *me* around, boy," Rudhira said.

"Don't hurt him!" Hanner called as he ran up panting. "We don't know whether he's done anything . . ."

"I haven't," the boy gasped.

"He tried to knock me down," Rudhira said. "I felt it."

"I was just pushing you away," the boy said. "You frightened me!"

"Why?" Rudhira asked angrily. "Why should you be scared of me?"

"You were flying!"

"So were you!"

"But I . . . you're *bigger* than me."

This was just barely true, given Rudhira's rather small stature, but she was definitely an adult, while the boy definitely was not.

"And my magic is stronger," Rudhira said, finally letting the boy sit up. "Don't you forget it, either."

As Hanner went down on one knee beside the boy he glanced up at Rudhira, but said nothing in reply. He was not happy to hear her words; she sounded a little too assertive about her newfound abilities. Apparently she *was* the most powerful of his group of warlocks, but that didn't mean she had the right to push anyone around.

"Are you all right?" Hanner asked the boy, offering a hand to help him up.

"I guess so," he said, taking the hand and getting to his feet. Hanner noticed that the boy was looking past him; he glanced over his shoulder and saw that the rest of his party had turned the corner and was watching intently. The other two flyers, the old man in the linen shirt and a plump nondescript woman, were on the ground now.

Hanner wished he had taken the trouble to learn everyone's name, so he could call instructions, but he hadn't. He turned back to the boy.

"What are you doing out on the streets at this time of night? Shouldn't you be at home with your parents or your master?"

"My parents told me to stay outside until I stopped moving things and bumping into things. I was trying to learn how to control this magic."

"Warlockry," Hanner said. "That's what the witches call it."

"Well, *whatever* it is, I didn't ask for it!" the boy said in a thoroughly aggrieved tone. "I had a nightmare and I woke up in midair over my bed, and I knocked the pitcher off the nightstand when I let myself fall, and it broke all over the floor and woke up my brothers, and then my mother came and ordered me out of the way while she cleaned up the mess, and I stumbled on the stairs and went flying and knocked over a lamp, and my father yelled at me and told me to go outside if I was going to bump into things. So I did, and I've been practicing flying. And other stuff." He looked at Rudhira. "How did you make me fall? I know how to push things, but you did something different."

"It's easy enough," Rudhira said. "I'm not sure how to explain it, though. I used some of my magic to . . . to erase yours, sort of."

"Can you teach me how? And how to fly better?"

"I don't think this is the time or place for that," Hanner interjected firmly as the rest of the party came up to join them. "I think it's time you went home and went back to bed. If this magic hasn't gone away by morning come to the Palace and ask for Lord Hanner, and I'll see if someone wants to teach you some tricks."

"You're Lord Hanner?"

"Yes, I am. Now, go home. On foot."

"Yes, my lord." The boy glanced at the motley collection of people staring at him, then turned and ran down Circus Street. At a corner he turned again and was out of sight.

That left Hanner standing at the front of his little mob of warlocks. "You didn't ask him to join us," the guardsman said.

"He's just a child," Hanner said, "and it's the middle of the night." He glanced at the soldier. "What did you say your name is?"

"Yorn of Ethshar, my lord."

"That's right, Rudhira told me. Yorn, don't you think we have enough warlocks already?" He gestured at the others.

"I suppose so, my lord," Yorn admitted.

"*I* think so," Hanner said. "If something happens to prove I'm wrong, you're welcome to say you told me so."

Yorn didn't answer that.

"Come on," Rudhira said, rising into the air. "Let's get

to the Palace." She swooped overhead like an immense red bird, back toward Arena Street.

With a sigh, Hanner followed, the others trooping or gliding along—the other flyers were airborne again.

They had gone another dozen blocks when a woman came running out of Fish Street onto Arena, glancing about wildly. She stopped at the sight of Hanner's group, hesitated, her attention clearly focused on Yorn's uniform.

"What's wrong?" Hanner called.

"You're . . . you . . ." She stared about wildly, and then froze, speechless, when she saw Rudhira and the other two flyers.

"Yorn, tell her we won't hurt her," Hanner ordered.

"It's all right, ma'am," Yorn said. "These people are all under control. Now, tell Lord Hanner what's wrong."

"Down there," the woman said, pointing back along Fish Street. "It's horrible! Two of them, throwing everything around . . ."

"I think we'd better take a look . . ." Hanner began—but then he stopped. Rudhira was already swooping around the corner, flying down Fish Street. Hanner sighed again. "Come on," he told the others, waving them forward as he ran after Rudhira.

The entire party broke into a run—or a glide, for those capable of flight—in pursuit of Rudhira. They were not evenly matched; the faster quickly left the slower behind.

They heard the confrontation before they saw it—people shouting, glass shattering, loud thumping. At last Hanner rounded a curve and stopped.

Rudhira was still airborne, but only a few feet off the ground, her waist roughly even with the top of Hanner's head. Her hands were flung up defensively, guarding her face as a storm of hard and heavy objects flung themselves at her—bricks, stones, broken furniture. All turned aside before they reached her, to drop harmlessly to the hard-packed dirt.

Fifty feet farther down Fish Street two men hung in the air, one scarcely out of his teens and dressed in a fine velvet tunic that was at least a size too small, the other middle-aged and wearing good brown homespun. The street beneath them was strewn with debris—and bodies. At least four people lay motionless amid the rubble, and Hanner could not tell whether they were alive or dead.

It was from this field of rubble that objects were rising and accelerating toward Rudhira.

The entire scene was eerily lit by the flames of burning buildings; several of the houses and shops here had been torn open, their doors, walls, and windows ripped out into the street, and spilled lamps or flung torches had set curtains, carpets, and other furnishings ablaze in the ruined interiors thus exposed. One thatched roof had caught as well; fortunately, Hanner noticed, the surrounding roofs were proper tile, so the flames might not spread—though burning wisps of straw might be carried on the hot winds . . .

"Gods!" someone behind Hanner said.

"Don't just stand there," Hanner snapped. "Stop them!"

The other two flyers in Hanner's party had already come up alongside Rudhira; now the three of them formed a united front, and the hail of flying rubble slowed and stopped. Rudhira lowered her hands and glared at the two men.

"You shouldn't have done that," she said in a voice that carried unnaturally, echoing from the walls still standing on either side.

"Mind your own business, witch!" the young man bellowed back.

"*Warlock,*" Rudhira answered. "Not witch. I'm a warlock now, just as you are."

"Oh, no," the man replied. "Not like *me*. I'm the most powerful of all!"

"You haven't proved that to *my* satisfaction," the older man barked.

"I would have, if she hadn't interrrupted!" He turned his attention from Rudhira to the older man. "I already knocked down three people who thought they could match me—"

"You're forgetting something," Rudhira interrupted. "It took *both* of you to stop me—and now I have help!" She raised her hands again—not in a defensive gesture, but spread wide in defiance.

The young man dropped heavily to the ground and fell back, lying supine across a smashed window frame.

"The rest of you keep the other one busy," Rudhira ordered as she glided forward, toward her downed opponent.

The older man looked alarmed and started to turn away.

"Stop him!" Hanner ordered. "All of you but Rudhira—knock him down!"

It was as if a gigantic hand had swatted him from the sky; the older man smashed into the ground flat on his face and lay stunned.

Hanner was somewhat stunned as well, though for only an instant. He had not realized how effectively his warlocks could work together.

"Just hold him," Hanner said. "Don't hurt him." Then he turned to Rudhira.

She loomed over the young man, her red dress catching the firelight vividly, almost seeming to glow—in fact, Hanner thought it might *be* glowing. Given how little was known about this new magic, this so-called warlockry, that would hardly be surprising.

Rudhira hovered about five feet up, arms spread, glaring down at the young man struggling to rise—not to sit up, but to lift himself off the ground. He fluttered slightly, like a fallen leaf stirred by the wind, but could not levitate himself more than an inch or two against Rudhira's resistance.

At last he let himself fall back. "You killed *more* than three, then?" he asked.

Hanner gasped—but Rudhira snapped, "I didn't kill anyone!"

"But then how can you be so *strong*?"

Rudhira frowned more deeply. "What are you talking about?" she demanded.

"Isn't that how it works?" the man asked. "I got stronger

each time I fought and defeated another one of us . . . a warlock, you said?"

"That's what the witches called us," Rudhira said. "It's as good a name as any."

"And you didn't kill other warlocks?"

"You're a fool," Rudhira said. "I didn't kill anyone. We're all different—some stronger than others. I was just lucky."

"But I got *stronger*," the man protested. "I know I did! I felt more powerful after each fight!"

Rudhira stared down at him for a moment.

"Yes, I'm sure you did," she said, disgust plain in her voice. "Have you ever heard of *practice*? I don't know what warlockry is, but I know it gets easier with practice—the more I use, the more I can feel it waiting to be used. You were stronger after each of your stupid fights because of *that*, you idiot, not because you were stealing your enemies' power!"

"Is that really how it works?" Hanner asked, but neither Rudhira nor her opponent heard him.

If it was so, then any hope he might have had that these warlocks would all use up their power and return to normal was gone.

He turned to the older man and stepped forward, picking his way through the wreckage. "Hold him down," he called to Yorn and the others as he approached.

Hanner's route took him past one of the bodies, an old woman, and from the glassy staring eyes and bloodless complexion he was fairly certain she was dead. He didn't look; instead he focused on the older warlock.

The man was recovering from his fall—enough to turn his head and look up at Hanner.

"My lord," he said, recognizing Hanner's attire.

"Let me go," Rudhira's foe said. "I'll go away if you let me up!"

"Just keep him there for now," Hanner called back over his shoulder. Then he returned his attention to the older man.

"That one says he killed three people," Hanner said, indicating the other downed warlock with a jerk of his head. "How many did *you* kill?"

"I didn't *try* to kill anyone," the older warlock said.

"Just let me go!" the younger warlock said. "If you're right that it's just practice, then there's no reason to hurt me!"

"Shut up!" Hanner bellowed at him. "Rudhira, you keep him right where he is." He turned back to the older man.

"You didn't *try* to," he said. "*Did* you?"

"I might have," the warlock admitted. "I did make some of the mess, I admit it—I was defending myself against that lunatic!"

"Why did you help him fight Rudhira?"

The older man shrugged. "A mistake," he said. "That fool attacked me—*challenged* me, he said, for control of the street. I got caught up in it, and when she interrupted us it seemed like an unwelcome nuisance."

Hanner nodded. "The heat of battle," he said. "I've heard it can make a person do stupid things."

"Yes, exactly, my lord."

"And now that the battle's over, what do you intend to do?"

The man glanced around at the rubble-strewn street, the burning buildings, the old woman's corpse.

"I suspect I will stand trial before a city magistrate, where I will plead for leniency because I was driven mad by my nightmares and this new magic." He sighed. "And then I suppose I'll spend the rest of my life as a slave or in a dungeon somewhere, if I'm not simply hanged."

"If your plea for leniency is accepted, you might just be flogged or exiled from the city," Hanner said. "And I think you can reasonably point to all the others who ran wild tonight as evidence to support your case. I take it you're surrendering to us?"

"I don't have much of a choice."

Hanner smiled slightly. "No, you don't," he agreed.

Then he turned to the other man. "What do you have to say for yourself?" he asked.

"I went mad too, I think," the younger man said. "I thought I was *chosen*, that the dreams meant I had to do something with this power I was given. I thought I would fight my way up, killing the others and taking their power, until I was the most powerful magician in the World, and then I would rule all of Ethshar."

"What about the overlord?" Rudhira demanded. "*He* rules Ethshar, and he's not a magician at all!"

"I was going to kill him," the man admitted.

"That's treason," Yorn said.

"Lord Azrad's a fat old fool!" the warlock shouted, sitting up—Hanner saw Rudhira's startled expression when he was able to do so; she had clearly not intended to let him up.

"He's still the overlord," Hanner said.

"Not *my* overlord," the warlock said, struggling against something invisible.

"Stop fighting," Hanner ordered him.

"May demons gnaw your bones," the warlock said. He raised a hand—and suddenly his head twisted around to one side, impossibly far, and Hanner heard the snap of breaking bone. The warlock fell back, limp and lifeless.

Rudhira smiled with satisfaction. Hanner stared up at her. "You didn't have to kill him!" he shouted.

"He was a traitor and a murderer and I was defending myself," Rudhira said flatly.

That was obviously true, but Hanner was still upset by her actions. He started to phrase a further protest when the older warlock said, "I helped her."

"He did," Rudhira agreed.

Hanner looked from one to the other. He had the distinct feeling that his control of the situation was not as secure as it should be, and that any further disputes would only erode it further.

"Well, what's done is done," he said. "Get up, you, and come along—we're heading for the Palace, and if you co-operate we'll put in a good word for you when the time comes." He reached down a hand to help the warlock up.

The older man rolled over and took Hanner's hand.

A moment later the entire party was once again marching down Fish Street, leaving the surviving inhabitants of the neighborhood, now warily emerging from their ruined homes, to put out the fires and clean up the mess.

Chapter Eight

Kirsha sat in the middle of the street, wrapped in wine-red velvet while a cluster of stolen jewelry orbited slowly above her head, and shivered, despite the warmth of the summer night and the heat from the burning tannery a block to the north. Bolts of cloth lay strewn on the street around her.

It wasn't a dream. She was sure of that now. She had begun to doubt it some time ago, when she realized she could feel the heat of the flames and the hard ground beneath her bare feet when she landed. Her dreams were never so detailed as this.

It was magic, some terrible magic, and she had been caught up in it and done crazy things. She had stolen all this pretty cloth, a dozen silver rounds' worth at the very least, and the jewelry, which was probably worth the same in gold. She had smashed in people's shop windows, and had flung broken window glass at people who annoyed her . . .

She shuddered at that, and thanked the gods that she hadn't hit anyone.

At least, she didn't *think* she had.

Just then she heard voices and looked up to see a woman flying.

For a moment she almost reconsidered, and decided she

was dreaming after all. The woman practically glowed red in the torchlight and moonlight and firelight; her clothing was all red and gold, her very hair was an orange color Kirsha had never seen before, her face was heavily made up so that her cheeks shone red, and she was flying along as casually as a hummingbird.

Then the woman called to her, "Are you all right?" and she knew it wasn't a dream.

"No," Kirsha said miserably, huddling down under her stolen velvet.

"Lord Hanner!" the woman in red called. "This way!"

Two more flying apparitions appeared around the corner, and a small crowd of people on foot. Kirsha felt something close around her, and suddenly the spinning, flying jewelry fell to the ground.

A plump, curly-haired young man in a silk-trimmed tunic came trotting up to her. "Are you injured?" he asked.

"She's fine, physically," the woman in red replied.

"Just upset," said the other flying woman, who wore green and brown and was fatter and older than the first.

"Who are you?" Kirsha asked.

"I am Lord Hanner," the plump young man said. "These are warlocks under my command—people affected by this magic."

"Like me?" Kirsha asked.

"More or less," Lord Hanner said. He frowned. "It looks to me as if you've been . . ."

"Stealing," Kirsha said, lifting up a length of velvet. "I know. I went a little crazy, and thought it was all a dream, or that the whole World had gone mad."

"We've seen quite a bit of that," Lord Hanner said. "I think you'll have to come with us—the overlord's magistrates will want to talk to you." He looked around at the scattered fabric. "First, though—do you know where all this came from? We should take it back to its rightful owners."

Kirsha nodded. "I think I remember it all."

"Good," Hanner said—and the bolts of cloth rose into the

air around them, like a tent being lifted into place or banners being raised. Kirsha's eyes widened.

She wasn't doing this.

"Lead the way," Hanner said, offering a hand to help her up.

Lord Faran straightened his tunic slightly as he stepped into the lesser audience chamber, and tried his best to look completely untroubled by all the madness around him. Lord Azrad looked up at him.

"Well, it's about time you got here!" the overlord said.

"Your pardon, my lord," Faran said, essaying a small bow. "I was attending to urgent business elsewhere in the Palace."

Azrad eyed him suspiciously. The overlord was always foul-tempered when his sleep was interrupted, but his expression seemed unusually sour even so.

"In the Palace?" Azrad asked.

"Yes, my lord. Attending to a few personal matters, and then checking to see who had been awakened and who had not, who was where, and so on—seeing to the overlord's business as best I could."

The personal matters had been discovering that while Nerra and Alris were secure in their own beds, Hanner had never returned from his walk; and that Isia had left the Palace before the overlord had ordered the entrances to be sealed and no one to be permitted in or out.

The girls had been awakened by the noise and were probably still up, chattering, but they were safe at home while Hanner was not, and while Isia might or might not have reached her parents' house safely.

Faran was not pleased at the thought that his nephew and his mistress were somewhere out in the city while magic-wielding lunatics were rampaging through the streets, but there wasn't much he could do about it.

At least, not that he knew of—but of course, he could

apparently wield that same magic, and he had no idea what that might make possible.

"Good," Azrad said. "*Nobody* is to leave, not even you, Faran. And no one's to enter. I don't want to risk this thing, whatever it is, contaminating my home!"

"Of course, my lord," Faran said. Long years of practice allowed him to keep his expression utterly calm as he realized that Azrad did not know that whatever had happened had already affected people inside the Palace.

So far he knew of two people who had been awakened by a nightmare and found themselves able to do strange magic—himself, and a serving girl in the kitchens by the name of Hinda. Faran had gone down to the kitchens to make sure there was sufficient food available for the extra guards and anyone else summoned from their beds, should they become hungry, and had found three of the cooks making a fuss over the little orphan.

Hinda had demonstrated that she could send a spoon skittering across the table or hopping up and down like a frightened flea. Faran had told her not to worry about it right now, but to get the cooking fires hot and see what was in the stores.

"I don't like this," Azrad said, shaking his head. "Wild magic running loose, people flying around like wizards—it's not good, not good at all. Someone's up to something, some magician somewhere. I won't have it. The wizards say we can't mix magic and government, so they've been watching the government—but maybe they haven't been watching the right magicians, *hai*?"

"Maybe," Faran agreed. "Has someone spoken to any of our hired magicians to ask if they know what's going on?"

"My brother's attending to it."

"Ah . . . which brother, my lord?"

"Lord Karannin, of course. He's Lord High Magistrate."

"The Lord of the Household works with magicians as well, my lord."

"Clurim has enough to do."

Faran started to ask just what Lord Clurim had to do,

then decided not to. If Azrad wanted to tell him, he would—and if he didn't, Lord Faran would find out elsewhere.

"Lord Karannin deals with several magicians, but none of them are of any great note, my lord. Perhaps I should go speak to Guildmaster Ithinia—"

"If you leave the Palace you won't get back in," Azrad interrupted. "Not even you, my lord."

"Then I won't go," Faran said promptly.

He didn't like it, though. If *he* couldn't get back in, then no one could. He wondered where Hanner was—not in the Palace, according to the guards at the entrance, but that left all the rest of the World.

Faran hoped he was safe in Mavi's bed, but somehow he doubted that Hanner had managed that.

"We'll send Ithinia a messenger later," Azrad said. "For now, though, I want to get back to my bed, and when you've answered one more question I plan to do exactly that." He shifted in his seat and then continued, "Tell me, then—do you know anything about this magic that's running loose?"

Faran hesitated.

Sooner or later he might want to admit the truth—or he might not; if the magic turned out to be temporary, something that vanished at sunrise, then perhaps it would be best quickly forgotten.

Right now, though, Faran was not about to tell Azrad that he, the overlord's chief advisor, was one of the people touched by the mysterious power. Lord Azrad was clearly in no mood to tolerate such a revelation.

"Not a thing, I'm afraid," Lord Faran said.

Elken the Beggar smiled to himself as he hurried along Wall Street.

Those other fools back in the Wizards' Quarter had obeyed when that fat little lordling told them to follow him to the Palace, but Elken wasn't stupid enough to do that. He had other plans.

Nobody knew what this new magic was or what it could do, but they were already trying to find ways to control it. Lord Hanner and his party, Mother Perréa and the witches, all the wizards and guardsmen and the rest, they just wanted to put everything back the way it was.

And they would probably succeed. The new magic would be erased or controlled all through the city streets, and everything would once again obey the overlord's laws.

Except that there were places where the overlord's laws had never meant much, and Elken lived in one of them.

Other people with the new magic would want to improve themselves with it. They would probably pretend to be real magicians and would go into the streets looking for ways to use it to earn money. They would obey the law.

They wouldn't stay in the Hundred-Foot Field with the thieves and beggars.

Which meant, Elken thought, that there was an opportunity here. Being one magician among many was nothing special, but being the *only* magician in the Hundred-Foot Field would be another matter.

He smiled again, looked out across the Field, and casually, purely for the enjoyment of the sensation of control, tipped over someone's tent fifty feet away before hurrying on.

The streets were quieter now. Kennan had been grabbing passersby, if they were on foot rather than airborne and didn't look dangerous, and asking them if they knew what was happening; so far he hadn't gotten anything close to a decent answer. The mad ones, the ones flying by or flinging objects in all directions, he had sometimes hidden from, sometimes shouted at, but they had not been any better.

Some sort of magic was loose in the city, clearly—but nobody seemed to know what. People had disappeared— Aken was not the only one—but no one knew who had taken them or why.

The only guardsman Kennan had seen had pulled away,

saying he was too busy to worry about one missing man.

Kennan stood in the doorway of his house, looking out at the empty street, with Sanda pressing up behind him, peering over his shoulder. He was thinking.

At last he reached a decision.

"Someone has to know what's going on," he said, "and someone has to be doing something about it. I'm going to go to the Palace and demand an explanation."

"I'll come with you," Sanda said.

Kennan turned and pushed her back inside.

"No, you won't," he said. "You'll stay here and look after the children."

"They're all asleep . . ."

"No, I said!" Kennan glowered at her, his hand still pushing at her shoulder. "What if little Sarai wakes up and wants her mother? What if one of them gets sick? What if the magic tries to take one of *them*?"

"I couldn't stop it . . ." Sanda began halfheartedly—but she was no longer resisting the pressure of Kennan's hand.

"And what if Aken comes back as soon as I'm out of sight around the corner and finds us *both* gone?"

Sanda blinked, suddenly silent, and stepped back into the house.

"I'll stay here until you come back," she said.

"Good," Kennan said, lowering his hand. "Good." He tried to smile at her, without much success. "Don't worry, Sanda. I'll find him. I don't know why the magicians took him or what they did with him, but I'll find out." He stepped back inside long enough to give her a quick, reassuring hug, then turned and marched out of the house, closing the door tightly behind him.

The overlord would probably be asleep at this hour, closer to dawn than sunset, but *someone* at the Palace was surely awake, and someone there would either give him the answers he wanted or direct him to where they could be found.

If they didn't, they would regret it.

Chapter Nine

The walk to the Palace took Hanner's company more than two hours—they made detour after detour as they encountered one incident after another. Hanner took the time along the way to ask a few questions and learned that his other two flyers were Varrin the Weaver and Desset of Eastwark. He learned the names of about half the others, as well, including the four warlocks they had taken prisoner: the girl who had stolen jewelry was Kirsha the Younger; Saldan of Southgate had dueled with the warlock Rudhira killed; Roggit Rayel's son had been looting cash from shops and taverns, and Gror of the Crooked Teeth had been smashing windows more or less at random.

Three other warlocks had fled and not been deemed worth pursuing; half a dozen had been calmed down and sent home. Had Hanner realized how many he would encounter, he thought, he might not have chosen to take Kirsha and Gror as prisoners, since they had not harmed anyone and seemed to have regretted their crimes—but having already made the decision, he was not inclined to reverse it.

The journey seemed interminable, but at last Hanner, at the head of his party, emerged from Arena Street into the torchlit plaza—and found himself facing a wall of guardsmen, lined up six deep, armed with spears.

Spears were either for show or for serious fighting and putting down riots or insurrections; swords and truncheons were standard for the far more usual patrol and police work.

"What's going on?" Hanner demanded as the rest of his group, including the prisoners, emerged from the dark street and gathered behind him. Rudhira was still flying and swept up to hover above him.

The rows of guards promptly aimed their spears in her general direction.

"Put those down!" Hanner bellowed as best he could—he was exhausted, and at its best his voice had never been the commanding roar his uncle could produce, so the result was not very impressive. "She's with me."

"That's Rudhira," one of the soldiers said. "I know her."

"Who is *he*?" someone else asked.

"I am Lord Hanner," Hanner shouted. "Nephew and heir to Lord Faran, the overlord's chief advisor. Now, what's going on here? Who's in charge?"

The lines of spearmen shuffled for a moment, then parted, and a captain, gold-trimmed breastplate over his yellow tunic, stepped forward. He bore no spear, but his hand was on the hilt of his sheathed sword.

The face was familiar; Hanner, tired as he was, needed a few seconds before he could attach a name.

"Lord Hanner," the captain said, before the name came to Hanner's lips.

"Captain Naral," Hanner said. "May I ask what is going on here, and why all these men are on parade in the middle of the night?"

"It's no parade, my lord. Surely you're aware of the mad magicians running riot through the city—you appear to have brought at least one of them with you." He nodded toward Rudhira.

"Of course I'm aware!" Hanner said. "And I've brought some of them here for the overlord to deal with." He gestured at his party. "We've taken four criminal warlocks prisoner and brought them for trial."

"Warlocks?"

"That's what the witches call them. Nobody else seems to have a name for them."

"You've spoken to a witch about them, then?"

Hanner nodded. "When I saw what was happening I went to the Wizards' Quarter for advice. The magicians there are as puzzled as the rest of us, but Mother Perréa said this new magic resembles a technique used by witches in the Great War, and she called it war-locking."

Naral frowned. "No one knew what caused this outbreak?"

"No one I spoke with," Hanner confirmed.

"That's bad." The captain frowned again, then turned up an empty hand. "Well, perhaps by morning someone will have divined more."

"And in the meantime, Captain, I have gathered several warlocks of goodwill, and with their aid taken four criminals prisoner, and I would like to bring them all into the Palace and get some sleep."

Naral hesitated. "I'm afraid I can't allow that," he said at last.

Hanner had expected and dreaded this answer. "Why not?" he asked.

"We have been ordered to allow no one to enter the Palace, and most particularly not to allow any of these mad magicians—these warlocks, as you call them—near it."

"I'm sure my uncle didn't mean that to include *me* . . ."

"It wasn't Lord Faran who gave the order, my lord," Naral interrupted. "It was Lord Azrad himself. The overlord."

Hanner blinked. "Oh," he said.

That explained the apparent overreaction of lining up several hundred guards in the square. Lord Faran would probably have been more conservative of manpower; Lord Azrad, though, had never demonstrated any sense of proportion, nor shown any inclination to conserve anything but his own energy.

Right now Hanner was very much in the mood to conserve what little energy he had left himself—preferably while comfortably tucked into his own bed. He glanced up over his shoulder at Rudhira, and wondered how much she could carry.

"You realize that a warlock could probably just fly over your heads to reach the Palace?" he asked.

"She would have to fly through a storm of spears," Naral said, his tone almost apologetic.

Hanner was not at all certain that would bother Rudhira, but decided against asking her. Instead he said, "Could someone please petition the overlord on my behalf? I'd very much like to get some sleep."

"The overlord has retired for the night," Naral said. "He gave *very* strict orders that he was not to be disturbed except in the event of dire emergency."

Hanner sighed deeply. "Then could someone send a message to my uncle, please? Lord Faran?"

Captain Naral considered that for a moment, then nodded. "I'll send someone. What's the message?"

"Simply that I'm out here, with several friends and four prisoners, and we would like to enter the Palace—at the very least, *I* would like to enter, to go to bed."

"I'll tell him, but I doubt he'll defy the overlord's edict. Lord Azrad was quite emphatic."

"Just send the message, please, Captain."

Naral bowed. "As you wish, my lord." He turned away, beckoned to a guardsman apparently at random, and explained the errand.

While he did, Hanner turned to his own party.

"It appears we'll have a wait, at the very least," he said. "I'd suggest sitting down and getting a little rest." He pointed at the curbstones surrounding a shrine set in the corner of the wall at Arena Street and Aristocrat Circle. "I'll be right here if anyone needs me."

With that, he settled himself on the nearest curbstone and leaned back, his head just touching the underside of the shrine's offering shelf.

Just getting his weight off his aching feet for a moment felt wonderful.

Yorn settled beside him, but had to duck slightly and lean forward to avoid banging his head on the shelf. He looked out at the neat lines of guardsmen and remarked, "I don't see anyone from my company."

"Well, that's good," Hanner said. "Then you probably

aren't disobeying any orders by being here with me."

Another of the warlocks, a weather-beaten fellow in gray homespun, settled on Hanner's other side, not on the curbstones but squatting with his back against the wall.

"We could all go out to the Hundred-Foot Field," he said. "No one there would bother us once they realized we're magicians."

Hanner looked at him. "I don't think I heard your name," he said.

"Zarek," the other replied. "Zarek the Homeless, for the past few years."

"Then you've slept in the Hundred-Foot Field before," Hanner said.

"Every night," Zarek replied. "That's where I was tonight when the screaming started, over in Westwark. I went to the Wizards' Quarter thinking I might be able to trade the news of mysterious screaming for a free meal, but then I found out the whole city had been affected and everyone already knew. And *then* I found out that I could do this new magic, and while I was trying to think of some way to use it you made your announcement, and I came along with you in hopes it might mean a roof over my head for the night."

Hanner stared at him.

Like everyone in Ethshar of the Spices, Hanner knew about the Hundred-Foot Field. More than two hundred years ago Azrad the Great had decreed that no permanent structure could be built in the hundred feet between Wall Street and the city wall—the area was to be kept clear so that troops could move freely along the defenses in time of war.

Of course, the Hegemony of the Three Ethshars hadn't been in a real war for two centuries, not since the Great War finally ended, and empty space inside the city walls was too precious to be left empty. The law said no permanent structures could be built there, but it made no mention of *temporary* ones, and Ethshar was crowded; accordingly, within days of the edict the city's poor and homeless had begun to set up crude huts and flimsy tents in that hundred-foot gap.

The entire length of the Hundred-Foot Field, estimated at nine or ten miles, was a refuge for the outcasts of the Hegemony. Beggars, thieves, cripples, madmen—and those honest people who, for one reason or another, couldn't afford to rent a room and had no wealthier friends or relatives who would take them in.

Hanner had seen the Hundred-Foot Field on those few occasions when his business had taken him to any of the city's gates or within a block or so of Wall Street, but he had never gotten any closer than he had to. He had no intention of sleeping in the Hundred-Foot Field or even of setting foot in it. Zarek might be safe enough there, but Zarek wasn't one of the city's lords. Walking into the Field wearing silk embroidery and bay-leaf insignia was asking to be robbed; wearing worn homespun would attract far less interest.

On the other hand, Zarek wasn't as filthy and miserable as Hanner would have expected a dweller in the Field to be. His hair and beard were desperately in need of washing and trimming, but they weren't tangled or matted, and his hands and face were fairly clean, his skin clear of any lesions. He certainly looked far better than that rag-clad fellow Hanner had seen back in Witch Alley—*that* person Hanner would expect to sleep in the Hundred-Foot Field.

Legend had it that at one time the Field was green with grass and wildflowers, but now it was all bare dirt—hard-packed and dusty in dry summer heat, a sodden mass of sticky mud in the spring rains, icy in winter—trodden by hundreds, or more likely thousands, of feet. Despite that Zarek, while hardly dapper, was reasonably clean and presentable, and his account of his actions was direct and clear. He had plainly kept himself mentally and physically intact, despite the hardships of his life.

Perhaps, Hanner thought, Zarek knew secrets for living relatively well in the Hundred-Foot Field—or perhaps he had somehow managed to clean himself up tonight before venturing into the Wizards' Quarter.

Asking him directly how he had achieved this seemed

rude, and Hanner was too tired to really take that much of an interest. Instead he said, "I think we can find somewhere better to stay than the Field."

Zarek turned up a hand. "I can't afford to pay anything."

"*I* can," Hanner said. "But I hope we won't have to." He looked toward the Palace, hoping to see his uncle or a messenger approaching.

Instead he saw the ranks of spear-carrying guardsmen, standing ready to face the strange magic that threatened the city's peace.

Hanner wondered just how effective those spears would be against warlocks. Oh, some warlocks were undoubtedly too weak or unskilled to fend off a solid thrust or well-aimed throw, but he had no doubt that Rudhira, for one, could have easily turned aside any single attack.

At that thought he looked around for Rudhira and spotted her perched, catlike, atop a garden wall, looking not out at the waiting soldiers, but inward, into the darkened garden of one of the mansions facing upon the square.

Hanner wondered what she saw there—hedges and fountains and flowers, presumably. Hanner took a moment to orient himself and realized that the garden belonged to Adagan, Lord of the Shipyard. Hanner knew Adagan, of course, but had never seen his gardens. They had no special reputation for excellence.

Rudhira, though, was a Camptown streetwalker—or had been until tonight, at any rate. She might well have never seen a real garden before.

A streetwalker. And Zarek was a homeless beggar. Hanner frowned. What was he doing among these people? He was a lord, an assistant to the overlord's chief advisor, specializing in the relationship between government and magic; what business did he have with these beggars and whores?

But of course, they were magicians now. Whoever was responsible for this new magic had certainly shaken up the natural order of things.

Hanner did not appreciate that. Apparently Lord Azrad didn't much like it, either. Hanner wondered how long this

warlockry business would last—hours? Days? Years? Forever?

Short of divination there was no way to know, and Hanner had no intention of waking up a wizard or theurgist at
this hour to buy a divination that might not even work, as
predictive magic about magic was notoriously unreliable.
Tomorrow he might go back to the Wizards' Quarter and
inquire, but now he just wanted to sleep.

He wasn't quite as exhausted as he might ordinarily have
expected after staying up so late and walking all over the
city, but he supposed that was just the excitement.

He stood up and stretched, and was about to settle back
on the curbstone when the line of soldiers parted, and his
sister, Lady Alris, appeared.

"Hanner?" she called uncertainly, eyeing the warlocks
scattered around the intersection. Hanner realized that he
was standing in the shadow of the little shrine, where the
soldiers' torchlight didn't really reach; he stepped forward
and called, "Here I am!"

"Oh!" Alris hesitated, then ran to him, stopping a few
feet away.

"Uncle Faran sent you?"

Alris nodded. "He can't leave the Palace."

That wasn't really a surprise; Hanner supposed his uncle
was closeted with the overlord somewhere, discussing the
situation—though Naral had said the overlord had retired.

Well, perhaps Faran was talking to underlings, preparing
them for whatever was to be done in the morning.

"May we enter, then?" Hanner asked.

"No, of course not," Alris said, startled. "*No one* may
enter! That's why Uncle Faran can't leave—the overlord
isn't letting *anyone* in, not even him! Not the guards, not
messengers—they have to call their messages through the
door without stepping inside. No exceptions *at all*."

"Oh," Hanner said, startled. "But then how will *you* get
back in?"

"I won't," Alris said. "I'll be staying with you." She

smiled, the brightest smile Hanner had seen from her in months. "It'll be an adventure!"

"Staying where?" Hanner asked.

"Oh, well, that's why Uncle Faran sent me," Alris said. She reached into the purse on her belt and produced an ornate black key. "He didn't trust anyone but us with this, and Nerra refused to come, so I volunteered."

Hanner had never seen the key before, but he knew immediately what it must be for. Lord Faran's official residence was in the Palace, where he was easily available when Lord Azrad wanted him, but he was not, in fact, always available. He was only home in the Palace perhaps four nights in ten. Hanner and his sisters had long suspected that he maintained an unofficial residence as well, where he could indulge himself in interests that might not please the overlord and might not be welcome in the Palace.

None of them knew where this other residence was, though—or at least, none of them had until now.

"He told you where it is?" Hanner asked.

Alris nodded. "It's at the corner of High Street and Coronet Street. The northeast corner."

That was about half a dozen blocks to the southwest of where they now stood, in the New City.

"Lead the way," Hanner said. Then he raised his voice and called, "Yorn! Rudhira! Varrin! All of you! Follow me!"

Alris started and looked about nervously as the warlocks rose—some of them well into the air—and assembled. "Uncle Faran said *we* could stay there, Hanner," she said. "You and me, not all these people."

"They need to stay *somewhere*," Hanner replied. "I ordered them to follow me, back in the Wizards' Quarter; that makes me responsible for them. They can sleep on the floor; I'm sure we can squeeze them all in."

Hanner knew enough of his uncle's tastes to be sure of that; Faran was not the sort to settle for a mere furnished room for his trysts. Hanner expected a fair-sized apartment.

"I don't—" Alris began.

"Alris," Hanner said, cutting her off, "we're *all* going. It's my decision, not yours; if Uncle Faran doesn't like it we can deal with that later. Now, lead the way."

Reluctantly, Alris obeyed, and the entire party trudged out of the torchlit square into the shadowy streets.

Chapter Ten

Kennan stood in the corner of the plaza, staring in frustration at the ranked soldiers.

They wouldn't let him *near* the Palace. When he had told them he had to speak with the Lord High Magistrate about his stolen son, they had told him that a hundred other people were in line ahead of him, and the overlord wasn't letting *anyone* see Lord Karannin.

And then when those people had come flying up Arena Street the soldiers hadn't taken them prisoner or tried to kill them—instead they had just sent someone to *talk* to them.

Kennan stood up on his toes, trying to see clearly, as the officer talked to the chubby young man in the fancy tunic.

As he watched, the officer turned and beckoned to another soldier. They spoke quietly for a moment, and then the second soldier began pushing his way toward the Palace.

Kennan watched, fuming—was that guardsman going to be permitted in, where he, an honest citizen with a legitimate grievance, was not?

But then the guardsman was stopped on the bridge, and his message, whatever it was, was relayed from there.

So even messengers weren't being permitted inside.

Then he couldn't hope to get inside the Palace tonight. He looked at the motley bunch of people gathered at the mouth of Arena Street—the young man in the fancy tunic, the flying whore, the worried-looking guardsman, and the rest.

If the guards could talk to them, Kennan decided, so could he. They might know what was going on, and where Aken had been taken. He began making his way around the side of the square.

By the time he reached Arena Street the others had retreated slightly, and it took a moment before he could locate them again. There were people scattered about, some standing, some sitting against walls, but he couldn't tell which were magicians; no one was hanging in the air anymore.

At last he spotted the redheaded whore perched atop the wall surrounding a mansion on Aristocrat Circle. He walked up to her and called up, "*Hai!* I'd like to talk to you."

She turned and looked down at him.

"Go away," she said. "I'm not available."

Kennan felt his ears redden. "I'm not a customer," he snapped. "I need to ask you something, about my son."

The redhead looked bored. "What name was he using?" she asked.

"He wasn't a customer, either," Kennan said, exasperated. "It's not about *you.*"

"If it's not about *me*, then why are you *asking* me?" she demanded.

"I saw you flying," Kennan said. "I thought you might know something."

The whore sighed. "Then ask. But I probably don't."

"His name is Aken of the Strong Arm. He was taken from his bed earlier tonight, snatched out the window by magic."

The woman turned up an empty palm. "I never heard of him," she said. "Don't know anything about anyone being snatched out a bedroom window. Sorry."

"Is there someone I could ask? Some magician?"

The woman turned up her palm again.

"Gods, woman, don't you have any compassion?" Kennan shouted. "My son is missing, and I want to know who's responsible!"

"None of us *know* who's responsible, old man!" the redhead shouted back. "We don't know you and we don't know your son, and in case you haven't noticed, half the city has gone raving mad tonight, prancing about smashing shop windows and setting things on fire, and some of us have had this magic thrust upon us, and we don't know any more about it than *you* do!"

Kennan stared up at her in silent anger, fists clenching and unclenching.

"Go away," she said, and Kennan found himself forced back, against his will, toward the plaza.

He fought at first, but it did no good, so at last he turned and walked away under his own power. When he had rounded the corner, out of sight of the woman in red, he stopped, took a deep breath, and collected himself.

He didn't know who those people were, but they *owed* him an explanation.

Just then he heard a commotion behind him, and he turned to see a girl in her early teens step out of the lines of soldiers and call, "Hanner?"

Kennan turned and watched as the man in the silk-trimmed tunic appeared out of the shadows and spoke to the girl—who, Kennan realized, must have come from the Palace.

There was something going on here, definitely. All of these people were working together, he was sure of it. He watched them closely, trying to hear as much as he could of their conversation.

"*No one* may enter!" the girl said. Kennan couldn't make out her next sentence, but that was clear. He listened and heard her conclude, "No exceptions *at all*."

Kennan didn't hear the next exchange, but then the girl said, "It'll be an adventure!" She reached into her purse and showed the man something Kennan couldn't see.

More words Kennan couldn't catch, and then the man raised his voice and called, "Yorn! Rudhira! Varrin! All of you! Follow me!"

The girl made a protest Kennan couldn't hear, and for a moment the two argued, but the man clearly won. The girl turned and began walking away from the square, into the darkness of Aristocrat Circle.

Several of the people who had been standing or sitting around arose and followed—including the redheaded whore, and two others who flew rather than walked.

Kennan hesitated only briefly, then followed.

"You'll do what I tell you!" Elken the Beggar bellowed, hovering above the Hundred-Foot Field, pointing down at the thirty or so people he had gathered.

"Elken, this is stupid," Tanna the Thief said. "If you're such a powerful magician now, why are you staying *here*?" She pointed at Wall Street. "Why don't you go into the city and make a place *there*?"

"Shut up!" Elken said. "I know better than that. I *went* into the city, and I came back. There are hundreds of magicians in the city, and lords ordering them around. But *here*, there's just me—me, and the bunch of you, and you're all going to be my slaves now."

"All right, fine," an old woman said. "What do you want us to do?"

"That's better," Elken said, mollified. "I want you to put together the tents and make a place worthy of me! And I want all the food you've got stashed away. And if anyone has any *oushka*, I want that, too."

The others looked at one another. A few whispered comments were exchanged, empty palms turned up.

Twenty minutes later Elken lay on a pile of mismatched bedding—a *big* pile, collected from at least a dozen of the residents of the Hundred-Foot Field—beneath a canopy made out of Old Man Kelder's tent stretched across the poles from Anaran the Thief's hut. He had a strip of dried salt beef in one hand, a half-full bottle of *oushka* in the other.

He took a gulp of liquor and smiled broadly. "The gods have smiled on me," he said. "It's as if they wanted to pay me back for making me suffer through that nightmare."

The memory of the dream, of the sensations of falling and burning and being buried, was unpleasant; his smile vanished and he took another long draught of *oushka*.

"The gods are just," Tanna said, from where she sat—just out of his reach, deliberately so.

"Of course," Elken said, then drained the rest of the bottle. "Come here, woman."

Reluctantly Tanna came, before Elken could use his mysterious magic to drag her. She cuddled up beside him.

As she had expected, though, he was now too drunk to do anything more than give her a squeeze before falling into a booze-induced stupor. After a few fumbling moments his head rolled back, his eyes closed, and he began snoring.

Tanna waited another five minutes, just to be sure.

Then she took the sharp little paring knife from her belt, reached around, and neatly sliced open Elken's left carotid artery.

He jerked awake, and she cut his throat from ear to ear as he stared up at her and clapped a hand to the initial wound.

She was flung back by his magic, smashing through the jury-rigged framework of his beggar's palace and landing on hard ground. She rolled aside—she had had years of practice dodging attacks, and a magical one wasn't really so different.

By the time she got to her feet and made her way cautiously back inside, Elken was still and limp, his eyes staring and lifeless.

"It's all right," she called. "He's dead."

The others emerged from their refuges to gather around her and look at Elken's corpse.

"I'm sorry about the ruined bedding," Tanna said as she stared down at the body. "What a waste!"

No one was sure whether she meant the bloodstained bedding or Elken's magic.

*   *   *

"I can't believe you sent her out there!" Nerra said, staring at her uncle.

Faran pointedly did not stare back, but instead studied the reports Captain Vengar had given him.

"She'll be fine," he said. "She just has to go a few blocks, and she'll have Hanner with her, and then they'll both be safe at my house."

"You really have a house in the New City?"

"I really do. I've had it since you were a baby."

"That's where you go when you aren't here and don't take us with you?"

"Usually, yes."

"So Hanner and Alris will live there from now on?"

Faran put down the reports. "I certainly hope not," he said. "I expect Lord Azrad will come to his senses once he's had some sleep and daylight has brightened the World, and then Hanner and Alris will come back here where they belong, and my house will be private again."

"But now they'll know where it is."

Faran sighed. "Nerra, there are scores of people in this city who know where it is. Anyone who really wants to know could find out easily enough. I don't think anyone really *cares*, though."

"Then why didn't you ever tell *us* about it?"

"Because it wasn't any of your concern."

"But . . ."

Faran had had enough of her questions—and he had *not* had enough sleep. His temper gave out, and he glared at her as he cut her off.

"Go to sleep, Nerra," he said. "If you really *must* ask me impertinent questions, do it in the morning." He got to his feet and marched into his bedroom.

Nerra watched him go, then looked around, realizing that she was alone in the room.

And she would be alone in her bedroom, with Alris out of the Palace. She would be alone, and these mad magicians, or demons in human guise or whatever they were, were roaming the streets and skies. The city guard was out in force, keeping the plaza clear—but what could they do against a demon? What good would they be if a mad magician flew across the canal to Nerra's bedroom window?

She shuddered at the thought—but she didn't have much choice. Reluctantly, she wandered back to her own bed, climbed in, closed the curtains, and buried herself under the coverlet, certain she would get no more sleep that night.

Ten minutes later she was snoring quietly.

Chapter Eleven

Hanner stood in the shadows of Coronet Street and looked up at the looming black facade beyond the garden wall.

"It's the entire house?" he asked.

"That's what he said," Alris replied.

Hanner grimaced. He should have known, he told himself. Fitting his entire party—himself, his sister, his fifteen recruits, and his four prisoners—would not be a problem. It was entirely possible there would even be enough beds for each to sleep alone. Lord Faran's unofficial residence stood four stories high, and the garden wall extended along Coronet Street from High Street almost to the corner of Merchant Street.

"Where's the gate?" one of the warlocks asked.

"Who needs a gate?" Rudhira asked, flying over the wall.

"*Some* of us do," Yorn replied grumpily.

"It's on High Street," Alris said, pointing.

They trudged on up Coronet Street, and around the corner onto High Street. The garden wall that had hidden the ground floor from them ended a few feet from the corner, to be replaced by an iron fence topped with spikes. Peering between the bars of the fence Hanner could see broad, many-paned windows in a brick and black stone wall just the other side of a dooryard perhaps five or six feet wide. Rudhira was in the dooryard, moving quickly toward the front door, but Hanner took a moment to look the place over.

All the windows were dark, and no torches or lanterns hung at the entrance, but that was hardly a surprise.

An elegant iron gate guarded the entrance, a dozen yards from the end of the garden wall. To Hanner's surprise it wasn't locked; it swung open at his touch, silently, without the slightest creak or rattle. Hanner stepped through into the dooryard to find Rudhira standing by the door, tapping her foot impatiently.

"I could have opened this myself," she said.

"Without breaking it?" Hanner asked, curious about just what warlockry could and couldn't do.

"I *think* so—but I'm not sure, and you've got the key, so I waited."

"Thank you," Hanner said. Then it registered that no one was opening the door, and he turned. Alris was standing just behind him, the key in her hand, watching Rudhira warily and not approaching the door.

"I'll do it, Alris," he said, taking the key from her. He found the lock, and a moment later the door swung open.

The hallway beyond was dark, of course. Hanner stepped in and beckoned to the others, then stood still for a moment to let his eyes adjust.

A red glow appeared to one side, dimly illuminating the hall. Hanner turned, startled, and found Rudhira standing beside him, one hand raised—and that hand was glowing.

By that dull red light Hanner could see a look of intense concentration on Rudhira's face. Her lips parted to reveal tightly clenched teeth as she grimaced and sucked in air.

The glow brightened from red to orange—and then brightened further, but stayed orange. Rudhira let out her breath in a long, ragged sigh and relaxed; the glow steadied.

Hanner quickly turned his attention to their surroundings and spotted a candle on a table by the door. "Does anyone have tinder?" he asked, pointing. "We don't want to wear Rudhira out."

Rudhira followed his finger and saw the candle. "I might be able to light it," she said, starting to lower her glowing hand.

"No, don't strain yourself," Hanner said. Alris was already pulling a tinderbox from her purse, and a moment later the candle flared to life.

"You can relax now," Hanner told Rudhira, nodding at her still-glowing hand as he picked up the candle.

"It's no trouble," she said, but the glow blinked out.

"It looked like an effort," Hanner said.

"Only at first, when I tried to see how to do it," Rudhira said. "Once I started, it got easier. That's how this magic always seems to work—the more you use it, the easier it is. The hard part is in understanding *how* to do something new."

"You seem to be doing well at that," Hanner said. "I haven't seen anyone else make anything glow. Mostly they just seem to throw things around." As he spoke he was looking around at the broad hallway.

As he would have expected from Uncle Faran, it was magnificent, but tasteful. It was perhaps fifteen feet across, with a twelve-foot ceiling, and he couldn't see the far end by the single candle's light. The walls were papered in gold and white above polished dark wood wainscoting, broken by ornately modeled plaster and gilt pilasters. Gleaming brass sconces were spaced evenly between the columns, except where arched doorways opened into other rooms. A splendid staircase, dark wood carpeted in red, rose ahead of Hanner and his party. To the left an archway opened into a darkened parlor; to the right was a closed door, painted white and trimmed with gilt.

"May a hundred gods bless me," Zarek muttered as he looked at this opulence.

"Well, it's a roof over our heads," Hanner said wryly. He turned and beckoned everyone inside—some were still hesitating on the front walk. "Come in, all of you!" he said.

He counted off the party. Rudhira and Alris had come in with him; Zarek and Yorn were close behind. He still hadn't learned the names of all the others, but he counted the four prisoners and the other twelve warlocks, and once they were all inside he stepped past them all to take a final look outside—he didn't think he had missed anyone, but he wanted to be sure.

An elderly man was walking slowly past and glanced at him, but said nothing. Other than that the street was empty; satisfied, Hanner closed and locked the door.

As he did, he finally noticed the bell pull hanging just inside the door, a few inches from where the candle had been waiting.

"Oh, for . . ." he began. Then he bit the oath off short and tugged at the cord.

Somewhere he heard a distant tinkle.

It was possible that there were no servants in residence at present, but it seemed unlikely—the place was obviously clean and well maintained, and Uncle Faran would probably want to be able to drop in at any time, without notice, with his latest conquest on his arm, and be properly attended.

That done, Hanner turned to face the crowd gathered in the hallway. Some of them were barely visible by the lone candle's light, but Hanner was sure they were all there. He cleared his throat, and every face turned toward him.

"All right," Hanner said, "I don't know whether anyone will answer that bell, but if someone does, he or she will know better than I what sleeping accommodations are available here. I, on the other hand, feel qualified to explain a few things that you ought to know before you agree to stay here.

"This is my uncle's house—my uncle Faran's. Yes, that's the same Lord Faran who is chief advisor to the overlord. Knowing my uncle as I do, I'm sure he knows the exact location and value of every item in this house. Now, most of you are honest citizens who were caught up in tonight's madness through no fault of your own, but a few of you are . . . well, perhaps not entirely honest, and you've suddenly had magical abilities thrust upon you. Furthermore, I'm sure *most* of you have never before been in such luxurious surroundings and may find yourself tempted to borrow a trinket or two, or to tamper with some unfamiliar device.

"Don't.

"I know my uncle. If you interfere with any of his possessions, if you damage or break or steal anything, you're risking your very life. We're trusting you all to be on your very best behavior for your stay here.

"Thank you."

"But we're warlocks," a young man—a boy, really—said. "Don't we . . . won't that mean anything?"

"I don't know," Hanner said honestly. "I don't know much of anything about it. But I *do* know not to fool around with my uncle's belongings."

Because he was standing by the door and facing down the hallway, and the others were all turned to face him, Hanner was the first to see the light that sprang up beneath the stairs. "Ah!" he said, stepping forward.

A man in fine white linen and black breeches appeared from beneath the stairs, holding a copper lamp; the hallway brightened considerably. He stopped dead and stared at the crowd in the hallway in ill-concealed astonishment.

"*Hai!*" Hanner said, striding through the gathered warlocks. "I'm Lord Hanner, Lord Faran's nephew." He held up the key to the front door. "An emergency has come up, and my uncle agreed to let me and my companions stay the night here."

"My lord," the man mumbled, still looking about in confusion at the unexpected throng.

"This is my sister, Lady Alris," Hanner said as he came even with his sibling. "And your name is . . . ?"

"Bern, my lord."

"Bern," Hanner said as he came up to the man and clapped him on the shoulder. "Excellent. There are twenty-one of us in all, but if there aren't sufficient beds for so many we'll be glad to share, or to make do with couches or carpets."

"There are . . . there are ten guest rooms, my lord, and Lord Faran's own bed." Bern was clearly hesitant, unsure how he should deal with this horde of unanticipated guests.

They did have a key, though, Hanner thought, and a gang of thieves would hardly have so many ill-assorted members. Hanner was fairly sure Bern would accept him at his word, and was trying hard to convey an attitude of absolute certainty.

"Excellent!" Hanner smiled broadly. "Lead the way, then, and we'll settle in. It's late, and we don't wish to impose on my uncle's hospitality any more than necessary."

"Of course, my lord," Bern said, finally recovering his aplomb. "This way."

It took another half hour to get the entire party properly distributed, at two to a room. All the bedchambers were on the second floor—Hanner was briefly puzzled and asked Bern, "Why aren't there any beds on the third and fourth floor?"

"There may be beds there, my lord," Bern replied, "but I am not permitted on the top two floors. Those are Lord Faran's private rooms, and no one but he is allowed up there."

"Oh," Hanner said. He was too tired to pursue the matter further and returned his attention to sleeping arrangements. In the end Alris and Rudhira took the chief guest room and Hanner took Faran's own bed for himself, while the others were paired off more or less randomly in the other nine chambers.

Each room was tastefully lush and equipped with enough bedding for two—sometimes one large bed, sometimes more than one. No one complained about the accommodations; in fact, some rooms were greeted with awed silence. What delays did occur were the result of getting lamps or candles lit, locating chamber pots, and arguing over who would share which room.

Hanner was unspeakably weary, almost staggering, when

Bern finally swung open the door of the master bedroom and led Hanner in.

Hanner stopped dead in his tracks and simply stared while Bern crossed to a bedside table to light the lamp there.

He had known that his uncle had a sybaritic streak, and had often heard Faran complain about the size, arrangement, and condition of their apartments in the Palace, but he had always assumed those complaints to be largely empty rhetoric. Hanner had seen the interiors of several other mansions in the New City and knew they were more luxurious than the rooms in the Palace, but he had always found Faran's official quarters comfortable enough. Despite the grumbles, he had thought his uncle did, too.

Now he changed his mind.

It was not a matter of size; the grand bedchamber was large, but not outrageously so. It was, rather, the furnishings that impressed him.

The bed was thick and soft, mattresses piled waist-high within the carved ebony frame, and was wide enough that Hanner could have lain across the black silken coverlet with neither head nor feet hanging over the side. Lengthwise, he could not stretch far enough to reach both footboard and headboard simultaneously. Wine-red velvet curtains trimmed in black and gold hung from a silk and velvet canopy, tied back on either side with elaborate gold-braid rosettes.

At each corner of the bed stood a table. The two at the head held the usual appurtenances—lamps, basin, pitcher, mirrors, and so on. The two at the foot held bronze statues, each of a nude couple engaged in amorous play. Chests of drawers, trimmed with intricate carvings, stood against one wall, and two enormous wardrobes, their doors elaborately painted, occupied another. A marble statue of a woman stood in the center of the room. A small, extraordinarily fine shrine was built into the wall near the head of the bed. Two broad windows, shuttered and curtained, pierced the north side of the room. A large marble and gilt mantel topped a carved marble fireplace above an elegant tile hearth; a gold and ivory screen blocked the opening, since no one would want a fire for months. Half a dozen fine small carpets hid much of the polished parquet floor, and a dozen painted panels adorned the walls; the paintings mostly seemed to involve beautiful people in states of undress. Everywhere were detailed carvings, fine woods, rich textures and colors.

Hanner had seen the overlord's own bedchamber once; it was not so lush and ornate as this.

"Gods," he murmured.

Then he realized that Bern had been talking and had stopped. He had asked Hanner a question.

"What?" Hanner asked.

"Breakfast arrangements, my lord," Bern said. "What shall I do?"

"Do you . . ." Hanner began, then he remembered some of what Bern had already said. He hadn't really been listening, but some of it had registered anyway.

Bern was merely the chief caretaker; other servants came in sometimes during the day to clean and maintain the place, and when Faran was in residence a full staff was on call.

Hanner had been about to ask about Bern's cooking skills, but now he thought better of it.

"Just something simple," he said. "Cold salt ham and small beer, perhaps. Or fruit and bread, if any is on hand, but you needn't light the oven."

"Thank you, my lord," Bern said. He bowed and departed—Hanner stepped into the room, out of Bern's way, when the servant reached the doorway.

Bern closed the door softly behind him, leaving Hanner staring at his uncle's private bedchamber.

Hanner had never realized that Faran would *want* a place like this. He had known his uncle pursued women whenever he had the time free from his work, and affected expensive tastes, but somehow Hanner had still thought of Faran as a frugal and common-sensical man, not the sort of sybarite who would maintain so elaborate a hideaway.

He wondered how, after a dozen years living with his uncle, he could have understood him so little. It was somehow the biggest surprise of the entire long, strange night.

And a very long, very strange night it had been. Walking Mavi home had been only very slightly out of the ordinary, a natural progression in a normal relationship, but from then on the night had grown ever more bizarre. Strange new magic erupting all over the city, people running amok with it, the magicians of the Wizards' Quarter confounded, Hanner making himself the leader of a posse set upon restoring order, being refused admission to his home in the overlord's palace, being sent here instead—and finding that his uncle was not the man Hanner had thought him, all these years.

Hanner let out a long, shuddering sigh, then headed for the bed, pulling off his tunic.

Perhaps in the morning everything would be back to normal. Perhaps this strange new magic would pass with the dawn, perhaps the overlord's orders would have changed, perhaps everyone could go back to their own proper homes . . .

But, Hanner realized, as he pulled off his boots, Uncle Faran would still be capable of having maintained this amazing secret retreat. *That* wasn't going to go away.

But it might not seem to matter by daylight. Hanner crawled under the coverlet, straightened the pillow under his head, blew out the lamp, and fell instantly asleep.

Chapter Twelve

Ulpen of North Herris arose early from a night of troubled dreams, while the sun was still red in the east. Half-asleep, he stumbled to the kitchen to stir up the fire and get his master's breakfast.

He felt strange and awkward as he moved through the familiar rooms of the wizard's house in the slanting orange light, and the walls seemed almost to close in on him, suffocating him—an image he knew came from one particular nightmare that still haunted him.

He used the poker to spread out the banked coals in the bottom of the stove, then returned it to its hook and fetched wood and tinder from the bin. He threw a handful of tinder onto the coals, but when it flared up suddenly he started back involuntarily; the fire was too much like one of his dreams. He backed unthinkingly away from the stove, blinking mazily, rather than adding the sticks he held to the fire.

His foot hit an obstruction—Deathbringer, the wizard's cat. Deathbringer yowled in protest. Trying desperately not to hurt the cat, trying not to drop the firewood, Ulpen lost his balance and began to fall backward. The sticks tumbled from his arms as he belatedly flung out his hands to catch himself.

"Augh!" he said as he and the wood stopped falling.

Then he realized that he hadn't hit the plank floor, and that the sticks hadn't, either. The little stack of wood had somehow re-formed, balanced impossibly on his chest as he rested on one leg, one palm, and empty air.

Magic had broken his fall.

"Thank you, Master," he said, carefully lowering himself and the wood to the floor and turning to the doorway. Since he had hardly been in a position to cast a spell even had he thought quickly enough, he assumed his master had stopped his fall.

Sure enough, the wizard Abdaran stood in the kitchen doorway, staring down at his apprentice and frowning. The frown deepened as he said, "It was none of *my* doing."

Ulpen blinked. He gathered up the wood and set it on the floor, then sat up, turning to face his master.

"Until you spoke I had intended to ask you what spell you used," Abdaran said. "I didn't recognize it and thought perhaps you had been meddling in things best left alone."

"I haven't, Master," Ulpen protested. "I didn't do anything!"

"Yet you stopped falling in midair, and the wood did not scatter."

"It's definitely magic, Master, but it's not *mine*."

"Nor is it mine."

"But . . ." Ulpen looked around uneasily. "We're the only wizards in North Herris, aren't we?"

"To the best of my knowledge, we are," Abdaran agreed. "Nor are there any in South or East Herris. But are we sure that it was wizardry that stopped your fall?"

"No," Ulpen admitted. "But what, then?"

"You tell me, apprentice," Abdaran said, switching to his lecturing tone.

Ulpen chewed on his lower lip thoughtfully as he got to his feet and brushed off his breeches. Then he looked at his master. "It might be gods, demons, witchcraft, sorcery, some unknown natural phenomenon, or . . . well, or something we don't know about."

Abdaran smothered a smile. "I would say that covers the possibilities," he acknowledged. "That last category is perhaps a bit over-inclusive, though."

Ulpen did not bother responding to that; instead he said, "There aren't any sorcerers left around here, are there?"

"Not so far as I'm aware. There are four witches in East Herris, but no known sorcerers."

"Why would the witches have kept me from falling?"

"I can't imagine how they would know, or why they would bother," Abdaran replied. "We could ask them."

That idea did not appeal to Ulpen. Witches could read people's emotions, sometimes even their thoughts, and that made the apprentice nervous. "I'm sure they meant no harm," he said.

"And why do you assume it was the witches?" Abdaran asked. "You haven't eliminated all the other possibilities on your list."

"Well, we eliminated sorcery . . ."

"No, we did not," Abdaran interrupted. "We eliminated *known sorcerers*. There could be someone new in the area, using this as a rather unorthodox introduction, or perhaps a sorcerer has been hiding here all along, or perhaps this was some leftover bit of sorcery from some long-ago spell."

Ulpen considered that as he gathered up the wood. He tossed the first stick into the fire—just barely in time, as the tinder had all but burned away—and said, "But in that case, couldn't it just as well be some side effect of wizardry? A spell cast a hundred years ago, or a hundred leagues away?"

"Or to be cast at some time in the future," Abdaran agreed approvingly.

Ulpen threw another stick of wood on the fire as he absorbed that. The idea that a spell that hadn't been performed yet could somehow affect them was new to him, and he found it hard to think about.

"And gods or demons?" Abdaran prompted.

"Can't be demons unless there's a demonologist," Ulpen said. "The demons were shut out of the World after the Great War, and can't interfere in human affairs uninvited."

"There are demonologists in the World, though," Abdaran said.

"Not around *here*, are there?" He glanced at his master and saw the satisfied expression of a teacher about to reiterate a favorite point, and quickly added, "That we know of?"

Abdaran let out the breath he had drawn. "Not that we know of," he said.

"And the gods . . . well, they do favors for theurgists, but other than that they don't generally intervene in little things like stumbling over a cat."

"Not generally," Abdaran agreed.

"Do you think Sinassa might have asked a god to look after me?" Sinassa the Theurgist lived in South Herris; Ulpen had met her once when he was very young, when his mother had taken him to have a fever cured, and rumor had it that Abdaran had romanced her briefly many years ago.

"Do *you* think so?" Abdaran replied. "Have you paid her to do so, or even asked her?"

"No," Ulpen said as he threw in more wood. "I haven't

spoken to . . . blast!" He dropped the rest of the wood and knelt in front of the stove.

He had been careless, and most of the kindling had burned away while he was talking; his latest addition to the fire, rather than adding fuel, had smothered the flame. There were still glowing coals, but he knew those wouldn't be enough to light the new wood without help. He breathed gently into the stove, trying to coax a new flame.

"Come on, come on," he muttered to himself. "Come *on*!"

A wisp of smoke rose from the little heap of wood, then vanished.

Relighting the fire was not really a serious problem; if all else failed, he could douse it completely and start from scratch, using either flint and steel or Thrindle's Combustion.

That, however, would be a nuisance and would undoubtedly trigger a long lecture from Abdaran on the necessity of maintaining a proper household and not relying excessively on wizardry for everyday tasks.

If he had had any sulfur at hand he might have surreptitiously worked the Combustion anyway, but the nearest sulfur was in the workshop, and besides, using the Combustion on something that was already burning would produce an explosion. The iron stove *might* contain such a blast without damage—but it might not, and blowing the kitchen stove to bits would get him worse than a mere lecture.

He stared at the wood, *willing* it to burn . . .

And it did. It flared an eerie, unnatural orange, then smoldered, sizzled, spat sparks, and caught fire.

"What did you *do*?" Abdaran said, suddenly close at Ulpen's side.

"I . . . I don't *know*!" Ulpen said, staring into the stove.

"It glowed orange," Abdaran said.

"Yes," Ulpen agreed, still staring.

"*You* did it somehow, didn't you, boy?"

Ulpen nodded.

"Can you do it again?" Abdaran handed Ulpen another stick of wood.

Ulpen accepted it with unsteady fingers. He looked at the stick, then looked into the stove.

The fire was burning merrily—not the fragile, uneven flame of a newly lit fire, but a steady blaze, as if it had been burning half an hour; putting the stick in there would be more than enough to light it without any magic.

Instead, Ulpen stood up, backed away, then raised the stick like a torch. He stared at it, and *willed* it to burn.

The stick—and his *hand*—glowed orange; sparks flew, and flame burst from the wood. The sudden heat was far more than he had expected; startled, Ulpen dropped the stick . . .

And caught it a foot from the floor, without touching it.

"It's *you*," Abdaran said. "Something's enchanted you."

Ulpen nodded and, still without touching it, flung the burning stick into the stove.

"How did you do that?" Abdaran asked.

"I don't *know*, Master!" Ulpen wailed. "Can't *you* tell?"

Abdaran turned up an empty palm. "This is nothing *I've* ever seen before," he said. "Nor have I read of anything like this, and if my own master ever mentioned it, I either wasn't listening or forgot it long ago."

"But . . . can't you do *something*? You're a master wizard!"

Abdaran looked at Ulpen quizzically. "How do you feel?" he said.

"I . . ." Ulpen stopped, considering the question more carefully. "I feel fine, actually." To his surprise, he realized that he felt better than he had in days. The queasy residue of his nightmares and his usual morning grogginess had both vanished. His unhappiness was entirely due to the shock of discovering his unexpected abilities, not from any sort of physical discomfort.

"Not tired?"

"No."

"Then it's not that you've suddenly learned witchcraft—I

know from Cardel and Luralla that witches find fire-lighting exhausting."

"Then it's not witchcraft," Ulpen agreed. Aside from being frightening because it was strange, the fire-lighting experience had been more exhilarating than exhausting. "Isn't there some spell we can use to figure this out? Some divination?"

Abdaran snorted. "Ulpen, I may technically be a master wizard, but if I could do that sort of divination, do you really think I'd be out here in North Herris, selling love potions and treating cattle for mange and the like?"

The question startled Ulpen, who had never given the matter any thought at all. Abdaran had always been here, always been the town's one wizard, an unquestioned part of the community; it had never occurred to Ulpen that Abdaran might ever want to be somewhere else.

"No, this one is beyond me," Abdaran said, not waiting for Ulpen to answer. "I think you'd better see someone who knows far more magic than *I* do."

"But . . ." Ulpen began.

"I think this is a matter for the Wizards' Guild," Abdaran said, ignoring Ulpen's attempt to speak. "Unknown magic is always a Guild matter."

Ulpen's eyes widened. "It is?" he asked.

He had heard of the Wizards' Guild, of course, and he was technically a member—he had sworn half a dozen great and terrifying oaths to that effect when he first started his apprenticeship and began to learn the secrets of wizardry. Every wizard was required to join the Guild; the penalty for practicing wizardry without joining, vigorously enforced by the Guild itself, was death.

But Ulpen had never had any real contact with the Guild outside his apprenticeship with Abdaran. He had met perhaps three other wizards in his life, all very briefly, and each had been an ordinary hedgerow wizard like Abdaran, not anyone Ulpen thought of as representing the Guild. The Guild had seemed to him this mysterious, all-powerful organization lurking somewhere beyond the horizon.

He had always known that upon completing his apprenticeship he would be presented to representatives of the Guild who would approve or disapprove his elevation to journeyman; he had known that someday, barring disaster, he would be examined by the Guild for the rank of master and the right to take on apprentices of his own.

Those, however, had been far-off matters—he assumed he still had a good two years left before he would be rated a journeyman—and quite intimidating enough.

"You'll have to see the Guildmaster," Abdaran said.

Ulpen's eyes widened farther. "You mean the head of the *entire Guild*?"

Abdaran started. "What? No, no, of course not. I mean Guildmaster Manrin, in Ethshar of the Sands. He's only responsible for this area, he's not the head of the entire Guild. There are dozens of Guildmasters in the World. I don't even *know* who's the head of the entire Guild—and I don't think I want to, and I think that if you're wise, *you* won't want to, either."

"Oh," Ulpen said. This was not helping his self-confidence at all.

"Come on, then," Abdaran said, turning away. "Pack your things. It's a long walk to the city, and we'd better get started."

"Wh . . ." Ulpen hesitated, tried to think of something intelligent to say, and finally could find no response more appropriate than "Yes, Master."

The two wizards, master and apprentice, had been gone for perhaps half an hour when several terrified villagers and folk from nearby farms came to Abdaran's home, seeking counsel regarding the bizarre nightmares a few of them had experienced the night before, the mysterious abilities that two of them had manifested, and the unexplained overnight disappearance of three people.

Chapter Thirteen

Lord Hanner did not realize immediately that he was actually awake; the view before him was so unfamiliar that at first he thought he was still dreaming. Gradually, though, memories of the night before drifted back, and he began to recognize his surroundings.

This was Uncle Faran's bedchamber, in his mansion on High Street—the mansion Faran had never admitted to Hanner that he owned.

Hanner was looking at a fine mirror framed in polished brass; it stood on a small bedside table, just visible past the edge of the bed curtains, and reflected in it Hanner could see a small bronze statue of a nude couple entangled with one another, and beyond that a larger marble statue of a naked woman.

That was why he had thought he was dreaming; in his waking life up until last night he had only seen such statuary in gardens and grand halls, never in bedrooms.

The room was dim, but the fact that he could see at all meant it was after dawn, since he had put out the lamp before going to sleep. He sat up.

Sunlight was leaking in through the shutters and curtains that hid the two large windows. Hanner pushed aside the black silk coverlet, slipped out of bed, and padded over to the nearer one. He opened the drapes and unlatched the shutters; the wooden panels swung open.

Light blazed in, forcing Hanner to squint and blink; at first he thought he had accidentally looked directly into the sun. When he could see clearly again, though, he realized that the sun was nowhere to be seen—in fact, thinking about the house's location and where the bedchamber was, he realized the windows faced north. It was simply the contrast between the bright light of a summer day and the dimness of a shuttered room that had fooled him.

The windows opened out onto a balcony overlooking the mansion's garden; Hanner unlatched one and stepped outside into the day's heat. To the left he could see over the garden wall and across Coronet Street; ahead and to the left he could see down Coronet to the intersection with Merchant Street. Directly ahead, beyond the garden, he could see the back of what he took to be a tradesman's home, with rooms above a shop, while to the right beyond the garden wall was another garden and the rear of another mansion.

From the shadows of the trees in the garden and shadows on the surrounding walls, he judged it to be midmorning, halfway betwen dawn and noon. He had never intended to sleep so late—but then, he had never intended to stay up so late the night before!

Half the morning was gone—the entire mess caused by the mysterious new magic might well have been straightened out and dealt with by now.

He certainly *hoped* it had been. He saw no signs of trouble on the visible portions of Coronet or Merchant Street. Traffic seemed perhaps a little light—but he didn't really know what was normal for this neighborhood, since he had rarely had any business here.

He didn't have a clear view of anything more than a block away, so he couldn't very well look for smoke from still-burning buildings or warlocks flying about, but the few people he did see in the street were walking, not running. That was a good sign, but hardly definitive.

It could all be over, or it could just be a lull.

Well, he told himself, he couldn't really expect to find out anything staring out at his uncle's garden—except that Uncle Faran had been far less imaginative and extravagant in arranging his garden than in furnishing his house, as the paths were broad and straight, the flowerbeds and hedges simple, the statuary sparse.

If he wanted to know what was happening, he would have to go out and see. He turned back inside and looked for his boots, wishing he had a clean pair of stockings to wear.

A moment later he was in the hallway, fully dressed. Unsurprisingly, Bern was nowhere at hand; a bellpull hung by the side of Uncle Faran's bed, but Hanner had not wanted to use it. None of the others—neither Alris nor any of the score of warlocks—was in sight, either, but Hanner could hear voices drifting up the stairs from below. He started down.

He was perhaps halfway down when Rudhira's head appeared around a door frame at the foot of the stairs. Her long hair was a mess, disarrayed and tangled—if her room had contained a hairbrush she obviously hadn't used it. She had cleaned off her makeup, however, and that, added to the difference between the bright morning sunlight spilling through the windows and the firelight Hanner had seen her by the night before, made her look almost a different person—a younger and more appealing one, so far as Hanner was concerned.

Hanner noticed that she was wearing the same red tunic and skirt as the night before, somewhat the worse for having been slept in—but of course, what else would she have to wear? He was still in the same clothes himself.

The difference, he thought to himself, was that his clothes were far more appropriate to these surroundings, and to daylight, than Rudhira's.

"*There* you are!" she said. "We've been waiting!"

Hanner really didn't know how to answer that, so he didn't; instead he simply nodded and continued down the steps.

Rudhira met him at the foot of the staircase and took his arm to lead him into what he discovered to be the mansion's dining hall.

"My lord," Bern said, appearing as Hanner stepped through the door. He bowed discreetly. "I have kept the head of the table for you—I assume your uncle will not be joining us?"

"So far as I know, he'll be staying in the Palace until further notice," Hanner agreed.

"And will your party be staying on?"

"I don't know," Hanner said. "We'll have to discuss that later."

"If I may say so, so large a group is really more than I can care for single-handed at even a minimal level. If you do stay, I feel it would be advisable to call in more servants. Your uncle has a fine staff on call."

"I'll let you know what we decide," Hanner said, moving past and turning his attention to the others in the room—and to the room itself.

The dining hall was large—which was hardly surprising in a house this size. A splendid table of gleaming unfamiliar wood inlaid with ivory took up the center of the room, with a dozen oaken chairs spaced along its sides and one larger chair at the far end. Four ornate cabinets were arranged along the east and west walls, each with various drawers and compartments glittering with brass and ivory inlay; three of the four included glass-fronted upper sections, and Hanner could see something moving behind one of those panels, but the glass was so elaborately cut and beveled that he could not tell what it was. Since that was hardly an appropriate place to keep a pet, he supposed Uncle Faran had indulged in some variety of magically animated tableware.

Mirrors hung on all four walls; the south wall was pierced by three generous multipaned windows partially obscured by lace curtains, looking out on the dooryard and High Street. At the north end a large sliding door was closed tightly, while two small doors to the east stood open.

Seven people were seated around the table—three warlocks on either side, and his sister Lady Alris at the foot of the far side. Four more warlocks stood or leaned elsewhere around the room, not counting Rudhira, who was at his shoulder. They had obviously been talking earlier, when he had heard voices, but now they were all staring silently at him.

None of the four prisoners they had taken were present. "Where are the . . ." he began.

"We locked the prisoners in their rooms," Rudhira said before he could finish the sentence. "The others are still asleep."

"I'll wake them if you like, my lord," Yorn said. He was standing to one side.

"It's not necessary," Hanner said. Hesitantly, uneasy under the silent scrutiny of a dozen watchers, he crossed the room and took his seat at the head of the table.

He had never been at the head of a table before, and wasn't entirely comfortable with the idea; this was properly his uncle's place. As a nobleman Hanner had grown up giving orders to servants and soldiers and expecting a certain amount of deference, but he had also almost always been subordinate to someone else—his parents, his uncle, the overlord, the various other lords who ran the city. The only times he had been the highest-ranking person at a meal had been in the palace kitchens or in the city's inns—never in a formal dining room. It felt odd to sit in the big carved oak chair and look down the length of the table.

An empty plate lay ready for him, while half-empty platters of bread and ham and a pitcher of small beer stood close at hand. Hanner could see that the others had not waited for him to appear before eating; Bern had not yet cleared away the used plates and scattered crumbs.

Hanner speared a slice of ham with his belt knife and transferred it to his plate, then reached for the beer and a pewter mug Bern had provided.

"My lord," Yorn said as Hanner poured, "I should return to my company."

Hanner looked up, startled. "Has the warlockry gone away?" he asked, putting down the pitcher.

He should have asked that sooner, he realized. It should have been the first thing he said when he came down the stairs and found Rudhira waiting. It was obviously the most important question, the single thing that would most affect what he did that day.

"No," Yorn said.

"No," Zarek agreed. He was seated on Hanner's left. "Look!"

Zarek's plate lifted into the air, then hovered and began to spin—which flung bread crumbs in all directions. One landed in Hanner's beer.

"Sorry," Zarek said as the plate dropped the foot or so to the table and landed with a ringing clatter.

"It's nothing," Hanner said, picking up the mug and staring at the floating crumb. He glanced up and noticed Bern's silent but intense disapproval of Zarek's action.

Well, Bern was the servant and Zarek the guest, despite Zarek's ragged attire; Bern would just have to tolerate such behavior. With a grimace Hanner gulped beer, then set the mug down again.

"So the magic is still here," he said. "Has *anything* changed since last night?"

The others looked at one another; no one spoke at first, then Zarek offered, "I've had the best night's sleep I've had in years, thanks to that lovely bed you let me use, but other than that, nothing."

"Has there been any word from the Palace?" He directed this at Alris, but she turned to Bern.

"There have been no callers since your arrival, my lord," Bern replied.

"Did anyone receive any messages by other means, then?" Hanner looked around the table and at the others beyond. "A wizard-sent dream, perhaps?"

A few empty hands turned up; no one spoke.

"Alris?"

"I haven't heard a thing," she said. "If I had any dreams I don't remember them."

"I had dreams," Rudhira volunteered. "Not messages, though—nightmares. Bad ones. Fire and falling and suffocation, all jumbled together, and something calling to me."

"So did I!"

"Me, too!"

Half a dozen voices chimed in, startled.

"But those were *before*," one young woman said, over-riding the others. "That was what woke me up in the first place, when I first found out I could do magic. I dreamed I was flying but burning as I flew, and then I fell and fell and fell and dove into the earth as if it were a pond, but then it fell in on me and I was buried, I was trapped and smothered, and that was when I woke up and discovered my bedsheets were floating in midair."

Again, several voices spoke at once, but this time not all were agreeing—some were protesting that their dreams had been later, here in the mansion.

"Silence!" Hanner bellowed. He stood up and pointed at Rudhira. "When did you dream?"

"I was awake when the magic came," Rudhira said. "It was like a flash in my mind, and I could fly and . . . well, you all know about that. It was here, in this house, that I had dreams about burning and falling and strangling."

Hanner nodded and pointed to Yorn.

"I had no dreams," the soldier said. "I was awake when the screams came, and it was when I tried to help one of the others in my barracks that I found I could move things."

The next man, Alar Agor's son, had been asleep when the magic came and had been awakened by nightmares, and the nightmares had recurred, far less intensely, after going back to sleep in Lord Faran's mansion.

The next person, the young woman whose bedsheets had floated above her, had been awakened by the dreams, but they had not recurred. Hanner asked her name, which she gave as Artalda the Fair.

In the end, of the eleven warlocks in the room, four had been awake when the magic came, and all seven of the others had been awakened by the same nightmare of a fiery plunge into entrapment in the ground. Four of them—two who had originally been awake and two who had been asleep—had had milder nightmares afterward, here in the house on High Street.

Neither Hanner nor Alris nor Bern had dreamed at all, so far as they could recall.

"The later dreams were different," said Desset of East-wark, a plump woman who was one of the two who had experienced both, and who was one of the three who had been flying steadily last night. "Something was *calling* me. I don't think it was the first time."

"Something was definitely calling me," Rudhira agreed.

"I think something called me *both* times," said Varrin the Weaver, the last of the three flyers, the other who had dreamed twice, and the one whose initial experience, destroying his entire bedroom, had been the most violent.

Just then another warlock, newly arisen from his borrowed bed, wandered in, to be immediately confronted by Rudhira.

"Did *you* have any strange dreams last night?" she demanded.

Startled, the warlock—a youth named Othisen Okko's son—said, "What?"

Rudhira repeated the question. The boy, a farmer's son who had been in the city consulting a theurgist when the new magic appeared, looked around at the crowd staring at him.

"Sort of," he said. "I don't really remember."

Rudhira looked ready to interrogate Othisen further, but Hanner interrupted.

"I don't think it matters," he said. "I think it's clear that there is some common phenomenon at work here, something that happened last night that caused these nightmares and that gave you all this strange magic. And it's clear that it's affected different people differently, which is why some of you have much more powerful magic than others, some have more intense dreams, and so on. Finding out exactly which effect it's had on whom isn't important. Finding out what it was, and whether the effects are permanent, and whether there are *other* effects we don't know about, *might* be important. So we know that the magic hasn't gone away, and the dreams haven't gone away—but not everyone had the dreams, and they do seem to be a little less intense the second time around. Now, has anyone noticed anything else out of the ordinary? Has the magic faded at all?"

The warlocks looked at one another. Rudhira ventured, "There was a lot of screaming last night, when it all first started."

"That was because of the nightmares," Zarek said. "I woke up screaming. So did some of the people around me. I was terrified and thought for a moment I was going mad."

"Maybe you did go mad," someone suggested. "Maybe we *all* did, and we're just imagining this."

"I don't think so," Hanner said, dismissing the suggestion with a wave of his hand. "Anything else?"

No one had any other observations to report.

"Fine," Hanner said. "Then is the magic weakening with time?"

There was a sudden rustling, and a surreal flurry of motion as most of the warlocks began testing themselves by lifting up from the floor, levitating random objects, sliding furniture around, and so on.

Rudhira did not move, which Hanner found interesting; she merely watched.

Yorn rose gently from the floor until an upstretched arm reached the ceiling; he was the first to speak.

"If anything, my lord, it's stronger," he said.

There was a chorus of agreement.

Hanner nodded, considering what should be done next. He had no idea how long this warlockry would last or how widespread it was—and whether it was really his problem. He was here, rather than safely home in the Palace, because he had been outside when it all began and had taken it upon himself to try to do something, but was it really his responsibility?

"My lord," Yorn said urgently, "I should go now. I was due to report for duty hours ago."

"And I should go home," Othisen said. "Once I've eaten," he added hastily, eyeing the ham and bread.

"But you're warlocks," Hanner said.

"I'm a soldier," Yorn said.

"And magicians are forbidden to serve as common soldiers," Hanner said.

"But I'm not a magician," Yorn protested. "I served no apprenticeship, I'm not a wizard or a witch or a sorcerer, I don't summon gods or demons—I can just do a few things. Someone put a spell on me, but that doesn't make me a magician!"

"And I'm not a magician *or* a soldier," Othisen said as he snatched a chunk of bread and a slice of ham.

"Are we prisoners here?" Rudhira demanded.

"No, of course not," Hanner said. He had been thinking that the group he had gathered would stay together for as long as the warlockry and its mystery remained, but now he saw that was foolish—the magic might *never* go away, the mystery might *never* be solved. He had said the wrong thing again. "You're right, and I'm sorry. You're free to go, all of you who choose to—and you're also free to stay, for now. Thank you all for your help last night, and if any of you want to stay and help me handle the prisoners and try to figure out more about what's happened, I would be glad of it. I promised those who aided me a reward, but since the overlord has refused us admission to the Palace, or any recognition of your efforts, all I can offer to fulfill that promise is food and lodging here."

"Thank you, my lord, but I have food and lodging elsewhere," Yorn said. "If you have no objections, I'll leave at once." He suited his actions to his words and trotted out of the room; a moment later Hanner heard the front door open and close.

"I'll go when I've finished eating," Othisen said.

Hanner took a bite of ham, then a swig of beer, and looked around at the others.

"I'll stay," Rudhira said.

That was a comfort for Hanner; he had been beginning to worry that if all the warlocks left he would be unable to control the vandals they had captured the night before. He had a responsibility to keep them safe until they were properly delivered to a magistrate.

If not for the prisoners Hanner might have simply chased everyone but Bern out, locked up the house, and gone home himself, but as long as those four were locked in upstairs and he had no instructions as to what should be done with them, he was stuck here. And he had to keep them secure. Yorn was the only trained guardsman in the group, and his absence would be felt if the prisoners were to attempt escape or otherwise cause trouble, but Rudhira appeared to be the most powerful warlock of them all—though Varrin might be close—and could almost certainly keep all four in line.

"And the rest of you?" Hanner asked.

Zarek laughed. "If you think I'm going back to the Hundred-Foot Field when I can sleep in a mansion, you're mad."

"I'm going back to the Palace as soon as they let me in," Alris said.

Hanner nodded. He assumed that Alris would be admitted, that the overlord's panicky edict had been revoked by now, but it would not have surprised him if warlocks were still banned from the Palace. That was why he couldn't just march the prisoners there.

"I'd appreciate it, Alris, if you could go see what's happening there, then come back and tell me," Hanner said. "I need to know what to do with those four we have locked in upstairs, for one thing." The sooner they were out of his custody, the better, so far as he was concerned, and Rudhira might not want to stay around indefinitely.

"If I go," Desset said, "can I come back later? I don't want my family to worry, but I want to find out what's happened, and you people seem . . . well, you know."

"You can come back so long as I'm here," Hanner assured her. "If my uncle chases me out, or we all just get bored and go home, come to the Palace and see me there."

Desset nodded.

In the end, everyone but Rudhira and Zarek decided to go—but several promised to return.

And Othisen, after he had eaten, changed his mind.

"No one in my village is expecting me back for a few

days anyway," he said. "If I can *fly* home, I can be there in plenty of time even if I don't leave until tomorrow or even the day after, and . . . well, I want to see what happens."

"*Can* you fly?" Hanner asked. "You didn't fly last night that I saw."

"I did a little," Othisen said as he sawed at the ham. "And I'm learning to do it better, I think."

"You're welcome to stay," Hanner assured him, "but if you're going to practice flying, please do it in the garden, not the house."

Othisen smiled and nodded, his mouth too full of ham to reply in words.

Well before midday the others had gone, and Hanner had finished his breakfast. The three remaining warlocks—Rudhira, Zarek, and Othisen—helped Bern in clearing away the remains of the meal and tidying up the dining room, while Hanner sat there, thinking.

He tried to concentrate on what he should do about the warlocks, especially the prisoners, but he found his thoughts straying to wondering just why Uncle Faran had so big and luxurious a house, and why he had kept it secret at all—he wasn't married, after all, so taking a variety of lovers was no great offense against morals or custom. Eleven bedrooms, not counting Bern's! Four stories . . .

And what was on the top two floors? Hanner remembered that Bern had said no one but Faran was permitted above the second. What did Faran have up there?

It was none of his business, he told himself, and antagonizing his uncle by investigating wasn't going to do anyone any good. He forced his attention back to the warlocks.

Were they magicians? Were they, perhaps, truly warlocked witches, the magic bestowed upon them against their will? If so, had Rudhira's free use of her powers the night before killed witches somewhere?

How did the dreams fit in? And the screaming?

He remembered the night before, when he had been walking on Newmarket Street after seeing Mavi home . . .

Was Mavi all right? Had she been caught up in the night's

insanity? He would need to check on that at the first opportunity.

In fact, he thought, perhaps he should go right now . . .

But there were the prisoners, all of them with dangerous magical abilities, and he couldn't very well leave them in his uncle's house guarded only by a beggar, a streetwalker, a farmboy, and the housekeeper.

For that matter, he couldn't very well leave the beggar, the streetwalker, and the farmboy unattended here. He didn't know them well enough to trust them alone with so many valuable furnishings.

He would have to send Alris or Nerra to check on Mavi. That would be less awkward in any case.

He hoped she was all right. He remembered how he had stumbled for no reason just as the screaming began; if she had been similarly affected while climbing stairs she might have fallen . . .

And why had he stumbled?

He frowned, and started over.

What should he do, if anything, about the warlocks?

Chapter Fourteen

Kennan had finally given up and gone home after all the lights in the mansion had gone out, but this was not, he swore, over.

Sanda had fallen asleep waiting in a chair by the front door; he left her there and went up to his own bed, where he slept uneasily for a few hours.

When he awoke he checked to make sure that Aken had not returned, and that Sanda and the children were still safe; he ate a hasty breakfast of bread and cheese, then set out for the Palace.

Once again he was refused admission.

He stood staring across the canal at the gleaming marble walls, wondering what was happening in there.

As he did, Lord Azrad slumped in his seat and glowered unhappily at his brother Clurim. He then turned his gaze to the others in the lesser audience chamber.

"Where's Lord Faran?" he demanded.

"Asleep, I believe," Captain Vengar reported. "He was up most of the night, after all."

"So was I, confound it, and *I'm* here!"

Vengar hesitated, then said, "My lord, you retired perhaps an hour or two after midnight. Lord Faran was still receiving reports when the eastern sky was light. I think he finally returned to his apartments just as the sun rose."

"He won't be much use to you if he's half-asleep," Lord Clurim remarked.

"I don't think he's much use in any case," Azrad the Younger muttered. His sister Imra slapped his arm at that.

The overlord had gathered his entire available family together for this morning conference—his three brothers and both his children. His four surviving sisters had all long since been married off—Zarréa, the youngest, to Ederd IV, overlord of Ethshar of the Sands, and the other three to various kings and barons elsewhere—and of course his wife, Thera of Alorria, and his second eldest sister, Lura, had both been dead for years.

Captain Vengar, present commander of the contingent of the city guard inside the Palace, was also present—and Azrad had wanted Lord Faran there as well.

Most of his other advisors and the other important lords of Ethshar did not live in the Palace, but in their own mansions in the New City, so they could not attend the meeting—Azrad did not trust them not to bring in whatever contagion had spread madness and magic through the city. Lord Faran, though, was in the Palace, and had spoken to the overlord briefly during the night; it was very annoying that he was not here.

Azrad decided he would have to make the best of it. He looked at his brothers.

"Do any of you have the slightest idea what's going on out there?"

Lord Karannin and Lord Ildirin exchanged glances.

"No more than you do," Clurim said. "There's some sort of wild magic that got loose last night, and some people ran wild with it, and things have quieted down now, but the magic is still loose."

"I know *that*," Azrad shouted. "Do you know anything *more*?"

"I'm afraid not," Clurim said.

"All we know is what we hear from the messengers," Karannin said.

"Since you won't let anyone in," Ildirin added.

"None of my regular magicians were in the Palace last night," Karannin said. "I'd let old Tarissa visit her granddaughter. I haven't been able to talk to any of them."

"You sent messages, didn't you?" Azrad asked.

"Yes, but I haven't gotten any useful answers yet. The only reply I've received so far was from Orodrin of the Scarred Hand, that demonologist you don't like. He said he doesn't know anything about it except that no demons were involved."

Azrad snorted. He turned his attention to Ildirin.

"I've sent messages to all the gates, and to Guildmaster Ithinia, as you asked," Ildirin said. "So far we have no word back from any of them."

"Send word to the Guild again," Azrad said. "Tell them it's urgent I meet with their representatives."

"Azrad, I don't even know whether Ithinia is in the city at present . . ."

"Then send messages to *all* the Guildmasters, and any other important wizards you can think of!" Azrad demanded. "They claim to regulate magicians, don't they?

Then they had better regulate *those* people, those . . . those . . ."

"Warlocks," Captain Vengar offered.

The others all turned to stare at him.

"That's what they're called," Vengar said, looking around uneasily at the inquiring faces. "Someone told the guards in the plaza last night. It's a witch name, apparently."

"The witches know something about them?" Azrad asked.

"I don't know, my lord," Vengar said.

"Who told the guards about this?"

"I'm not sure, my lord. I believe it was someone in Lord Hanner's party, perhaps Lord Hanner himself."

"Faran's nephew? That Lord Hanner?"

"Yes, my lord."

"I want to know everything you can tell me about that— where is Lord Hanner, and what is he doing? How did he know that name?"

Vengar hesitated. "My lord, Lord Hanner came to the plaza last night, after you were asleep, in the company of several strangers, some of whom were warlocks. The party was stopped well before approaching the bridge. He asked permission to enter, but was refused, in accordance with your orders. Lord Faran sent Lady Alris out to talk to him and accompany him to someplace where they could spend the night safely. That's all I know."

"Faran sent *Alris* out, in the middle of the night?"

"Yes, my lord."

Azrad stroked his short-trimmed beard. "That's odd. I wonder where they went?"

No one answered.

"Lord Hanner had some of these warlocks with him?"

"So I am told, my lord."

"That's *very* odd. Do you think . . ." Azrad broke off, frowning, in midsentence. Then he turned to Clurim. "Did you find any more of these warlocks?"

"No," Clurim said. "Just the one girl in the kitchen, Hinda the Orphan. We sent her out of the Palace, as you ordered. No one else in the Palace has admitted to having this new magic, as yet, and I haven't found any evidence that anyone is lying."

"Just the girl," Azrad said. "No one among the nobility?"

"No, Azrad. Not that we know of."

"Are there any signs that it might have spread to anyone else in the kitchens?"

"No. It doesn't appear to be contagious."

"Well, thank the gods for *that* much, anyway!" Azrad said. "You checked *everyone* in the Palace?"

"Yes. That's what you ordered, and that's what I did. It took me all night. I just finished half an hour ago, and then you came and ordered me to get this meeting together; I haven't been to bed yet. I'm at least as sleepy as Lord Faran, I would think."

"If that's a hint that I should let you go, I'm sorry, Clurim, but you'll have to wait." He turned his attention to the others. "Captain Vengar, I know there are unhappy citizens out there in the plaza. Do you know the nature of their complaints? Arson, vandalism, rape?"

"Arson, vandalism, theft, and murder, my lord," Vengar said. "We haven't had any reports of rape that I know of— but they may well be coming. Mostly, though, it's the disappearances that people are complaining about."

Azrad blinked. "Disappearances?" he said. "I don't believe I've heard about this."

"I told you I was sleepy," Clurim muttered. "Forgot to mention it."

"My lord," Vengar said, "we have had *numerous* reports of people who vanished last night, at the same time that people began screaming and the magic first manifested itself. Some people simply walked away and never came back; others appear to have been snatched out through windows or even through holes torn in the roof. Captain Naral started keeping a count eventually; the last time I checked with him, we had reports of over three hundred missing people."

"Three *hundred*?"

"Yes, my lord."

"The warlocks took them?"

"That would appear to be the logical assumption, yes. Certainly it's what many of the complainants believe."

"Three hundred people."

"At least."

Azrad sat back on his throne and stared silently at Vengar for a moment, then said, "I want reports. I want written reports from Captain Naral, and whoever spoke to Lord Hanner, and anyone who knows anything about these disappearances. I will not *stand* for this in my city! If these warlocks are responsible, I want them all removed."

"Yes, my lord," Vengar said.

"Go and get on with it!" the overlord said, waving a hand in dismissal. Vengar turned.

As he did, Azrad pointed at Clurim.

"You," he said. "Go get me Lord Faran. I don't care if he's asleep; I want to talk to him *now*. Get him down here— and then get some sleep yourself."

"Yes, Azrad," Clurim said.

He left the room scarcely a step behind Captain Vengar.

"Send those messages to the wizards," Azrad ordered Ildirin.

Then he looked at the others—Karannin, Imra, and Azrad the Younger.

"And you three," he said, "find something useful to do. Elsewhere."

A moment later the room was empty save for Azrad, sprawled unhappily in his throne, contemplating hours, perhaps days, of activity before he would be rid of all this and able to return to his usual comfortable indolence.

Chapter Fifteen

Lord Hanner had not yet reached any useful conclusions regarding what he should do about the warlocks by the time Alris returned.

He had been wandering about the house—or at any rate the first two floors—marveling at the place and trying to think of whether he ought to be doing anything more.

He had first checked on the prisoners and made sure they had food and clean water; they seemed resigned to their fate and willing to face the magistrates. Kirsha, the teenaged girl they had caught amid a cloud of stolen jewelry and fabric, asked whether there was any way to send a message to her family, and was told that it would have to wait a little longer.

When that was done Hanner went back downstairs and explored further. He discovered that the big doors at the back of the dining hall led to a vast ballroom, which in turn opened on the garden, and he noticed that the inlays in the ballroom floor included a mystic circle, suitable for ritual dancing; that was more of Uncle Faran's obsession with magic, he supposed. He wondered at first whether it had ever actually been used; then he found the traces of old chalk markings, imperfectly erased, and concluded that it had.

He wondered whether ritual dance was included in the Wizards' Guild's prohibition on government use of magic—but he had no idea who the dancers had been or what the dance had been intended for, which made it hard to guess whether it might have violated Guild rules.

The small doors on the east side of the dining hall led to a warren of kitchens and pantries, where Bern spent much of his time. Here, too, there were signs of an interest in magic—or perhaps just in ostentation—in the form of animated crockery and a never-empty water jug.

The west side of the house, beyond the big front parlor, held an assortment of salons, studies, and libraries.

When the front door lock rattled Hanner was two rooms away, admiring a collection of glassware that was either from Shan on the Desert or an extremely good imitation—and Hanner doubted Faran would own any imitations. He was holding a delicate little purple cruet made in the shape of an orchid, studying the way the color faded from almost indigo at the base to almost red at the top, when he heard the key turn. He looked up—and the cruet slipped from his hands.

He started to grab for it, then realized he might crush it and hesitated, and it was too late, it was out of his grasp. He reached for it anyway, desperately *willing* it not to fall . . .

And it didn't. Instead it sank slowly through the air as if it were sinking in oil, and Hanner was easily able to catch it before it hit the hard parquet floor.

He plucked it from the air and set it carefully back on its shelf, then stared at it.

It was obvious what he had done, of course. He, too, was a warlock.

He was a warlock after all; he merely hadn't realized it before.

This concept demanded some thought. How was he a warlock? Why was he a warlock?

Was *everyone* a warlock, then, and most people just hadn't noticed it yet? Or was it spreading, like an infection, and he had caught it from the warlocks he had gathered?

At first Hanner couldn't begin to answer any of these questions. He hadn't felt any change in himself—but he remembered he had staggered the night before, at the instant before the screaming began.

It had probably happened then, and he just hadn't known it until now.

How many other people, he wondered, were in the same situation?

Bern and Alris were speaking in the entryway, and Alris's voice interrupted his thoughts.

"Hanner? Are you here?"

He tore his attention away from the glassware and his newly discovered abilities and called back, "I'll be right there." He gave the cruet one final glance, then turned and left the room.

He met his sister in the front parlor, and saw immediately that she was both excited and worried—which worried *him*, since Alris's usual mood was irritated boredom.

"Did you speak to Uncle Faran?" Hanner asked.

"No," Alris said. "He was too busy to come to the door, and I wasn't allowed inside."

Hanner blinked in surprise. "Inside? You mean you weren't allowed inside the Palace?"

"That's right," Alris said. "They still aren't letting anyone in, for any reason. The overlord hasn't rescinded the order, and it doesn't look as if he intends to. And Uncle Faran hasn't done anything about it, either—the guard said he thought Faran *agreed* with the overlord!"

"He does sometimes," Hanner said dryly. "So who did you talk to?"

"The guards, mostly," Alris said. "Hanner, it's bad, really bad."

"What is?"

"Everything. The whole city. What happened last night."

Hanner sank into a nearby armchair and gestured for his sister to take another. "Tell me about it," he said. "What happened last night? Was there something besides the looting and fighting?"

Alris nodded.

"People disappeared," she said. "*Hundreds* of them!"

Hanner frowned. "Disappeared how?" he asked. "Just vanished? Was there a flash or a bang or smoke or anything? I didn't see or hear anything like that."

"Not *vanished* vanished," Alris said. "Or at least, not necessarily. Maybe some of them disappeared that way, but most of them are just gone. They weren't there in the morning when their families or neighbors went to find them. And there are stories about seeing dozens of them flying away, and the guards who were on duty at Westgate supposedly reported dozens of people marching out the gate in the middle of the night without saying anything, without any baggage—some of them weren't even dressed!"

Hanner felt a cold knot forming in his stomach. He remembered seeing the flying figures overhead the night before, and wondered how many of them had never returned.

"Magic," he said. "A compulsion, maybe."

Alris nodded. "Probably," she said. "That's what most of the people think, anyway. There's a big crowd of their friends and relatives in the square, waiting for the overlord to do something, and they just about all think it was magic—after all, what *else* could make people just leave in the middle of the night and not come back?"

Hanner made a wordless noise of agreement.

"What nobody agrees on is what *kind* of magic," Alris said. "Most of them think it was the warlocks who did it."

"That's silly," Hanner said. "There weren't any warlocks until last night; the warlocks didn't have time to *plan* anything like that!"

Alris turned up a palm. "Well, just about everyone thinks there's *some* connection. Some people think it was the Wizards' Guild behind it all, for some secret reason of their own, and some think it was a coven of demonologists paying for some huge spell, and I heard someone saying it was Northern sorcerers left over from the Great War, out for revenge."

"I don't think sorcery could do that," Hanner said.

"But *Northern* sorcery . . ."

". . . is a lost art, yes. Partly. It's not as lost as some people would like to think, though—most of our sorcerers are using Northern relics. Anyway, where would these Northerners have hidden all this time? It's been two hundred years since the war ended!"

"Somewhere in the northern wilderness, I suppose," Alris said. "Tazmor or Srigmor, maybe."

"It seems pretty unlikely."

"I thought so, too—but a lot of the people who disappeared were last seen going north."

"That doesn't mean there are any Northerners involved," Hanner pointed out. "It could just as easily be some wizard somewhere in Sardiron. Maybe someone's spell went wrong—I know that happens sometimes."

"I guess you're right," Alris said. "So maybe it was the Wizards' Guild or the demonologists. But whatever it is, *something* big happened!"

"Obviously," Hanner agreed dryly.

"Anyway, Uncle Faran and old Azrad have been conferring all morning, listening to reports and everything, trying to figure it out. And anyone in the Palace who can do this warlock stuff is ordered out—they threw little Hinda from the kitchens out on the street, and you *know* she doesn't have any family. She's just sitting in the square, crying. One of the guards gave her some bread, so at least she won't starve right away, but if something doesn't happen she might have to go to the Hundred-Foot Field tonight, and who knows what will happen to her there?"

Hanner felt his shoulders tense, and his skin suddenly felt cold despite the summer warmth.

He had seen the cruet slow to a stop in midair because he wanted it to, and knew that he, too, was a warlock. Did that mean he could never go home to the Palace?

But surely the overlord would rescind his decree eventually and let Hanner and Hinda back in. When Uncle Faran learned that his only nephew was a warlock . . .

Well, how *would* Faran react? Hanner had to admit he didn't know. Despite years of living in his uncle's apartments, Hanner still couldn't always predict Faran's actions—especially where magic was concerned. Warlockry was unquestionably a kind of magic, and Faran's attitude toward magic was a complicated stew of jealousy, desire, and distrust.

"If you see Hinda again, tell her she can come here," Hanner said. "Were there any other warlocks in the Palace?"

"Not that I've heard of," Alris said.

"There might be some who had the sense not to tell anyone," Hanner said.

Alris shivered. "I suppose so," she said, glancing across toward the dining hall. The significance was unmistakable—she was remembering all the warlocks who had been here earlier, and who were now scattered across the city.

"They're just people," Hanner said. "Some of them got a little carried away at first, that's all."

"I don't know," Alris said. "All those missing people—what if it *was* the warlocks who took them all, or killed them?"

"Why would they do that? How could they plan it? Besides, if a lot of the people who disappeared *flew* away, weren't they warlocks themselves? I'd guess that some of them just flew off somewhere and got lost, and they'll be back as soon as they find their way home."

"You think so?"

Hanner nodded. "And you know, I'd wager there are people out there who are warlocks and don't even know it yet. After all, they don't *have* to use the magic."

Alris shuddered more visibly. "That's creepy," she said. "I know *I'm* not a warlock!"

"*How* do you know?" Hanner asked.

Startled, she looked him in the eye, then turned away. "Shut up, Hanner," she said. "You're scaring me."

"Well, have you *tried* moving things without touching them?" Hanner asked. "That seems to be the basic thing that warlocks can do."

"Of course not!" Alris snapped. "Have *you*?"

"No," Hanner said—he hadn't, after all. He had made something *stop* without touching it. "But I'm not the one saying I know I'm not a warlock."

Because he knew he *was* a warlock—but he wasn't ready to tell Alris that.

He was a warlock—but he was also a noble in the city's

government, and if warlocks were magicians then he was violating the Wizards' Guild's rules simply by existing. Hereditary nobles could not be magicians.

"Well, I'm *not* a warlock," Alris said. She turned and glowered at the doily on a nearby table. "See? It doesn't move."

"I'll take your word that you were trying," Hanner said. That was another item to add to the information he was accumulating—presumably some people really *weren't* warlocks. He wondered what percentage of the population had been affected.

And how long would the effect last?

And what had caused it?

A thought struck Hanner. Alris seemed not only certain that she wasn't a warlock, but that she didn't want to be one. "I thought you *wanted* to be a magician," he said. "Didn't you beg Uncle Faran to apprentice you to a magician, any sort of magician?"

"That was months ago," Alris said, "and I meant a *real* magician, not a warlock!"

"Being a warlock is so terrible?"

"Yes! After what I heard at the Palace ... well, I guess the ones here are all right, but warlocks sound horrible!"

"Oh? So what else did you hear at the Palace?" Hanner asked.

"Oh, lots of stories—warlocks hurt and killed people last night, and smashed and stole things. There were a dozen fires, at least, and bodies and wreckage in the streets, and that's not counting all those hundreds of people who just disappeared. Everyone's scared and upset—a lot of people were calling for the overlord to have all the warlocks hunted down and killed."

Hanner frowned. That did not sound good at *all*. "But most of them didn't do anything wrong," he said. "The ones I brought here didn't."

Except, he remembered, the four prisoners still locked in a room upstairs.

Alris turned up a palm. "I don't think anyone cares," she

said. "Warlocks did a lot of damage last night, and the people I heard talking weren't interested in sorting out the good ones from the bad ones. Or the ones who haven't done anything *yet* from the ones who already went wild. What if tonight they all start screaming again and go berserk?"

Hanner had not thought of that, and did not like the suggestion. "But how would anyone hunt them down?"

"Magic, of course," Alris said. "Don't be stupid. The wizards and demonologists could do it."

"Maybe," Hanner admitted. He sighed. "Did you ask what we should do with the prisoners?"

"They aren't getting into the Palace," Alris said. "Even if they start letting other people in, I don't think the overlord's *ever* going to let any warlocks in. The guard suggested we take them to one of the local magistrates."

"I suppose that would be easiest," Hanner said. The possibility had occurred to him earlier, but he had wanted to be sure first that no one at the Palace wanted them. And besides, he had captured them while acting in the overlord's name, which meant that they were supposed to be the overlord's responsibility.

Obviously, though, Azrad didn't *want* that particular responsibility.

Hanner sighed again, and got to his feet. "I think the closest magistrate would be in the Old Merchants' Quarter; I don't want to try to figure out whose district we caught them in. I'll need to find the others to help me . . ."

"I'm right here," Rudhira said from the doorway.

Hanner turned, startled, then smiled at her.

She was wearing a different outfit—a white silk tunic embroidered with green and a long green skirt—and had removed the remains of her makeup and brushed her hair. The clothes fit her well, and nothing marked her as anything but a respectable woman. Hanner had not looked forward to confronting a magistrate with the sorry crew he had on hand, and this transformation on Rudhira's part was a welcome improvement.

It wasn't really a surprise that Uncle Faran kept extra

women's clothes on hand, given his probable use for this second home of his. Hanner supposed he ought to protest what amounted to theft, but he was too pleased by the results.

"Good," he said, meaning both her presence and her appearance. "Let's find the others and get those four out of here."

The sooner the prisoners were gone, Hanner told himself, the sooner he could concentrate on other matters . . .

Such as his own unwanted magic.

Chapter Sixteen

The Lord Magistrate of the Old Merchants' Quarter leaned on his desk and looked unhappily at Hanner.

"Vandalism, theft, assault, and unruly behavior," he said. "Disobeying the orders of a representative of the overlord."

"That's right," Hanner answered.

"You aren't mentioning the use of forbidden magic."

Hanner frowned and glanced at Rudhira. She was keeping both feet firmly on the plank floor. Beside her, Zarek and Othisen were standing silently, listening and watching carefully. The four prisoners were arrayed on the bench, their wrists and ankles chained. Hanner had not asked Bern why Uncle Faran had had chains and cuffs in his house; he didn't want to know.

"I'm not aware that the magic they used is forbidden by any statute or edict," Hanner said.

"But they do have this new magic that was running wild last night."

"Yes," Hanner conceded.

"Then if they're magicians, why haven't they resisted imprisonment? How did you bring them here?"

"By hiring other magic, of course," Hanner said. "These other three assisted me in capturing and holding the prisoners." He gestured at his remaining aides.

"They're magicians, too?"

Hanner nodded.

The magistrate sighed. "To the best of my knowledge the overlord has not yet issued instructions as to whether this new magic is criminal in nature."

"Then it isn't," Hanner said. "And you need only rule on the actual crimes involved—theft, vandalism, assault, unruly behavior, and the refusal of orders from the overlord's representative."

"That would be you?"

"Yes."

"Lord Hanner, to the best of my knowledge you hold no official position in the overlord's service, as yet."

"That's true."

"Then I can't rule on that—only the overlord can say whether you were correct in acting in his name." He brightened up suddenly. "Which means that I must, regrettably, refer this case to a higher authority . . ."

"But you can't!" Hanner said. "The overlord won't allow anyone into the Palace, and I don't think Lord Karannin is going to come out and rule on this case."

"To be blunt, my lord, that's not my problem."

Hanner glowered at the magistrate. "Fine, then! I hereby drop that charge. Deal with the others."

"I do not see the aggrieved parties—the owners of the stolen and vandalized property—here . . ."

That was the pebble that sank the barge.

"By all the gods and demons!" Hanner roared, startling everyone, including himself. He stepped forward to the desk and only at the last instant refrained from leaning across and grabbing the magistrate by the throat. "You're one of Lord Azrad's magistrates! Will you stop making excuses and do your accursed job, sir? I have brought you three men and a young woman caught in the act of wantonly stealing anything they pleased and smashing anything in their way,

I have brought you three eyewitnesses in addition to myself, and I *demand* that you deal with the matter!"

"I *can't*!" the magistrate insisted. "The overlord might outlaw this new magic at any moment and order them all to be hanged!"

"Well, he hasn't done it *yet*!" Hanner bellowed, leaning forward until his nose almost met the magistrate's own. "I've been holding these four prisoner in my uncle's house, and I can't hold them forever! I have no idea when Azrad will finally make up his mind, and neither do you, and the entire city can't just wait around doing nothing until he reaches a decision! Just *forget* about the magic, will you? Treat them as ordinary thieves and vandals!"

"And what if I let them go, and the overlord . . ."

"*I'll* take the responsibility for that!" Hanner shouted. "You just get on with it!"

"You'll take responsibility, before these witnesses?"

"*Yes*, blast you!"

"Very well, then. Ordinary thieves and vandals." He looked at the waiting prisoners, pointed at the first one, and said, "You! Do you deny any part of what Lord Hanner has said of your actions last night?"

He had chosen Kirsha, the only female. "No, my lord," she said.

"Are there any extenuating circumstances you believe should be considered in determining your punishment?"

The girl hesitated, glanced at Rudhira, then said, "I thought I was dreaming, my lord."

The magistrate sat back in his chair. "*Did* you?" he said. "How interesting! Why?"

"Well . . . I *had* been dreaming, a nightmare about falling and burning and smothering, and then I woke up but I was hanging in midair—my lord, I'd never even spoken to a magician before; the only flying I'd ever done was in dreams. So I thought I was still dreaming."

"And you didn't notice that the World was its usual solid self?"

"But it wasn't! Not at first, anyway. I could fly and make

other things fly, and there were people screaming everywhere—everything seemed mad, so I thought it was either a dream or the end of the World, and I could do anything I pleased."

"So you went rampaging through the street, looting shops."

The girl nodded unhappily.

"That doesn't say much for your upbringing or your common sense."

"I know," she whispered.

"Five lashes, and you will compensate your victims as best you can."

The girl flinched, but Hanner thought the sentence was fair enough.

He didn't comment, though; he was too busy regaining his own composure. He had never before yelled at anyone like that in public. Not since childhood had he lost his temper so completely.

He hoped it wasn't connected to becoming a warlock; the idea that he might eventually go rampaging through the streets, as so many warlocks had done the night before, was profoundly disturbing.

On the other hand, he had seen Uncle Faran lose his temper that way once or twice, usually when he was short on sleep and severely overworked, so perhaps it ran in the family and he just hadn't had the occasion to experience it before.

The next prisoner to be brought forward was a young man, Roggit Rayel's son. He had known he was awake, but claimed he had thought the city was being destroyed by screaming demons, and had wanted to gather enough treasure to live on when he fled to Aldagmor.

"Aldagmor?" the magistrate asked. "Why Aldagmor? Do you have family there?"

"No, my lord."

"Then why Aldagmor, and not the Small Kingdoms, or Tintallion, or somewhere?"

"I don't know, my lord," Roggit said, head bowed. "It just seemed right."

Hanner heard this with intense interest. Aldagmor, the easternmost of the Baronies of Sardiron, was almost due north of the city, and many of the people who had disappeared had last been seen heading north. Was there some significant connection, perhaps?

"You're old enough to know better," the magistrate said. "Seven lashes, and whatever restitution you can make."

The third prisoner, Gror of the Crooked Teeth, merely said that he had been profoundly disturbed by nightmares, had awakened to see others running wild, and had followed their example; he received a sentence of eight lashes. The fourth was Saldan of Southgate, the older man who had been dueling with the man Rudhira killed; he had no excuse at all. He also received eight lashes.

Hanner hesitated, uncertain whether he should point out that Saldan might have killed someone in the chaos and could therefore deserve something more than a relatively light flogging, but in the end he said nothing. As far as Hanner could tell no one, including Saldan, really *knew* whether he had killed anyone, and while the magistrate might bring in a magician who could settle the matter Hanner thought it would be better to give Saldan the benefit of the doubt.

Besides, he didn't want to drag magic back into the proceedings once he had finally convinced the magistrate to ignore it.

The guards led the four prisoners away; unless the convicts could demonstrate poor health or wanted particular witnesses, the floggings would take place immediately, and the prisoners would be released as soon afterward as they were able to put their tunics back on and walk out.

Hanner had no desire to watch; instead he took his leave, and he and the three warlocks—the three *other* warlocks, he silently reminded himself—left the magistrate's home and turned their steps eastward.

"I'd like to see what's happening at the Palace," Hanner said. "Would you three care to join me?"

"I don't think so," Zarek said uneasily. "There are too many guards around the Palace. I'll just go back to the house, if you don't mind." He hesitated. "Will that housekeeper let me back in?"

"Bern?" Hanner had not given specific orders, but Bern had seemed a very sensible person, and had heard Hanner invite the others to stay that morning. "I would think so— but if he doesn't, just stay nearby, and I'll be back eventually."

Zarek nodded and turned right at the next corner, back toward High Street.

Rudhira and Othisen stayed with Hanner, though. Hanner looked at the farmboy with mild interest as the threesome walked down Merchant Street. "I thought you were in a hurry to get home," he said.

"I changed my mind," Othisen replied. "This is all pretty exciting, you know. And I don't mind another look at the Palace; it's an impressive building."

Hanner blinked and didn't reply, but that was not because the boy's words had no effect. On the contrary, Hanner found them startling and distracting.

Impressive? He had never thought of the Palace as impressive; he had just thought of it as home. He had been born there, after all, and had lived his entire life within those familiar halls and chambers.

Othisen had presumably grown up on a farm somewhere; visiting the city was probably a special occasion for him, where Hanner had never yet slept outside Ethshar's walls. Hanner supposed that the entire city would probably be impressive to someone who had never seen it before, and the Palace was, after all, perhaps the largest single building in all Ethshar of the Spices.

But it was still just home to Hanner; he couldn't really think of it in any other way.

Of course, right now, he reminded himself, it was *not* home—he was banned from the Palace, by Azrad's order, until further notice. He was sure this was just a temporary aberration, though, and that everything would be back to normal in a few days.

He looked around, trying to judge whether the city looked any different.

The streets appeared to be much as they were on any other day, though perhaps the crowds were a bit thinner than average and the people a little more nervous, a little more prone to hurry. There were a few looted shops visible down one side street, their smashed display windows hastily boarded up, and one old house on Lower Street in the New City had been burned out, but most of the city seemed untouched by the previous night's insanity.

There had been a spasm of violence and wild behavior, clearly, but it was past. Things should return to normal soon enough. Magical mishaps had happened before, though perhaps not on quite so large a scale, and Ethshar had always recovered quickly.

It was tragic that those hundreds of people had disappeared, of course, but there wasn't much to be done about it unless some magician could determine where they had gone and bring them back. Surely, Azrad would see that. Hanner peered down the street toward the Palace.

He could see the parapet atop the facade, but the surrounding structures and the people on the street blocked his view of most of the building.

He could *hear* something, though.

He frowned at that. He could very definitely hear the sound of the crowds ahead—and it was not a good sound, but an angry buzz.

"Come on," he said, picking up the pace and trying not to pant. He glanced over to see whether the others were keeping up with him, and noticed that Rudhira, who had been walking normally up to that point, was now airborne.

Hanner came to an abrupt halt and turned to her.

She stopped as well and hovered a foot off the ground, looking down at him slightly.

"I don't think that's a good idea," he said, pointing at her dangling feet.

"I can't walk that fast," she replied.

"Then run."

"Running is undignified. Especially if I trip. I don't want to get these clothes muddy; your uncle's mistress wouldn't like it."

"I don't think my uncle's current mistress ever saw them," Hanner retorted. "I think they're leftovers from a few women back." He pointed toward the Palace. "Do you hear that crowd in the square there? I do, and I don't think they sound happy. I think they sound dangerous. And angry. And one of the things they're angry about is warlocks. Flying in there right now, openly announcing that you're a warlock, is likely to start a riot and get us all killed. I don't know about you, but I would prefer to get through today alive."

Rudhira tossed her head dramatically. "I don't think they *can* kill me!" she said. "Because I *am* a warlock, and going by what I've seen so far I'm one of the most powerful warlocks in Ethshar!"

"That's probably true," Hanner agreed, "but you're still one person, and there are hundreds, maybe thousands, of people over there, and while I doubt any of them are warlocks, since I assume most warlocks have more sense than you, some of them might well be wizards. Or witches. Or sorcerers, or demonologists, or other sorts of magicians. *I* don't know how warlockry matches up against the ordinary kinds of magic—do *you*?"

Rudhira looked quickly toward the square, then dropped to the ground. "You've made your point," she said as she started walking.

Othisen had observed this exchange silently; now, as the three of them walked quickly—though not quite as quickly as before—toward the Palace, he asked, "Do you really think it's dangerous? Will there really be magicians?"

"Yes, it's dangerous," Hanner said. "I don't know whether there will be magicians."

Othisen smiled at this and trotted forward enthusiastically.

A moment later the three of them reached not the square, but the rear of the crowd, a good fifty feet outside the square itself.

"What's going on?" Hanner asked the first man he reached who appeared to be part of the crowd itself.

The man threw him a glance. "I don't know," he said. "I can't see. Someone's talking, but I can't hear."

That reply was singularly lacking in useful information; Hanner bit back a sarcastic retort. "Excuse me," he said, pushing forward.

The crowd was large, but not very tightly packed; Hanner was able to force his way through without too much difficulty. Once or twice he caught himself pushing people aside without touching them, and each time he felt a chill of fear as he clenched his teeth and stopped the magic.

Now that he knew he could do it, it was hard to resist using warlockry. It was no surprise Rudhira liked to fly; this strange magic was oddly addictive. It *wanted* to be used. When he hadn't known it was there Hanner had felt no urge to try it, but now he kept thinking how easy it would be to reach out with it, to pick up this or move that . . .

He wondered whether other magic had the same appeal. None of the magicians he had interviewed on his uncle's behalf had ever mentioned anything of the sort, but that didn't mean much either way.

He glanced back and discovered that he had left Othisen and Rudhira back on Merchant Street.

Othisen was a country boy; he had probably never seen so many people in one place in his life. Rudhira was fairly small, and while she could undoubtedly have used her warlockry to protect her from any random jostling, Hanner had just talked her out of doing that.

Well, they were not children; Rudhira was probably a year or two older than he was. They could look after themselves for the moment. He pressed on.

Last night the square had been full of soldiers. Today the

guards were lined up along the north side of the square, shielding the canal, the bridge, and the Palace, and leaving the rest of the square open to the horde of unhappy citizens.

Someone was indeed addressing the crowd over there, right at the mouth of the bridge. Hanner strained to catch the words.

". . . questions! You can hire magicians—maybe they'll be able to tell you!"

Someone in the crowd shouted an angry and unintelligible response to that, which was followed by a rumble of agreement.

"Oh, death," Hanner muttered as he pushed onward. He didn't know who was speaking, but whoever it was didn't seem to be very good at it.

"It's *your* job to protect us!" someone roared.

"And we *are* protecting you!" the man on the bridge replied. "Do you see any warlocks here?"

"How can we tell?" a woman shouted back.

A chorus of agreement rolled over the crowd like a wave, echoing from the facade of the Palace.

"Look, it's *magic*," the man on the bridge said, clearly exasperated. Hanner could see now that he wore a captain's uniform. "We don't know any more about it than *you* do until the magicians tell us! Lord Azrad has sent a message to the Wizards' Guild, demanding an explanation, and we're waiting for their reply!"

"They probably *started* it!"

"It's the demonologists!"

"Northern sorcery!"

"What does Lord Faran say?"

That question was one Hanner wished someone would answer. What would his uncle say if he ever found out that Hanner was one of these troublesome new magicians?

For that matter, what would the Wizards' Guild say?

Not that Hanner had any intention of telling anyone.

He wished he knew just where Faran was, and what he was doing.

Chapter Seventeen

L ord Faran's voice was almost pleading—which was utterly unheard of. He sat in his usual seat in the lesser audience chamber, but leaned forward toward the overlord's throne rather than sprawling comfortably as he usually did.

"Lord Azrad," he said, "they aren't *all* criminals!"

"They're all dangerous," the overlord replied. He remained slumped on his throne in his customary slouch, but he was glaring at his chief advisor with unusual intensity. The two of them were alone in the room and able to speak freely. "I am struck by your concern, my lord Faran—it's hardly your usual style. Is your latest mistress one of them, then? Or perhaps that useless nephew of yours?"

"No, Lord Azrad," Faran replied. "Or at least, I think not, but since you have not seen fit to allow Lord Hanner to reenter the Palace, I can't say with any real certainty that he is not."

"And your woman?"

"Oh, I can attest to Isia's utter lack of any magic beyond the usual charms natural to young women."

He had not, in fact, tested that, but certainly there had been no sign that she, too, had acquired this strange new magic that the witches called warlockry.

And if she had, he was not particularly concerned about it; she was pleasant enough company, but so were any number of women, and she had not uniquely endeared herself to Faran any more than had her dozens of predecessors.

"Then why are you so determined to let these mad magicians live?"

"Because, my lord, they have done no wrong, and when the crowd's madness has passed the people of Ethshar will remember that. While none of them are my own family, nonetheless they do have families and friends, and in time those families and friends would begin to wonder why old Uncle Kelder or little Sarai from down the street was put to death for the crime of being a magician. Why warlocks, and not demonologists? After all, they dabble with the darkest of forces. Why not sorcerers, who were the favored of the Northern Empire and who may yet bear the Northern taint? Why not wizards, who meddle with truly incomprehensible forces and whose Guild dares to dictate terms to all the World's governments? Oh, the warlocks broke into a few shops, burned a few homes, raped a few women— but *Uncle Kelder* did none of that, and an ordinary thief gets off with a flogging, a rapist with enslavement. Why are warlocks so dire that they must be exterminated?"

"Faran, you're being deliberately dense. You *know* why— because we don't know what they can do! Because they're completely uncontrolled. Because they seem to have made at least four hundred people simply *disappear* overnight, which even the wizards have never done. There are reports that a warlock can stop a man's heart with a look—what if one of them decides that he doesn't like the way we run the city? A glance, an apparent heart attack, and that useless son of mine is on this throne instead of me!"

"Oh, I agree they're dangerous, my lord, but so are ordinary people, and when they've had time to reflect I believe that those ordinary people will regret hanging all the warlocks, and they'll blame *you* for doing it."

Azrad frowned deeply.

"I agree that it's a bad situation either way," Faran said quickly. "But really, what threat does a warlock pose that a wizard or demonologist does not? A glance that kills—is that really any more lethal than the Rune of the Implacable Stalker, or a demon like Spesforis the Hunter?"

"I wouldn't know," Azrad growled. "Unlike you, *I* never even *heard* of that rune, or this Spessris you mention."

"Spesforis," Faran corrected.

"Whatever. Faran, I sometimes think your researches

have gone too far—you're entirely too fond of magicians, even these warlocks."

"Knowledge is a tool, my lord," Faran protested. "I like to have a full toolbox ready."

"Hmph."

"In this case, my lord, if I may extend the metaphor, my toolbox has nothing in it but rust and wood shavings. We don't know anything about this warlockry. It may all vanish tomorrow—and what will people say *then* if we've hanged a hundred innocent people? For that matter, warlocks can fly—what if they can't be hanged?"

"Then cut off their heads. That's easy enough. A rope's traditional, but it's hardly the only means at our disposal."

"True, but really not my point. I would . . ."

Azrad held up a hand, and Faran stopped in midsentence.

"You may be right," the overlord said. "I don't want the blame for hanging everyone's Uncle Kelder. So we need to put the blame somewhere else. If the Wizards' Guild wants the warlocks wiped out, then it's not *our* fault."

Faran fingered his beard in silence for a moment as he considered this.

"I see your point," he said at last. "You think, I take it, that it would be very convenient if the Wizards' Guild declared warlockry a menace to be destroyed. You would reluctantly yield to their authority, since magic is their area of expertise."

"And we would be blameless. And if people are unhappy with the Wizards' Guild, it won't make *my* beer taste any worse."

"Of course not."

"So, Lord Faran, would *that* suit you? Or do you still argue that the warlocks must live?"

"It would seem my stated objections have been countered," Faran admitted.

He did not sound pleased about this; in fact, he realized that he still sounded unconvinced, and that Azrad knew him well enough to recognize that.

He had been working closely with the overlord for more

than twenty years—Azrad had come to power upon his father's death twenty-eight years ago, and Faran had spent his entire adult life in the Palace, working his way up in Azrad's esteem. Lying successfully to the overlord would take a little more effort than his usual casual facade.

"You have unstated objections, then?"

Faran certainly did—foremost among them that he was himself a warlock, but of course he couldn't admit that. He knew Azrad too well to think that knowing his chief advisor was a warlock would change the overlord's opinion of warlocks; it would instead, he was sure, change his opinion of Faran. Azrad always chose the more negative option in such cases.

Especially when he was scared, which he clearly was.

"Nothing I can put into words," Faran said. "It just seems wasteful."

"Better wasteful than dangerous," Azrad replied.

"What if the Wizards' Guild decides the warlocks pose no great threat?"

"You deal with the Guild more than I," Azrad said. "Do you think it likely?" He shifted heavily on the throne. "And if it's likely, can you change that?"

"I don't know," Faran admitted.

"Then find out," Azrad snapped. "I have sent several messages to the Guild, asking their representatives to wait upon me at their earliest possible convenience, and I expect them to oblige me no later than tomorrow."

"Lord Azrad, you've cut off many of my best sources of information by forbidding all entry to the Palace. Might you relent, perhaps, in the case of my nephew Hanner and my niece Alris?"

Azrad considered that, chewing his lip and staring at Faran.

Faran gazed serenely back, but internally he was seething. The fat old fool didn't see the possibilities in warlockry! He didn't realize how hard it would be to detect warlocks, didn't see that he had one right here beside him—he would never be able to exterminate them all, but would instead drive them into hiding.

Warlocks would make perfect spies, ideal assassins. They could fly over walls, break locks with their magic—Faran wasn't sure yet whether they could open locks without breaking them—and could kill anyone from a distance, leaving no mark.

If the Hegemony were to *use* those abilities they could rule the World, retake the Small Kingdoms and the Pirate Towns and the northern lands. If they tried to stamp warlockry out those abilities would be turned against them instead.

Saying that would be unwise, though—Azrad clearly had his mind made up, and would almost certainly prefer a handful of openly hostile warlocks in hiding to hundreds of undecided ones living openly in the city.

Faran, on the other hand, saw the possibilities clearly. All the other varieties of magic had drawbacks, weaknesses, limitations—wizardry required exotic materials and intricate rituals; witchcraft strong enough to be any use left the user exhausted and weak; theurgy was limited to coaxing whimsical and rule-bound gods to cooperate, and so on, while a warlock need merely *think* of what he wanted, think hard and it would happen. With this magic at his disposal, an ambitious man could accomplish almost anything.

If Faran were to reach out with his mind now, and grip Lord Azrad's overworked heart . . .

But it was too soon to move so openly. Besides, Azrad the Younger, Azrad's son and heir, who would someday be Azrad VII if all went as expected, was a vigorous man of thirty-five, far less familiar and far less easily manipulated than the present bloated and slothful overlord.

"I don't think so," Azrad said at last. "From what I've heard, both of them have been associating with several warlocks. I don't think we can trust them until those warlocks have been disposed of."

"But they can probably tell us a great deal about the warlocks! We could learn just how big a danger they actually are . . ."

"*That* subject is *closed*, Lord Faran," Azrad said. "They've shown themselves to be dangerous enough that they must be removed."

Faran had never before been so irked with his master; the temptation to squeeze that heart was growing.

"Of course, my lord," he said.

"When this is all over, Lord Hanner and Lady Alris will be permitted into the Palace again—that is, assuming *they* aren't warlocks."

"But not before?"

"Not before."

"In that case, my lord, I think I had best set about finding others I can send on certain errands."

Perhaps the throat, rather than the heart. Perhaps if Azrad were to choke slightly, but recover . . .

No. That wouldn't change anything, except to make the overlord suspicious.

"Be about it, then," Azrad said with a wave of dismissal.

"Yes, my lord." Faran rose, bowed slightly, and turned to go.

As he crossed the room his fingers were clenching and unclenching. He could feel the power in his mind, like rising dough, pressing outward, eager to be used. It took an effort to reach for the door handle with his hand, rather than with magic . . .

And then the door swung open before he reached it, almost slamming into his nose, and his mind lashed out, shoving it closed again. He stepped back, startled.

The door opened again, more slowly this time, and Captain Vengar stepped in, peering around the panel at Faran.

"I'm sorry, my lord," he said, "I didn't know you were there. Lord Azrad signaled for me."

"You still should have knocked!" Lord Faran said angrily.

"Captain," the overlord called sharply, in a tone Lord Faran had never heard before in all his years in the Palace.

Startled, Faran turned to see the overlord sitting bolt upright on the throne.

"Yes, my lord?" Vengar said.

"Captain, this man is a warlock," Azrad said, speaking slowly and clearly and louder than his wont—and not entirely steadily. "When he closed that door on you just now he did not touch it. Remove him from the Palace at once and see that he is not readmitted without my specific permission."

"What?" Faran burst out. "Azrad, that's absurd!"

"I saw what I saw, my lord. Your hands were at your sides when that door slammed shut. Why you did not see fit to tell me of your altered circumstances I do not know, but it's quite obvious I can't trust you anymore. Go peacefully—and I might suggest that you consider leaving the city, as well as the Palace, for your own safety."

The overlord's eyes were unnaturally wide and staring, Faran saw—and wet, as if he were on the verge of tears.

"But it's . . . you couldn't, from across the room . . ."

"Captain."

Vengar reached for Faran's arm. "If you would come with me, my lord," he said nervously.

Faran looked at the soldier's familiar worried face, then back at Azrad, sitting up straight, eyes wide, for the first time in years. He looked at the tapestried walls, the tessellated stone floor, that symbolized the wealth and power of the triumvirate that ruled the Hegemony of the Three Ethshars.

It was too soon to fight openly. He was the only warlock in the Palace, and there were at least a hundred guards on hand, not counting the company out in the square and leaving the building's other inhabitants out of consideration. He did not know just how strong his magic actually was—he had been telling himself there were no limits, but he had not had a chance to test the truth of that. Since the overlord's immediate decree, the moment he heard of the troubles the night before, that no warlocks were to be permitted in the Palace, Faran had had to hide his abilities, and what with the crisis demanding his attention he had had no opportunities to experiment in private.

"Lord Azrad," he said, making one more try, "I am no threat . . ."

"*Out!*" Azrad bellowed, rising to his feet and pointing. "Get out of my home, traitor!"

Stung, Faran glared silently for a moment longer, then whirled back to the door.

"Lead the way, Captain," he said. "I will leave it to others to try to talk sense to the overlord." He stalked out.

A moment later he paused in the central hallway and asked, "Captain, may I send for my belongings later? I'll provide a list of what I need, and my niece Nerra will attend to locating it all."

"I'll have to check with the overlord, Lord Faran," Vengar said. "I'm sure you understand."

"Of course," Faran replied. "Of course. I'll send a messenger to inquire when I've settled into my new quarters."

Vengar hesitated. "My lord," he said, "are you really a warlock?"

Faran gazed at the soldier, then smiled a crooked little smile.

"Yes, I am," he said. It was a relief to admit it openly and put an end to pretense.

It was with an oddly light heart that he marched out the door onto the bridge, into the slanting sunlight of the afternoon.

Chapter Eighteen

Hanner had spotted a familiar face in the crowd, and after much shoving—with both hands and magic—he had finally reached her side.

"What are *you* doing here?" he asked.

Mavi turned, startled. "Lord Hanner!" she said. "I didn't expect to see *you* out here! I thought you'd be inside with the others."

Hanner grimaced. "I *could* say that was your fault," he said. "I didn't make it back in time last night, after I saw you home, and I've been locked out by the overlord's edict. Alris is locked out, too."

"That applies to *you*? But you *live* there!"

"Lord Azrad makes no exceptions," Hanner replied. "What about you, though—are you all right? Was anyone in your family hurt?"

"Oh, we're fine," Mavi said quickly. "There was some disturbance, certainly, and I didn't sleep at all well, due to the shouting and so on, but nobody troubled us. I heard all the neighbors talking, though, so I thought I'd come up here to see what was happening."

"Not very much, from what I can see," Hanner said. Then someone bumped against him, and he turned to find that Rudhira had finally worked her way through the crowd, caught up with him, and shoved her way up to his side.

"Who is this?" Rudhira asked.

"Ah," Hanner said. He spread his hands as best he could in the crowded circumstances. "Rudhira of Camptown, this is Mavi of Newmarket. She's a friend—a friend of my sister Nerra, I mean."

"Pleased to meet you," Rudhira said, though she did not look especially pleased. "Hanner, why are we here? They aren't saying anything new."

"You don't have to stay," Hanner told her, a trifle resentfully. "You can go home or go back to Uncle Faran's house."

"Uncle Faran's house?" Mavi asked, puzzled. "But your uncle lives in the Palace."

"He has a house on High Street, as well," Hanner explained. "That's where Alris and I are staying until the guards let us back in."

"Oh, I assumed you'd found an inn."

"I didn't need to . . ."

"We wouldn't all have *fit* at an inn!" Rudhira interrupted.

"We?" Mavi asked, puzzled.

"I collected a group of people to help out last night," Hanner explained. "Rudhira was one of them." Othisen was approaching as well; Hanner pointed him out and said, "And Othisen Okko's son was another. Most of the rest have gone home now, but these two stayed."

"*I* could have helped!" Mavi said. "You should have come to get me!"

"Are you a warlock?" Rudhira demanded, before Hanner could reply. Hanner raised a hand to hush her.

"No, of course not," Mavi said.

"*We* are," Rudhira said, gesturing at herself and Othisen. "Lord Hanner found us in the Wizards' Quarter—we were trying to figure out what had happened to us, and he came and told us to help him stop the *bad* warlocks."

At that, a stranger in the crowd turned and stared. "What did you say?" she asked.

"Did you say you're a warlock?" another said.

"A warlock? Here?"

Hanner looked around worriedly and quickly threw a protective arm around Mavi. Several faces were turning toward them, and Rudhira was standing defiantly, hands on her hips, glaring back at them all.

"We were *helping*," she said. "Lord Hanner invoked the overlord's name and told us to help, and we did! We've just come from turning four of the warlocks who went smashing things over to a magistrate!"

Mavi threw Hanner an uncertain glance.

"I'll explain later," he said. "Right now, I think we should—"

The end of his sentence was drowned out by a sudden roar from the crowd, followed by a hush. Hanner turned, startled, trying to see what had happened.

The palace door had opened, and a figure had emerged onto the bridge, a figure dressed in a magnificent green velvet cloak that was probably swelteringly uncomfortable in the summer heat.

Hanner recognized him immediately—as had several others in the crowd.

"Lord Faran," someone said.

An expectant silence spread quickly as Faran strode across the bridge. The lines of soldiers parted at his approach, and he marched on into the square. Everyone waited for him to stop and begin speaking.

He didn't. He kept right on marching.

The crowd stepped back, splitting down the middle to give him room, and then, much more slowly, filled back in behind him.

Faran paid no heed to any of them; he strode onward as if the square were empty, directly across the center without looking to either side, and finally out of the square and onto Center Avenue, as if he intended to simply march straight on to Southmarket.

The silence broke as people began to ask one another what the Lord Counselor was doing, and Hanner had to shout to be heard over the babble.

"Come on!" he said, taking Mavi's hand. "I think I know where he's going, and we'd best meet him there."

Mavi didn't try to answer over the noise, but followed as he led the way.

Rudhira and Othisen followed as well, and the foursome fought their way quickly through the milling throng—not toward Center Avenue, as that was mobbed, but to Aristocrat Circle.

Hanner was sure that Faran was headed for the house on High Street, and there were other routes that would take one there more quickly than going straight up Center and then turning right onto High Street.

Even as he hurried, he was aware of the feel of Mavi's hand in his—cool and soft, her touch delicate but not weak.

He also noticed that Rudhira was opening a path through the crowd by unnatural means; he considered protesting, but then decided against it. The mob was already stirred up by

Faran's silent appearance, and too busy to notice that they were being pushed not by hands, but by magic.

In fact . . .

"Rudhira," Hanner called, "maybe you should fly."

Rudhira turned to look at him, and then smiled a broad, not entirely pleasant smile.

"We all will," she said.

Before Hanner could protest he found himself snatched off his feet; the surrounding crowd fell away, the buildings around the square dropped away and shrank. His hand tightened—and so did Mavi's. Hanner turned to find her wide-eyed with fright, staring down, but saying nothing.

"It's all right!" Hanner shouted. "Just stay calm!"

She lifted her gaze to him, her expression making it plain that she thought he was completely insane to tell her this. "But we're flying," she said.

"Yes, I know," Hanner said. "But it's safe."

She did not look convinced. "You've done this before?" she asked.

"Well, no," Hanner admitted, "but *Rudhira* has."

Honesty, he decided upon seeing her reaction, had not been the right choice.

Below them voices were shouting angrily.

"Which way?" Rudhira called to him.

Startled, he stopped watching Mavi's face and looked around.

The four of them, he and Mavi and Rudhira and Othisen, were hanging in midair perhaps fifty or sixty feet up, well above most of the rooftops. Below them in the square people were churning about and shouting and pointing, and a few were throwing things at the hovering clump of people; fortunately, none were able to actually hit anything so far off the ground.

To the north was the golden facade of the Palace and the dark water of the Grand Canal, and on all other sides the rooftops of the city stretched out, all brightly lit. There were no shadows up here, nothing to keep off the summer sun, and the expanse of red tile seemed vast and shimmering, pocked and split almost randomly by the dark separations between buildings. The Old City was a tangled patch of red tile, golden thatch, and black slate to the northeast.

On the ground he knew half a dozen routes to the corner of High Street and Coronet, but from up here he didn't recognize any of them. One tile rooftop looked much like another.

He could work it out logically, he told himself. If the Palace was that way, they wanted to go the opposite, into the New City, up the slope past Short Street and Second Street and Lower Street . . .

He tried to pick out the streets from the rooftops, but the alleys and gardens and courtyards confused matters, and he settled for pointing south and saying, "That way."

Immediately they were whisked away, swooping after Rudhira as if they were on strings.

Once they were moving Hanner was able to spot a few details he had missed before. There was Lord Anduron's estate with its eccentric assortment of turrets and wrought-iron spires, at the corner of Canal Avenue and Second Street . . .

"Bear right," he called.

Rudhira obliged, and they cut diagonally across a block, over assorted gardens and courtyards. He recognized a facade on Central Avenue.

"Farther right," he said.

That sufficed; they were then aimed as directly as he could ask toward Lord Faran's house. A moment later they descended gracefully toward the packed dirt of High Street.

"Wait," Hanner said. He glanced to the left, toward Center Avenue, and could see people moving about—not the usual gentle movement of people going about their business, but pushing and running. He could hear shouting as well.

Rudhira stopped, and the four hung in midair. All of them followed Hanner's gaze.

"What should we do?" Rudhira asked.

"Back up," Hanner said. "We'll land in the garden out back, and go in that way, where we can't be seen."

"Good idea," Othisen said.

Rudhira nodded, and the foursome swooped upward again, over the roof and down into the garden.

Mavi stumbled when they landed; she had tucked her legs up and did not straighten them quickly enough. Hanner caught her, then quickly released her.

"Sorry," he said.

"Thank you," she replied.

"Now what?" Othisen asked.

Hanner looked around at the neatly trimmed hedges and flowerbeds. They had traveled far faster by air than a man could on foot and had been able to cut across the roofs instead of following the streets, so they had undoubtedly gotten here before Lord Faran, but he would be arriving any minute.

"We go inside, of course," Hanner said. He led the way to one of the garden doors and knocked vigorously, hoping someone was within earshot.

Bern answered the door. He tried to say something, but Hanner was in no mood for polite greeting and pushed past him, leading his party quickly into the house and through the long gallery toward the front. As he passed, Hanner told Bern, "Uncle Faran's coming."

Alris, sprawled on a divan in the front parlor, heard that. "He is?" she called, startled. "He's not still in the Palace?"

Hanner turned up an empty palm as he stood in the doorway to the parlor. "He'll be here any minute," he said.

"Is Nerra with him?" Alris asked, rising.

"No," Hanner said. "He was alone."

"No guards to take charge of the prisoners?" Zarek asked from the parlor—he had been seated not far from Alris. "Does he know what you did with them?"

"He's alone," Hanner said. "I don't know any more than that. I don't know why he left the Palace or why he's coming here or why he's alone."

Bern arrived as Hanner finished this speech.

"My lord," he said, "I really think you should know, *before* your uncle arrives, that we have additional guests."

Startled, Hanner turned to face him.

"They're upstairs, resting," Alris said. "Two of those people you had here last night, who went home this morning. They came back. Their neighbors were shouting at them and throwing mud."

"What? Why?" Hanner asked.

"Because they're warlocks, of course," Zarek said.

There was a moment of awkward silence as the seven of them—Hanner, Mavi, Rudhira, Othisen, Alris, Zarek, and Bern—stood scattered about the parlor and hallway, looking at one another, seeking some clue as to what was happening and what they should do.

And then the front door opened, and Lord Faran stepped in.

"My lord," Bern said with a bow. "May I take your . . ."

He had not yet said the word "cloak" when Faran flung the garment at him. Bern caught it and began smoothing and dusting it as Faran looked around at the others. Hanner, from years of experience, saw that his uncle was regaining control of a lost temper; he suspected the others saw nothing but a man relaxing after the exertion of a brisk walk in the summer sun.

"Hanner, my boy," Faran said. "A pleasure to see you here. Would you introduce me to your friends?"

"Of course, my lord uncle," Hanner said, bowing. Formalities that he never bothered with if he could help it, that he almost never used when he was surrounded entirely by family or entirely by outsiders, seemed necessary and natural in this particular setting. "Lord Counselor Faran, may I present Rudhira of Camptown?"

Rudhira had the wit to curtsy.

"I believe you have already met Mavi of Newmarket, who I had the good fortune to meet in the square just now and invite to accompany us. This young man is Othisen Okko's son, and that is Zarek, known at present as the Homeless."

Neither man managed a decent bow, but Zarek did make a belated and halfhearted attempt, while Othisen just gaped.

"I understand you are the master of this house," Rudhira

said. "Our thanks for your hospitality, my lord." She smiled warmly—a little too warmly, Hanner thought.

Faran smiled in return, a smile that Hanner had seen many times before, and Hanner knew where that would lead. He cleared his throat.

"It's a pleasure to welcome guests such as you," Faran said. He looked around. "And are there any others? My understanding was that my nephew had brought more than a dozen visitors here last night."

Hanner hesitated. "The others left, my lord," he said. "The four criminals have been turned over to the Lord Magistrate of the Old Merchants' Quarter, since Lord Azrad refused them entry, and the others, now that the excitement has subsided somewhat, went home. But two of them have come back."

Faran raised one eyebrow. "The excitement, my boy, has scarcely begun."

"That's why the two returned," Hanner said.

Faran nodded. "Tell me, are all my guests here possessed of the new magic that appeared last night, this so-called warlockry?"

Hanner swallowed and looked at the others.

"I am," Rudhira said proudly, spreading her arms and rising a few inches from the floor. To Hanner's surprise, Faran's smile broadened.

"I'm not as powerful as Rudhira, but I'm a warlock," Othisen said.

"So am I," Zarek admitted.

Faran looked at Mavi, who turned up both hands. "Not I," she said. "I was just talking with Hanner in the square when we saw you leave the Palace, and I was brought along."

"The two upstairs are warlocks, though," Hanner said.

"Ah," Faran said. "Then counting that mysterious unnamed pair, there are six of us."

"Us?" Hanner said, startled.

Faran's smile vanished. "Us," he said. "I, too, am a warlock. Thus Lord Azrad, that useless old fool, has cast me out."

Hanner's mouth fell open, and he could see Alris's eyes widen with shock.

The revelation that their uncle was a warlock was perhaps the biggest shock, but it was by no means the only one. That Faran had called Azrad a fool before these near-total strangers was another, almost as great. They had both heard their uncle speak disparagingly of the overlord before—quite often, in fact—but never before where anyone outside the family could hear. In fact, it had been pounded into Hanner from an early age that as a hereditary lord he must never, ever speak ill of Lord Azrad in public; whatever they might think or say among themselves, the nobility had an obligation to present a united front to the World at large, so as never to undermine the public trust.

And the idea that Azrad would evict Uncle Faran from the Palace was almost more than Hanner could comprehend. For as far back as he could remember Azrad had relied on Faran, had trusted him to make all the decisions that would keep the city running smoothly. That even strange new magic could shatter that trust in a single day was hard to grasp.

"He threw you out of the Palace?" Alris gasped.

"Oh, he has done more than that, my dear niece," Faran said. "It would seem that Lord Azrad the Sedentary, in his infinite stupidity, has sentenced the four of us, and all the others upon whom this new magic was bestowed, to die."

Chapter Nineteen

Die? For *what*?" Rudhira demanded.

"For endangering the peace of the Hegemony of Ethshar by the mere fact of our existence," Faran said. "Or perhaps for kidnapping or murdering a few hundred people—he didn't seem very concerned about a reason."

"But we haven't . . . well, *I* haven't hurt anyone!"

Zarek cleared his throat. "Rudhira, you killed a man last night," he pointed out.

Rudhira turned angrily, and Zarek staggered backward, catching himself on the door frame. "That was self-defense!" she shouted.

"He's still dead," Othisen said.

Rudhira whirled, and Othisen slammed back against the wall, his head narrowly missing a brass sconce.

"Rudhira," Hanner said, "don't hurt *them*."

Rudhira started to turn on Hanner, and he braced himself for whatever she might do, but instead she stopped. Her raised arms fell to her sides.

"You're right," she said. "It's those fools in the Palace I want to throw around, not you."

"Just one fool, really," Faran said, watching Rudhira appraisingly. "It's Azrad himself who's behind this, not any of the rest of us."

Rudhira met Faran's gaze. "Is he really as fat and lazy as they say?" she asked.

Faran smiled knowingly. "Since I don't know who 'they' are or what they say," he said, "I can't answer that exactly, but I can certainly say that Lord Azrad the Sixth weighs perhaps twice what most men his height do, and exerts himself as little as humanly possible."

"If I ever get at him, he'll exert himself!" Rudhira snapped.

"And I hope to see it happen," Faran replied, his calm facade slipping.

"Lord Faran!" Mavi gasped. "He's the overlord! The triumvir!"

"He's an idiot," Faran said. "Oh, his great-great-great-great grandfather* was a great man, a military genius, the founder of this city—but the blood has obviously thinned, and I think it's time to do something about it. You know

---

*Four greats is correct. Azrad the Great outlived both his sons; Azrad II was his grandson.

who's really been running this city the past ten years, Hanner." His temper was visibly wearing thin again.

"You have," Hanner said. "But still . . ."

"That's right, *I* have!" Faran said angrily, cutting Hanner short. "And what does it get me? A *death sentence*, because some mad wizard somewhere got careless and spilled magic everywhere!"

"I don't think it was a wizard . . ."

"Fine! *Whatever* did it!" Faran flung his hands in the air, no longer making any pretense of composure. "And do you want to know something even more despicable, my boy? Our dear Lord Azrad won't even take responsibility for his own actions. He intends to arrange for the Wizards' Guild to outlaw this new magic, and let *them* take the blame when the people realize how unjust this all is!"

Hanner blinked, digesting this new information, as Faran glared at him. Then he said, "That's not so foolish. It's actually sort of clever . . ."

"It's *insane*!" Faran said. "Give the Wizards' Guild even *more* power?"

"But it won't . . ." Hanner began, intending to point out that the Wizards' Guild would be weakened when they were indeed blamed for the proposed slaughter, but Faran wasn't listening.

"I won't have it," Faran said. "I have no intention of letting Azrad or his soldiers or the wizards kill me—or kill you, Rudhira, or Othisen, or Zarek, or anyone else who innocently got warlockry bestowed upon him." He glowered at Hanner and Alris and Mavi. "*You* three don't have anything to worry about—by the gods, Hanner, that fat old man might well name you my successor! But *we*"—he gestured at the three acknowledged warlocks—"are fighting for our lives!"

"I know," Hanner said, "but what can you—"

"I could fly us away," Rudhira said. "North, maybe, to . . . to Aldagmor." She looked slightly puzzled at her own words.

Hanner felt oddly uncomfortable at that suggestion. Faran, too, reacted strangely, jerking his head slightly before replying, "No. I'm not giving up my home without a fight."

"But, Uncle," Alris said, "what can you do? Even if you're a warlock, you can't fight the entire city guard *and* the Wizards' Guild!"

Rudhira shuddered. "No one can fight the Wizards' Guild," she said.

"Why not?" Faran said. "They're only mortal—well, most of them, anyway. *We* have magic now, too! And maybe we can get the other magicians to join us—the sorcerers and theurgists and witches . . ."

"Why would *they* help?" Hanner asked.

"Because they're tired of the Wizards' Guild ordering them around," Faran said. "Keeping them out of government, telling them no one can learn more than one kind of magic . . ."

"They don't care, Uncle," Hanner said. "They like things the way they are . . . or at least the way they *were*, before last night."

"I don't believe it," Faran said.

"But they *do*," Hanner insisted. "You've had me talking to them, day after day, for *years* now, and they really, truly don't care about the Wizards' Guild."

"Maybe, when we tell them what's going to happen to us, their fellow magicians . . ." Rudhira said hesitantly.

"Right!" Faran said, pointing at her. "Exactly right! Rudhira, you understand the situation better than my nephew, and he's spent his life in the Palace." He smiled at Rudhira, then looked expectantly at Hanner.

Hanner knew that look. Uncle Faran expected him to yield now, to say that of course Faran was right, and everyone would do what he told them to do—but Hanner was not ready to yield. He was thinking.

Lord Faran's expectant smile was starting to slip into a frown when Hanner said, "Uncle? You said that the overlord intends to blame the Wizards' Guild for ordering all the warlocks executed?"

"Yes. That's exactly—"

"He hasn't done it yet?"

Faran blinked, startled, and Hanner realized that this was the first time in years that he had dared to interrupt his uncle.

"No," Faran said. "He hasn't had time yet. He's asked the Wizards' Guild to attend him as soon as possible, and expects to meet with them by tomorrow. So we have a few hours—"

"Uncle," Hanner said, interrupting again. Faran's eyes widened. "Why are you so sure the Wizards' Guild will cooperate with the overlord? After all, warlocks are arguably their fellow magicians."

Faran's mouth opened, then closed.

"We should talk to them," Othisen said. "Maybe they're on *our* side!"

"Maybe some of *them* are warlocks," Hanner suggested. "There's no reason it couldn't happen, is there?"

"Who knows?" Faran asked. "Maybe wizards were immune."

"But even so, they still might be sympathetic," Hanner said. "You didn't *ask* to be a warlock."

"They don't allow magicians in the government," Faran said.

"But most of the warlocks *aren't* in the government," Hanner pointed out. "*You* are, but Rudhira and Zarek and Othisen aren't—they're just ordinary people. They have just as much right to be magicians as any wizard's apprentice."

Hanner, long familiar with his uncle, could see Faran resisting the impulse to say that that didn't help *him*, that he wanted to keep both his post and his new magic. Faran never admitted to selfish motives—but Hanner knew they were always there.

"You'd have to renounce your title, of course, Uncle," Hanner said.

"I suppose I would," Faran said slowly. "That would still be preferable to execution, of course."

Hanner wasn't at all sure Uncle Faran actually believed that.

"You should talk to them, Lord Faran," Othisen said. "Maybe they'd make an exception."

"They *never*"—Hanner, Faran, and Alris all began in unison; they looked at one another, and Hanner finished—"make exceptions."

"But I should talk to them," Faran added. "You're quite right—we really don't know what position the Wizards' Guild will take on all this."

"We don't know how long the warlockry will last," Hanner pointed out. "Maybe if you emphasize that, that it's probably just a temporary thing, they'll be lenient. Wizards take the long view, and even if the people who are warlocks now *do* stay warlocks for the rest of their lives, which you probably won't, it's not as if anyone's going to take apprentices and train *new* warlocks."

"But it could happen again," Rudhira said. "Whatever happened last night, I mean. For all we know it'll happen again tonight or tomorrow."

"Well, don't tell *them* that," Alris said.

"Do you want me to go speak to Guildmaster Ithinia?" Hanner asked.

"That won't be necessary," Faran said.

"But—" Rudhira began.

Faran silenced her protest with an upraised hand.

"I'll speak to Guildmaster Ithinia myself," Faran said.

"Will you need your cloak, my lord?" Bern asked.

Faran smiled. "No, Bern," he said. "I won't be going out."

"But—" Mavi began. Hanner hushed her.

"That's what's on the top two floors, Uncle?" he asked.

Faran threw him a glance. "Shrewd, my boy," he said. "Unless you've been snooping?"

"I haven't been up there," Hanner said. "But what else

could you have there that you'd keep so secret? You've been collecting magic."

"Exactly." Faran smiled crookedly. "And if I'm an outlaw now anyway, through no fault of my own, and must either renounce my title or put an end to the Guild's prohibition on the nobility's use of magic, there's no point in concealing it anymore. Using a spell to contact Guildmaster Ithinia should demonstrate that we are indeed her fellow magicians, and not merely rabble."

Hanner was not sure his uncle, in his anger, had thought this through properly—possession of illegal magic other than warlockry might merely demonstrate that Faran was even more dangerous than the overlord believed.

"I don't understand," Mavi said. "What are you talking about?"

"You explain it, Hanner," Faran said as he turned toward the stairs. "I have matters to attend to."

Hanner sighed and explained.

"My uncle has been interested in magic for years," he said. "So have I, for that matter, and when he's too busy with other city business I've taken charge of handling the magical stuff. It really annoys him that the Wizards' Guild forbids any reigning triumvir or monarch, or any hereditary official of any government, to learn magic or to use magic for direct personal benefit. The limits do seem arbitrary sometimes—for example, we can use magic in the city courts to determine what's true, but we can't use it as punishment. The magistrates can't sentence a murderer to be turned to stone or order a thief to spend a year as a cat, no matter how appropriate that might be. And a hereditary lord can decorate his mansion with, say, talking statuary or seal his strongbox with a rune, because those just enhance possessions he'd have anyway, but he can't hire a magician to cure his warts, because that enhances *him*. Uncle Faran can hire a seer to spy on a traitor, because that benefits the entire city, but not on one of Azrad's other advisors, because that would be to his own political benefit. The exact rules are complex, and sometimes they don't seem entirely consistent—the Guild judges some cases individually, and sometimes it seems as if the ruling depends more on how annoying the wizards find the person asking than on what's actually asked."

"I knew part of that," Mavi said. "Not the details, since I'm neither a lady nor a wizard, but I knew the overlord couldn't just order the wizards to do whatever he wants."

"Oh, he can't *order* them to do *anything*," Hanner said. "He has to pay them, just like anyone else does, and they're always free to refuse a job, even if it's something the Guild has approved."

"Oh," Mavi said.

"Tell her about mixing magic," Alris said.

"That's another thing that annoys our uncle," Hanner said. "The Wizards' Guild insists that each magician should only learn one kind of magic. Witches aren't allowed to learn wizardry, sorcerers aren't allowed to learn theurgy, and so on. The Guild hasn't always managed to make that one go—I've seen witches and wizards use a little sorcery, and demonologists and theurgists have been known to trade invocations occasionally. Mostly, though, that's accepted— you won't find wizards summoning demons, or witches turning people into newts." He sighed. "Sometimes I think they don't allow the nobility to use anything else because they consider political power a sort of magic itself, and it would be mixing magic."

"I didn't know it was a *rule*, that no one could learn two kinds of magic," Mavi said. "I thought it was just too hard, learning more than one."

"It may be that, too," Hanner admitted. "Uncle Faran doesn't believe it, but I'm the one who's talked to dozens and dozens of magicians, and most of them are far too busy learning more of their regular arts to worry about other disciplines. I've never heard of the Wizards' Guild really enforcing that one—they don't need to."

"All right," Mavi said, "but what does that have to do with Lord Faran going upstairs?"

Hanner sighed. "This house has four floors," he said.

"The first two are where Uncle Faran brings women he doesn't want in the Palace, for one reason or another. He may do other things here as well, I don't know—for all I know he could meet with a secret cult of assassins every sixnight. Bern, here, takes care of the two lower floors when Uncle Faran isn't using them."

Bern acknowledged the mention of his name with a quick bow.

"But the top two floors are kept locked up," Hanner continued. "Bern isn't allowed up there. Faran's women don't go up there. Nobody does but Uncle Faran. So what could he possibly have that he needs to keep secret? He's *Lord Faran*, chief advisor to the overlord of Ethshar of the Spices—he can do pretty much anything he wants . . ."

"Except magic," Mavi said.

"Right. So he's been secretly collecting magical stuff, I would guess, and hiding it up there, and now he's going to go use something up there to contact the Wizards' Guild and talk to them about warlockry."

"He said something about someone named Ithinia?"

"That's our local Guildmaster. At least, the one we know about."

"What's a Guildmaster?" Rudhira asked.

Hanner was getting tired of explaining things that everyone he ordinarily dealt with had known since childhood, but he carried on. After all, some of these people might be magicians of a sort, but they hadn't had any training, and there was no reason for anyone but an aristocrat or a magician to have learned any of this.

"All wizards are members of the Wizards' Guild," he said. "They kill anyone who practices wizardry without joining, or who breaks other Guild rules—the rulers of Old Ethshar gave them that authority hundreds of years ago, maybe thousands, and nobody argues with it. Most of them are just ordinary members, though, the same way most people are just ordinary citizens of Ethshar. A few wizards are chosen as Guildmasters—we don't know who does the choosing, or how, and apparently anyone who told us would be put to death. The Guildmasters have more authority. We don't know how much—maybe the Guildmasters run everything, but there are rumors that there's some secret higher rank. We don't even know whether there are different levels of Guildmaster, or how many Guildmasters there are in the city, or who they are—again, that's all kept secret. But we do know the names of a few, so that we know who to talk to if we need to consult the Wizards' Guild and don't want to work our way up from the bottom. The highest-ranking Guildmaster we know of in Ethshar of the Spices—and really, we're just *assuming* she's ranked higher than the other two we know about—is named Ithinia, and she has a mansion on Lower Street, near Arena."

Rudhira said, "That's less than half a mile from here."

"I know," Hanner said. "Much less. That's why I offered to take a message."

"Uncle Faran would rather do it himself," Alris said. "He likes showing off."

"It sounds dangerous to me," Mavi said. "If he has magical things up there and he uses them to send a message to Ithinia, isn't he admitting he's broken their rules?"

"Yes," Hanner said. He glanced uncomfortably up the stairs; Faran was long since out of sight. "I hope he knows what he's doing."

Hanner thought it all too likely that his uncle did *not* know—that after being cast out by the overlord he had lost his temper so thoroughly that he wasn't thinking clearly, and was more concerned with demonstrating that he still had power than with the best long-term strategy.

Or maybe he had simply gotten fed up with keeping so many secrets.

Or maybe he did know what he was doing, after all. He had far more experience than Hanner in these matters.

"I *really* hope so," Hanner said.

Chapter Twenty

Ithinia of the Isle was not happy. She was short on sleep, having been rousted out earlier than her wont by panicky messages from various lords, magistrates, and magicians, and she had spent the entire day dealing with people who expected her to know far more than she did, which she always found wearing.

Furthermore, she didn't approve of changes in the normal routine of Ethsharitic life. Whatever had happened the night before had disrupted any number of things, and Ithinia resented that.

And finally, she had spent the whole day talking to people instead of doing magic. She hadn't cast a single decent spell. Oh, she had used a few simple tricks and applied some existing artifacts, but she hadn't worked anything more difficult than a third-order incantation, and she *hated* that. She had become a wizard because she loved magic, and she was *good* at it, which was how she'd become a Guildmaster, and she considered it completely unfair that her duties as senior Guildmaster for the World's largest city so often meant she had no time to spend in her workshop, animating bric-a-brac or talking to ghosts she had trapped, or otherwise enjoying the miraculous abilities she had spent her life acquiring.

She thought now that she should have used some sort of time-distortion spell to find a few extra hours she could use to catch up on her sleep, but she hadn't done it—at least, not yet, and she still wasn't sure when she would have a chance.

So her mood was already quite sour enough when she arrived home, transported magically into her downstairs solarium, to hear a loud, unnatural buzzing in the garden behind her house.

It was not a pleasant buzz. It was a harsh, insistent noise that Ithinia found intensely grating. She thrust a hand into the pouch on her belt, fumbled with a vial, and opened the garden door of the solarium with a pinch of brimstone in her fingers, ready to fling Thrindle's Combustion at this annoyance, whatever it was, and burn it into silence.

She stepped out, looking for the source of the buzz, and spotted it almost immediately—a shiny black *thing* lying atop the garden wall, gleaming darkly in the bright warm light of the setting sun. It was roughly the size of a woman's sandal, but with odd little wings on either side. Two of her magical guardians, stone carvings she had animated years ago, crouched at the foot of the wall, watching it.

The mysterious buzzing device was not anything she recognized, but she knew the general category of objects that had that peculiar slick finish. It was a sorcerous talisman of some kind.

She was tempted to go ahead and fry it—but Thrindle's Combustion didn't always work on talismans, and might well backfire. She dropped the bit of brimstone and wiped her hands on the skirt of her formal robe as she cautiously approached the still-buzzing object.

Poking it with her athame, the ritual dagger she wore on her belt, would probably silence it—sorcery and wizardry did not *like* each other much, and an athame was virtually pure wizardry, able to ruin most sorcerous devices with a touch without taking any noticeable harm itself.

If she did that, though, she wouldn't know who sent it, or why, and it might be important. Some sorcerer somewhere might know something about what had caused last night's ferocious and mysterious magical outburst. She couldn't afford to throw away that knowledge.

And she really doubted it was dangerous. No sorcerer would be stupid enough to try to harm her—attacking a Guildmaster was a good way to die. Even if an attack succeeded, which was unlikely given the protective spells she always wore, the rest of the Wizards' Guild would retaliate, quickly and lethally.

She stopped several yards away. The two stone guardians turned to glance up at her, but then returned to watching the talisman.

"How long has that thing been here, making that noise?" she asked the nearest of the gargoyles that crouched on the various corners and protrusions of her house.

The gargoyle turned its head with a creak, looking at her. "About an hour, Mistress," it said in its grating voice. It was difficult to distinguish the words over the constant noise, but Ithinia was accustomed to her creations' peculiar speech.

The neighbors must have loved that, Ithinia thought. Most of them wouldn't dare complain—one expected occasional annoyances when one lived near a wizard—but it would hardly have generated any goodwill.

"It's been sitting there buzzing the whole time?"

"No, Mistress. It descended from the sky and approached the house, and Old Rocky warned it away, as you instructed us to do when intruders enter the garden. It ignored the warning, so Rocky and Glitter climbed down to frighten it away. It retreated to where it is now, and began calling your name. When you did not answer, after a few minutes it stopped speaking and began buzzing."

Old Rocky and Glitter were the two creatures still guarding it. Ithinia glanced at Old Rocky's niche, on the southwest corner of the house.

"Did you see where it came from?"

"No, mistress. It came down out of the sun while we were meditating."

"You were sleeping, not meditating," Ithinia said. "I've told you not to try to fool me. Stone *should* sleep—it's nothing to hide."

"Yes, Mistress," the gargoyle said, abashed.

"It called my name? Did it say anything else?"

"It said it needed to speak with you."

Ithinia sighed. Another one.

"I might as well get it over with," she said. She lifted her skirt slightly to keep it from getting dusty on the little-used bricks, then marched down the garden path to the wall.

Glitter and Old Rocky stepped aside at her approach, and she took a moment to pat Rocky on the smooth patch of granite behind its carved curving horns. "Good job," she said. "You, too, Glitter. Go on back to your places now."

Glitter's mouth was so full of fangs and tongue that it couldn't speak, but Rocky growled, "Thank you, Mistress," before retreating up the walkway.

When they had left Ithinia said sharply, "All right, I'm here. Stop that infernal buzzing and tell me what you want."

The buzzing continued.

"Stop it!" Ithinia shouted, her hand falling to the hilt of her athame.

The buzzing stopped abruptly. "Guildmaster?" a voice said from the black device.

"Yes," Ithinia said angrily. The voice sounded familiar—it was definitely that of a native of the city, with the lilting quality affected by the wealthy and powerful. She couldn't quite place it, and was in no mood to be subtle or even polite. "Who are you?"

"Your pardon, Guildmaster," the voice said. "I am Lord Faran, formerly the overlord's chief advisor."

Ithinia closed her eyes and muttered, "Oh, blood and death."

She had already received word that Lord Azrad wished to consult the Wizards' Guild on an urgent matter, which of course meant that the overlord wanted the Guild to do something about the warlocks. She had put that meeting off until at least tomorrow—it was always best, when dealing with Azrad the Sedentary, to delay the meeting for a time to give the man's natural lethargy time to assert itself. Azrad was always less demanding when he had had time to cool down from whatever event had provoked him. An early morning meeting accentuated this, so Ithinia had been planning to arrive at the Palace perhaps an hour after dawn, either tomorrow or the day after.

Besides, that would give her a little more time to learn about the situation and think about what should be done.

This communication from Lord Faran, though, complicated the situation. "*Formerly* the overlord's chief advisor" meant that there had been a serious falling out within the inner circles of the city's government, and Ithinia suspected the Wizards' Guild was about to be dragged into a factional squabble, whether they wanted to be or not.

One of the secondary reasons for the Guild's rule against magicians meddling in government, or rulers fooling around with magic, was precisely so that the Guild would *not* be dragged into factional squabbles, but it appeared that the participants in this one wanted the Guild involved.

Presumably it had something to do with the warlocks.

And then there was the fact that Lord Faran was using sorcery to speak to her. He knew perfectly well that the Guild wouldn't approve of a nobleman in the overlord's government using magic like this; he was obviously doing it on purpose, to make a point.

What point, she didn't know. She had dealt with Lord Faran before; he had a twisty mind that she did not understand and didn't particularly want to. He seemed constitutionally unable to accept a direct statement of the Guild's intent at face value, no matter what the circumstances, which annoyed her, since she always made an effort to deal openly with the government of the Hegemony. She would have preferred to never speak with him again.

But she was obviously going to have to deal with him. Even if he was no longer the overlord's right hand, he was still likely to remain a powerful man—and he clearly had sorcery at his disposal.

And he had decided to rub the Guild's nose in his sorcery. Ithinia would have considered that utter folly for most people, but for Lord Faran she couldn't be sure.

"Yes, my lord," she said, addressing the little black device in as even a voice as she could manage. "What can I do for you?"

"I'm sure you're aware of last night's events, and the

outbreak of what appears to be an entirely new form of magic."

"Yes." She bit off the "of course" that would naturally have followed.

"I believe that Lord Azrad has requested a consultation with representatives of the Wizards' Guild to consider what should be done about this development—in fact, I know he has, and that this consultation, if it has not already taken place, will be held within the next day or so."

"Most likely, yes. We have not agreed upon a time."

"Of course," the talisman said. "Whenever it happens, though, I thought that you might be interested in knowing just what the overlord plans, in terms far blunter than he'll express it to you himself, in advance of the meeting. I would also like to confer with the Guild's representatives myself, as the spokesman for another group."

"And what group would that be?"

"The warlocks."

Ithinia stared at the talisman for a moment, then closed her eyes and put a hand to her forehead, where she massaged her temple with three fingers.

That was all she needed. Now the warlocks were getting organized and had found themselves a leader—perhaps the best, most experienced politician in the city.

"Guildmaster?" the voice from the talisman asked.

"I'm here," she said, opening her eyes but keeping her hand where it was. "I was just thinking." She sighed. "Very well, my lord—did you wish to meet with me or shall we simply converse as we are, over this forbidden apparatus you have intruded into my garden?"

"Guildmaster, I am no longer a part of Lord Azrad's government. I do not believe that sorcery is still forbidden to me."

"Fine," Ithinia said. "We can argue about it later, if necessary. Shall we meet?"

"It's not necessary, but whatever pleases you. It might be more convenient."

"It might. For now, though, let's just talk as we are."

"As you wish."

"So tell me what the overlord intends."

"He intends, Guildmaster, to outlaw warlockry and order the extermination of all warlocks within the walls, guilty or innocent, lest they disturb the city's peace. He further intends to place all responsibility for this decision and these actions on the Wizards' Guild, the self-appointed authority in all matters magical. Need I say what this will do to the Guild's standing in the public's estimation when the initial panic has subsided, and the knowledge that hundreds of innocents have been slaughtered registers?"

Ithinia closed her eyes again.

"No," she said. "I can imagine."

"Last night, Guildmaster, as you may have heard, some of the new-made warlocks did not join in the night's madness, the looting and mayhem, but instead acted to limit the damage and tried to put themselves at the overlord's disposal. In his confusion, Lord Azrad forbade them entry to the Palace. I have now taken this group in hand, at a location known only to a few, and am speaking to you on their behalf. We see no reason we should be penalized for last night's misbehavior—we did not participate in it and did what we could to restrain it, even turning four of our fellow warlocks over to the Lord Magistrate of the Old Merchants' Quarter. While we won't defend the lawlessness some warlocks displayed, *we* are innocent of any wrongdoing—yet Lord Azrad has made clear to me that he intends to seek *our* deaths, along with those of the criminals. I am speaking to you now, Guildmaster, to ask the Wizards' Guild to refuse any part in this appalling injustice. I am asking all of you to come to the aid of your fellow magicians . . ."

"You aren't magicians," Ithinia interrupted angrily. "You aren't trained, you never apprenticed, you aren't any recognized school. You're people with some strange new spell on you; that doesn't make you magicians."

"Not magicians, then, but people involved with magic, through no fault of their own."

"Yes, quite," Ithinia said. "I see your point."

Unfortunately, she could also see the overlord's view, if Faran had presented it accurately. She had seen the corpses of a dozen people killed by rampaging warlocks. She had seen one poor boy who had had dozens of shards of glass embedded in his flesh by a warlock; a priestess had been trying to invoke Blukros to heal the child, and a witch had been suppressing the pain, but even if the god answered and restored the boy to perfect health nothing would ever make up for the terror and suffering he had been through.

She didn't want to talk to Faran anymore—his voice, as relayed by the talisman, was smooth and calm, but suddenly she found it intensely irritating.

"I will need to talk to others," she said. "If you're no longer at the Palace, how can we contact you? I assume you'd prefer something other than the Spell of Invaded Dreams, and would rather we did not track down your location known only to a few."

"I could hardly expect to keep my location secret from the Guild," Faran said, "but rather than put you to any trouble, let me suggest that you take this talisman and place it somewhere safe. When you wish to speak to me, pick it up, and the warmth of your hand will activate it and alert me."

"Clever," Ithinia said. Ordinarily she didn't think much of sorcery, which had a tendency to have peculiar limitations and to fail spectacularly at inopportune times, but this particular device—assuming it worked as advertised—could be rather convenient.

"It may be a few moments before I can respond, of course," Faran said.

"Of course," Ithinia said. It occurred to her that she wouldn't really *want* a device that could demand her attention at any moment, and once again she was glad she had taken up wizardry, rather than one of the other magicks. "I'll speak to you later, then."

"Thank you," Faran's voice replied.

Ithinia picked up the talisman and tucked it into the purse on her belt, then turned and headed back toward her house.

Chapter Twenty-one

On the morning of the sixth of Summerheat Mavi ambled out into the courtyard behind her family home, nominally to dump her chamber pot and the kitchen slop bucket in the public sewer but really to hear the morning gossip—and to tell the story of her own adventures the previous day.

She had hoped, when she went to bed on the fourth, that being walked home by Lord Hanner and giving him a goodnight kiss would be the juiciest item in the morning chatter on the fifth. Instead there had been so much excitement about the night's madness that she had never even gotten around to mentioning it.

Today, though, she had the tale of her adventures with Hanner and his collection of warlocks to tell, and *that* was certainly going to be worth mentioning no matter *what* Thetta and Aniara and Oria had to report. She had *flown through the air*, and met all those warlocks, and spent *hours* with Lord Faran and Lord Hanner, and heard Lord Faran say all those terrible traitorous things about the overlord . . .

She grinned at the thought.

And Hanner had walked her home again, and this time they had kissed *each other* good night, and not just a quick little peck, either.

Lord Hanner wasn't quite the impressive catch he had been before the Night of Madness, now that his uncle was an outcast warlock rather than the Lord Counselor, but Mavi didn't really care; he was still a sweet young man, always ready to help, so sincere and eager to please that she couldn't help but enjoy his company. He was a little soft and plump, a little unsure of himself, but in general she found him very satisfactory. He had lovely dark eyes and curly black hair and a funny smile.

If he had a good position, rather than just being his uncle's assistant, he would be a fine candidate for her husband.

She opened the sewer lid and dumped in the waste, then closed the lid again. When she straightened up and turned around she saw Oria approaching.

The two waved to each other, and after Oria had disposed of her own burden the two young women settled on the bench by old Skig's chicken coop, in the shade of an ancient gum tree, to talk.

The conversation stayed very light at first—the usual exchange of rumors about who might be pregnant, whose marriage might be in trouble, and the like. Anything more interesting would be saved until the others had arrived.

But then Thetta arrived—almost running.

"What's wrong?" Oria asked her as Thetta hurried up to the bench.

"Did you hear about Pancha?" Thetta asked as she squeezed onto the end of the bench beside Oria.

"What about her?" Mavi asked. Pancha was Aniara's slightly older half sister.

"She's a warlock!"

"You're joking!" Oria said, shocked.

Mavi, who had spent the previous day practically surrounded by warlocks, was less surprised—especially since Aniara had mentioned the day before that Pancha had been one of the people who woke up screaming about a nightmare.

Pancha hadn't run out into the street smashing windows, though.

"Is she all right?" Mavi asked.

"Aniara? Oh, she's upset, but . . ."

"I meant Pancha."

"Oh." Thetta looked confused for a moment, then said, "I guess so. They've locked her in her room and sent for a priest."

"A priest? A theurgist? Why?"

"To try to cure her, of course!" Thetta said, leaning forward to look past Oria at Mavi.

"Is Aniara all right?" Oria asked. "*She* isn't a warlock, is she?"

"She says she isn't," Thetta said, "and she seems to be holding up, but she's not leaving the house until the theurgist is done."

"She won't be here this morning, then?" Mavi asked.

"No," Thetta said. "I thought we might go by there later to comfort her, though."

"Oh, we should," Oria agreed. She shuddered. "Her own sister a warlock! How dreadful."

"Oh, warlocks aren't really so terrible," Mavi said.

"How would you know?" Thetta asked.

Mavi smiled and began explaining how she had spent the previous day. The others were suitably impressed.

"Maybe you should tell Pancha about that house full of warlocks," Oria said thoughtfully when Mavi had finished.

"They're going to cure her!" Thetta protested.

"If they can," Mavi said. "I don't know whether you *can* cure warlocks."

"Why don't we go see?" Oria asked, getting to her feet. "Just let me put a few things away . . ."

The others quickly agreed, and half an hour later the three of them were in Aniara's parlor, talking to Aniara and her mother, pretending not to listen to the chanting faintly audible from upstairs.

"I hope it works," Aniara said, looking up the stairs.

"It's not really so horrible, being a warlock," Mavi said. "Some of the people at Lord Faran's house seemed almost proud of it. And it must be handy sometimes, being able to do magic like that."

Aniara shuddered. "It's *creepy*," she said. "What if she goes mad, like those others, and starts breaking things? Or what if people start disappearing around her? What if . . ."

Just then the daylight seemed almost to flicker, and Mavi and the others felt a sudden pressure.

Mavi swallowed. "I think the theurgist's invocation

worked," she said. The notion that there was an actual god—or at least a partial manifestation of one—in Pancha's room upstairs made her at least as nervous as the houseful of warlocks had.

"I wonder which god he was summoning?" Oria asked, glancing at the stairs.

"I remember that when Diriel was sick, the priestess summoned Blukros," Thetta said. "She said Blukros was god of healing."

"I'm not sure warlockry is something that needs healing," Mavi said doubtfully. She glanced at Aniara's mother—Pancha's mother, as well—who was sitting in the rocking chair in the corner, rocking steadily in unhappy silence.

The five women did not speak for a moment after that; the knowledge of a god's presence was affecting them all, in various ways. At last Aniara said, "Mavi, tell me more about what Lord Faran said!"

Welcoming the distraction, Mavi began a detailed account of Lord Faran's actions the previous day. She had gotten to his sorcerous conversation with the wizard Ithinia when the air suddenly stirred, and an invisible pressure seemed to be lifted from the room.

All eyes turned to the stairs.

"It must be over," Oria said.

A moment later they all heard the sound of a door opening and of Pancha snuffling; then the theurgist came slowly down the stairs, straightening his white robe.

"What happened?" Aniara asked, leaping to her feet.

The theurgist took a deep breath, then said, "I consulted the goddess Unniel the Discerning, and I'm afraid the results are not what you hoped for."

"What do you mean?"

The theurgist sighed. "I mean the goddess could not even recognize your sister as human." Before anyone could respond, he raised a hand and continued. "This isn't as significant as it sounds—the gods see things differently than we do, and often don't perceive magicians other than theurgists as human. There are some people they can't see at all; we don't know why, and they have never managed to explain it in ways we can understand. Unniel could see Pancha, but not as a human being; she said Pancha was a thing she had no Ethsharitic word for."

Aniara made a strangled noise.

"Unniel could not tell me anything useful about this magic," the theurgist said. "She could not remove it, and assured me no other god or demon could. She said it was unlikely that any other magic could reverse Pancha's transformation, due to something she called an *ursettor fwal* in Pancha's brain, but reminded me that even the gods don't understand wizardry or know exactly what it can and cannot do."

"So she's still a warlock?" Aniara's mother demanded. Mavi turned, startled, to see that the older woman had stopped rocking and was staring intently at the priest.

"Yes, she's still a warlock," the theurgist replied. "There's nothing more I can do about it."

"I don't want a warlock in my house," the old woman said.

"Mother, she's your own daughter!" Aniara said.

"Not anymore," her mother said. "You heard the priest— she's not even human anymore! She's a *thing* that used to be my daughter."

"I didn't say . . ." the theurgist began.

"Human or not, she might go berserk at any time," the old woman said. "Did any of you hear about the house in Seacorner where Varrin the Weaver smashed the entire top floor in an instant? He almost crushed his own wife!"

The other women looked at one another.

"Please, Mother, this is her home," Aniara said. "Where else would she go?"

Mavi immediately knew what would happen then, and sure enough, Thetta and Oria turned to look at her. Pancha's mother pointed at her, and Aniara turned as well.

The puzzled theurgist also looked at Mavi, simply because everyone else did.

"All right," Mavi said. "I can take her there." That this

would not only be a kindness to Pancha but would give her another chance to see Lord Hanner did not escape her.

"May I ask where?" the theurgist said.

"You explain," Aniara said, heading for the stairs. "I'll go help Pancha pack."

As Tanna the Thief worked the crowd in the plaza, cutting purses from people's belts and slipping them into her own shoulder bag, she was still trying to decide who she should tell about Elken—if anyone. Her original intention in coming here had been to warn the magistrates about the warlocks, but it had been instantly clear that they already knew. The guards in front of the Palace, the shouting crowds, made it plain that *everyone* knew about the warlocks.

No one was going to pay her for the information.

She wished she hadn't taken a day to bury Elken, clean herself up, steal new clothes, and get up her nerve—if she had arrived yesterday she might still have gotten a couple of bits for her report.

Of course, she was doing fairly well at her customary trade, certainly taking more than a few copper bits. The crowd was large and angry, which meant it was also more careless than usual, and she had gotten half a dozen purses. Still, it was the *principle* of the thing—she had something that *ought* to be worth money, and she wasn't able to collect.

Of course, she told herself, in a way it was paying off. Ordinarily she would never have come *here*, right in front of the Palace, where any number of guards and magicians might be watching, and she would never have found this crowd of unsuspecting prospective victims.

Just then she was distracted as someone shouted, "*Hai!* My purse!"

Tanna turned to see who spoke, ready to flee if anyone pointed her out as the culprit. Perhaps these people hadn't been quite so unsuspecting as she thought.

An elderly man was staring down at the severed cords

dangling from his belt; then he raised his head and looked around at the crowd.

"Who did that?" he bellowed. "Did anyone see who took my purse?"

Suddenly inspired, Tanna called, "The warlocks!"

The elderly man's head snapped around, and he stared directly at her.

"It vanished," Tanna said. "I saw it! It just disappeared. It must be the warlocks!"

"The warlocks?" the old man said. "First they took my son, and now they take my purse?" He turned to look at the guards on the north side of the square. "Blast it, it's time something was *done* about this!"

"You tell them, sir!" Tanna said as she slipped behind a tall man.

A moment later she had worked her way well away from the angry old man, who was arguing with the nearest soldier. It was time to go, she decided. She had tried to do her civic duty by reporting Elken's attempt to take over the Hundred-Foot Field, and she had gathered a few fat purses for her efforts, and that was enough; it was time to go, before things got really ugly.

Ten minutes later she was trotting down Arena Street, trying to ignore the shouting behind her.

Kennan was absolutely furious. The guards had referred him to their captain, who had stolidly listened to his story, then told him to go away.

"But they stole my purse!" he shouted.

"Sir, I doubt it was a warlock who stole your purse," the captain said. "It looks to me like the work of an ordinary cutpurse."

"But that girl *saw* it!"

"More likely she was the one who took it."

"Captain, I have been robbed of my child and my money by these people, and I *demand* that you do something about it!"

"The overlord is consulting his advisors and magicians as to what action to take."

"What action to take? Go *get* them, and demand they return what they've taken!" Kennan said. "They're all right there in that big black stone house on High Street, at the corner of Coronet!"

"Sir, I doubt that *all* the warlocks are there," the captain said dryly.

"Well, *some* of them are!" Kennan raged. "Lord Faran went there, and that fat man, and that redheaded whore . . ."

"Sir, I have my orders," the captain said. "I am to guard the plaza and the Palace. Unless you have real proof that those particular warlocks took your purse or your son, I am not going to arrest them. If you really do have a witness, I suggest you bring her here to testify."

Kennan glowered at the soldier, then turned to look for the thin, long-haired girl in the brown tunic.

He couldn't see her anywhere.

He fumed silently for a moment, then growled. "I've had enough of this," he said. He stamped away from the captain.

"Excuse me," someone said.

Kennan turned to see a stocky man in a tan tunic. "Yes?"

"Did I hear you say that you know where the warlocks live?"

"Yes," Kennan said. "What of it?"

"They took my brother," the stocky man said. "Can you show me where this place is?"

Kennan scanned the crowd again, but could not see the girl anywhere.

It wasn't as if he were accomplishing anything here, he told himself.

"Come on," he said. "We'll go there together. At the very least we can keep an eye on the place."

Chapter Twenty-two

Manrin the Mage, Guildmaster of Ethshar of the Sands, charged with overseeing and representing all those wizards who dwelt outside the city walls but within two days' travel, was not happy at all. He was even less happy than his colleague Ithinia in Ethshar of the Spices, forty leagues to the east, had been the afternoon before when she heard from Lord Faran.

The Night of Madness, as it was now referred to, had initially hit Ethshar of the Sands roughly as hard as it had hit Ethshar of the Spices; hundreds of people had vanished, dozens had been killed, shops and homes had been looted and burned. However, unlike the disturbances in its sister city, the rioting in Ethshar of the Sands had lasted until dawn. No party of well-intentioned warlocks had roamed the streets, suppressing their wilder compatriots; Ederd IV had not called out the guard to defend his palace as his brother-in-law Azrad VI had, but had instead dispersed them through the streets, which had in many cases only inflamed the situation.

That, however, was not the major reason why Manrin was even less cheerful than Ithinia.

Lord Ederd's people were now ranging up and down Wizard Street, questioning every magician they could find, hoping to find an explanation for the outburst of magic. Ederd himself was in conference with several well-respected magicians of various sorts at the Palace, while Ederd's wife, Zarréa of the Spices, was roaming the city organizing rebuilding efforts, sometimes conscripting magicians into service.

Manrin had been questioned at considerable length in his

home by Lord Kalthon, son of the Minister of Justice, which had not been pleasant. The general impression Manrin had received was that the people of the city did not trust *any* magicians right now.

That was not the major reason why Manrin was unhappy, either.

Manrin's own daughter Ferris was among the missing; she had not been seen since the moment the screaming began.

Even that, though, was not what *most* upset him, though it was a close second. Ferris was a grown woman, aging but still well able to take care of herself, and Manrin told himself that she was probably safely in hiding, waiting for things to return to normal. Even if she was truly among the vanished, nobody knew what had become of them; they might all be alive and well somewhere.

And Manrin's other three children, their spouses, his dozen grandchildren, and his half-dozen great-grandchildren were all unharmed and safe in their homes. He was not concerned about any of them.

What worried Manrin most was his magic. He had tried to perform several different spells in the past day or so, and far too many of them had not worked. That the Spell of the Revealed Power had yielded nothing when applied to the debris in the street was not particularly alarming—that was a tricky ninth-order spell, and the debris might simply not have carried any traces that the spell recognized. That the Spell of Omniscient Vision had failed, though, meant something was wrong. That was an easy third-order incantation—he had learned that as an *apprentice*, almost a hundred years ago, and he hadn't had any problem with it since he was a journeyman! He was a Guildmaster now; how could he have made a mess of something so trivial? The ingredients were basic. He knew the dagger and incense were exactly what they should be; could the stone have somehow been exposed to sunlight, destroying its virtue?

His magic wasn't *totally* gone—he had tested himself with a few quick little first-order spells that had all worked properly—but it had become completely unreliable for anything complex enough to be useful.

And then there were things that had moved about his workshop, apparently by themselves—the chair that had slid into place, his Book of Spells leaping to his hand, and a handful of other incidents. All these movements had been harmless or even beneficial, but they shouldn't have happened. Had he left some spell unfinished, some magical being unrestrained? Could the Aerial Servitor he'd conjured up a sixnight before still be lingering, trying to be helpful? He had set it the required three tasks, and it had performed all three—it should have been dismissed thereafter.

These failures and movements were worrisome. Anytime magic misbehaved there was good cause for concern; the forces involved could be catastrophically powerful.

Was age starting to catch up with him again? It had been a long time since his youth spell; he might well be due for another. He could scarcely expect to perform anything that difficult for himself under the circumstances, though, and hiring another wizard to do it would be troublesome and expensive. He almost wished he had gone for *eternal* youth the first time, rather than mere rejuvenation.

Or it might not have anything to do with age. Could there be any connection between his own problems and the mysterious magical power that had so disrupted the city's life?

Well, he was a wizard; when he had a question, no matter what it was, he could get an answer—if the spell worked. And if it didn't, he wasn't really much of a wizard.

He had gathered the necessary ingredients—salt, cock's blood, his athame, and a cake of the appropriate incense—and was working out the exact phrasing of the question he intended to address with Fendel's Divination, assuming he could indeed get the Divination to work, when someone knocked on his workshop door.

Manrin sighed and put down his athame. "Yes?" he called.

The door opened and his servant Derneth peered in. "Master? You have visitors."

"Lord Kalthon? Or Lady Zarréa?"

"No, Master. A wizard by the name of Abdaran the White, and his apprentice, Ulpen of North Herris."

Manrin frowned. "Abdaran? Oh, yes. I know him. He has an apprentice?"

"Apparently, Master."

"Send them in."

Derneth hesitated—ordinarily, Manrin met visitors in one of the parlors. Still, the order was clear enough. "Yes, Master," he said, closing the door.

Manrin looked at his question again, debating whether "explain" or "describe" would be the better verb—or whether either of them would transform the question to a request, which the Divination would not handle properly. Perhaps "What is the nature of . . ."

The door opened again and two wizards stepped in—a man who appeared to be perhaps half a century in age, with snow-white hair, and a black-haired lad of sixteen or so, both in formal robes. Abdaran wore deep red, while the boy—presumably Ulpen—wore apprentice gray.

"Guildmaster," the older man said with a bow.

"Abdaran," Manrin said, pushing aside the paper. "What brings you to Ethshar?"

Abdaran smiled wryly. "My feet, actually," he said. "I had no transportation spells on hand, and the matter seemed urgent. May we sit down?"

"If you can find somewhere to sit, by all means," Manrin said, gesturing broadly. "What was it that seemed urgent?"

Abdaran looked significantly at a chair, and Ulpen hurriedly cleared several books and a neatly tied bundle of small bones off it, so that his master could sit. When Abdaran had settled comfortably, he said, "My apprentice, Ulpen, has developed some curious new abilities."

Ulpen was busily clearing jars from another chair—there were only three chairs, in addition to Manrin's own stool, and a great many things were stacked on them—and didn't see Manrin look questioningly at him.

"What sort of abilities?" Manrin asked.

"Primarily, the ability to move physical objects by the power of thought alone," Abdaran replied.

"Warlockry," Manrin said. He looked at Ulpen. "But surely, he has his athame?"

"Of course he does, Guildmaster," Abdaran said. "Right there on his belt. I'm afraid I don't see the relevance, however, nor do I recognize the word 'warlockry.' We heard it mentioned by the guards in Grandgate, but we don't know the term."

Ulpen finally got the chair cleared and sat down, turning to face his elders expectantly.

Manrin stared at the two in surprise. "Gods!" he said. "Where have you two been?"

"North Herris," Abdaran said sharply. "A village some eight leagues northeast of here, as you certainly ought to know."

"Master," Ulpen whispered loudly, "he's a *Guildmaster*!"

Manrin sighed. "No, he's right, boy," he said. "I'm sorry, it's been so much in evidence here that . . . well, obviously you somehow missed it."

"Missed what?" Abdaran said, keeping his tone more civil this time.

"The Night of Madness," Manrin said. "That's what people are calling it. The night before last—late on the fourth day of Summerheat, and into the morning of the fifth."

Abdaran looked at him expectantly, and Manrin continued, "Somewhere after sunset, but still a little before midnight on that night, *something* happened. We still don't know what; attempts at divination have been unsuccessful, apparently blocked by some *very* powerful, and completely unfamiliar, magic. Hundreds, perhaps thousands of people who were sleeping were awakened by intense nightmares; some people who were awake report an odd sensation, as if hit by something invisible. Many of both groups began screaming, though they often couldn't explain why, and many of them panicked. Almost everyone who screamed, and some who did not, discovered that like your apprentice here they could now move objects about without touching them. And those who panicked went rampaging through their homes and the streets, using their new power to smash anything in their way and snatch whatever caught their fancy. Some who hadn't panicked did the same, simply because the opportunity was there and they could see others running wild in this fashion. Dozens of people were killed, shops and houses were smashed or burned—it was *very* bad, and you're lucky to have missed it."

Ulpen's face had gone pale, and Abdaran frowned deeply.

"I see," he said. "And you think this thing has affected my apprentice?"

"Yes, I do," Manrin said. "Assuming that he can, in fact, move things in this fashion. If so, then yes, he's a warlock."

"Show him," Abdaran said, turning to Ulpen.

Ulpen swallowed, looked around, and pointed at the bundle of bones he had moved from Abdaran's chair. "Will that do?"

"Certainly," Manrin said—and before the word had entirely left his lips the bundle was floating in midair, a foot or so off the floor. It moved tentatively back and forth, then lowered itself back to the planking.

"And have you had bad dreams these past two nights?" Manrin asked. "Dreams of falling, or burning, or being buried alive?"

"Not last night," Ulpen said. "The night before, yes."

Manrin turned back to Abdaran. "He's definitely a warlock," he said.

"This word 'warlock,' " Abdaran asked, "where is it from?"

"The witches in Ethshar of the Spices reportedly say that this magic resembles a secret they used during the Great War, centuries ago. The name has caught on, though it appears the resemblance is only superficial."

"Are there many people affected this way?"

"Lord Ederd's people estimate there could be hundreds, perhaps as many as a thousand, just in Ethshar of the Sands, and reports from Ethshar of the Spices indicate they have a similar number. Ethshar of the Rocks has fewer—perhaps a few hundred at most. We have no word as yet from the Small Kingdoms or the northern territories." He hesitated, then added, "I haven't told you the worst of it. When this first happened, hundreds of people simply disappeared. Some were seen walking or running or even flying, using their new abilities, to the north—north by northeast, to be precise. Others were just gone when their families awoke the next day. None of them have returned; we have no idea what became of them. Most people assume the warlocks are responsible, and Ederd is considering ordering them all into exile—or perhaps killing the lot of them, though I doubt anyone would want to be *that* drastic. Apparently the other two members of the triumvirate favor this solution, as well."

"Can't you find out what caused all this?" Abdaran asked.

Manrin turned up an empty palm. "We're trying," he said. "So far we've established that it wasn't the work of a god, that despite the similarities it's not witchcraft, that it isn't any recognizable form of wizardry that's responsible." He looked at Ulpen again. "And we *thought* that it didn't affect wizards. You do have a proper athame, don't you, lad?"

Ulpen nodded and patted the sheathed dagger on his belt.

"Well, then we have a puzzle," Manrin said. "A part of your soul is in that knife, and we thought that meant that wizards can't do any other kind of magic. That's why we forbid anyone to learn more than one kind of magic—because we thought we couldn't do it, and we didn't want anyone else to have an advantage over us. We know we can't summon gods or demons, or learn witchcraft, because of our divided souls—but it would appear we can still be warlocks. Interesting!"

Ulpen swallowed hard, then said, "Guildmaster?"

"Yes? Speak freely, my boy."

"I'm not sure I *am* a wizard anymore."

Manrin eyed the boy thoughtfully.

"Explain that, if you please," he said.

Ulpen glanced at his master, took a deep breath, and said, "I haven't worked a real spell since the night before last— since this thing happened. And I've tried four times. When it didn't work I used the new magic instead."

Manrin and Abdaran both stared at him for a moment. Then Manrin said, "Abdaran, would you be so kind as to test the boy's athame?"

Abdaran turned, puzzled. "Test it? How?"

Manrin sighed. How in the World had Abdaran ever qualified as a master wizard without learning these simple tricks? "Touch the tip of his athame with the tip of yours. We should see a clear reaction."

Abdaran frowned, but drew his dagger. Ulpen drew his own and held it out, remembering at the last moment to offer it point first, instead of the standard polite hilt first.

Abdaran touched the knives together.

A sudden loud crackle sounded, and a burst of green and blue sparks appeared from the point of contact, spraying in all directions and then vanishing. Abdaran was so startled he dropped his own athame, but he caught it before it hit the floor.

Manrin frowned. "That's odd," he said. "You never tried that before?"

"No, Guildmaster," Abdaran said, his tone more respectful than it had been a moment ago.

"It should have been more of a *bang*, and there should have been more colors," Manrin said unhappily. "So the boy is a wizard, but there is something not *right* about his athame. Was he a good student before this?"

"Competent enough," Abdaran admitted. "Not brilliant, but he could work a dozen spells reliably."

"Well, there's definitely something wrong." He picked up his own athame from the workbench. "Here, I'll show you." He held out the knife.

Abdaran rose from his chair and approached cautiously until at last the knife points touched. The air crackled again, and a shower of blue and purple sparks exploded from nowhere and vanished into nothingness.

Manrin stared. "But *that's* not right!" he said. "That wasn't any better at all. It must be *your* athame that's damaged! Here, boy, come try yours."

Ulpen obeyed—but when his athame touched Manrin's there was only a fizzing hiss, and a handful of indigo sparks trickled.

"Oh, no," Manrin said, staring at the daggers. "Oh, *please*, no!"

The pieces had fallen into place.

"Guildmaster?" Abdaran said, puzzled.

"Get out!" Manrin bellowed, waving his free hand wildly. "Get out of here, right now! I must talk to the boy *alone*!"

Baffled and clearly upset, Abdaran retreated to the door. "I don't . . ." he began.

"Out!"

"But he's *my* apprentice . . ."

Manrin brandished his athame. "Get out now, or I'll turn you into a toad, I swear by all the gods!"

Abdaran got. Manrin closed the door behind him and locked it securely.

Then he turned to Ulpen.

"Now," he said, "I want you to tell me how you move things, how you do your warlockry."

"I don't understand," Ulpen said. His face was ashen with terror. "What's going on?"

"What's going on, boy, is that you and I have something in common, though I didn't realize it until I saw that *both* our athames are somehow depleted. I was so *sure* that wizards would be immune that I missed the obvious!"

"The obvious *what*, Guildmaster?"

"That *I'm* a warlock, too! And that's why I haven't been able to work any high-order magic for the past two days!" He gestured with the athame. "We're still wizards, you and I—we know the spells, and we have our athames—but this new magic is suppressing our skills."

"It is? How can you be sure?"

Manrin had been on the verge of dancing around the room, but now he stopped and stared at Ulpen.

"I can be *sure* with a simple divination," he said. He looked at the Book of Spells, and the waiting salt, incense, and blood. "But we may need to have someone else perform the spell."

"Should I call Abdaran back?"

Manrin held up a palm. "No," he said. "I don't think we want Abdaran involved; he's just a country wizard. This is a Guild matter." He thought for a moment, then said, "Serem should do."

Chapter Twenty-three

S erem the Wise kept no servants; instead he had animated objects of various sorts that he considered sufficient for his needs.

Manrin disagreed. Self-pouring teapots and perpetually moving fan trees were all very well, but the door did not answer itself. When Serem was training an apprentice that was no problem, but Kalinna was a journeyman now, and Serem had not yet taken on anyone new. That left Serem himself and his wife Gita as the only occupants of the big house at the corner of Grand and Wizard Streets.

And neither of them was rushing to answer the door.

Ulpen stood beside Manrin, staring up at the house's many gables, as Manrin waited impatiently. After a moment he rapped on the black enamel of the door, since the bellpull had gotten no response.

If he had still been able to use magic properly he would have done something to verify that Serem was home, but that option was no longer reliable. He looked at the miniature shrines carved into the stone of the door frame, with their magically generated fire and water; when the house would be empty for an extended period Serem usually extinguished the flames and turned off the fountains, but right now both flames still burned behind the tiny altars, and water still flowed around the bases.

Idly, he used his mysterious new abilities to twist the left-hand flame into a spiral. Now that he *knew* he was a warlock he could consciously control the power, and such a trick was easy and, he had to admit, fun. Becoming a warlock was by no means entirely bad.

Ulpen's gaze had worked its way down the painted cornerposts to the stone arch, and now he noticed what Manrin was doing.

"We could open the door ourselves, Guildmaster," he said.

Startled, Manrin looked at him. The thought had not occurred to him, but of course Ulpen was right—unless there were magical protections Manrin didn't know about, either of them could use warlockry to release the lock and open the door. He could sense the shape of the lock's mechanism, and moving it without a key would be simple.

He didn't do it, though.

"Yes, we could," he said, "but that would be trespassing. In a wizard's house."

"Oh . . ." Ulpen began—but just then the door opened, and Serem looked out at his two guests.

"Oh, it's you, Manrin," he said. "Do you have any word of Gita?"

Manrin was caught completely off guard by the question. "What?" he asked.

"My wife," Serem said. "Gita. She's missing."

"Oh," Manrin said. He swallowed a sudden lump in his throat. "Since the night before last?"

"That's right." Serem sighed. "Then that's not why you're here?"

"Not exactly, no." He added, "My daughter Ferris is missing as well. I hope they're safe."

"So do I," Serem said. He stood aside. "Come in, and tell me why you *are* here."

Manrin and Ulpen were ushered into the parlor, where Ulpen stared at the potted palm that endlessly fanned the big wicker chair. Manrin had seen it countless times before and ignored it as he said, "We *are* here about the results of the Night of Madness," he said, "though not about poor Gita. I hadn't realized she was one of those who vanished."

"She was," Serem said. "Stolen by those damned warlocks, probably."

Ulpen threw Manrin a worried glance at that. Manrin, whose confidence and enthusiasm had already taken blows from both the necessity of walking the three long blocks from Gate Street to knock at Serem's front door like an ordinary customer and the discovery that Gita was among the hundreds who had disappeared, decided that a direct request that Serem perform a divination to ascertain that Manrin and Ulpen were indeed warlocks and that that was the cause of their difficulties in performing wizardry was out of the question, at least for the moment.

They couldn't just turn around and leave, though. And the subject of the disappearances was of considerable importance.

"I hadn't thought it was the warlocks who took Ferris—" Manrin began.

"Who else could it be?" Serem interrupted angrily. "The warlocks appeared, hundreds of innocent people disappeared—I think there's clearly a connection."

"Oh, I suppose there's a connection, but I don't see that the warlocks are necessarily at fault. We really don't *know* what happened."

"*I* don't, certainly, but someone probably does," Serem said. "I'd hoped it was you, and you'd come to tell me about it."

"I'm afraid not."

"Then you just came to compare notes?" Serem asked. "I've been doing that—I talked to Kendrik and Perinan and Ithinia, and one of Zerréa's servants." He glanced at Ulpen as if suddenly realizing that he didn't recognize the youth, and asked, "Who is this?"

"This is Ulpen of North Herris," Manrin said. "He came to Ethshar to discuss the situation in his home village—they hadn't realized that the Night of Madness had been so wide-spread."

"It seems to have been *everywhere*," Serem said. "Though it was worse some places than others. Apparently the Baronies of Sardiron were hit harder than we were, and in Aldagmor entire villages were reportedly depopulated. The survivors have been seeking shelter elsewhere, bringing the news."

"How are they dealing with it?" Manrin asked.

"The Council of Barons is meeting in Sardiron of the Waters in a sixnight to discuss the matter, and meanwhile some of them are putting to death every warlock they catch—which strikes me as a good idea."

Ulpen went pale, but Serem was looking at Manrin, not at the apprentice, and didn't notice. The Guildmaster hid his own reaction.

Serem continued, "Ithinia says Lord Azrad wants the warlocks exterminated, and Ederd is debating exile—but exiling them is just pushing the problem on someone else, so he may well come around to hanging the lot of them, too."

That meant, Manrin thought, that he and Ulpen would not be welcome in two of the three cities in the Hegemony. "What about Lord Wulran?" he asked.

"Dithering," Serem said. "Hardly a surprise. He's had less than three years as overlord—this is the first real crisis he's faced since his father died. And Ethshar of the Rocks apparently didn't suffer anywhere near as badly as the other two cities, so he doesn't have the same urgency."

Manrin nodded. "Execution seems a bit *drastic*," he said mildly. "After all, not all the warlocks committed any crimes, and they have family and friends . . ."

"Ithinia mentioned that," Serem said. "In fact, she says that Lord Faran, Azrad's chief advisor, brought it to her attention. Apparently he's gathered a party of warlocks he says haven't hurt anyone, and is speaking on their behalf. For myself, I still think they're all involved in the disappearances somehow. Until I see Gita again, I'm not inclined to be merciful."

Ulpen threw Manrin a look, and Manrin stroked his beard thoughtfully.

He had lived in Ethshar of the Sands for eighty-some years, since he was only a journeyman, but if Lord Ederd was considering exiling or hanging warlocks it might be time to leave, and Serem's news suggested an obvious destination. Talking to other warlocks, comparing notes, might be very useful, and having Lord Faran's protection would be welcome. Manrin had not visited Ethshar of the Spices for almost thirty years, so he had never met Lord Faran, but the man's reputation for energetic leadership was known throughout the Hegemony.

The next question was how to get there, given that his wizardry was unreliable. The journey by ordinary methods would take at least a sixnight, and the delay might be dangerous.

Manrin knew warlocks could fly, at least some of them, but he didn't know yet whether *he* could fly, especially for a distance as great as the forty leagues to Ethshar of the Spices.

And flying openly might attract unwanted attention—though of course, as a wizard, he could always lie about how he was doing it.

Another method of travel would be a good idea—and as a Guildmaster, he saw an obvious possibility.

It was slightly risky, since he had no idea what his superiors in the Guild thought of warlocks, or whether they had developed any easy methods for recognizing them. Serem apparently hadn't noticed anything different about Manrin, or seen anything unusual about Ulpen—but Serem was distracted by the loss of his wife, and was not the most perceptive wizard in the World.

Still, Manrin thought, using the Guild's transportation methods would be fastest and easiest. "You know, I think I'd like to speak to Ithinia," he said. "In fact, I think I'd like to visit her, in Ethshar of the Spices. Does Perinan still have the tapestry in his attic?"

"Of course," Serem said.

"In that case," Manrin said, "I think we had better be going." He bowed. "Our thanks for your help."

"But you just got here!" Serem protested. "Could I get you a cup of tea before you go? Some grapes?"

Manrin held up a hand. "No, no. Thank you, but we really must go. We were just stopping by to see how you were faring in all this."

Baffled, Serem turned up a palm. "If you must," he said.

Five minutes later Manrin and Ulpen were hurrying south on Wizard Street, through sparse and nervous crowds. "We'll stop at my house," Manrin said. "I want to fetch a few things. Did you bring anything at all with you?"

"Not much," Ulpen said. "I'm just an apprentice, after all—"

"You're something rather different now, I would say," Manrin interrupted. "And whatever you are, I want you to have everything you brought with you when we use the tapestry. I'm not sure we'll be coming back."

"I don't understand," Ulpen said, struggling to keep up— Manrin was old, but he still walked fast enough to give Ulpen a challenge. "What tapestry? Come back from where? What's going on?"

They had reached Manrin's own front door; there he pulled Ulpen into the tiny portico and said, "Perinan has a Transporting Tapestry—anyone who touches it is instantly transported to a shop in Ethshar of the Spices, in the neighborhood they call the Old City. We are going to use it to get ourselves out of this city. You heard Serem—he thinks warlocks murdered his wife, so he wants us exterminated, and thinks Ederd can be convinced to hang us all. I don't think it was warlocks who made poor Gita disappear, but he's probably right about Ederd."

"But he said *Lord Azrad* wanted to kill us all, too! Isn't Azrad the overlord of Ethshar of the Spices? Shouldn't we be going somewhere else? What about that Wulran person?"

"Wulran II is overlord of Ethshar of the Rocks," Manrin said. "And while his city may be safer now, if the other two triumvirs agree that warlocks should be exterminated throughout the Hegemony of the Three Ethshars, he'll go along. He'll have to; that's how the triumvirate works on issues that affect all three cities, by majority vote."

"But—" Ulpen began.

"But maybe they *won't* agree," Manrin said before Ulpen could get another word out, "because Lord Azrad may well change his mind. By all accounts he's let Lord Faran run Ethshar of the Spices for him for the past ten years, and Lord Faran wants to protect warlocks. We're going there to find Lord Faran, and join up with him, and do everything we can to help him convince Lord Azrad." He hesitated, then added, "Besides, if we're to have any chance of influencing the *Guild's* position on all this, we need to talk to Ithinia. She's the senior Guildmaster in Ethshar of the Spices."

"But *you're* a Guildmaster!"

"I am the *junior* Guildmaster here," Manrin said. "That's why I'm responsible for rural wizards like yourself. Perinan is the senior, and there are four others that I know of, all of whom outrank me."

"That you *know* of?" Ulpen's voice cracked.

"The Guild is a little too fond of secrets for its own good, my boy. There is a great deal going on within it that the ordinary members never hear about, and there are things that not even a Guildmaster necessarily knows." He knocked on the door. "You know, Serem may be a Guild-master, or if he is not as yet, he'll probably become one soon. Now, let's move along."

Derneth opened the door, and Manrin stepped in, telling Derneth, "Pack me a bag—I need to take a trip. I'll be gone for at least a few days; I'm not sure exactly how long."

"In the city, Master?"

"In Ethshar of the Spices."

Derneth nodded. "As you say."

Twenty minutes later Abdaran had been sent home without his apprentice, and Manrin was waiting impatiently at the door while Ulpen stared about, still trying to comprehend what was happening. Events were moving far too quickly for him. He had his pack on his shoulders; it was far lighter than it had been on the walk from North Herris, since he was no longer carrying any of Abdaran's belongings.

It was discomfiting to be out of Abdaran's keeping and in a strange place. He had only met Manrin an hour or two before, yet he had put himself entirely in the Guildmaster's hands. He wondered whether that was really proper and in keeping with the terms of his apprenticeship and his oaths to the Guild.

At last Derneth appeared with yet another bag. Manrin picked up the two he had already had, and reached for this new bundle, but Ulpen took it from Derneth. "If I might help, Guildmaster?" he said.

"Good," Manrin said. "Good." He looked at Derneth. "Take care of the place," he said. "I really don't know when I'll be back. Tell my children not to worry. If Ferris returns, tell one of the neighbors to let me know with the Spell of Invaded Dreams."

"Yes, Master," Derneth said.

"And take care of yourself, Derneth," Manrin said. "I know I've treated you rudely much of the time, but you've always done a fine job and never complained."

Ulpen watched as the expression of weary resignation that had been on Derneth's face every time Ulpen had seen him suddenly cracked into real concern. "It's that serious, Master?"

"It might be—but you aren't involved. You'll be fine. And it might all come to nothing. We'll see." With that, he hefted his two bags up on his shoulders and marched out the door.

Ulpen hurried after him.

He glanced back when they were half a block down Gate Street and saw Derneth still standing in the open doorway, staring after them.

Chapter Twenty-four

Shouldn't we have heard something by now?" Hanner asked, looking at the odd black talisman that Uncle Faran said was his link to Guildmaster Ithinia.

They were sitting in the front parlor of the house on High Street, in a pair of chairs by the mantel that Hanner supposed would be cozy in the winter, with the black talisman on a small table between them. Right now, in the heat of summer, with no fire on the hearth, the main virtue of this location was that it was out of the way of the various warlocks moving hither and yon through the house.

Lord Faran turned up an empty palm. "They're wizards," he replied. "What did you expect?"

Hanner could hardly argue with that; he knew well that most wizards kept their own schedules, ignoring the convenience of lesser beings—though he had never been able to decide whether this was arrogance or sloppiness. "If they don't reach a decision soon Lord Azrad may get tired of waiting," he said. "He's never struck me as a patient man."

"He's not," Faran agreed. "He gets bored easily and hates waiting for anything. That's why he let me and his three brothers and his other advisors run everything. But he hates doing his own work even more, usually." He tapped the talisman, but it remained inert. He frowned. "Maybe I should see if I have some other way to determine whether she's trying to contact me."

"Can't you just use that?" Hanner said, gesturing at the talisman. It occurred to him for the first time that his uncle might not actually know everything about how the sorcerous device worked; perhaps Faran wasn't confident that the thing would do what it was supposed to.

"It might interrupt something," Faran said. "If she's meeting with other Guildmasters I don't want to suddenly start talking to her from the talisman. That would be rude." He grimaced. "I can't think what I might use, but I can't remember everything I've got up there." He rose from his chair and picked up the talisman. "You know something about magic—or at least you ought to, after all the time you've spent in the Wizards' Quarter on my behalf. Why don't you come upstairs with me and see if you have any suggestions?"

"I'd be glad to," Hanner said, getting to his feet.

That was the simple truth, for several reasons.

First off, he was eager to help out. He doubted he really knew enough about magic to be helpful, but he would be happy to try.

Second, he was desperately curious about just what Uncle Faran had stashed away up there. The sorcerous device that let two people speak to one another despite any intervening distance was completely unlike anything Hanner had seen before—most of the sorcerers he knew specialized in healing, or in consulting oracles, or in working with odd little things like fire-starters and lost-object locators. A few offered the use of magical weapons. None had ever mentioned anything like Faran's talisman. Hanner wanted very much to see what else Faran might have acquired in his years of research.

Third, the mansion's ground floor was getting almost crowded. Warlocks had been drifting in, one or two at a time, all day; word was circulating through the city that this was a refuge for them, a place they could come when their former homes cast them out or their neighbors made them unwelcome. As news of disappearances and destruction spread, more and more warlocks were being cast out or made unwelcome.

Faran and Hanner—and Bern when he was there; at the moment he had gone out to market to replenish the pantries—had made them all welcome.

Most of Hanner's party from the Night of Madness had

returned, along with assorted friends and neighbors and various other warlocks who had somehow heard about the refuge at the corner of High Street and Coronet. Mavi, though not a warlock herself, had brought an afflicted friend, a young woman named Pancha; after seeing Pancha introduced and settled in, Mavi had stayed on to visit with Alris. They were upstairs, in the room Alris shared with Rudhira.

Hanner had hoped that Mavi would also visit with *him*, but Uncle Faran had had him running errands at the time, assigning new arrivals to various guest rooms, which had kept him too busy to socialize.

Hinda, the little kitchen girl from the Palace, was now busily cleaning out the kitchens here, eager to earn her keep; Rudhira and half a dozen others were out in the garden, holding some sort of competition in the use of warlockry.

That left a score of others wandering about the parlors, salons, and halls of the ground floor. While Hanner had grown up amid the bustle of the overlord's palace, he still felt a little strained by this population of strangers.

Fourth, he wanted to get farther away from the front windows and their view of High Street.

The influx of warlocks had not gone unnoticed; Hanner supposed that people had followed Faran from the square when he first arrived. Certainly, ever since shortly after that there had been a varying number of observers, standing in the street and watching the house intently. Individuals came and went, but whenever Hanner looked out someone was there—usually about half a dozen at a time. One old man seemed particularly determined, and was there at the dooryard fence, glowering at the house, every time Hanner looked.

Hanner was not at all sure what these people thought they were accomplishing by this unrelenting scrutiny, but apparently they had something in mind—and he was fairly sure, from the looks they gave anyone entering or leaving the house, that their intentions were hostile. Warlocks who were capable of flight had mostly been arriving by way of the garden, rather than passing this group; earthbound warlocks had been approaching cautiously, then making a dash through the gate to the front door.

Nobody in the house liked the presence of these stubborn sentinels, but there really wasn't much that could be done about it. A person had the right to stand in the public street, after all. So long as they stayed outside the iron fence, Faran could not order them to leave.

And there they stood, making Hanner uncomfortable. Going up to the third or fourth floor would get him away from the watchers, and away from the crowd of warlocks.

"Come on, then," Faran said as he started toward the stairs.

But just then the hum of street noise suddenly rose in volume, and Faran and Hanner both paused. They looked at each other as the conversation among the warlocks around them faded away.

Everyone had heard the change. The people out front of the house were yelling now, though no one inside could make out words. The motley collection of warlocks looked about nervously. Several went to the front windows and peered around the drapes.

"Blood and death," Faran said. "What are they doing now?" He redirected his steps to the front door.

Hanner followed.

Faran swung the door wide and stood in the doorway, looking out—and leaving Hanner no good way to see past his uncle.

"What is it?" Hanner asked.

"It would appear we have company coming," Faran replied. "Company in wizards' robes."

"Ithinia?"

"No," Faran said. "It's someone I never saw before, an old man with an apprentice."

"How would they know where we are?" someone Hanner didn't know asked from the parlor.

Hanner could see Faran struggling to stay polite.

"They're wizards," he said. "You're no wizard, and *you*

found it. And those people out front certainly aren't making much of an effort to keep it secret."

". . . teach those warlocks about magic!" someone shouted from the street.

"One wizard and an apprentice coming here can't be much of a threat," Othisen said, coming up beside Hanner.

Hanner snorted. "If the Guild had decided to kill us they wouldn't need to come here in person at all," he said. "I'd guess they're bringing a message." He glanced at Faran. "Maybe that talisman isn't working properly."

"I'd think Ithinia would have come herself or sent . . ." Faran stopped in midsentence as the strangers turned and stepped through the open gate into the little dooryard under the intense scrutiny of various observers. "Greetings," he said. "I am Lord Faran, formerly chief advisor to Lord Azrad."

"I am Manrin the Mage," replied one of the strangers—a stocky old man of medium height wearing a white and gold wizard's robe. "This young man is Ulpen of North Herris. I understand you've been gathering warlocks here."

Faran cocked his head. "If you'll excuse me for asking, Master Wizard, if I have, how does this concern you? Are you here to speak on behalf of the Wizards' Guild?"

"I am here on my own behalf, not the Guild's," Manrin said. "If we could enter and perhaps speak privately, I will be glad to explain myself." He glanced over his shoulder at the old man staring through the fence at them.

Faran followed Manrin's gaze, then bowed and stepped aside. "Enter, then, and be welcome."

The wizards were plainly startled by what they found inside, though Hanner was not sure whether they were most surprised by the opulent furnishings, the number of warlocks milling about, or the bizarre assortment of attire on display, ranging from Faran's fine court silk to Zarek's rags. Manrin quickly hid his reaction, but Ulpen stared about openly.

"You wanted to speak privately?" Faran said.

"If we could," Manrin said.

"If you'll come upstairs to my study, then?" Faran gestured toward the stairs and took a step in that direction.

"Of course." Manrin beckoned to Ulpen to accompany him as he followed Faran.

Faran, seeing this, beckoned to Hanner. "Lord Hanner will accompany us," he said.

Othisen threw Hanner an envious glance, then stepped aside and let the foursome ascend.

Hanner was not sure at first just what study his uncle was referring to—there was a study on the ground floor, he knew, but not one on the second so far as he had observed. That question was answered, however, when Faran unlocked the door to the second staircase, the one leading to the third story.

"I hope you'll forgive the dust," Faran said. "I don't allow the servants to clean up here."

Manrin made a polite wordless noise in reply. Hanner ran his hand along the left-hand banister, then sneezed—the dust was indeed plentiful. Ulpen didn't say or touch anything; he looked frightened. Hanner wondered whether Ulpen's discomfort came merely from being among warlocks or from something else entirely.

At the top of the stairs Faran led the way down a broad passageway. The walls were painted white and a worn red and gold carpet ran the length of the corridor; the luxurious furnishings of the two lower floors were notably absent, and a long scorch mark on one wall had been left unrepaired. Hanner noticed that the burn was obviously not recent, as dust and cobwebs were just as thick there as elsewhere.

Faran opened a door and ushered the party into a good-sized but dim room. As the others stood around uncertainly Faran opened the heavy drapes on two big west-facing windows, letting in the late-afternoon sunlight; it cut through the room in bright shafts alive with dancing dust and illuminated several chairs and walls lined with chests of drawers.

It didn't look much like a study to Hanner, as there was no desk and the only books were a set of ledgers atop one of the chests. It didn't look particularly magical, either, and there was no obvious reason to have kept it so carefully locked, though Hanner supposed the drawers might contain almost anything.

But it was somewhere private to talk.

Faran gestured to the chairs and pulled one forward for himself. "Now, Master," he said as he seated himself, "why have you come here?"

"I understand that you are gathering warlocks here, and that you have undertaken to defend them against over-reaction regarding the disturbances on the Night of Madness," Manrin said as he settled carefully onto a chair.

"That's more or less the situation," Faran agreed. "What of it?"

Manrin and Ulpen glanced nervously at each other.

"In that case," Manrin said, "we would like to join your group."

Faran cocked his head to one side. Hanner said, "But you're wizards, aren't you?"

"We are," Manrin agreed. "However, we are also war-locks." He looked around for a convenient demonstration, and one of the ledgers lifted itself from the chest of drawers. It hovered for a moment, then settled back into place.

Faran and Hanner watched this silently; then Faran turned back to the wizards and asked, "Your apprentice, too?"

"He's not *my* apprentice," Manrin said. "He's Abdaran's apprentice—Abdaran the White, a village wizard of no particular significance. But the boy's a warlock, as I am, so I brought him along."

"Is that so?" Faran asked Ulpen.

"Yes, mas . . . yes, my lord," Ulpen replied. "Master Ab-daran took me to the Guildmaster for a consultation, and Guildmaster Manrin took me to Guildmaster Perinan, and Guildmaster Perinan sent us to Guildmaster Ithinia, and then we came here."

"So all these people know you're warlocks?" Faran frowned. "Then why did you want to see me *in private*?"

"They *don't* know," Manrin said quickly. "Abdaran

knows about Ulpen, but I don't believe any of the others know it's possible for a wizard to have been contaminated in this fashion. I claimed to be acting from disinterested motives in consulting the others, and had Perinan send us to Ithinia—or rather to Ethshar of the Spices. That was the fastest way to get here."

"A Transporting Tapestry?" Faran asked.

"You know of them?" Manrin asked, startled.

"I've heard of them," Faran said. "I've never seen one in operation."

"They're very handy; we stepped forty leagues in a heartbeat."

"It was amazing!" Ulpen said, showing the first sign of enthusiasm—very nearly the first sign of *life*—Hanner had seen from him. "We just *touched* it!"

"Yes, yes," Manrin said. He turned his attention back to Faran. "At any rate, we arrived in the city, stopped by Ithinia's home to maintain the fiction that we came to consult her, and then came here." He hesitated. "You understand why we came?"

"I'd prefer you to make it explicit," Faran said.

Manrin sighed. "It's simple enough. We want to live. And right now, it's not clear that we'll be permitted to. Ithinia says your overlord here, Lord Azrad, is determined to kill all the warlocks; our Lord Ederd isn't so certain, but was talking about exile."

"Then haven't you just made your situation worse by coming here?" Hanner asked.

"We came to seek shelter, young man," Manrin said.

"But if you stayed out of Ethshar of the Spices, you wouldn't necessarily *need* shelter . . ."

"I think we would, no matter what Ederd decides," Manrin replied. "The triumvirate isn't the only power in Ethshar. Don't forget—we are wizards. And wizards are forbidden by Guild rules to learn any other magic. And violations of Guild rules are punishable by death."

"But you didn't *ask* to be warlocks!" Hanner exclaimed.

"I'm afraid that the Guild often does not worry about intentions, but only results."

"Then they're no better than Lord Azrad!"

Manrin blinked at him in surprise. "Did anyone ever claim they were?"

"My nephew has something of an idealistic streak," Faran said dryly. "I've been telling him for years that the Wizards' Guild is not as benign as it would like to appear, but he was not inclined to believe me."

"So I see," Manrin said. "Well, in any case, it seems to me that if we, as both warlocks and wizards, want to survive, we had best find some support. We can't keep our situation a secret forever—"

"Why not?" Hanner interrupted, startling everyone, including himself. He had just been thinking that in Manrin's position he would simply never have admitted to being a warlock.

After all, *he* hadn't told anyone *he* was a warlock, and didn't intend to.

Manrin looked at him in surprise. "Because warlockry wants to be used! Hasn't anyone told you that, out of all these warlocks? It's easy to use it quite unintentionally—we've both done it several times. One can even use it inadvertently in one's sleep. Sooner or later we would slip somewhere we could be seen—and that's quite aside from the fact that Ulpen's master Abdaran already knows that Ulpen is a warlock."

Lord Faran was nodding, and Hanner remembered that his uncle had, in fact, given away his own warlock nature by accident. The possibility that Hanner would give away his own secret the way Manrin described worried him, but just now he didn't see much he could do about it.

Manrin frowned. "And there's another factor, as well. It would seem that warlockry and wizardry do interfere with each other to some extent. Most of my spells have been going wrong for the past two days, and it may well get worse. I'm a Guildmaster—people expect me to use my magic every day. If I begin to refuse, or if my spells begin to fail regularly, questions will arise."

"Oh," Hanner said. He glanced at his uncle.

Faran was looking thoughtfully at the wizards.

"Your spells don't work?" he said. "Then are you really still a wizard?"

Manrin sighed. "I'm afraid so," he said. "I can still work *some* spells, and besides, one can't stop being a wizard, not really. I know a good many Guild secrets, including some that it's death for a nonwizard to know. So if I'm still a wizard, then I must die for being a warlock; if I am no longer a wizard, then I must die for knowing Guild secrets. Unless, that is, I can find some way to convince the Guild to relent."

"The Guild *never* relents, does it?" Ulpen asked. "Abdaran told me it didn't."

"Not unless it's forced to," Manrin agreed. "And that's why we've come here. I'm not sure just what you intend with this group you're gathering, my lord, but whatever it is, we'd like to offer our services in exchange for whatever protection you can give us."

"Your services," Faran said. "But you just said that your magic is damaged."

"My *mind* isn't," Manrin snapped. "And it's wizardry that's damaged; I'm still as much a warlock as any of those others downstairs. And I'm also still a Guildmaster, until they find out what's happened to me—I really *do* know secrets, and for now I am able to speak with Ithinia and Perinan about matters that an outsider would never dare broach."

"That could indeed be valuable," Faran admitted. "I spoke to Ithinia yesterday and asked for an audience to discuss the warlocks' situation; when you came to the door I thought you were here as her representative, to deliver an ultimatum or escort me to a meeting or otherwise respond to my request. You obviously aren't her representative—do you know why she hasn't responded? Has she met with the overlord, as he requested?"

"No, she hasn't," Manrin said. "I *do* know that much. She hasn't met with any of you because she's been busy meeting with other wizards—the Guild wants to present a consistent response to the warlock problem, throughout not just the Hegemony of the Three Ethshars, but the entire World. So the—"

He stopped abruptly in midsentence, glanced at Ulpen, then continued.

"I am about to break an oath," he said. "I think this is really a very minor point, compared to some, but I'm going to tell you a Guild secret, and I have sworn never to reveal any of the Guild's secrets. If this is unacceptable, tell me now—I do not want to be forsworn for nothing."

"Go on," Faran said. "If it's any comfort, I would guess you were about to say something about the Inner Circle."

"Ah!" Manrin looked relieved. "Then you already know, and I'm not breaking my vow after all. Yes. The Inner Circle is meeting to discuss this matter, or at least part of it is. I don't know where, but it's not in Ethshar. Ithinia and Perinan and the others are gone, and won't return until there's a decision; I caught her just before she left and asked her where you could be found. She thinks I'm here to see what you're up to with all these warlocks, so that I can report back to her—but I have no intention of reporting back."

"Then there really *is* an Inner Circle, and you're not a member?" Faran asked. "I'm afraid I'd only heard rumors."

"There really is an Inner Circle, and I'm not a member," Manrin confirmed. "I had hoped that I might someday be invited in—but obviously, that can't happen *now*."

Hanner heard the bitterness in the wizard's voice. It was quite clear that whatever this Inner Circle might be, Manrin thought he *should* have been a member by now.

Hanner noticed that Ulpen looked more confused than ever, and in the apprentice's interest as much as his own he asked, "Just what *is* the Inner Circle?"

Manrin bit his lower lip, causing his beard to thrust out, and looked at Lord Faran.

"The rumors I've heard," Faran said, "were that while ostensibly the Wizards' Guild is run by all the Guildmasters, in fact there is secretly a select group within the Guildmasters that is the true ruling council of the Guild. This council is called the Inner Circle."

Manrin opened his mouth, hesitated, then said, "That's essentially correct."

"I never heard anything about that," Ulpen said.

"You're just an apprentice," Hanner said. "I'm sure you'd have heard about it eventually."

Actually, he wasn't sure of anything of the kind, but there was no reason to say so. Ulpen did not look happy about any of this.

In fact, Hanner noticed that Manrin had done virtually all the talking, and it occurred to him that Ulpen might not even have wanted to come here. As an apprentice he had to do as he was told, and Manrin had told him to come here—but he might not *like* it.

That would be something to keep in mind; they might want to keep an eye on the boy.

"So the Inner Circle is meeting to discuss the situation?" Faran said. "Do you have any idea how long this might take?"

Manrin grimaced. "It could be *years*," he said. "These are master wizards, the least of them my equal. I'm one hundred and eleven years old, and expect to live many years yet, and by the standards of the Inner Circle I'm scarcely more than a journeyman. They have the Spell of Sustenance, so they needn't worry about food or drink; they have youth spells, at the very least, and some of them have genuine eternal life. Time does not mean the same thing to them that it does to ordinary people like you."

"But . . ." Hanner began.

Manrin held up a hand to silence him. "I don't think it *will* take years," he said. "I think they'll recognize the urgency of the situation and act quickly. But how quickly, I have no idea."

Hanner bit back a protest.

He didn't want this to drag on for years, or months, or even another sixnight. He wanted everyone to come to their senses and simply treat warlocks as *people*.

All Hanner really wanted was to go back home to the Palace and sleep in his own bed—well, that, and to get to know Mavi better, and eventually to find himself a career other than palace parasite. He had walked Mavi home again the night before. She had turned up again today, bringing her friend Pancha, and he had been very pleased to see her, even though they hadn't had a chance to talk.

He would have been even more pleased if they were all back in the Palace, and none of them were warlocks.

He didn't say that, of course. He looked silently at his uncle.

"Then the question is—" Faran began.

Hanner never found out what the question was; just then a crash sounded from the hallway, like a door being smashed open, and Rudhira's voice called, "I think you better get down here right now!"

Chapter Twenty-five

The crowd of warlocks at the foot of the stairs parted as the four men hurried down.

The front door stood open, and in the gate beyond stood Captain Naral of the city guard, with some twenty fully armed guardsmen arrayed behind him. The street beyond this party was crowded with curious onlookers of every description. Lord Hanner, looking over his uncle's shoulder, spotted the persistent old man there, his expression annoyingly satisfied.

"Lord Faran?" Naral called when he saw the foursome appear.

"Yes, of course, Captain," Faran said. "What can I do for you?"

Naral took a deep breath, puffing out his armored chest, then proclaimed loudly, "By order of Azrad the Sixth, Overlord of Ethshar of the Spices, Triumvir of the Hegemony of the Three Ethshars, Commander of the Holy Navies and Defender of the Gods, you are hereby required to depart from this city of Ethshar immediately, by which is meant that you must be without the city walls within the hour. You are to take with you any and all persons of your acquaintance who are in any degree affected by the magic known as 'warlockry.' You are furthermore forbidden to return within the city walls at any time or for any reason until written permission has been given in the overlord's own hand. Any property you leave within the city will be sold, and the net proceeds sent to you in your place of exile. I am here to escort you to one of the city gates or to a departing vessel. Failure to comply with this command will be punished with death, at such time and by such means as shall be expedient."

He managed to deliver the entire speech at a fairly impressive volume without taking a breath, which Hanner found remarkable. He was also surprised that Naral had managed to deliver the formal wording perfectly, including the added sentence about warlocks, without stumbling or hesitating. The rest was the standard sentence of exile, which Hanner had heard pronounced once or twice before, but usually it went directly from "within the hour" to "you are furthermore forbidden."

"You can't be serious," Lord Faran said, leaning gracefully against the door frame.

"I'm completely serious, my lord," Captain Naral said. "Lord Azrad wants you out of the city at once."

"Lord Azrad can go juggle fish," Faran replied.

Half those listening gasped at that; the other half was stunned into silence.

"Now, you see?" Naral said when he had regained his composure. "I'm sure that's exactly the sort of thing that's gotten Lord Azrad so annoyed." He drew his sword. "I'm afraid, my lord, that I must escort you to the gate, either peacefully or by force. It's your choice. I assume that West-gate will suit you?"

"I'm not going anywhere," Faran said. He nodded once, and the sword in Naral's hand suddenly twisted out of the soldier's grip and fell to the hard-packed dirt of the street beyond the fence.

Naral quickly stooped and grabbed it up again.

"Captain," Faran said, "I'm a warlock. This house is *full* of warlocks. I can easily handle you. I might not be able to handle all your men, but I'm sure some of the others here would be glad to help me out with that."

"Don't kill anyone," Hanner whispered over his uncle's shoulder.

"I wasn't planning to," Faran said back without turning his head, speaking in a voice so low no one more than a yard away could hear it.

Hanner turned, looking over the other warlocks. He was at Faran's right shoulder; Manrin was at the left, and Ulpen stood just behind Manrin, looking very unhappy indeed. The others had all hung back slightly; Rudhira was closest, a step behind Hanner, while a dozen others were gathered in the adjoining rooms, watching through the windows or listening from the doorways.

Rudhira was the obvious choice to ask for assistance; Hanner knew her, trusted her to keep control, and knew her warlock abilities were among the most powerful of anyone present. "Rudhira," Hanner whispered, beckoning. "Come here—my uncle may need some help."

Rudhira came up behind Hanner—literally up; she lifted herself off the floor so that she could see past the men in the doorway, and hung several inches off the floor as she peered out at the guards.

"Don't kill them," Hanner said. "They're just following orders."

Rudhira nodded.

Naral was clearly thinking it over, but at last he called,

"Lord Faran, please reconsider. I'm just carrying out the overlord's commands. Maybe you can stop *me*, but you can't stop the entire city!"

"I really doubt we'll have to," Faran said with a smile. "But if we do—you know, I'm not sure we can't. We don't know just what warlockry can do. We're only just starting to learn. Are you *sure* we can't stop the entire city?"

Naral sighed.

"I have my orders," he said. "Now, will you come peacefully?"

"I won't come at all," Faran said. He straightened up and stepped back, inside the threshold.

He couldn't close the door; Manrin was in the way, standing with his back to the door handle. The wizard had been staring out at the soldiers and took a moment to realize that Faran was glaring at him, and another moment to realize why. He said, "Oh," then started to move aside.

By then it was too late—Naral was leading a charge, the entire score of guardsmen rushing toward the gate, yelling at the top of their lungs. The watching crowd was enthusiastically cheering them on.

Faran and Manrin were distracted, Hanner had no idea what to do, but it didn't matter. Rudhira waved a hand, and the soldiers were swept off their feet, tumbling backward as if a huge wave had struck them head-on, spears and swords clattering as they fell to the ground.

The yelling stopped abruptly, the cheering crowd fell suddenly silent, and for a moment the rattle and thudding of the soldiers, their weapons, and their armor hitting the ground were clearly audible.

Then the street was completely still for several seconds, the only sound the distant buzz of the rest of the city going about its business.

Faran and Manrin and Hanner stared out at the sprawled guardsmen; some of the soldiers tentatively moved to sit up while others lay still, fearing that any motion might provoke another attack.

"Go away!" Rudhira shouted over the heads of the three

men, her voice seeming impossibly loud to Hanner. "We're magicians, and we demand the respect due to magicians! You can't just run in here with your swords and spears as if we were a bunch of drunken rowdies smashing up a tavern!"

Hanner smothered a sudden urge to laugh hysterically. He was quite sure that Rudhira was not speaking theoretically, that she had seen guardsmen deal with rowdies smashing up taverns at least once before.

Captain Naral got carefully to his feet, brushed himself off, picked up his sword, brushed *that* off, then turned and looked over his men. Most of them were sitting up now; a few had even retrieved weapons.

He turned back toward the doorway.

"Lord Faran," he said.

"Captain Naral," Faran acknowledged.

"It appears you intend to defy the overlord's orders, and that we can't stop you."

"Captain, we could kill the lot of you quite easily. Please don't force us to demonstrate."

Naral turned up a palm. "I won't," he said. "But I will have to report back to Lord Azrad, and he may try something more drastic next time."

"I would be happy to negotiate with the overlord's representative; I understand that there are serious matters at stake here, and I'm eager for a peaceful resolution."

"Of course." Naral hesitated, then added, "Leaving the city would be peaceful."

"I'm afraid I'm not eager for that *particular* peaceful resolution," Faran said. "I hope we can find another."

"I hope so, my lord," Naral said. Then he turned and bellowed at his men, "All right, you, up on your feet! Let's see some order here!"

Hanner watched silently at Faran's side as the soldiers got upright and organized, and started to march off, with Naral at the rear.

"Wait a minute!" the persistent old man in the street shouted. He no longer looked satisfied; he looked distraught.

"You can't give up! Get them! Arrest them! My son disappeared two nights ago, and they're responsible!"

"We are *not*," Hanner shouted back.

Captain Naral pointedly ignored the exchange as he and his men marched away.

Hanner watched them go and kept an eye on the civilians in the street as well as the departing guardsmen; the expressions he saw there were mostly sullen and angry, though that one man appeared truly outraged.

The warlocks had driven off the overlord's men and avoided exile for the moment, but it was plain to Hanner that they hadn't made any friends.

"Thank you, Rudhira," Faran said as he gently pushed Hanner aside and finally managed to close the door. "That was well timed and neatly done."

Rudhira smiled and curtsied—a flouncing little-girl curtsy, not the subtler, more graceful dip of a noblewoman. Hanner supposed it was something she'd learned to please her customers, since ordinary folk hardly ever bothered with such formalities.

"Uncle," Hanner said, "they'll be back with magicians."

"I know," Faran said. "I hope that without me there to insist on speed that they won't be quick about it—you know how lazy Azrad and Ildirin and the rest are."

"But if Lord Azrad's angry . . ."

"Yes. Then he wants it over as quickly as possible." He turned to Manrin. "What wizardry can you still perform?"

Manrin snorted. "Not much. Even if I could rely on it, where would I get the ingredients for anything more potent than Felshen's First Hypnotic?"

"Upstairs," Faran replied. "I should have everything you need."

Manrin stared at him silently for a moment.

"Oh," he said at last.

Hanner listened but said nothing more just yet. He was beginning to see just how completely his uncle was cutting himself off. He was defying the overlord *and* the Wizards' Guild, disobeying the city guard, and openly admitting that he had studied forbidden magic. There could be no possible return for Lord Faran—either he would triumph as something new, as a master warlock no longer bound by the old rules, or he would almost certainly die, as a traitor and rogue magician.

Hanner just hoped that if Faran lost he wouldn't take the entire family down with him. The Hegemony of Ethshar had never believed in punishing the family of a criminal for his crimes, but Uncle Faran was a special case—the city's second-highest official, committing the highest of crimes.

And Hanner and Alris were here, helping him.

More than ever Hanner wished he were safely home with Nerra in their palace apartment, and that he wasn't a warlock.

"Wizardly ingredients are stored in the rooms on the west side of the third floor," Faran said. "I think you'll find everything properly catalogued; the index is in the bound volumes in the room where we spoke earlier." His full attention was apparently focused on Manrin, but Hanner knew his uncle well enough to be sure that he knew other people were listening. Rudhira and Ulpen and half a dozen other warlocks were in fact listening intently.

Faran was deliberately letting them know about his dabbling in magic, and that Manrin, a wizard, was on their side—presumably to hearten them in the face of the knowledge that the overlord knew where they were and wanted them gone. Knowing that they had resources beyond their own mysterious and untrained magic . . .

Untrained. Hanner thought about that for a moment.

"Uncle," he said as Manrin and Ulpen started toward the stairs, and Faran turned to follow them.

Faran turned back to his nephew. "Yes?"

"I think that you had best leave the wizardry to the wizards—but if you're expecting a confrontation, shouldn't you find out just what other resources we have?"

"We have a houseful of warlocks," Faran said.

"Yes, but shouldn't you find out *how many* warlocks, and what they can do? We really don't know what they're capable of." He waved at Rudhira. "They can't *all* stop a dozen guardsmen in their tracks the way she can—but some of them may be able to do other things."

Faran looked at Hanner, then around at the clustered warlocks listening in, then wistfully at Manrin and Ulpen as they mounted the stairs.

"You're right," he said. "We should do that. Better an army than a mob, eh?" He gestured and called, "All right, everyone! Into the dining hall, so we can see just who we have here."

As the crowd began to move in the indicated direction someone knocked on the door, the rapping barely audible over the shuffling feet. Hanner looked at Faran.

They could both hear shouting out in the street, but it was not close to the door.

Faran looked at Rudhira, who brushed her hair back from her face and said, "I'm ready."

Hanner bit his lower lip. Faran and Rudhira obviously thought there might be another enemy out there, but Hanner thought it far more likely it was either Bern, his hands too full of groceries to work the latch, or another warlock arriving.

But there were those people who hung around, watching. It was probably just as well to have Rudhira ready to use her warlockry to defend the house.

Faran nodded, and Hanner opened the door.

The shouting was suddenly louder, and for the first time Hanner made out words.

"Where's my husband? What did you warlocks do with him?" a woman was shrieking.

She was not at the door, though, nor anywhere near it. The shouters were all outside the fence, on the street. The only person *inside* the fence was a black-haired girl of perhaps thirteen or fourteen, wearing a drab grey dress. She stood in the dooryard just outside, her knuckles raised to knock again.

Rudhira made a derisive little snort and turned away.

Hanner was annoyed by this rudeness and determined to

make up for it. "Good afternoon to you," he said. "I'm Lord Hanner; may I help you?"

"I'm Shella the Apprentice," the girl said. "Are you . . . are warlocks welcome here?"

"Yes, indeed," Hanner said, swinging the door wide. "Come in!"

"Thank you," Shella said. She stepped inside, then stopped dead, staring at the lush furnishings and the motley collection of people marching through the hallway into the dining hall.

"Apprenticed to what trade?" Hanner asked politely as he closed the door, to distract her and put her at ease.

"Witch," she said.

Uncle Faran, who had been ignoring the girl as he ushered his other guests into the dining room, suddenly turned to stare at her.

Hanner smiled.

"Come right this way," he said as he led her past Uncle Faran to the head of the table.

Chapter Twenty-six

I was standing out there for hours, trying to get up my nerve," Shella explained quietly to Hanner as Lord Faran tried to get everyone lined up neatly. Faran had decided to leave her to his nephew for the moment; she spoke so softly that it took an effort to carry on a conversation, especially over the background noise the crowd of warlocks made, and he had other matters to attend to. "When I saw you send the soldiers away, I decided maybe you *can* protect me."

"Protect you from what?"

"Everything," the girl said, waving a hand vaguely. "I mean, I'm sure it's bad enough for anyone, being a warlock, but being a witch *and* a warlock . . . well, that's against the Wizards' Guild law, isn't it? My master thought so. He thought it might be against Sisterhood rules, as well."

"I don't think the Sisterhood could possibly have rules about warlocks yet," Hanner said. He knew little about the loose organization of female witches, but from what little he did know, he couldn't believe they were sufficiently organized to have made such a rule in just two days. "Besides, you don't need to join the Sisterhood if you don't want to."

"But . . . well, don't their rules apply to everyone, the way Wizards' Guild rules do?"

"No, no," Hanner said. "In order to be a wizard you have to join the Guild, and they kill anyone who breaks their rules about wizardry, but the Sisterhood isn't like that at all. I'm not even sure they *have* rules, and if they do—well, they don't apply to anyone but members. Besides, the Sisterhood doesn't kill anyone, so far as I've ever heard. It's more a social group than a guild."

"The Brotherhood has rules," Shella said doubtfully. "My master told me some of them. He used to be a member."

"But he's not a member now?"

"No, he left. They didn't like him taking a female apprentice."

"And they didn't kill him, did they?"

It was like watching a cloud blow away from the sun to see her face as this sank in.

"No," she said.

Then the cloud returned. "But the Wizards' Guild still doesn't allow mixing magic."

"And the overlord doesn't want warlocks in the city at all," Hanner agreed. "But we're here to fight that."

Shella nodded, but her expression remained worried and uncertain.

"So," Hanner said, hoping to cheer her—and himself—up, "who's your master? Does he know you're here?"

"Kelder of Crookwall," she said. "I don't think he knows where I am—and I don't think he cares." She blinked rapidly, her mouth working, and Hanner realized she was on the verge of tears. "He threw me out."

"But he can't do that!" Hanner said. "A master is responsible for his apprentice!"

Shella snuffled and wiped her nose with her sleeve, then dabbed at one eye. "He did, though," she said. "He said I wasn't a witch anymore, and never could be."

"Because you're a warlock?"

She nodded silently.

A thought struck Hanner.

Warlocks could move things without touching them; most warlocks, himself included, discovered what they were by finding themselves able to do this.

But *witches* could move things without touching them, too. After all, the name "warlock" came from the resemblance to war-locked witches in the first place. Witches only levitated fairly small things, but still, what could this girl have moved that a witch couldn't?

"How does he *know* you're a warlock?" he asked.

"Because of what I did," Shella said, so softly Hanner could barely hear her.

"Hanner, my boy," Faran called, "could you and your young friend pay attention? We're ready to begin."

Hanner looked up. "In a moment, Uncle," he said. Then he turned back to Shella. "What did you do?"

"I turned Thellesh the Butcher into a warlock."

Hanner blinked.

"Hanner," Faran said warningly.

Hanner held up a hand. "You did *what*?" he said.

"I was trying to *heal* him!" Shella said loudly. Then her voice dropped back to its usual near inaudibility and the words spilled out in a rush, so fast Hanner had trouble keeping up. "He'd cut himself, and then slipped on the blood and hit his head on the wall, and Master Kelder said it was time I started to learn healing, so we fixed up Thellesh's hand together, and then Master told me to study his head and see whether we could do anything there, so I tried to, but my witch sight wasn't . . . I couldn't *see* properly, and then I did something, I don't know what, and I *could* see, but it was all different, and I could see inside Thellesh's head, and I looked at how it was different from mine, because I thought mine would be working right, and I . . . I did something, I don't know how to explain it, but it was like opening a tap, sort of, except I couldn't close it again. And then Thellesh sat up, and he was better, but he felt funny, and he said he heard voices, and then he reached for his purse, and it jumped into his hand, and Master Kelder looked at us both and . . ."

At that point she finally lost control and began crying, quick soft little sobs and gasps.

"Hanner!" Faran barked.

Hanner looked up. "I'm sorry, Uncle," he said. "I'll take her to the parlor to calm down. We'll be back."

Faran glared at him. "Go on, then," he said.

Hanner put an arm around Shella's shoulders and led her out of the dining room, across the hallway to the front parlor. He closed the dining-hall door on his way out.

If Shella was telling the truth, then this might have huge significance. Up until now Hanner—and probably everyone else—had assumed that the people who had become warlocks on the Night of Madness were all the warlocks there would ever be, at least unless that same mysterious phenomenon happened again and created a whole new batch.

But if warlocks could *make* new warlocks, the way witches could train apprentice witches and wizards could help their apprentices make the ritual daggers they needed to become wizards, then . . . well, exterminating warlocks might not be as easy as Lord Azrad thought, and perhaps warlocks really *were* true magicians.

Hanner saw that Mavi had come downstairs, but still not gone home again—he wondered whether she might be waiting for him to accompany her. She and Alris were sitting in the front parlor, talking; they fell silent as Hanner and Shella entered.

"Did Uncle throw you out with the rest of us nonwarlocks, then?" Alris asked.

Mavi got to her feet and stepped toward Shella, apparently seeing the signs that she had been crying and seeking to comfort her, but the girl shied away, and Mavi stopped.

"I brought Shella in here to calm down," Hanner explained. "She's had a very hard day. Her master threw her out."

"She's a warlock?" Alris asked Hanner.

"Are you all right?" Mavi asked Shella.

"She's a warlock," Hanner said as Mavi took Shella's hand.

"Then shouldn't she be in there with the others?" Alris demanded.

"Maybe when she's feeling better," Hanner said. He had had some thought that maybe Alris would like having Shella around, since they were roughly the same age, but it didn't appear that was going to work.

"I'm Mavi," Mavi said.

Shella swallowed and managed to stop crying long enough to reply, "I'm Shella."

"This is Lady Alris," Mavi said. "She's Lord Hanner's sister."

Shella glanced at Alris, then stared intently at Mavi for a moment.

Hanner felt suddenly uneasy; something was happening, he could sense it, but he didn't know what.

"You're not a warlock," Shella said. It wasn't a question.

"No, I'm not," Mavi said. "Neither is Lady Alris nor Lord Hanner, but they live in the Palace, and the overlord won't let them back in because he's scared of the warlocks, so they're staying here with their uncle. I'm just visiting, to keep them company; I live in Newmarket."

"But . . ." Shella threw Hanner a sharp, puzzled glance, her tears apparently forgotten.

She knew, he realized. She knew he was a warlock.

"I'll explain later," Hanner said quickly.

"Explain what?" Alris demanded.

"None of your business," Hanner snapped.

Alris looked at Hanner, then at Mavi, then said, "I'll bet

I know, though I don't know why you told *her* before you said anything to your own sister!"

Mavi started. "No, Alris, it's not—I mean, we haven't . . ." Her voice trailed off in confusion.

"Just shut up, Alris," Hanner said wearily. He hadn't expected to find these two in the parlor, and much as he ordinarily enjoyed Mavi's presence, he wished they weren't there. He turned to Shella.

"You were telling me what happened after you healed Thellesh," he said.

"Oh," Shella said. "Well, Master Kelder tried to undo what I'd done, but he couldn't, and I couldn't see how I could, either, when he told me to try, so finally he sent Thellesh home, and we talked for a while, and then he told me to get my things and get out, that I wasn't a witch anymore and I was too dangerous to stay in his house. I think he thought it might be catching."

"So you left?"

"I didn't even get my stuff," Shella said. "I was too upset. I just ran out the door. And later I listened to people talking and asked some questions, and I heard about the Warlock House and came to see."

"The Warlock House?" Alris asked.

"That's what they call it," Shella said.

"This house, you mean," Hanner said.

"That's right."

"So much for keeping anything secret," Alris said.

Hanner hoped those words weren't prophetic; he still had secrets he wanted to keep. The location of Uncle Faran's house, the refuge for warlocks, wasn't one of them, though. "We already knew the guards had found us," he said. "And there were those people in the street."

"*Are* you still a witch?" Mavi asked Shella.

"No," Shella said. "At least, I don't think so. When I try to do witchcraft it all feels different, so I think I'm doing warlockry instead. I can't do some things at all, like reading moods. And I don't get tired—instead it makes me feel stronger."

That certainly fit what Hanner knew of warlockry.

"When did it start?" he asked.

"I don't know," Shella said. "I felt funny all day yesterday, but I wasn't sure anything was wrong until today."

"Did you have any strange dreams last night?"

She looked up at him, startled, and her eyes grew wide. "What kind of dreams?" she asked.

"About falling and being buried alive," Hanner said.

"You know about that?" Shella said breathlessly.

"Tell us about it," Mavi said.

"It wasn't last night, but the night before I did! I dreamed about falling through the air burning, and then falling down under the ground until I was buried and couldn't breathe, and all the time I knew there was something I had to do, but I didn't know what it was." She shuddered. "I knew it was a magical dream, but I didn't know what kind or where it came from."

"It's the same dream," Alris said. "I've heard everyone talking about it over and over. All the warlocks who were asleep when the Night of Madness started had it, and some of them have had it again since then."

Hanner glanced at her. "Have *you* had it?"

"*Me?*" Alris clapped a hand to her chest. "*I'm* not a warlock! Of course I haven't had any dreams like that." She snorted. "Now I probably *will*, not because of any magic but just because you said that."

Hanner watched his sister's face for a second, trying to decide whether perhaps she was being a little *too* emphatic, but then dismissed it. She was probably telling the truth, and any excess drama was just because she was thirteen.

He still found her attitude toward warlockry puzzling, though. She had been so insistent for so long that she wanted to be a magician, and she didn't seem to mind being in a house full of warlocks—she had friends she could stay with if she really wanted to—yet she seemed to be very determined to dislike the *idea* of warlockry.

Hanner couldn't figure it out and gave up trying. He turned his attention back to Shella.

"Well, I don't think you need to worry too much, Shella. You're a warlock now, that's all. All this—the dreams, the strange magic, trouble with your old magic—that's all the same sort of thing that the other warlocks have been through. All of it except what you did to Thellesh; no one else did that."

"Were any of the others witches?"

"No," Hanner admitted, "but two of them are wizards."

Shella drew in her breath, her eyes widening again. "Oh," she said. "*Wizards* can be warlocks?"

"Sort of. It interferes with their old magic, just as it did with your witchcraft. Or almost; they can still do a *few* spells."

"That's so *strange!*"

Hanner sighed. "I suppose so. Now, if you can stand the crowd, I think we should go back to the other room, where my uncle, Lord Faran, is getting things organized."

"All right," she said.

She and Hanner were just turning around when someone knocked on the front door.

Alris hopped onto a chair by one of the front windows and pressed her cheek to the panes so that she could peer sideways for a look at their visitor.

"It's a guardsman," she said. "Should I call Uncle Faran?"

"*One* guardsman?" Hanner asked. "Just one?"

"I just see one," Alris confirmed.

Hanner frowned and crossed to the door. He opened it a crack.

The crowd in the street had fallen silent, presumably waiting to see what would happen—as Alris had said, a single guardsman stood just outside, inside the gate.

At first, distracted by the yellow tunic of a soldier, Hanner failed to recognize the man's face, but before the new arrival could speak the familiar features registered, and Hanner flung the door wide.

"Yorn!" he said. "Come in, come in!"

The soldier obeyed, closing the door gently behind himself. "Am I still welcome?" he asked.

"Of course!" Hanner said, clapping Yorn on the shoulder. "As long as you're not here to order us all into exile."

"Uh . . . actually, I was . . . those orders . . . that's why I'm here," Yorn said.

Hanner frowned. "We already chased away Captain Naral and an entire squad," he said. "Why would they send just you?"

"Oh, that's not what I meant!" Yorn said hastily. "I mean, they told us to find any warlocks we knew of and order them out of the city, and that was when I realized I couldn't stay in the city guard anymore, not until the lords change their minds. And I didn't have anywhere to go but here." He looked around. "Is everyone else gone?" He noticed the others and said, "I mean, besides these three."

"No," Hanner said, "they're still here. But first, this is Shella." He told her, "This is Yorn of Ethshar. He's a warlock, too."

"Not much of one, really," Yorn said.

"This is Mavi of Newmarket," Hanner said. "She's *not* a warlock, just a friend."

Yorn bowed. "And I know Lady Alris," he said.

"Shella and I were just about to join the others," Hanner said. He beckoned for Yorn and Shella to follow, then opened the door to the dining hall.

The murmur of voices and the scent of crowded bodies spilled out.

"Gods, there are a *lot* of them!" Yorn said as he followed Hanner into the crowded room.

"Thirty-two," Lord Faran announced. "And the apprentice witch is thirty-three, and you, sir—are you a warlock?"

"I am," Yorn admitted.

"Thirty-four," Faran said.

"Against a city of thousands," Rudhira said.

"Most of them won't trouble us," Faran said. "Just the guard."

"How many is that?" Othisen asked.

"Eight thousand," Yorn replied, speaking up loud and clear.

A horrified silence fell.

Chapter Twenty-seven

Eight thousand soldiers?" someone squeaked at last. "That's what they tell us," Yorn confirmed.

"It's supposed to be *ten* thousand," Lord Faran said, "but Lord Azrad has never bothered to put in the money to get the guard to full strength."

"There's no reason he should," Yorn said. "There are plenty of us as it is."

"I didn't know there were ten thousand people in the *World*," Othisen said.

"Oh, there are *hundreds* of thousands in Ethshar," Yorn said. "Nobody knows the exact number."

"The wizards might," Rudhira suggested.

"My master says that if it weren't for the wizards, there couldn't be a city this big," Shella said. "It's wizardry that keeps the water clean and keeps the food good through the winter and empties the privies where the sewers don't go."

"The theurgists do some of it," an elderly woman Hanner didn't recognize protested mildly.

"This is all very interesting," Lord Faran said, "but if we could get back to business, there are thirty-four of us here, of varying abilities. All of us can move small objects by sheer force of will, but some of us can do more than that, and I think it would be wise to find out just who can do what, and how well. Now, who here can fly?"

A dozen voices spoke up, and hands were raised; Lord Faran shouted over the babble, "If you can fly, please go to *that* end of the room!" He pointed at the windows. "If you *cannot* fly, go to *that* end!" He pointed at the ballroom. "If you don't know, please stand near the table!"

"I can lift myself off the ground," said the woman who had mentioned theurgists, "but I can't really *fly* so much as *float*."

Faran looked at her, then said, "What's your name?"

"Alladia of Shiphaven."

"Alladia. Thank you. For now, just stand near the table." She obeyed.

Shella also went to stand by the table, and Hanner accompanied her. He found himself standing next to Alladia.

"I'm Lord Hanner," he said. "I'm pleased to meet you."

"I could wish it were under other circumstances," Alladia said, looking around as the others sorted themselves out.

"You'd rather not be a warlock?" Hanner asked.

"That's right," Alladia said.

This was interesting; Hanner wondered whether he could gain any insight into Alris or the others. "Is it just because of the overlord's threats?" he asked. "Suppose no one knew—wouldn't you like it then?"

Alladia turned to look him in the eye. "No, I wouldn't," she said.

"Why not? After all, you have magic now, without even serving an apprenticeship."

"I had magic *before*," Alladia replied angrily. "I was a priestess!"

"A theurgist?" Understanding dawned. Warlockry interfered with witchcraft and wizardry; presumably it interfered with theurgy, as well.

"That's right. And a good one, if I do say so myself. But ever since this *thing* got inside my head, the gods won't listen to me. The simplest invocation goes unanswered. I tried to consult Unniel to find out what was wrong, and even *she* ignores my prayers!"

"Unniel?" The name was vaguely familiar.

"Unniel the Discerning. She's one of the easiest of all the gods to contact; any halfway competent apprentice can speak to Unniel. But since the night before last, *I* can't! In the past I've successfully summoned Asham and Govet, and now I can't even call Unniel!"

"And you think it's because you're a warlock?"

"Of course. What else could it be? Something's put this curse on us, and it's cut me off from the gods. Before I could open gateways to another world, heal the sick, reveal any secret; now I can send plates flying about the room. Do *you* consider that a good exchange?"

"No," Hanner admitted.

Before he could say any more, Faran called for attention.

"I count ten who can't fly, thirteen who can, eleven who don't know," he announced. "Let's see if we can sort out those eleven. Hanner, if you would step aside?"

Hanner glanced at Shella and Alladia, but then stepped away from the table.

"In fact, Hanner," Faran said, "if you don't mind, would you wait in the parlor with Alris and Mavi? And if Manrin and Ulpen come back down, send them in."

"You only want warlocks in here," Hanner said.

"That's right. No need to crowd things any more than necessary."

Hanner hesitated. This was a moment when he could admit that he was a warlock after all—and he really *should* admit it, shouldn't he? Sooner or later the truth would come out.

But if it did, he would be either exiled or put to death, or would find himself caught in Uncle Faran's schemes permanently, and he would never get back to his own bed, his own rooms, in the Palace.

He bowed, patted Shella reassuringly on the shoulder, and left the room, closing the door behind him.

In the parlor, Alris asked, "What are they doing in there?"

"Sorting warlocks," Hanner replied. "Seeing who can do what."

Mavi shuddered. Hanner looked at her, startled.

"Oh, I'm sorry," she said. "I know they're just people, that they didn't *ask* for this spell or power or whatever it is, but they make me nervous. Even your uncle, and poor Pancha. It's just so . . ." She turned up her palms, unable to find the right word.

And here was another reason not to admit he was a warlock, Hanner thought. He did not want to make Mavi nervous, nor did he want her to find him repulsive.

He hadn't realized she felt this way.

"The theurgist said Pancha wasn't even human anymore," Mavi said.

"Alladia said that?"

Mavi blinked at him. "No—who's Alladia?"

"The theurgist turned warlock in there," Hanner said, pointing at the dining-hall door. "Who did *you* mean?"

"The theurgist who tried to cure Pancha this morning," Mavi explained. "He said the goddess he summoned didn't even think Pancha was still human!"

That, Hanner thought, would indeed be a reason to find warlocks unpleasant to be around. He wondered why the goddess had thought so, and whether that was why Alladia couldn't summon Unniel. The pact made at the end of the Great War said only humans could invoke the gods.

"And the dreams," Mavi continued. "*Why* do they have those dreams? Do they mean something?"

"They don't *all* have the dreams," Hanner said.

"But *most* of them did. And they sound so terrible—falling *and* burning *and* being buried alive. It's just . . . I don't know, excessive."

"I suppose it is," Hanner agreed, glancing at the closed door.

There was a sudden loud thump from the other room; Mavi started. Hanner glanced at the closed door of the dining hall, but otherwise didn't move.

What he *wanted* to do was reach out with his will and open the door, to see what was happening—but he refused to use his magic.

If it was his at all. No one knew what had caused the Night of Madness; all this warlockry might just be something some mad wizard had done.

"Do you think it's permanent?" Mavi asked.

Startled, Hanner turned back to her. "Do I think what's permanent?"

"This warlockry. Maybe it's just temporary."

"That would certainly simplify matters," Hanner said.

"I stayed around today, hoping it would all just *stop*," Mavi said, staring at the closed door. "I wanted to be here, to help when it ended—I thought some of them would be upset. And I thought I could take Pancha home. But it isn't stopping."

"No, it isn't," Hanner agreed. "At least, not yet."

But it could, at any time. They couldn't know. That was the thing about magic—it didn't have to make sense. Sometimes it *did* make sense, and it was predictable enough that magicians could use it, and the whole city could rely on it, but sometimes it was just bizarre. A wizard could make a living creature out of powdered bone and feathers, or put a man to sleep with a pinch of dust and a single word—where was the logic in that? More than a hundred years ago a simple fire-lighting spell went wrong in the Small Kingdoms, and the resulting tower of flame was reportedly still burning, without fuel—how could it be? Why would virgin's tears work in certain spells, when the same woman's tears shed after her wedding night would be as useless as well water?

Wizardry was the strangest, but where was the logic in sorcery, where certain devices would perform their functions flawlessly for centuries, and then simply stop? And other devices that appeared perfectly identical didn't work at all, or did something different.

Or theurgy—why did the gods only grant certain requests? Why would they listen to some people and not others? Why did demons sometimes answer theurgical invocations?

Magic was not far from madness—and in the case of warlockry, the distinction had initially been invisible. The warlocks who went rampaging through the city that first night had certainly appeared mad.

So how could they know what warlockry would do? Uncle Faran was in there, trying to make sense of it—but what if there was no sense to be made? What if it were to simply vanish again, as abruptly as it had appeared? What if it changed form? What if there were another Night of Madness, but affecting an entirely different assortment of people?

But then, all of life was like that, really. Even when Hanner had been sleeping in his own bed in the Palace, as safe as anyone could be, at any moment some mad magician's spell could have turned him to stone, or transformed him into a cat, or simply killed him.

Even without magic, his own heart could just stop, or he could catch a fever, as his mother had, and be dead in a sixnight.

One just had to make the best of the situation, forge ahead as best one could, try to learn how things worked, and accept it when the rules changed and learn the new rules.

Warlockry wasn't any different. It could vanish at any time, but while it was here, it would be useful to know how it worked and what it could do.

He should be in there with Uncle Faran, studying the situation, he thought—but then he looked at Mavi's eyes, dark brown and shining.

Uncle Faran had chased him out, and now Uncle Faran would have to do without him for a while.

"Would you like me to walk you home?" he asked. "Get away from the warlocks?"

She smiled. "I'd like that very much," she said.

Alris made a gagging noise. "You two," she said. "What if I came along? That would ruin all your fun, wouldn't it?"

"No, of course not!" Mavi said, turning and reaching out a welcoming arm. "We'd be happy to have you join us."

Hanner didn't say anything at first; he was too busy struggling not to glare at his sister.

Alris looked at him.

"We'd be glad of your company," Hanner managed at last.

She snorted. "No, you wouldn't. And I don't want to walk all the way to Newmarket, anyway, and someone should be here in case more warlocks show up, or Uncle Faran wants to know where you've gone, or those wizards come back down here looking for help."

"I'm sure Bern's around somewhere," Hanner said.

"No, you go ahead," Alris said with a wave. "I'll stay here."

"As you please." Hanner turned to Mavi. "Shall we?"

Chapter Twenty-eight

As Hanner and Mavi stepped out the door into the streets of Ethshar a score of wizards were gathered around a table, discussing the situation, in a place that was not part of Ethshar, nor even of the World.

"We still have no idea what caused it," a white-haired wizard said. "I have had a dozen of my best people working every divination we can find for the past two days, approaching the question from every angle we can think of, and we haven't learned a thing about its origins. That magical aura around the Source blocks everything."

"We have consulted the dead, and with the aid of several theurgists we have consulted the gods," a cadaverous figure with a shaven skull said. "They know nothing of it."

"I've spoken with Irith the Flyer, and of course with Valder," a beautiful woman who appeared to be only in her twenties said. "They don't remember anything that might help. If anyone knows of any other immortals who aren't wizards, please tell me. And I've sent a message to Fendel the Great, but as yet he hasn't replied."

"We have some thirty warlocks aiding us in our experiments," another wizard reported. "Most volunteered; a few are prisoners taken on the Night of Madness who were, at our request, sentenced to serve us. So far, while we are learning a great deal about how warlockry operates, we don't have any idea what it *is*, where it came from, or whether it will remain as it is, go away, or change into something else."

The litany continued—although they had learned a great deal about the events surrounding its appearance, nothing the wizards had tried had revealed anything important about the nature of warlockry itself.

"I've gone through the histories and the forbidden lore. Nothing like this is recorded anywhere."

"We spoke with half a dozen demonologists, and questioned a few demons ourselves, but learned nothing."

"We have charted the paths of some two hundred of those who were summoned on the Night of Madness, and have found no subtle deviations, no hidden patterns—they all simply headed toward the Source by the most direct routes available to them."

"We have studied the histories of a randomly chosen sample of known warlocks and have found no links, nothing to indicate why these people were chosen while others were not. We have noticed that there is a slight tendency for a family with a warlock in it to have more than one—that is, a warlock's cousin or sibling is more likely to be a warlock than the average person is—but what trait in the blood might explain this we cannot determine. We have also found that magicians of every sort were afflicted."

"Wizards, too?" someone asked.

"Wizards, too," the speaker replied. "We are currently attempting to divine exactly who in the Guild has become a warlock."

"None of *us*, surely?"

"That remains to be determined."

That created a stir, and for a moment the formal recitation was interrupted. Finally a red-robed figure at the head of the table rose to his feet and spoke.

"While we must continue our investigations," he said, "I

think it would be expedient to also begin to take action in certain cases where it is clearly appropriate."

"Lord Azrad would certainly like us to do something," Ithinia of the Isle said, from her seat near the far end of the table. "He expected me to attend him yesterday."

"Lord Azrad presumes too much," the red-robed wizard said. "We are not ready to enforce his sentences of exile or join in any campaign of annihilation, nor do we have time to waste in listening to his complaints. However, by our own rules, we are bound to restrain forbidden uses of magic. We have not yet established whether warlockry itself is forbidden by any of our covenants, but there have certainly been uses of it, and instances of its presence, that violate Guild laws. It is time we began to deal with these on a case-by-case basis." He took a deep breath, then continued, "For one thing, it may be educational to see whether we *can* deal with them—it may be that warlocks are more formidable than we think." He pointed at one of the others. "You, Kaligir—choose a warlock who is unquestionably guilty of serious crimes and send someone to deal with him. Let us see just what happens when wizard and warlock meet in combat."

"*Any* warlock?" Kaligir asked.

"Use your judgment, man."

"Rather, use a divination," the white-haired wizard suggested.

"An excellent suggestion," the red-robed wizard agreed.

"Very well," Kaligir said, slumping in his chair.

"And, Kaligir," the man in red said, "I expect a report—remember, a part of your task is to discover just how great a threat to us these warlocks truly are."

"As you say," Kaligir replied. He straightened, then stood. "I had best get on with it, then."

"As had we all," the red-robed wizard said. "I will remain here to coordinate, but the rest of you, begone, and press onward your researches!"

Robes rustled, chairs creaked, and the wizards arose and scattered.

*   *   *

Shemder Parl's son watched his intended victim with an unpleasant smile. Kirris was going about her business, hanging her laundry out on the line in the courtyard behind the house she shared with her husband and two young children, blithely unaware of her old suitor's presence on a nearby rooftop.

Shemder debated just what he would do to her. Perhaps a roofing tile could fall and break her skull.

It was a shame, he thought, that he had not had this wonderful magic a month ago, when she bore her second daughter; if he had caught her in childbirth he could have done something really slow and unpleasant without fear of detection.

Perhaps a roofing tile might cause an injury that would not kill her instantly, and he could then find some way to ensure that she never recovered.

But that was risky; her husband might hire a magician to treat her, and the magician might notice some invisible sign that warlockry was involved. Shemder did not know just what traces warlockry left, if any; he knew there were none visible to an ordinary person, but magicians could often see things others could not—as he could see things now that ordinary people could not.

A shadow fell across his vision, blocking the light of the setting sun, and he looked up.

As if summoned by his thoughts, a magician was standing in the air beside him, looking down at him—a man in blue robes. Shemder didn't know much about magic, but he guessed this must be a wizard—demonologists wore black or perhaps red, theurgists wore white or gold, sorcerers didn't wear robes, and he didn't think a witch could stand in midair so effortlessly.

"You are Shemder Parl's son?" the magician asked.

"No!" Shemder said. "My name's Kelder. Why? Who's this Shemder you're looking for?"

The magician hesitated. Shemder did not; he reached out

with his own magic and found the man's heart, beating steadily in his chest.

It was harder than usual; something was in the way, some other sort of magic. Shemder did not let that stop him.

A simple squeeze, and the magician gasped, eyes widening, arms flung wide; he toppled backward, tumbled down the sloping tile roof, and flopped over the eaves.

A second later Shemder heard the dull crunch of the body landing in the alleyway below.

He hesitated only a moment, wondering who the magician had been and who had sent him—had some friend or relative of one of the half-dozen people he had already killed hired a magical avenger?

If so, whoever it was had chosen the wrong hired hero.

Perhaps Kirris or her husband had made a contract for magical protection? They couldn't have known about Shemder's plans, but young parents sometimes did foolishly extravagant things out of worry about their infant children.

Either way, this rooftop was no longer somewhere Shemder wanted to stay. Kirris was safe for now—though once he knew what was going on, and how to deal with it, Shemder intended to come back for her.

Staying nearby after killing a wizard, though—Shemder wasn't fool enough to do *that*! He slid down the roof, on the far side from where the magician had fallen, and lowered himself over the edge. Then he caught himself in the air and settled slowly and gently to the ground, landing in the deserted street—though he knew he couldn't count on it staying deserted. Someone might happen along at any minute, hurrying home to supper, and Shemder did not want to be in the area when someone glanced in that alley and found a dead wizard. He turned, took a step toward the corner . . .

And felt himself shrinking, twisting, his skin crawling as fur grew, a tail thrusting out behind him, his clothes vanishing and the warm air against his skin. The houses reared up hugely around him, towering over him.

He squeaked in terror and scampered for shelter, running

on all fours. He scurried into the shadowy corner beside someone's front steps, then paused, once he was out of sight of most of the street, to try to see what had happened to him.

It was hard to think, but he struggled to hold on to himself to see what had become of him, to think of a way he might survive and undo whatever it was.

He knew he had somehow been transformed—that wizard must have had a spell of some kind that did this. He looked down at his paws, curled his tail around . . .

His tail was long and thin and bare, ending in a point. His paws had long, thin claws. He could see whiskers when he wiggled his nose. He measured his height against the steps, and concluded that he was now a rat. A large brown one.

That was bad, that was very bad, but it could be worse. He was still alive. He remembered who he was. And . . . was he still a warlock?

He found a pebble, and concentrated on it with all his might, trying to see it in that special way that let warlocks move things—and nothing happened. The pebble lay where it was.

He heard voices, human voices, and ducked back into the corner, baring his teeth.

The voices passed, but he waited several minutes, just to be sure.

He could hear rustlings and thumpings and the other sounds of the city, of the neighborhood going about its ordinary business, but he had trouble, in his transformed condition, identifying them and locating them. He was also distracted by smells—rats, he discovered, had a far better sense of smell than humans did.

At last, though, he decided the time had come to venture out. He was hungry and frightened, and wanted to get somewhere safer than a corner in the street. He could see no openings in the foundation of the house he crouched beside, nowhere he could take shelter.

His own room was only a few blocks away. If he could

get inside there, he would be safe. He couldn't unlock the door in his present condition, especially since the purse containing the key had vanished along with his clothes, but perhaps he could find a rat-sized entrance.

And the spell might wear off.

He crept out of the corner, then dashed forward, intending to make a run for the next street—and found himself confronted by a pair of suede slippers.

He looked up and found a robed man staring down at him.

"Shemder Parl's son," the man said. "This is very interesting—it seems the structure in your brain that makes you a warlock is still there in your new form, though greatly reduced in size, but it's completely inert."

Shemder squeaked furiously and bared his teeth. A rat's vocabulary was, he found, rather limited.

"Now," the wizard said, "what would happen if you were restored to human form? Would it remain inert?"

Shemder squeaked again.

"We'll have to try the experiment on someone, but I'm afraid that it won't be you," the wizard said. "You're too dangerous. I would never have thought you could kill a respectable wizard so quickly, despite a handful of protections and wards! I'm going to have a ghastly time explaining his death to his family, and to the Guild!"

As he spoke he drew a dagger, and Shemder began backing away.

He was just turning to flee when the wizard spoke a *word*, and flung the dagger.

The blade impaled the rat that had been the man called Shemder Parl's son, pinning him to the earth; the rat twisted, trying to escape the blade, trying to see some way to remove it, but succeeding only in injuring himself further. He squirmed in agony, and in his extremity forgot who he was, forgot that he had ever been anything more than a rat. He writhed, and the world around him dimmed, and he knew it was not because the sun was down.

And then the rat was dead, and Kaligir of the New Quarter stood looking down at it.

It remained a rat; sometimes, when Asherel's Transformation was done quickly from a distance like this, death broke the spell. Kaligir had thought that the rat might turn back into Shemder.

That it hadn't simplified matters; disposing of a dead rat was much easier than disposing of a dead person.

Of course, Shemder had apparently had the morals of a rat all along. Kaligir had chosen him because Fendel's Divination had named him as the warlock who had killed more innocents than any other in the World. His death was no loss.

The death of poor Lopin, on the other hand, was a tragedy. Kaligir frowned.

There was no longer any question—the warlocks were dangerous. Shemder had reached through Lopin's protective spells as if they were hardly there.

This was not reassuring news that he would be bringing back to the rest of the Guild.

Kaligir kicked the dead rat into the gutter, then turned to go.

Chapter Twenty-nine

As Lord Hanner trotted through the night, back along High Street through the New City, his heart was light and his features were brightened with a smile— until he neared the mansion now known as Warlock House.

Although there had been some uneasy moments when he and Mavi left and walked past the waiting, watching people gathered out front, a few shouts of "We were just visiting! We aren't warlocks!" had gotten them safely to the corner.

No one had followed them, and once they were out of sight of the house the city had seemed almost normal.

Oh, there were still a few burned-out buildings, and more guardsmen on the streets than usual, but in general things were back to what they should be. He and Mavi had strolled to Newmarket without incident, where he had had a delightful supper with Mavi's family. Much of the time he had been able to forget all about warlocks and exile orders and all the other unpleasantness of the past few days. Even when Mavi's parents had asked about his uncle's collection of warlocks, and had spoken with horror of the depredations that befell their neighbors on the Night of Madness, he had been able to remain happily detached, as if none of it concerned him.

The mob in front of his uncle's house, though, reminded him that it concerned him very much.

There were more of them than before, and they had torches. Torches were hardly unreasonable, since full night had fallen, but there seemed to be more of them than any reasonable need for light would justify.

And they were no longer standing out in the street, just watching; now they were pressed up against the fence, leaning through it, just a few feet from the front door and several windows.

Hanner's smile vanished.

"Where did you take them?" someone shouted.

"Give me back my son!"

Hanner stopped where he was, a block away, and decided that he was not going to walk in the front door. He would see if there was a rear gate—he didn't remember seeing one, but surely there was a servants' entrance somewhere. If he couldn't find one, he would climb the garden wall.

Or, perhaps, fly over it, though he had yet to attempt to fly under his own power.

Instead of continuing on High Street he turned right on West Second Street, then left on Lower Street and left again on Coronet, and walked up the block.

There was no torch-bearing mob on this side of the house.

Light spilled from the corner, burying the garden wall and the mansion's west face in shadow.

He didn't see any doors or gates, any more than he had two nights before. The garden wall was solid brick. He looked up at the top, a foot or two over his head.

He couldn't climb that. The brick was smooth and solidly mortared; he couldn't find toeholds or fingerholds in the dark. He could call for help and hope a warlock heard him and helped him over the wall before that mob out front heard him and came to investigate.

Or maybe he could fly over it. He *was* a warlock, and the power was there inside him, eager to be used.

Just thinking about it made it surge up, ready and waiting; he could *feel* it, could almost see it.

But how did one fly? He had seen Rudhira and the others do it often enough, but he hadn't really *observed* it.

Thinking that, he became consciously aware for the first time that he could perceive things he hadn't before, that he could use his magic to sense things—it wasn't seeing, and it wasn't feeling, but it was almost both. He realized this must be what Shella had meant when she talked about studying Thellesh's injuries with something that wasn't witch sight.

He could feel/see the bricks that made up the wall, the mortar that held them together, the grainy texture of the mortar, the smooth glaze on the bricks . . .

But it was dark, and he wasn't touching the wall; his hands were at his sides.

He blinked, and the perception faded slightly.

He didn't need to know how the wall was put together, he just needed to get over it. He still couldn't sense any toeholds, even with this new ability.

He turned his attention to himself, to see whether he could figure out how to fly. It should be easy—just lift himself off the ground. He had experimented with his magic a little in secret, earlier in the day, and he could move small objects around, but he hadn't tried lifting himself.

It wasn't as easy.

It wasn't so much the weight, although he had never tried lifting anything even close to his own size; instead, he realized, it was because he couldn't sense a relationship between himself and the object he was trying to move.

That was how a warlock moved things. He had done it without understanding it before, without being aware of how he was doing it, but now he saw it clearly. His new sense showed him the relationship in space between himself and the object he wanted to affect, and then he manipulated that relationship—warlockry was all a matter of using this new sense to find the magical connections between himself and the rest of the World, and then forcing them to change. He had caught that cruet by blocking its connection to the floor.

But finding the magical connections between himself and himself didn't seem to work.

Rudhira and the others had done it, though. There had to be a way.

He studied himself with his newly recognized warlock sight, and finally figured out what he would have to do. In order to fly, Hanner saw, a warlock didn't move himself; he moved the rest of the World.

Hanner reached out and tried to do that, to move the street and wall away—and caught himself just before he fell over backward.

He straightened up, frowned, looked down at his feet, and tried again, concentrating on pressing the ground away from the soles of his sandals.

He rose unsteadily for an inch or two, then wobbled and started to fall backward. Again, he used his warlockry to catch himself.

He could *catch* himself easily enough, he thought. It was annoying; it was as if his magic worked better when he didn't think about it.

But if he didn't think about it, he couldn't fly!

He heard footsteps and turned to see a patrolling guardsman marching toward him. Quickly he tugged up his tunic and untied his breeches, to provide the obvious excuse for why someone was standing inches from a blank wall at night.

"Hai!" the soldier called. "Go find somewhere better!"

"Sorry!" Hanner called, retying his breeches. "Drank too much ale at supper."

"Well, get rid of it somewhere else."

"Yes, sir."

He hesitated, then took a step toward Merchant Avenue. The guardsman marched on.

Hanner turned back to the wall, studying it with his warlock sense, wondering whether he could somehow brace against it to stay upright while he lifted himself over it. Bricks and mortar, bricks and . . .

"Oh," he said.

The service entrance was right there, a few yards to his right, a wooden gate with an iron latch. How had he missed it?

He hurried to it, reached out—and realized he couldn't see any gate. The brick was solid and unbroken . . .

To normal eyes. To a warlock, there was a gate.

At last Hanner figured it out. Uncle Faran had had his gate enchanted, had a protective illusion put on it. He reached out and felt the "wall."

Sure enough, it was wood, not brick. The illusion wasn't so complete it fooled his fingers. He found the latch by feel, and tried to open it.

It was locked. He could sense the mechanism, a bolt that could be worked from the inside. There was a slot below it; presumably Bern carried a tool that could reach through the slot and work the bolt from the outside.

Hanner had no such tool—but he was a warlock.

The bolt slid back, and the gate opened, and he was inside. He closed the gate carefully, hoping he hadn't disrupted the undoubtedly costly illusion, and headed for a door from the garden into the house.

A moment later he was inside, making his way along the central hallway. He could hear voices ahead.

He found half a dozen people in the candlelit front parlor; they turned to look at him as he entered.

"Lord Hanner!" Rudhira said from a chair by one of the front windows where she had been watching the crowd in the street outside. "I'm glad you got back inside safely."

"I'm not sure how safe it really is," Hanner replied as he looked around. Besides Rudhira and himself, the room held Alladia, Othisen, and three other warlocks whose names he didn't recall immediately. "Where's Uncle Faran?" he asked.

"Upstairs with the wizards," Rudhira said. "He has us on guard duty for now, making sure those people outside don't do any harm." She pointed at the top of the window by her chair. "Someone caught us off guard and threw a brick through there about an hour ago, but we fixed it. You can hardly tell the glass was ever broken."

"You fixed it?" Hanner stared at the panes, which appeared completely intact. "How?"

One of the others giggled, and Othisen said gently, "We're warlocks, remember?"

"Yes, but . . . I know you can move things, but I didn't know you could fix them."

"We can do a lot of things," Rudhira said. "Move things, break things, unbreak them. We can make light, as you've seen." She held up an orange-glowing hand to demonstrate. "We've been teaching each other. We can open locks and heal wounds and heat things up or cool them down. We can harden things, or dissolve them, or set them on fire. We can see things too small to be seen without magic, see the insides of things, and feel things without touching them. It's *wonderful*, my lord! I thought it was good enough just being able to throw things around and fly, but there's so much more!"

"That's . . . that's wonderful," Hanner said, hoping he sounded more convinced than he felt.

He didn't know how to do all that—but presumably, if everyone else had learned these things, he could learn them. All he had to do was admit he was a warlock, throw in his lot with the others—and put himself at risk of exile or death, not to mention being something that Mavi found repulsive.

It was tempting, all the same—he could feel the magic in him calling out to be used, to be trained and built up.

But he wasn't going to do it.

At least, not yet.

"That girl, Shella, who was apprenticed to a witch," Othisen said, "she said we could make more warlocks, and sort of showed us how, but we didn't have anyone to experiment on."

"Lady Alris wouldn't volunteer," Rudhira said. "And you weren't here."

"And I'm not volunteering now," Hanner said, heading off any such suggestion and hoping none of these people were as attuned to warlockry's presence as Shella had been. "But what about those people out there?" he asked with a wave at the windows. "Maybe you could change one of *them*. That might convince them warlocks aren't monsters."

"Them?" Rudhira glanced toward the window, and the drapes flapped aside, though there was no wind in the closed room. The glow from her hand vanished. "I wouldn't do them the favor!" she said angrily.

"Besides," Othisen said, "you need to be very close to do it. Touching, if possible."

"Still, it's interesting that it's possible," Hanner said. "And you can learn different . . . different spells from each other." He didn't really think "spells" was the right word, but he couldn't think of a better one. "That means that if this stays around, warlocks could take on apprentices and train them, just like other magicians."

"Yes!" Rudhira said.

"I suppose that's true," Alladia said slowly.

"I'm so glad you found me in the Wizards' Quarter, my lord," Rudhira said. "Without you I wouldn't have come here, and I wouldn't have met Lord Faran, and I might never have learned all these things."

"I'm happy you're pleased," Hanner said, a bit taken

aback by this enthusiasm. After all, there was an angry mob just outside, ready to throw more bricks at a moment's notice; it hardly struck Hanner as an enviable situation. It felt as if they were besieged—and that was without even mentioning the sentence of exile hanging over their heads, and the possibility that Lord Azrad or the Wizards' Guild might decide even exile wasn't enough and demand their deaths.

This was certainly not his idea of a decent way to live, trapped here, awaiting an uncertain fate, and it was no improvement at all over his previous existence—but then, he'd never been a Camptown streetwalker.

"Lord Faran's quite a man," Alladia said.

"He's saved us all," Rudhira said. "Without him I'd never have had the nerve to fight back. I'd be an exile outside the walls by now, begging travelers for crusts of bread."

Hanner somehow found that unlikely; he couldn't imagine Rudhira giving up without a fight, and her warlockry was the most powerful he had yet seen. If she had accepted exile, he still thought she would probably have done something a little less passive than begging to earn her keep.

"He's had experience," Hanner said.

"Yes, of course!" Alladia said. "It's obvious when he speaks."

"He's a natural leader," Rudhira said. "You're a lucky young man to be his nephew."

"I'm sure I am," Hanner said. He did not add anything more, though he was tempted.

He had had experience himself—not at leading, but at being the Great Man's nephew. He was used to living in his uncle's shadow, and knew that anything he might say other than vague agreement could easily be misinterpreted. A disparaging word about Uncle Faran would mark him as a disloyal and jealous ingrate, while an injudicious, overly positive one would brand him a sycophant with no self-respect. If he were to point out that he, not Faran, had first thought of gathering warlocks together as a force for order and mutual defense, he'd be seen as a braggart.

He had a knack for saying the wrong thing, but right now he really didn't *want* to say the wrong thing. So he said nothing more on the subject.

"I think I'll go upstairs," he said instead. "To talk to my uncle."

"Tell him we're still guarding the house," Othisen said. "No one's getting past Rudhira and me!"

"I'll tell him," Hanner said, turning away.

He didn't mention that *he* had gotten in while they were on watch.

As he headed for the stairs he glanced back and saw the six warlocks gazing out the windows at the angry crowd outside. This couldn't go on indefinitely, Hanner knew. Something would have to be done.

Outside, Kennan stared in through the window at the people in the parlor. The redheaded whore was there, and the tall old woman, and the farmboy.

And the fat nobleman, Lord Hanner, had spoken to them, but he was gone now.

Those people had taken his son, he was certain of it, and somehow he was going to see them pay.

Chapter Thirty

Lord Faran had reclaimed his own bed, naturally, so Hanner awoke on the morning of the seventh day of Summerheat in one of the guest rooms, where he had shared a bed with Othisen. The farmboy had snored gently, but never moved once he was asleep; Hanner had on occasion shared beds with worse, when visiting.

He arose without disturbing his roommate and made his

way downstairs, to see whether the house was still besieged, and whether Bern was serving breakfast.

Four weary warlocks were in the parlor when Hanner walked past—Yorn, Hinda, one he didn't recognize . . .

And Kirsha, the girl who had gotten five lashes for theft and vandalism. Hanner stopped dead in his tracks and said, "What are you doing here?"

"Standing guard," Hinda said proudly.

Kirsha looked up. "Didn't you know, my lord?"

"How . . . ?" Hanner began, but then stopped; he knew perfectly well what they were guarding against. He had been asking why Kirsha was there.

Yorn glanced at Hanner and called, "Three bricks, a stone, and a flung torch so far this morning, my lord. All safely deflected."

Hanner asked, "Did you chase away the people who threw them?"

Yorn shook his head. "No," he said. "We four aren't all that strong; all the strong ones are asleep. And I thought it might just make them mad."

"Good thought," Hanner said. He hesitated, then asked, "What's Kirsha doing here?"

Yorn looked at Hanner, then at the girl, then back at Hanner. "She arrived last night," he said. "Along with Ilvin, here."

Ilvin, the warlock Hanner hadn't recognized, bowed slightly in acknowledgment. Hanner nodded in response, then returned to Kirsha. "But she . . . on the Night of Madness . . ."

"I went a little mad," Kirsha said. "Yes, I did. And you people caught me, and brought me to the magistrate, and he had me flogged and sent me home—and when the neighbors found out I was back, and that I was a warlock, I had to leave again unless I wanted to kill somebody, or let them kill me. I didn't want either one, so I came here." She patted Ilvin on the shoulder. "Ilvin's my cousin. He only realized he was a warlock yesterday."

"He's welcome, of course," Hanner said. "But you . . ."

"She's a warlock," Yorn said before Kirsha could speak. "She's one of us now. She made a mistake and she paid for it, but now she's come here for refuge, like the rest of us."

"You don't hold a grudge?" Hanner asked her.

Kirsha turned up a palm. "You did what you knew was right. I'd have been happier if you had let me go, or let me join your group, but you weren't unfair."

"We healed her," Hinda said.

"Well, Desset and Shella did most of it," Yorn said. "They were on guard when Kirsha got here, but the rest of us were here and did what we could to help. It was a chance for us all to learn how."

Hanner remembered Desset well, since he had seen her just hours earlier, when she had awakened screaming from another of those peculiar nightmares. She was a plump, dark-eyed woman who had been in the party that had captured Kirsha in the first place. She was one of the three who had learned to fly right away, along with Rudhira and Varrin the Weaver.

She had seen the damage Kirsha did, the smashed shop windows and stolen jewelry; if she had helped heal the scars left by the whip, it wasn't out of ignorance.

Criminals weren't supposed to be magically healed after a flogging—the long-lasting discomfort was intended to be a reminder of crime's consequences, and healing it theoretically lessened the effectiveness of the penalty. Wealthy lawbreakers, those who were willing to pay enough, could generally find some magician who could be "fooled" about the nature of the injury, of course.

But that wasn't what had happened here. The warlocks had healed one of their own, simply because she *was* one of them. They were uniting, leaving their old lives behind and forming a new community.

And Hanner somehow suspected they would not appreciate it if he, who did not admit to being one of them, objected.

Besides, Kirsha *had* gone a little mad when that first . . . whatever-it-was had struck and filled her with magic. She had thought she was dreaming, and had not meant anyone any harm. That was clearly an extenuating circumstance.

And she had been cast out by her neighbors, presumably by her own family. Hanner could *definitely* sympathize with that—after another night here he really missed his own bed in the Palace.

"Good," he said. "We're glad to have you. Guard well!" Then he waved and went on into breakfast.

He had missed Kirsha's arrival and healing, but even so, Hanner had had a long, busy night. The people in the street out front had been throwing things every so often, shouting, and occasionally charging the gate ever since Hanner's return; one old man, that persistent fellow who seemed to have been there longer than anyone else, had appeared to be leading them. The watch in the parlor to ward off these attacks was now permanent, with all the sufficiently capable warlocks in the house taking turns at it.

Manrin and Ulpen had attempted to put up magical wards around the rest of the house during the night, using what wizardry they could still make work, and the front gate, which was ordinarily left unlocked, was now sealed with three separate runes—though they were not certain how effective these would be, given their lessened wizardly abilities.

Hanner had not been involved in any of that; he had mostly stayed upstairs and out of the way, but he had been aware it was being done.

They truly were under siege here, trapped in the house until the situation improved—but at least now, with the wards and runes and the guards standing vigilant in the parlor, they were safe for the moment.

Apparently safe, anyway. For the moment everything appeared peaceful, but by Yorn's account it hadn't been for long.

And not everything upstairs had been peaceful during the night, either. A few of the warlocks were awakened by nightmares—not just Desset. The worst was Rudhira, who woke up screaming three separate times.

The first time she was merely confused when she awoke, insisting someone at the back of the house was calling her and she screamed to make it stop.

The second time she awakened in midair, bumping against the north wall of her room, saying she had to get out; her roommate Alris dragged her back to bed, displaying what Hanner thought was impressive courage.

The third time Rudhira smashed through her door and flew screaming down the hallway before smacking into a protective spell of some kind that Lord Faran had had placed on the door of his room. The noise roused the entire household, of course, and there were several theories about mysterious forces trying to use Rudhira against Lord Faran, or Lord Faran's magic somehow attracting Rudhira in her crazed and sleeping state.

Hanner didn't say so, but he thought Rudhira headed for Faran's room only because it was at the north end of the hall. He remembered that many of the people who vanished on the Night of Madness had headed north. He remembered how Roggit Rayel's son told the magistrate at his trial that he intended to flee to Aldagmor to escape the doom he thought was going to befall Ethshar, but couldn't explain why he chose Aldagmor.

Aldagmor was in the north. Hanner thought that was why Roggit chose it.

And Hanner could feel something in that direction himself, something very faint, very alien, and both slightly repulsive and slightly alluring.

But it was *very* faint. He could only sense it at all with his newfound warlock sight, and even with that it was like trying to hear the hum of a bee from a mile away.

After the third nightmare Uncle Faran went up to the fourth floor and came back down with something for Rudhira to drink, to help her sleep more soundly; she swallowed it without hesitation, and barely made it back to her bed before collapsing into unconsciousness.

The excitement over, everyone else retired again—except the handful on guard downstairs.

It took some time before Hanner got back to sleep after that. He wondered why Rudhira was affected more strongly than anyone else; was it because her warlockry was the most powerful of them all?

Was there a direct connection between the nightmares and the strength of a warlock's magic? He thought back, trying to remember that first breakfast gathering. There had been four warlocks there who had had the dreams after the initial experience on the Night of Madness—Rudhira, of course, and Desset of Eastwark, who had helped heal Kirsha, and Varrin the Weaver, and Alar Agor's son.

And, Hanner realized, Rudhira and Desset and Varrin had all had nightmares again this time, as well—Varrin had awakened twice, once in midair. Alar Agor's son was no longer in the house; he had left that first day, and had never come back.

At least, not yet, though Hanner supposed he might yet turn up.

Rudhira, Desset, and Varrin—those had been the three flyers in his party on the Night of Madness. When Uncle Faran had been sorting out who could fly and who couldn't Hanner had left the room before the sorting was complete, but he knew that Rudhira and Desset and Varrin had all been at the "can fly" end of the room.

There might well be a correlation between the nightmares and the power of a warlock's magic, then. Flying generally seemed to be something the stronger warlocks could do and the weaker could not.

That was interesting. Were the nightmares a sort of compensation, a disadvantage to balance out the advantages strong magic provided?

There were a dozen people seated at the dining table, eating a breakfast of sausages and cakes; Bern was hurrying in and out the door at the far side that led to the kitchens. Hanner exchanged greetings with the others—particularly Alris, who clearly had not slept well. She had shared a room with Rudhira, of course, which Hanner knew had hardly been restful.

Then Bern, returning with a tray of small beer, spotted Hanner.

"Lord Hanner!" he said. "Could I have a word with you, please?"

"Of course," Hanner said. "Though if you could spare me a sausage to eat while we talk, I would appreciate it."

"Yes, of course, my lord." Bern put down the tray, quickly distributed the mugs, and found a plate and a couple of fat sausages for Hanner. He handed Hanner the plate, then said, "Could you come with me, please, my lord?"

"We can't talk here?"

"There's something I need to show you. I had hoped to tell Lord Faran, but I haven't seen him yet this morning, and he may well be busy upstairs all day. Could you please accompany me?"

"Very well." Hanner followed, plate in hand, as Bern led him down a slanting stone passageway to a windowless, lamplit storeroom.

There they stopped. Bern simply stood for a moment, looking worried; Hanner glanced around, but could see nothing worrisome. It appeared to be a perfectly ordinary storeroom, though with more empty shelves than most.

"What is it, Bern?" Hanner asked.

"My lord," Bern said, "I don't dare disturb Lord Faran about this; he's far too busy with all the magicians. But I need to point it out to *someone*."

"Point out *what*?"

"Look, my lord," Bern said, gesturing at the empty shelves. "This house is accustomed to lodging your uncle, sometimes one or two of his friends, and of course anywhere from one to six servants. But right now I believe we have *forty* people here. I thought this could be managed if I made daily trips to Southmarket, and went to Fishertown Market or Westgate Market every so often, and picked up a few things at the shops in the Merchants' Quarters or the Old City."

"That's a great deal of walking," Hanner remarked. Southmarket was roughly a mile away, Westgate considerably farther. "Especially carrying food for forty people."

"I had thought I would hire a wagon," Bern said. "But, my lord, I can't."

"Why not?" Hanner said, but before the words were out of his mouth he remembered the mob on High Street, and the various magical protections sealing off the other three sides of the estate. "Oh," he said, before Bern could reply.

"My household funds are depleted, in any case," Bern said. "I'm not sure how good Lord Faran's credit is now—a few days ago his name was good anywhere, but now?"

"He probably has money," Hanner said, trying to sound more convinced than he was. "Gold, most likely, or silver at the very least."

"I hope so," Bern said, "but even if he does, how am I to get out to market, and safely back in?"

Hanner looked at him thoughtfully. It was plainly time for the warlocks to start earning their keep here.

"I think we can manage that," he said. "We can fly to the markets. And I don't think money will be a problem." He was sure Uncle Faran must have funds stashed somewhere in the house, or if not, some of the furnishings could be sold.

Or, being warlocks, they could simply demand credit. Hanner doubted any direct threats would be necessary. Inquiring about the possibility of credit while standing in front of a farmer's wagon doing something like juggling a knife without using one's hands ... well, that would be sufficiently intimidating that most people would probably agree to reasonable terms.

Most people. Merchants who didn't want to sell to warlocks at all, on credit or otherwise, would probably be more of a problem, but one that could be handled—by brute force, if necessary.

He was, Hanner realized, calmly contemplating a career of crime, something that would have been almost unthinkable a few days ago.

But a few days ago he hadn't known that his uncle had

been illegally collecting magic for years; he hadn't been evicted from his home by the overlord; he hadn't seen the overlord order Uncle Faran and the rest out of the city for no crime but being what they were.

A few days ago he hadn't been a warlock—and neither had anyone else. The Night of Madness had changed everything.

"Thank you, my lord," Bern said.

"We'll need a list of everything you need or want," Hanner said.

"Of course. I'll draw it up as soon as everyone's breakfasted."

"Good," Hanner said as he finally picked one of the sausages up from his plate. He took a healthy bite, smiled at the taste, and repeated, with a rather different emphasis, "Good!"

Chapter Thirty-one

The midday sun was hot as the people lined up in the garden; Lord Hanner held up a hand to shade his eyes.

Uncle Faran was sorting warlocks again. He had, he explained to Hanner, come to the conclusion that the ability to use warlockry really only had one variable: power. All the different things the magic could do, from healing to flying to warlock sight, could be learned, and once learned, the more powerful a warlock was, the better he could do any of them. A warlock couldn't be good at healing but a poor flyer, or a fast flyer unable to lift heavy weights; the magic simply didn't work that way.

Rudhira, the obvious example, was good at *everything*, once she learned how it was done. None of the others could match her in any use of warlockry. She simply had more power at her command than anyone else.

Faran therefore decided to rank everyone according to this simple measurement: How much could they lift to the height of their own heads? He brought a set of weights down from the fourth floor, ranging from tiny polished brass cylinders to immmense blocks of lead, and tested each of the warlocks with the idea of working up a scale of abilities so that he would know who could be called on for any given task.

Kirsha's cousin Ilvin turned out to be the weakest of them all; with anything over a quarter of a pound he was limited to sliding or bouncing it, rather than levitating it properly. He was unable to heal so much as a scratch, though he could soothe it slightly, and his warlock perceptions were so vague, so weak, and so limited by distance that no one, including Ilvin, was entirely certain he wasn't just imagining them.

Hinda was next in the rankings; she could bring a pound and a half to eye level, and was very proud of this accomplishment.

"I've gotten better!" she said happily. "When I started I could only lift a couple of spoons!"

Hanner smiled insincerely at her, and did not mention that she might have been better off *not* growing stronger. He watched as the others made their attempts.

Thirty-eight warlocks were tested on the weights—Hanner was uncomfortably aware that he should have been the thirty-ninth. He surreptitiously tried a few experiments with equipment that wasn't in use at the moment, and found he had no problem with a five-pound weight; he didn't get a chance to try anything heavier.

That meant he wasn't at the bottom, or even in the bottom five—he ranked at least sixth from last, ahead of Ilvin and four others.

Twenty-nine of the warlocks found their limits with the weights, though it took some doing—Othisen, the twenty-ninth, managed to lift the entire set of weights, a total of half a ton, to shoulder height before losing control and noisily dropping several.

Manrin placed slightly below the middle of the group, with a maximum of a hundred forty pounds. Lord Faran himself topped out around six hundred pounds.

Nine of the warlocks, however, hoisted the entire load. Ulpen, to everyone's surprise including his own, was one of them, as was Kirsha—and of course, Rudhira, Varrin, and Desset topped the list.

Now those nine were lined up in the garden while Lord Faran explained how he intended to test them further. Hanner had come along to watch.

"All of you can fly," Faran said. "Better than I can, in fact."

That, Hanner thought, given Faran's own conclusions about warlockry being simple, hardly needed saying. All these nine were far more powerful than Faran.

"What I propose," Faran said, "is that we fly out over the harbor and see how much water we can lift. That should tell us what our limits are—I think the entire Gulf of the East is too much for *any* of us." He smiled significantly at Rudhira.

The warlocks smiled back and nodded—or rather eight of them did; the ninth, Rudhira, was looking uneasily toward the back of the garden as if expecting someone to appear there, apparently unaware that Lord Faran was addressing her.

She had been nervous all morning; Hanner wasn't sure whether it was just the nightmares or whether something else was affecting her. He talked to her briefly while the others were being tested, and she said that she felt as if there were always someone talking somewhere behind her, just far enough away that she couldn't make out any words. She told Hanner that she had the feeling that there was something she should be doing—specifically that there was some *magic* she should be doing.

And she kept turning north.

It worried Hanner.

"So, follow me!" Faran said, lifting off the ground.

Desset and Kirsha and Varrin and the others rose as well, but Rudhira did not. As the other nine ascended Hanner hurried over to her and tapped her on the shoulder.

She blinked and turned to look at him.

"I have to go," she said.

"With the others," Hanner said. "You have to go with Uncle Faran and the others, to test your magic."

Her head was already starting to turn northward again, but she stopped herself. "Lord Faran?" she said. Then she looked up and gasped. "Oh!" She stared up at the others for a second, then shot upward herself.

"Be careful!" Hanner called after her.

She stopped dead and hovered, perhaps twenty feet off the ground. "Aren't you coming?" she called down to him.

"I can't fly," he called back.

"Oh!"

Before Hanner could say anything more he was snatched off his feet, as he had been the other day in the palace square, and swept upward. A moment later he found himself flying upward and northward at Rudhira's side.

They caught up with the others before they had gone more than a block. Rudhira whisked up to fly alongside Lord Faran, dragging Hanner in her wake.

Hanner noticed that his uncle, while able to fly under his own power, was none too steady about it, and clearly couldn't zip along at Rudhira's usual speed. Instead he was leading them all at a fairly casual pace, slow enough that people in the streets below noticed the shadows passing overhead and looked up.

To Hanner's dismay, several of them shook fists or shouted curses.

They crossed Merchant Avenue into the corner of the Old Merchants' Quarter nearest the Palace, sailing gently over the rooftops of the shops, then passed on into Spicetown, where Hanner looked down at the warehouses and alleys. Off to the right he could see the warm golden glow of the palace walls and sunlight blazing silver from the water of the Grand Canal.

Then they were beyond the Palace, and even here, seventy feet up and rising, Hanner could smell the perpetual tang of spices in the air—the warehouses below had been used to store all the spices brought across the Gulf of the East from the Small Kingdoms or down the Great River from the Baronies of Sardiron for the past two centuries, and even if they were abandoned tomorrow, Hanner suspected it would take another century before the odor faded completely.

The smell of salt mingled with the other scents; they were nearing the waterfront. Hanner could see the watery horizon ahead, beyond the buildings, spreading out before them. Sails dotted the waters of the Gulf.

The streets fell behind, the sea expanded, and then they passed over the wharves, Lord Faran's feet barely seeming to clear the highest masts of the ships tied up there. Hanner remembered his mother teaching him the names of the major docks—Thyme Wharf, Dill Wharf, Oregano, Balsam, Parsley, Mustard, then a stretch of open beach—he could see it now, just to his left—then the three diagonal wharves, Ginger, Nutmeg, and Cinnamon. Then there was the complex tangle of the Pepper Wharves, and the decaying row of the Tea Wharves, and just beyond that was the entrance to the New Canal that marked the western boundary of Spicetown. He wondered whether the names had ever really corresponded to what cargoes landed there; they certainly didn't now.

They were past the docks, past the line of half a dozen freighters standing off the coast awaiting a berth, and out over open water, and it suddenly occurred to Hanner to wonder whether he would be able to swim safely back to land if Rudhira were to drop him.

If warlockry were to cease to exist right now, as abruptly as it had begun, how many of the eleven of them would make it back to shore alive? The fall alone might kill them. They were at least eighty feet up.

Hanner took a breath, preparing to shout something, but just then Lord Faran slowed to almost a hover and called, "This should do."

The other warlocks slowed to a standstill in a cluster around Faran, but Rudhira continued on northward, Hanner in tow.

"Hai!" Hanner bellowed at her, startled. "Stop! Rudhira, stop!"

"Hm?" She turned, puzzled. "I have to go north," she said. "Lord Faran said so."

"No, he said to stop!" Hanner called. "See? He's back there!"

Rudhira blinked at him, but didn't stop.

Then Faran's voice came, unnaturally loud.

"Rudhira! Come back here!"

Hanner's eyes and mouth opened wide in shock; he had *never* heard his uncle shout so loudly. He had never heard *anyone* shout so loudly. He hadn't known it was possible.

Then he realized that it wasn't, ordinarily—Faran had somehow used warlockry to make his voice louder. He had heard Rudhira do the same thing to a much lesser degree more than once, though at the time he had been unsure whether it was magic or just an illusion.

It was definitely magic this time. And it had worked; Rudhira stopped and turned, as if waking from a dream.

"I'm sorry," she said to Hanner as she headed back to join the others. "I don't know what I was thinking—it just seemed as if I should keep going."

Hanner waved away her concern. "That's all right," he said.

But he was not sure it really *was* all right; Rudhira's recent behavior worried him. She seemed to be more and more distracted.

"Now we're all here," Lord Faran said as Rudhira and Hanner joined the hovering group, "I'd like to see just how powerful you are. Water is heavy, and should provide all the weight we need—I want each of you to try to pull up a column of water, as big around as your arms can reach, and see if you can raise it all the way up to this height." He looked over the group, then pointed. "Kirsha, you go first."

Kirsha hesitated, then looked down. "While flying?" she asked. "Can we do that?"

"Try," Faran said.

Kirsha stared down at the water below them—and so did Hanner and the others.

And as they watched, a wave curled itself into a spiral and rose upward, straightening itself into a vertical column of water as it climbed. Hanner held his breath at the sight.

It sparkled in the sun like a gigantic pillar of green liquid glass, rising up out of the sea.

When it was about thirty feet tall it began to wobble, and the rate of ascent slowed. At forty feet it stopped, swayed, and then shattered, falling back into the sea with an immense splash. Waves rippled out in expanding rings, swamping the shallow lines of waves that naturally rolled southward across the Gulf. The ships riding at anchor rocked gently as the waves passed beneath.

"Good!" Faran said. "Varrin, now you try."

Varrin looked down, took a deep breath, and spread his arms, and the waves seemed to reverse direction, drawing back in, re-forming the column that Kirsha had dropped. It rose upward, past the point where Kirsha had lost her hold, but began narrowing at the top.

Hanner could see the strain on Varrin's face, and could *feel* the magical power flowing through the air.

The column became a spire, the top narrowing to a point, but it continued to rise until at last Varrin reached out a hand and the water splashed upward against it, as if he held his hand over an impossible colossal fountain.

The column thickened, the top widening out into a rounded peak perhaps a foot across—and then it was too much, more than Varrin could handle, and water began spilling down the sides, splashing and spraying outward. The column swayed, split, and disintegrated, falling back not in a single great splash as Kirsha's had, but in a scattering shower of separate streams.

And Varrin had sunk partway himself; he was a good fifteen feet below the others and still losing altitude.

"Rudhira," Hanner called.

Rudhira had been looking off to the north, but she heard him, and Varrin's descent stopped abruptly.

"I'm sorry," he said as he rose gently to rejoin the others. "I misjudged. It felt as if I could still draw more power."

Faran held up a palm. "Don't worry about it," he said. "You did a fine job." He looked the others over, then pointed. "Luriaz," he said, "your turn."

Hanner watched with interest as the others each made the attempt. All but Ulpen bettered Kirsha's performance, but only Desset could match Varrin's—and she couldn't better it.

Rudhira watched with interest and caught anyone who started to fall. Her own turn, however, was left until last.

Finally, though, Faran turned to her and said, "Rudhira! Show us what you can do!"

Rudhira smiled. "Finally!" she said. She looked down.

Hanner could feel the wave of magical energy as if it were physical pressure; the hairs on his arms and face and body were all flattened against his skin.

And the water below them rose up.

This was not just a column; this was a mountain that soared upward. As it neared their feet it opened out into a ring but still continued, rising around them, surrounding them all in a roaring wall of water.

Rudhira laughed. No one else looked amused; Hanner forced himself to look away from Rudhira and look around at their faces, and saw only terror.

The water rose higher and higher, the circle of sky still visible above them receding and shrinking, until finally Lord Faran called, "That's enough!"

Rudhira smiled broadly and flung her arms wide, and the wall of water exploded outward. Water roared deafeningly as the entire structure disintegrated and fell back to earth—

but all of it *outward*; the eleven warlocks remained untouched and dry at the center.

Hanner looked out and down, and saw the freighters below, the wall of water sweeping down toward them.

"Rudhira," he called, pointing, "the ships!"

Rudhira looked, and to Hanner's astonishment the four closest ships rose up out of the water and hung dripping in the air while the torrent rushed beneath them. Hanner could see their crews, astonished and terrified, clinging to masts and ropes and railings as they watched.

And when the watery onslaught had passed, the ships settled neatly back to the surface.

Hanner watched the wave diminish with distance until at last it smashed into the city's docks, splashing up into the streets beyond—that was impressive, but no worse than a storm might do, and he doubted anyone was hurt or anything significantly damaged. Several people probably got soaked, but the sun would dry them quickly enough.

He felt himself suddenly drop several feet, but then he was caught again. He looked up at Rudhira.

"Sorry," she said. "That was . . . well, I think that was about my limit."

"It was *amazing*," Desset said admiringly.

"Indeed it was," Faran agreed. "Quite a spectacular performance! You should be proud."

Rudhira smiled wearily.

"I think we should go back," Hanner said. "Before everyone's too tired to hold me."

"Here," Desset said, dropping down. "Give me your hand! I'll take you, and let Rudhira get her breath back."

Hanner reached out gratefully and took Desset's hand. It was warm and soft.

Desset smiled at him. "It was very brave of you to come along, when you can't fly," she said.

"It wasn't my idea," Hanner said. "Rudhira brought me without asking."

Desset threw a startled glance up at Rudhira, who was

drifting southward, the others gathering closely around her, a few yards above Desset and Hanner.

"That really *was* amazing, what she did," Desset said. "I know that every time I use my magic it makes me a little stronger, so that each time I can do a little more than I could before, but I think it will be a *long* time before I can match *that*!"

"Probably," Hanner agreed. He suspected there might be some sort of limit to how much a warlock's power could increase, and Desset might *never* reach Rudhira's level— but he wasn't about to say that, and he wasn't sure that would be a bad thing. The idea of hundreds of warlocks strong enough to toss freighters around like toys was frightening, almost enough to make him think the overlord had a point.

But then, wizards had been working miracles for centuries, moving entire mountains on occasion. Why would warlocks be any worse?

And there might not be any limit; certainly, no one had found one yet, though of course it had only been a few days.

They were flying south now, back toward the city. Hanner glanced around to make sure Rudhira was accompanying them; he was fairly certain that whatever had made all those people fly off to the north on the Night of Madness was working on her.

She was there, flying south, above and behind him, but he could see her face, and her expression was ... well, "haunted" was the only word he could think of that fit.

Why was *she* particularly afflicted by this? Was it because she was so much more powerful than the others?

He glanced up at Desset, who was still carrying him. Either she or Varrin was the next most powerful warlock after Rudhira; if it *did* correlate to power, then she should be feeling some of the effects, though not to the same degree Rudhira was.

"Desset," he called, "do you hear someone calling you?"

Startled, she looked down at him, and their flight slowed.

"Then you hear it, too?" she asked. "I thought I was imagining it."

"No, I don't hear it," Hanner said. "But *Rudhira* does. I spoke to her about it earlier."

Desset glanced back at Rudhira.

"I think only the strongest warlocks hear it," Hanner said. "And I think it may be dangerous. I think that's what happened to those people who disappeared—I think they heard this calling, whatever it is."

"Oh," Desset said. "Do you really think so? I know *we* didn't take them, the way those awful people in the street say we did, but I hadn't thought *that* might have taken them." She shuddered. "It's not pleasant; I don't want to answer it. Is there some way I can make it go away?"

"I don't know," Hanner admitted. "Rudhira hasn't found one."

"Oh," Desset said again. Then she said, "Look!" She pointed.

They were over Spicetown now, and the streets were full of people—and they were all looking up at the warlocks, pointing and shaking fists.

"I don't think they liked our experiments," Hanner said.

"I guess not," Desset said. Then she smiled—a surprisingly nasty smile for such a motherly-looking person. "Not that there's anything they can do about it!"

Hanner didn't reply.

The overlord really might have a point, he thought—but with the warlocks all growing more powerful, all teaching one another more of what they could do, poor Azrad might have already missed his chance to do anything about it.

Chapter Thirty-two

The glowing images that floated in the air above the table faded away, leaving only the torchlight, but it was a moment before any of the wizards spoke.

"Impressive," the white-haired wizard said at last.

"Yes," said the beautiful woman. "Lifting loaded freighters as if they were toys . . ." She shuddered. "And there was the warlock in Ethshar of the Rocks who killed poor Lopin. I'm afraid we really must take this as a serious threat to the proper order of things. We can't put off acting indefinitely."

The red-robed man at the head of the table turned to Kaligir. "Was this Shemder of yours capable of anything like that?" he asked.

"I don't think so," Kaligir replied. "He relied on speed and subtlety, rather than power. And of course, the fact that there was absolutely no outward sign of preparation or action—he could be standing right there, kill someone, and no one would know who had done it."

"That worries me," the white-haired man said. "If we move prematurely, we might just drive the warlocks underground."

"There's no need to be hasty," the red-robed wizard said. "I would suggest that we acknowledge that warlocks are true magicians, powerful ones—anyone who can kill a wizard so quickly, by magic, is a powerful magician. Anyone who can raise a mountain of water is a powerful magician. The Guild has never forbidden an entire school of magic because, as our comrade from Sardiron says, that often merely drives it underground—but I don't believe we have ever before had any potential competition this powerful, this dangerous. Whether we forbid *this* one remains to be determined—but I believe it would be appropriate to enforce our existing strictures on magic."

"Carefully, though," Kaligir said. "I don't think any of us should forget what happened to Lopin."

"Carefully, of course," the red-robed wizard agreed.

Lord Azrad stood at the window of his favorite sitting room, staring northward, watching the waves slosh back and forth along the Grand Canal and seawater drip from the eaves of the warehouses.

Then he turned to face his brothers—it was Lord Clurim who had spotted the warlocks flying past and had called the overlord to the window to watch, and Karannin and Ildirin had joined them later.

"They're growing stronger," he said. "They must be stopped *now*. Clurim, call Captain Vengar—ready or not, I want Captain Naral to move *now*. And then go find Lady Nerra—maybe she can tell us something of what her mad uncle plans to do, other than inundate Spicetown." As Clurim bowed and turned to go, Azrad demanded, "Karannin, Ildirin, can't one of you get a response from the Wizards' Guild?"

"*I* certainly can't," Karannin said. "I've talked to dozens of wizards, and they assure me that the masters of the Guild are aware of the situation and discussing it, and that they know you want to talk to them, but beyond that—nothing."

"Have you spoken to the Sisterhood or the Brotherhood?" Azrad asked as Clurim quietly closed the door behind himself.

"The Brotherhood is terrified of the warlocks," Ildirin said. "They tell me that pitting them against Lord Faran's company would be like trying to boil a hundred gallons of soup with a single candle. The Sisterhood is not quite so frightened, but they agree that warlocks are far more powerful than witches; any campaign they might undertake would have to be slow and subtle."

"We don't have *time* for subtlety!" Azrad roared. "What about the others?"

"The gods can't even see most of the warlocks," Karannin said. "At least, that's what the theurgists tell me. And when they *can* see them, they still won't take action except purely defensively—you know how the gods are about not interfering. I don't know whether it's the oath they took two hundred years ago or just their nature, but they won't intervene."

"Demonologists aren't much better," Ildirin said. "I've corresponded with half a dozen since the Night. They don't agree on much of anything, but none of them seem inclined to go to war with the warlocks. Apparently demons can see warlocks just fine, but they can't tell them apart from ordinary people—naturally, they'd be the opposite of the gods. If you summon a demon and order it to kill a specific warlock, it will presumably do its best to obey, but we don't know how successful it would be, or what the repercussions might be, and you can't just tell one, 'Go kill all the warlocks.' It can't find them without names."

"We could at least have Lord Faran killed," Azrad said thoughtfully. "We know *his* name."

The other three looked at one another.

"Perhaps we could," Karannin said, "but would it be wise? First and least, there's the question of cost . . ."

"Which isn't trivial," Ildirin said. "Demonologists are expensive."

"The city treasury could surely afford it," Azrad said.

"Yes," Karannin said, "but that brings us to the second question, justification for doing so."

"He's a traitor," Azrad said. "That's good enough."

"My lord brother, our laws and customs require a trial for any capital offense, even treason, and the accused must be permitted the opportunity to defend himself. Sending a demonic assassin—"

"Can be justified," Azrad interrupted. "We can arrange for him to die resisting arrest. He *has* resisted arrest once, after all, and I'm sure he'll do it again."

"Perhaps," Karannin conceded. "But the third and most cogent question is what the Wizards' Guild will think and do if we hire a demonologist to carry out an execution. You know as well as I that that violates their rules against the governmental use of magic."

"Surely they'll make an exception!"

"The Wizards' Guild doesn't make exceptions," Ildirin said.

"And even if they might, you'd need to convince the demonologist of that beforehand," Karannin said. "I never met a demonologist who didn't consider himself more than the equal of a wizard, but I also never met one willing to take on the entire Guild. That's my fourth question—if the Guild *would* permit us to use a demon assassin, would the demonologist trust us—and them?"

"Surely *one* demonologist would—"

"My lord brother," Ildirin interrupted, "I think we're getting distracted here. The mechanism for killing individual warlocks is not really that important—if we have the Guild's approval we can simply let *them* handle executions, without needing to bring the added risk of dealing with demons into it. And if we *don't* have the Guild's approval, I doubt any other magicians will cooperate."

"Then we need their consent, and damn them all, why won't they *give* it?"

"They did agree we could hire wizards to aid in arresting warlocks," Karannin reminded him, pointing at the door where Clurim had vanished a moment before. "That's a start."

"Not much of one," Azrad grumbled.

"Azrad, you just sent Clurim out there with instructions to turn the entire city guard and every wizard we could hire to the task of removing Faran's company from the city. Why don't we wait and see what comes of that before we start worrying about involving the Guild more directly?"

Azrad glowered at him.

"Do you think it will *work*?" he demanded. "After what

we just saw out there?" He jerked a thumb at the window.

Ildirin grimaced.

"No," he said. He hesitated, and added, "And I don't know how Lord Faran will react to the attempt, either."

The overlord froze for a moment, then frowned. He slowly said, "I hadn't thought of that."

Chapter Thirty-three

There were soldiers marching in the streets of the New City, but the warlocks ignored them and flew easily back to the garden behind Lord Faran's mansion. Once they were safely back on the ground Hanner took the first opportunity to pull his uncle aside into an vacant room and talk to him privately.

"There's something out there, somewhere in the north, that's calling to your most powerful warlocks," Hanner said.

"I'd noticed there was something odd about Rudhira's behavior," Faran said.

"Yes, well, *talk* to her. I think she'll listen to you more than she will to me, and maybe you can get her to tell you something useful. And maybe get Manrin to do some checking—maybe he can do a divination and find out just what it is that she's hearing. I think it might be the same thing that causes those nightmares. And it's not just Rudhira—Desset's starting to hear it now. I suspect Varrin and some of the others are, too."

"You may be right, my boy." Faran's tone was reassuring, and he plainly intended to go on to say something more, but Hanner quickly cut him off. What he wanted to say was urgent; he couldn't risk being distracted.

"Uncle, I think that whatever is calling them is the same thing that called all those people on the Night of Madness—

the ones that disappeared. I think there's something out there that *wants* warlocks."

"It's possible," Faran agreed calmly. "It may be the same thing that made us into warlocks in the first place. A mad wizard, perhaps."

Hanner shuddered. "Could a wizard do all this? You saw Rudhira out there today."

"There's no known limit to what wizardry can do, Hanner. And from what I saw today I'm not sure there's any limit on what warlockry can do, either."

"But using it . . . well, when you get more powerful you start to get the nightmares and to hear that calling."

"That's a drawback," Faran admitted. "It's hardly fatal, though, and we may well find a way around it."

"I *hope* it's not fatal," Hanner said. "None of those people who disappeared has come back."

Faran was about to reply when someone shouted, "Lord Faran! Lord Faran!"

"We'll talk more later," Faran said. Then he turned and called, "I'm here. What is it?"

"Soldiers!"

Faran smiled, an unpleasant expression that reminded Hanner of the one he had seen on Desset's face half an hour before, over Spicetown.

"It would seem Azrad is trying again," he said.

"And we still haven't heard from the Wizards' Guild," Hanner said.

Faran's smile broadened. "You know, my boy," he said, "after what I saw Rudhira do today, I'm no longer concerned about the Wizards' Guild. I think we can handle Azrad and his men without their help."

Hanner opened his mouth, intending to say that he was not worried about the city guard but about the Guild itself, but Faran was already out of the room, striding briskly toward the front of the house. Hanner snapped his mouth shut and hurried to follow.

"Rudhira! Desset! Varrin!" Faran called as he walked. "Everyone, come with me! I think it's time we demonstrated to Lord Azrad that his authority does not extend to us!" He reached the front door and flung it open, the other warlocks gathering behind him. Rudhira stood by the door, looking slightly dazed—clearly, whatever was happening to her, whatever was calling her, had not stopped.

Hanner hesitated.

He wanted to see what would happen, but he didn't want to get in the way—he wasn't a known warlock, so he wouldn't participate in whatever the warlocks did. And it might be dangerous.

Besides, there was such a mob of warlocks in the hallway and at the parlor windows that he doubted he could get a decent view in any case.

And there were questions he needed answered. Two of the warlocks were notable by their absence, and Hanner thought this might be a good time to talk to them.

And there were windows upstairs; he might wind up with a better view that way.

He turned and started up the stairs at a trot. His weight and general lack of conditioning caught up with him by the time he had reached the second flight, though, and he slowed to a walk.

On the third floor he made his way down the central corridor, listening at each door; at the third one he heard voices and knocked.

One voice stopped, and Hanner heard footsteps approaching. Ulpen opened the door and peered out at him.

"I'd like to speak to you and Manrin," Hanner said. "May I come in?"

Ulpen swung the door open. "Don't interrupt him," he warned.

Hanner knew enough about wizards to not need the warning. He looked around the room with interest, being careful not to touch anything.

The room was lined with shelves and chests of drawers; several drawers stood open, displaying various powders and dried leaves. The shelves were jammed with jars, bags, boxes, and pots of various shapes and sizes. A table stood to one side, most of it covered with jars and boxes similar to the ones on the shelves; a large book lay open upon it next to an assortment of small tools. More tools were spread on the floor—two daggers, a wood-handled brush, a small iron tripod, a tinderbox, and three small metal implements Hanner couldn't identify.

Manrin was seated cross-legged on a silk carpet before a small brass pot. Something in the pot was smoking and smelled absolutely terrible; Manrin was weaving his fingers through the smoke while reciting an incantation.

". . . *gattu sa brutin fara . . . fara . . .* Oh, blast." Manrin spread his hands wide and leaned back.

"Didn't work?" Ulpen asked.

"Lost it completely," Manrin said. "I could tell it was going." He shook his head in dismay. "That spell was second nature to me a sixnight ago." He looked up and noticed Hanner. "My lord," he said. "What can I do for you?"

"I came to inform you that Lord Azrad has apparently sent soldiers to enforce my uncle's exile. More of them, this time. This may turn nasty." He frowned. "I thought you should know. And I had some questions I hoped you could answer."

Manrin uncrossed his legs, brushed dust from his robe, and with a little help from Ulpen, got to his feet. He nodded politely at Hanner.

"Let's have a look at these soldiers," he said. He led Ulpen and Hanner through two other rooms to a study with two windows overlooking High Street; there he swung open one casement and leaned out.

Hanner and Ulpen, not wishing to crowd a respected elder, took the other window.

Lord Faran stood in the dooryard below, wearing his magnificent green cloak, his hair newly brushed and tied; a soldier, a captain by his helmet, was standing in the gate, facing him. Hanner knew that gate had been locked, with runes supposedly sealing it, but now it stood open, and he doubted very much that Faran had unlocked it.

Beyond the iron fence, filling the street, were soldiers—

hundreds of them, all heavily armed. Lord Azrad had clearly decided not to waste any more time with half measures.

There were no civilian observers in sight this time—the soldiers had crowded them out of High Street completely. On the other hand, Hanner could see half a dozen figures in the array of guards who were not wearing tunic, helmet, kilt, and breastplate, but the colorful robes of wizards. He thought he recognized one of them as Ezrem of Arena, who had performed various spells around the Palace over the years.

Those wizards presumably explained how the wards and runes had been bypassed—assuming the wards and runes had really been there in the first place. It was also entirely possible that Ulpen and Manrin had botched the spells without even realizing it.

However it had happened, the wards were gone and the gate stood open. The soldiers held their spears at the ready—and the wizards clearly had spells ready to cast, as well. Ezrem, if it was really him, was holding a gleaming dagger with a blue gem in the pommel, and the others also held assorted knives or staves or crystals.

All eyes, though, were focused on Faran and the captain. The two men were speaking to each other, loudly enough to be heard over the muttering of the city, but Hanner didn't bother trying to make out the words. He knew what the gist of it would be. The captain would be ordering Faran out of the city, and Faran would be replying that he wouldn't go. Both would insist they wanted no trouble.

"I don't recognize anyone," Manrin remarked. "No Guildmasters there."

Hanner and Ulpen both glanced at him.

"You're sure?" Hanner asked.

"Unless Ithinia's promoted someone in the past few days, yes," Manrin said. "They don't look like much. Even as damaged as I am, I'm probably a match for any of those wizards down there."

"That was one of the questions I wanted to ask," Hanner said. "How damaged *are* you?"

Manrin snorted. "As a man, I'm fit and strong for my age, as healthy as anyone who's seen a century could ask. As a warlock, I seem to be adequate, if unimpressive—I believe Lord Faran ranked me twenty-first in the company here. But as a wizard, right now you'd probably do as well with a drunkard journeyman. It's frustrating, my lord, very frustrating—I'll be working a spell, some spell I know by heart and have performed a hundred times, I'll feel the magic building up and falling into place, and then the *wrong* magic will arise, and I'll be using warlock sight instead of wizard sight, or moving something by warlockry that I shouldn't touch yet because my thoughts strayed a little, and the wizardry will just vanish, poof! Like the shadows of night when the sun comes up, it's just gone and I can't get it back. I can still do *quick* spells, because there isn't time for them to go wrong, but anything that takes more than fifty heartbeats—well, I can't count on it. And anything that takes more than twenty minutes is completely hopeless. Fendel's Divination would be *so* useful right now, but I can't do it."

"Then you haven't been able to learn anything about the nature of warlockry?"

Manrin snorted. "Fendel's Divination is hardly the *only* way to learn things, young man! I've learned a little."

"Do you know what warlockry *is*, then?"

"Well, no," he admitted. "I know several things it's *not*, though. With little Shella's help, we have established irrefutably that the name is a misnomer—we are *not* war-locked witches, and warlockry is not witchcraft, though there are very definite similarities. And Alladia has helped us demonstrate conclusively that neither gods nor demons are responsible for its existence."

"Then . . . Rudhira and some of the others say there's something to the north somewhere calling to them. It's not a demon?"

"Not a demon, not a god," Manrin agreed. "But yes, there is something somewhere to the north of the city that we are all somehow linked to."

"A mad wizard, perhaps?"

Manrin shook his head. "No. Not a wizard. Because what-

ever is there, its magic blocks wizardry in a way that . . .
well, it's not wizardry. When one wizard's spell blocks another there are several ways it can work, but none of them
are anything like this."

"It *does* block wizardry?"

"Oh, yes."

"Then those wizards out there can't do anything to Uncle
Faran?" he asked hopefully.

"Oh, I didn't say *that*!" Manrin replied quickly, dashing
Hanner's hopes. "It's not like a wall. It's more like
drowning out a voice by shouting. Wizardry and warlockry
interfere with each other, like . . . like fire and water, almost.
That's how I know it wasn't wizardry that created warlocks.
But a hot enough flame will boil water away, and a well-
aimed squirt of water can pass right through a flame . . . the
analogy isn't exact, you understand."

"I understand," Hanner said. "I think. But about the thing
calling to Rudhira—can you do anything about it?"

Manrin frowned. "I don't know," he said. "If you could
bring her up here, so we could talk, and I could have a look
at her . . ."

"I think she's busy right now," Hanner said. He pointed
at the street below.

"Then later, perhaps," Manrin said.

"Something's happening," Ulpen called. While the others
spoke he had stayed at the window, leaning out the casement to watch the events below. Now Manrin and Hanner
leaned out as well.

Faran was striding out the gate into the street, and the
soldiers were being swept back, as if a gigantic invisible
bubble were expanding outward from the dooryard. They
were colliding with one another as they were forced back,
stumbling against each other, and some were falling to the
ground as they lost their balance. The captain was pressed
back flat against the iron fence, his helmet askew.

The wizards were reacting to this assault; orange flame
suddenly burst into being in the dooryard, only to be instantly smothered. A wizard gestured, and Lord Faran staggered briefly, then resumed his march.

"The first one, Thrindle's Combustion, was just silly," Manrin remarked. "And the second one was Felshen's First Hypnotic, which is a better choice but still not much of a spell. Even in my present condition I'm sure I could still do that one."

"Maybe we should get down there, Master," Ulpen said worriedly.

Manrin stroked his beard, considering, then nodded. "I think you're right," he said. "We could be useful. I'll just grab a few things."

Hanner, leaning out the casement, saw Rudhira marching out into the street behind Faran, still in her white silk tunic and long green skirt, and Varrin appeared behind Rudhira. The empty circle around them was thirty feet across now, the full width of the street; the sea of soldiers had been parted. The guards to the east were tumbled atop one another, trying to get themselves upright and scramble back; the guards to the west, on Coronet Street, had managed to keep more order, and were all still standing.

And Rudhira was looking back over her shoulder.

Looking north.

"I'll meet you down there," Hanner said, turning.

He didn't even take the time to close the casement before running for the stairs.

Chapter Thirty-four

At the foot of the stairs Hanner pushed his way through the little crowd of warlocks. At the door he looked out and saw that Lord Faran and at least a dozen others were marching eastward on High Street, away from the house, pushing the soldiers before them.

"Where are they going?" he asked.

"The Palace," someone said. Hanner turned to see little Hinda standing beside him. "Lord Faran said that he was tired of inter . . . interm . . ."

"Intermediaries," Hanner suggested.

"Yes, thank you, my lord. He said he was going to go talk to Lord Azrad face-to-face, to settle this once and for all."

Hanner looked out the door.

Desset was standing in the street directly in front of the house, facing west, and Hanner realized that she was single-handedly blocking the street so that none of the soldiers on that side could approach.

Off to the left the rest, with Faran, Rudhira, Varrin, Kirsha, and Yorn forming a line at the front, were marching slowly but steadily to the east, toward the Palace.

Hanner estimated that about half the warlocks who had gathered at the house were in that party; the other half were gathered in the hallway and at the parlor windows, watching eagerly.

This was, Hanner thought, monumentally stupid, or at the very least seriously overconfident. Faran and the others had no way of knowing what might be waiting for them there. There could be a trap. The wizards out here had apparently been nothing to worry about, but there might be far better wizards guarding the overlord. There could be witches, with their subtle spells, or sorcerers, with their mysterious talismans, or theurgists who could call the gods to their aid, or demonologists who could, of course, summon demons.

Warlockry might be powerful magic, but it was hardly the *only* magic.

"I had better go with them," Hanner said. "They may need someone else, someone who's not . . ."

He didn't finish the sentence, because he could not honestly say he wasn't on either side. He was his uncle's nephew—and he was a warlock, even if no one knew it.

If they were walking into a trap—well, he would try not to walk into it with them.

The sensible, safe thing to do would be to stay where he was, of course—or better still, slip out the back and head to Mavi's house, where he could wait out the coming confrontation. No one but Shella knew he was a warlock, so far as he knew; certainly the overlord didn't. He could just wait it out, and when everything was settled he could move back into the Palace, back where he belonged . . .

But Uncle Faran wouldn't be moving back into the family apartment with him. No matter what happened, he couldn't imagine that. Faran would be dead, or exiled—or if this march turned out the way Hanner thought Faran expected, Faran would be the city's new ruler, and would presumably be living in the overlord's apartments.

But, Hanner thought, he and Nerra and Alris could stay on at the Palace, surely. *They* hadn't done anything.

He wondered what was happening to Nerra, back in the Palace. Did she know what was happening out here? Was she frightened left alone there, her brother, sister, and uncle all locked out?

She was probably fine, he told himself. Alris was fine. They were safely out of the way.

But Uncle Faran was on his way to confront Lord Azrad the Sedentary, and Hanner couldn't just stand by and watch. He pushed past the other warlocks and out the door.

The air in the vacant stretch of street felt oddly still and lifeless—clearly, the warlocks were not just pushing the soldiers back, but had created barriers blocking *anything* from approaching Warlock House. Hanner began to sweat as he hurried through the dooryard and out the gate, then turned left and followed his uncle.

Desset glanced at him as he passed, but said nothing and stayed at her post, holding back the soldiers in Coronet Street. Hanner noticed that some of those soldiers were slipping away to the north, presumably planning to return to the Palace by another route.

He was also vaguely aware that a handful of the other

warlocks were following him, belatedly joining their comrades, but he didn't concern himself with them.

Faran's party of warlocks was marching relentlessly forward, side by side—not fast, but advancing steadily, pushing the soldiers back along High Street, regardless of whether those soldiers were standing or fallen. Most of the guards were retreating in disorder; some were standing their ground until actively dislodged by the advancing wall of magic, or were trying to help fallen comrades to their feet.

Some soldiers were no longer resisting at all, but just lying in the dirt, allowing themselves to be shoved or rolled along.

"Give me room!" someone shouted. The cry was strangely muffled, and Hanner realized it was coming from beyond the magical barrier the warlocks were pushing forward. He tried to see who had spoken.

It was one of the wizards, a man about Hanner's own age in a gold and white robe; soldiers were pushing and shoving to get out of his way, even more desperately then they were trying to avoid being knocked down by the warlock wall.

And Hanner could see why. The wizard was holding aloft a dagger, and miniature lightning was playing around the blade in crackling blue-white arcs. Hanner ran forward, calling a warning.

His cry was not necessary—Faran was already pointing the wizard out to his companions.

The wizard pointed the dagger at the warlocks, launching a bolt, at the same instant that Rudhira raised a hand in a warding gesture. A blaze of blue-white fire leaped from the knife blade—and spattered harmlessly into a shower of sparks against the invisible barrier.

The knife trembled in the wizard's hand, but did not fall. Lord Faran looked questioningly at Rudhira.

"It's enchanted," she said. "It's so full of wizardry that I can't affect it."

"Leave it, then. On to the Palace!"

"The Palace!" Varrin and Kirsha cried—but Hanner,

pushing through the group and panting up behind the five leaders, noticed that Yorn did not join in, but merely looked unhappy, while Rudhira's cry trailed off in midword.

She was looking northward—not toward the Palace, but beyond.

"Uncle Faran!" Hanner called.

Faran turned without stopping his steady march. "What are you doing here, boy?" he asked. "It's not safe."

"I can see that," Hanner said angrily. "But you might need another voice when you talk to the overlord."

Another miniature lightning bolt flared, but this time Faran did not bother pointing it out to anyone; again, it burst harmlessly against the barrier.

"I suppose we might," Faran agreed. "Azrad may want someone untainted—from what he said when last we spoke, and what Captain Naral has told me, he's quite convinced warlockry is inherently evil." He nodded. "Come along, then."

Hanner stepped up to join the line. Faran was in the center, Varrin on his right, Rudhira on his left, Kirsha beyond Rudhira, and Yorn beyond Varrin; Hanner squeezed in between Rudhira and his uncle. He was worried about Rudhira.

Behind them a score or more of other warlocks trailed along, looking like the undisciplined rabble they were, but this front line presented at least some semblance of order.

At least, it did until Faran suddenly stumbled, his hands falling to clutch at his belly.

Rudhira whirled and saw a wizard chanting. Her hand waved, and the wizard tumbled backward.

Faran straightened, coughed, and said, "Thank you. I do believe that was the Spell of Intestinal Turmoil." He swallowed, looking slightly pale, then adjusted his cloak and marched on.

A few seconds later the barrier had reached the corner of West Second Street and pressed on across the intersection. The party paused for a moment. Varrin asked, "Do we turn here? It's the shortest route."

"I think it would be more effective, more dramatic, to march down Center Avenue," Faran replied, pointing east. He started to continue—but then realized Rudhira had turned, ignoring his words.

"Rudhira!" he called. "*This* way!"

Rudhira shook her head, her red hair flying up wildly, as if a great wind were blowing around her—but the air inside the barrier was still unnaturally calm. "It's calling," she said. Hanner realized that her feet were no longer on the ground. "I can hear it. I can feel it. I can almost *see* it!" She was drifting northward along West Second Street, rising slowly, leaving the others behind. The barrier was splitting in two— one section, centered on Lord Faran and the others, remained motionless, while the other was pressing clear a swath down the center of West Second Street. Beyond it a disorganized crowd of soldiers and civilians watched in confusion; some turned to run, while others stood their ground.

"Rudhira, wait!" Kirsha called. "*What* is calling?"

"I hear it, too," Varrin said.

"But what *is* it?" Kirsha demanded. "We don't *know*! It might be something evil, something luring us in!"

The others were standing indecisively, and Hanner could take no more; he ran after Rudhira, calling her name.

She was well above the ground now; he jumped, and his hand brushed her foot, knocking off one green shoe. She didn't even look down; instead she began flying faster and higher, calling, "I'm coming!"

Hanner stopped, out of breath, and watched Rudhira's flying form dwindle with distance as she soared upward and northward, faster and faster, until she vanished above the rooftops of Spicetown.

The barrier that had cleared much of West Second Street vanished as well, and when Hanner lowered his gaze from the northern sky he saw half a dozen guardsmen advancing toward him, spears at ready.

"Oh, no," he said, backing up.

He didn't want to run; it was undignified to run away from one's enemies. He backed away, and the soldiers advanced. One of them kicked aside Rudhira's dropped shoe.

Then they stopped, as if they had just smacked into an invisible wall.

"This way, Lord Hanner," Kirsha called.

Hanner turned.

The four remaining warlocks were still standing in the intersection, waiting for him. He tried to pretend nothing disturbing had happened as he walked back to join them.

"She's gone," Yorn said, staring northward.

"I know," Hanner said. "Why didn't the rest of you try to stop her?"

"I *did*," Kirsha said. "Didn't you feel it? But she was always far stronger than me."

Hanner looked at Varrin.

"I didn't," he said quietly.

Faran turned, startled. "Why not? Maybe with the two of you . . ."

"I was maintaining the barrier, my lord—forgive me, but you aren't strong enough to have done it yourself." He hesitated, then added, "And besides, I couldn't have stopped her. If I had tried, I'd have gone *with* her. And I'm not ready yet."

"Not ready? Gone with her?" Hanner could see that Uncle Faran was trying to restrain his fury. "What are you *talking* about?"

"You haven't felt it yet, my lord?" Varrin asked. "The Calling?"

Hanner had heard Rudhira talking about a calling, but listening to Varrin he knew the warlock meant *the* Calling, something new and special.

"Felt what?" Faran said.

"Uncle," Hanner said, looking around, "maybe we should go back to the house."

"No!" Faran said angrily. "Yes, Rudhira has deserted us, but look!" He swept an arm around. "We still have the power to hold off the entire city guard!"

"But if Varrin hears this Calling . . ."

Faran and Hanner both turned to look at Varrin.

"I hear it," Varrin said. "I can still resist. But, my lord, the more I use my magic, the stronger the Calling becomes. If I do too much . . ."

"I hear it, too," Kirsha said. "But it's still weak for me."

"Uncle, it's the strongest warlocks who feel it the most," Hanner said. "The ones you need the most if you try to take the Palace."

"I didn't say I was going to *take* the Palace," Faran said quickly. "I intend to negotiate with Lord Azrad, not depose him." Magical energy crackled somewhere nearby; Faran turned and said, "Kirsha, you concentrate on the wizards, please. The rest of you, hold the soldiers back."

"Why do we *need* to negotiate?" Hanner asked. "Why not just wait him out? You've shown he can't hurt you."

"No, we haven't," Faran said, his voice dropping. "We've shown he can't just march in with his soldiers and take us, but what's to stop him from hiring wizards to kill us in our beds? We need to make an agreement *now*, in public, so he can't change his mind."

"What if the Wizards' Guild took our side? *Then* he couldn't hire wizards . . ."

"Demonologists, then. They have no Guild telling them what to do. I don't care to wake up one night to find a slimy horror from the Nethervoid sitting on my chest about to eat my face. No, we need to settle this *now*. Azrad's apparently called out the entire guard, and when that doesn't work, magic *has* to be next."

"If the Wizards' Guild—" Hanner began.

Faran cut him off. "Hanner, the Guild isn't going to help us in time, if they help us at all. If they were going to, Ithinia would have spoken to me by now. I have the talking talisman in my purse, and it's been silent. We're on our own, and we need to force an agreement from Azrad *now*."

"I agree, my lord," Yorn said, startling Hanner; he hadn't realized that several of the other warlocks had gathered around Faran and himself and were listening intently. "Timing is the key to control, Lieutenant Kensher always said— the best time to stop a fight is before it begins."

"I think this one's already started," Faran said, "but there's still time to keep it from getting worse."

"But we lost Rudhira," Kirsha said, glancing north.

"Another reason to hurry," Faran said, throwing Varrin a quick look. "Before we lose anyone else to this Calling, whatever it is."

"I still think it's foolish, Uncle," Hanner said. "Twenty or thirty warlocks against an entire city?"

"We work with what we have," Faran replied. "Now, come on!" He turned east, and gestured dramatically. "Onward to the Palace!"

Chapter Thirty-five

The march to the Palace seemed so strange to Hanner as to be almost unreal—an unruly gang of warlocks, of all ages, all sizes, and both sexes, dressed in everything from Lord Faran's best silk tunic and green velvet cloak to Zarek's ragged homespun, walking down High Street and Center Avenue as if no one else was present, while a few yards away yellow-tunicked soldiers and assorted civilians stood screaming and struggling, trying to hold their ground against the steady advance of the wall of warlockry. They were all forced back, some staying upright, others tumbling to the ground.

A few soldiers tried to get under the invisible barrier, without success.

A few wizards tried to levitate *over* the barrier, which might have been more successful, but rising out of the crowd made them immediately visible, and Kirsha or Varrin slapped each one down.

Desset had abandoned her post on the corner of Coronet Street not long after Rudhira's disappearance; trying to keep

the entire route clear was obviously impractical. She and a
few others were still acting as a rear guard, but were now
only about a hundred feet behind Faran and the others. A
few guardsmen and civilians had come around behind and
were following the warlocks, just beyond Desset's retreating
barrier.

Hanner walked along in the midst of this bizarre scene,
wondering how he had ever come to this. He could have
stayed at Warlock House. He could have fled to Mavi's
house. Why had he come?

It had seemed like the right thing to do—but it certainly
wasn't the safest.

When the party reached the mouth of Central Avenue and
marched out into the square before the Palace, Hanner
stopped so suddenly that Zarek, just behind him, bumped
into him. The two mumbled apologies to each other, then
walked on.

Both of them were staring at the crowd that had been
waiting for them in the square.

The overlord apparently had, indeed, called out the entire
guard—and more. A path from Central Avenue to the bridge
across the moat had been cleared, and on either side of it
stood a dozen rows of soldiers, all with pikes at the ready. Behind them stood hundreds, perhaps thousands, of ordinary
citizens, watching it all.

Faran marched out to the middle of the plaza, then
stopped and looked around; the other warlocks gathered
around him. Hanner, struck by an unhappy premonition,
hurried to his uncle's side.

"What now?" someone called.

"Why are we stopping?"

"I thought we were going to the Palace."

Faran did not answer; he stood, waiting silently, until all
the warlocks, even Desset, had collected into a fairly com-
pact group at the center of the square.

"Uncle," Hanner muttered, "what are you doing?"

"A thought struck me, Hanner," Faran muttered back.

Then he raised his voice and called out, "People of Ethshar! Men of the city guard! Listen to me!"

"Louder," Hanner whispered. "Use warlockry."

"I know," Faran said testily. "Shut up." He raised his arms and spoke again, and this time his words rang out supernaturally loud and clear.

"People of Ethshar! I am Faran the Warlock, who was once chief advisor to Lord Azrad the Sedentary! Around me you see other warlocks, your friends and neighbors, your sons and daughters, fathers and mothers, driven from their homes by mistrust!"

"Not *my* son!" an old man called from the crowd behind the soldiers to the west—an old man Hanner recognized as the one who had so often stood at the fence, staring at the house, during the past two days. "You took him!"

Faran turned to glance at the old man, then announced, "Some of you think we, the warlocks of Ethshar, were responsible for the disappearances on the Night of Madness. I give you my word, we are not! We know no more than you do of what happened to them!"

"Liar!" the old man called.

This time Faran ignored him and continued, "We have come here today to ask Lord Azrad, and to ask *you*, to forgive those of us who may have committed crimes on the Night of Madness, when this gift of magic was bestowed upon us by forces unknown. We have come to say that most of us took no part in that madness, we did *not* steal your children or neighbors, and despite our magic we are still just people like yourselves, no more inhuman or evil than wizards or sorcerers. Lord Azrad has ordered us into exile; we have refused to go, because we believe that sentence is unjust. We have done nothing to merit exile. We go now to ask Lord Azrad to reconsider his decision to cast us out, and we sincerely hope that he will."

Faran's words rolled out across the square and echoed from the surrounding buildings; no other sound could be heard while he spoke.

"*However*," Faran said, "I know Lord Azrad. I worked

with him for many years. He can be a stubborn man. He may refuse to hear us. I want you all to know, here and now, that if Lord Azrad *does* refuse to rescind our exile, we are nonetheless staying in Ethshar. This is our home. We will fight to stay here. We will try not to harm anyone, but we will do whatever it takes to stay here. I want to make that absolutely clear. I hope this can be settled without bloodshed, but we stand ready to fight, and if necessary, to kill."

"Uncle!" Hanner said.

"If we fight," Faran continued, "I want you to know that we will welcome anyone who chooses to fight on our side, whether he be warlock, or magician, or soldier, or ordinary citizen. Furthermore, we have learned how to train apprentices in warlockry, to pass on the gift of magic that we received on that night. Anyone who chooses to join us, and who wishes it, can become one of us!"

"Uncle!" Hanner looked around, horrified. He had thought that the knowledge that they could make more warlocks was a useful secret, to be held in reserve and perhaps brought out during negotiations.

The idea that they could make hundreds *more* warlocks would probably drive Lord Azrad into an even greater panic.

Of course, that might be exactly what Uncle Faran wanted, Hanner thought bitterly. Despite what he had said a few minutes ago, he might actually intend to go ahead and depose the overlord, maybe kill him outright. That statement that they would kill if necessary . . . the power of life and death theoretically belonged to the overlord and the Wizards' Guild, no one else. Faran was usurping it. He might intend to usurp more. Hanner knew his uncle had always been ambitious, always thought the city deserved better than fat old Azrad as its master—and Faran had clearly been disappointed that no position higher than Lord Counselor was open to him, short of a revolution.

Here, quite possibly, was his attempt at creating such a revolution.

"Now, we go to speak to the overlord!" Faran's arms dropped, and he began walking toward the Palace again.

"Now!" someone cried, and hundreds of spears were flung at the warlocks—only to bounce harmlessly from the invisible shield their magic still maintained. Soldiers marched forward, closing the path, only to be swept aside as Varrin and Kirsha advanced on either side of Lord Faran.

Hanner ignored all that; he was sure the warlocks could handle anything the guards might do. He ran forward, following his uncle, and called, "Uncle Faran!"

Lord Faran turned to listen to him, but did not stop walking.

"Uncle," Hanner said, speaking in low tones, "are you planning to take over the city?"

Faran glanced quickly around, then replied, "I might be considering the possibility."

"I wish you wouldn't," Hanner said. "I think you could do it well enough, but could you *hold* the city, once you took it?"

"Why not?" Faran said. He gestured at the soldiers. "*They* can't stop us."

"There are other powers to be considered," Hanner said. "The Wizards' Guild might accept you peacefully as another sort of magicians, like sorcerers or witches, but as the city's rulers? You know they won't allow that."

"Wizards have not been very effective against us so far," Faran said as they reached the bridge across the moat. The guards who ordinarily stood there were absent; presumably they had either been sent out with the others or had decided that being swept aside on a bridge was not as acceptable as being swept aside in the plaza and so had fled rather than risk being pinned against the stone railings or flung into the moat.

"Those?" Hanner snorted. "Those are nothing, and you know it. Those were the ordinary wizards the overlord could hire on short notice. I didn't see Ithinia or any of the other elder wizards out there on the streets."

"I think we can manage the Guild, all the same," Faran

said. "We might work out some power-sharing arrangement with them."

"I doubt it," Hanner said. "I don't think it's power they want, and it never was. But quite aside from that, Uncle, I think you're missing something important. All these plans of yours involve using a great deal of warlockry, don't they?"

"Yes, of course," Faran said. "It's all we have."

"And the more you use it, the more powerful you become."

"Yes."

"And the more powerful you become, the more prone to the nightmares."

Faran hesitated. He looked at Hanner, instead of staring ahead at the closed doors of the Palace.

"And the more powerful you become," Hanner continued, "the more you hear the Calling. And if you keep on using warlockry, flinging entire companies of guards about like so many rag dolls, sooner or later you'll reach Rudhira's level."

Faran stopped—but they were in the shelter of the palace entryway, close enough to the doors that Hanner wasn't sure whether it was his words or the physical barriers that were responsible. He frowned at Hanner.

"Uncle, that could happen to *you*, if you go through with this. You saw her today and yesterday—distracted, confused, and finally unable to stop herself. She flew off. We couldn't stop her. And I don't think she's coming back."

Faran waved to Varrin. "Open the door," he said. "Try not to smash it."

"Uncle, I think that's what happened to all those people who disappeared on the Night of Madness," Hanner said desperately. "I think they were the really *powerful* warlocks, the people who were more naturally attuned to it than you were." He gestured at the little crowd that had followed Faran onto the bridge. "You people are just the leftovers, the ones who only got a little bit of whatever it was. Whatever it was that did this, it was trying to summon people north, and some of you only got part of the message. But the more you listen, the more you'll hear, and sooner or later it will get through, and you'll fly off to the north."

"You're guessing," Faran said.

"Yes, I *am* guessing," Hanner admitted. "But do you want to risk it?"

Faran started to say something, then stopped. He turned slowly to look at the doors.

They were still closed.

He turned to look at Varrin, and found Varrin standing motionless, staring straight ahead—straight north.

"Varrin!" Faran barked. "The doors!"

"I'll do it," Kirsha said, and the doors sprang open.

Varrin was still staring blankly ahead; Hanner grabbed his sleeve. "Varrin," he said, "listen to me!"

"It's calling," Varrin said without looking at Hanner.

Hanner threw an angry glance at Faran, then turned his attention back to Varrin. "Varrin, *listen!* Turn away! And don't use any more magic, no matter what you do. Don't listen to it, listen to *me!*"

Varrin took a step forward, then stopped when Hanner's pull on his sleeve held him back. He paused, blinked, then looked at Hanner.

His eyes were haunted, almost glazed.

"Varrin, come on," Faran said. "We need to get to the audience chamber and talk to Azrad, get him to call off his war against warlocks. Then we can see whether a healer can do something about these dreams."

"A healer?" Hanner turned to stare at his uncle, but Faran paid no attention; he was waving his arm in a beckoning gesture.

"Come inside, all of you!" he called. Then he turned to Hanner. "If Varrin's inside he can't fly off the way Rudhira did, can he?"

"I hope not," Hanner said, unconvinced, as he followed Faran into the Palace.

What sort of a healer did his uncle have in mind? He knew that Alladia had said the gods wouldn't heal warlocks, and Shella had said witches couldn't touch the part of a warlock's brain that was presumably where the nightmares originated.

Faran wasn't thinking clearly, Hanner was sure of it; he was so caught up in the anger and exhilaration of using his magic to confront Azrad that he almost wasn't thinking at all.

Hanner wished he could think of the right thing to say, the words that would dissuade his uncle from a course Hanner was sure would end badly—but the words weren't there.

In the hallway beyond the doors the party of warlocks found Captain Vengar standing with raised spear. "I'm sorry, my lords," he began.

That was as far as he got before the spear splintered and fell to the floor in a dozen pieces; the steel spearhead bounced ringingly on the marble floor while the shattered fragments of the wooden shaft tumbled and rolled in various directions. Hanner had no idea which warlock had destroyed the weapon; it might have been a joint effort.

"Stand back, Captain," Faran said. "We're here to talk to the overlord."

Whether Vengar would have stood back voluntarily Hanner never found out; before the soldier could begin to respond he was picked up by invisible forces and slammed back against the tapestried wall, his helmet hitting the fabric with a loud, ugly thump. Hanner winced at the sound.

Vengar was a decent man, trying to do his job, Hanner thought; he didn't deserve such treatment. He glanced around, wondering which of the warlocks had done this.

There was no sign, no indication of whether it had been Varrin, or Kirsha, or Faran himself, or someone else in the group now straggling in.

Faran paid no more attention to Vengar, but marched down the grand hallway toward the golden doors of the main audience chamber with Varrin at his side and Kirsha on his heels. Hanner paused long enough to be sure Vengar was still breathing, then hurried after his uncle.

The other warlocks trailed into the Palace behind him,

and Hanner heard someone say, "Wow," at his first sight of the interior. He thought the voice might have been Othisen's, but he didn't take the time to look back and see.

He was too worried about what was about to happen. Uncle Faran was being overconfident, he was sure, and far too confrontational. The overlord might not be able to stop a gang of warlocks, but this sort of behavior was certain to eventually bring down the wrath of the Wizards' Guild, and despite what Uncle Faran said, Hanner did not think the warlocks were a match for the Guild.

Especially not when their most powerful members might vanish at any moment—Hanner noticed with dread that Varrin's sandals were a foot off the floor.

And before Faran could say a word to anyone Varrin spread his arms, and the golden doors did not merely open, but were smashed down, torn off their hinges, and then sent flying inward. Hanner winced at the sound of crashing metal; he had never heard anything quite like it. It was the sound of rattling pots and pans multiplied a thousandfold. He ran forward to grab Varrin, to try to calm him down.

It was too late; the weaver was flying now, ten feet up, soaring the length of the immense audience chamber in a matter of seconds, and smashing out through the great window above the overlord's vacant throne.

Faran and Hanner had both run forward into the audience chamber, hoping to catch Varrin; now, as the last shards of tumbling glass shattered on the stone, they both stopped and stood side by side on the long red carpet that ran from the door to the foot of the throne.

"May a thousand demons dance!" Faran said through gritted teeth.

Hanner managed to avoid saying "I told you so" only by clenching his own teeth hard.

Then he looked around, and realized that although the throne was empty and Lord Azrad not present, although the customary entourage of guards and servants was absent, the room was not totally deserted. Two figures stood to one side, cowering against the east wall below a tapestry showing someone directing the construction of a city wall.

One was Lord Clurim, one of Azrad's younger brothers. The other was Lady Nerra—Hanner's sister.

Chapter Thirty-six

Lord Faran waited impatiently until the entire party of warlocks had gathered in the center of the audience chamber, glancing now at his followers, now at his niece and Lord Clurim, now at the empty throne and the shattered window where Varrin had soared off into the northern sky. He made no attempt to address Clurim and Nerra—or for that matter anyone else. He simply waited.

Hanner watched the warlocks and estimated the crowd at about twenty; he studied their faces, trying to judge their mood. He looked especially closely at Desset, clearly the most powerful of them now that both Rudhira and Varrin were gone, to see whether she was yet acquiring that haunted look that meant the Calling was affecting her.

She seemed her usual self, so far. She, like most of the others, was looking around the room with awed curiosity.

None of them had ever seen the place before, and even Hanner, who had grown up in the Palace and been in the audience chamber at least a dozen times before, had to admit it was impressive. The coffered and gilded ceiling was almost thirty feet above the polished stone floor—a floor that had been magically hardened to prevent wear, so that it still appeared new more than two centuries after it was laid. The walls were hung with gigantic, lush tapestries depicting scenes from Ethsharitic history, and between each pair of tapestries stood a statue. Legend had it that the statues were various criminals or enemies of past overlords, petrified and put on permanent display here, but Hanner had no idea whether that was true.

Above some statues were balconies; above others were niches holding more statues.

Down the center of the chamber, for almost its entire sixty-yard length, was a thick carpet elaborately patterned in shades of red, some five yards across; most of the warlocks now stood on this. To either side of the carpet stood rows of fine chairs carved of black oak—though just now, several of these chairs had been knocked over or smashed by the massive ruined doors Varrin had flung from his path. Half a dozen oaken tables were arranged along the walls, widely spaced.

Daylight poured in from three windows at the north end of the room, above the great red and gilt throne. The two smaller windows, one on either side, were intact, while Varrin's departure had broken out the central portion of the central window, leaving intact the stained-glass rosettes around the border but reducing the lead tracery of the main section to twisted wreckage and allowing the salt-scented breeze to waft gently into the room.

On the east side of the room, not far from the south end, and not far from one of the small side doors, stood Lord Azrad's brother Clurim and Hanner's sister Nerra.

Lord Clurim was Lord of the Household, responsible for the smooth operation of the Palace; Lady Nerra had no official position as yet. Hanner had no idea why they were here in the audience chamber. They were not saying anything to the unruly bunch of warlocks that had just burst in; they were just standing there, watching.

"Lord Clurim," Faran said, turning to these two once the warlocks had gathered. He stepped off the red carpet toward them. "I seek an audience with your brother."

"Faran of Ethshar," Clurim said, his voice unsteady. "Lord Azrad has ordered you into exile; he is not interested in speaking with you."

Hanner noted Clurim's omission of the honorific in addressing Faran; that was a deliberate insult. Hanner had always considered Clurim little more than a harmless drudge, but he suddenly realized that the man had considerable courage. He knew Uncle Faran, knew his temper, and had just seen what warlocks could do to a set of doors weighing hundreds of pounds, but had intentionally insulted him.

"You mean he's hiding from me," Faran said.

Lord Clurim did not deign to reply, but Nerra made a wordless squeak of dismay. The warlocks watched silently. Hanner glanced at them and saw nervous faces—they had come this far following their leader, Lord Faran, but they clearly had not thought about what they expected to find.

They didn't know what they were supposed to do, so they were just watching, waiting for instructions.

"Am I to have no chance to appeal my sentence?" Faran said. "If not to the overlord himself, then at least to your other brother—Karannin, Lord High Magistrate?"

"You're not being exiled as a criminal, Faran," Clurim said. "You're being exiled for the good of the city. The overlord has the power to do that."

"Of course he does," Faran said. "But am I to have no opportunity to convince him that he's making a—"

"Lord Faran!" Kirsha shouted, suddenly bursting from her uncertain silence to interrupt. She pointed—not at Clurim, or Nerra, or any of the doors, but upward, at an angle.

Hanner and Faran and the others looked up to see a gray-robed figure hanging in midair before one of the balconies, a dozen yards north of Lord Clurim. The figure had a hood pulled up and forward, hiding its face, but Hanner had no doubt this was a wizard rather than a demon or anything else inhuman.

It stretched out a hand, pointing a long, bony finger at Faran. Hanner noticed that its other hand held a crystal goblet.

"Lord Faran of Ethshar!" the wizard said in a voice that rolled out across the hall and echoed from the walls. "You knew that as an official in the government of Ethshar of the Spices magic was forbidden to you, by the pact made between the Wizards' Guild and Lord Azrad the Great two hundred years ago, yet you gathered to you sorcerous talismans." His pointing hand dropped to the dagger on his belt. "The penalty is death, and I have been sent to carry out the ordained punishment . . ."

Lord Faran had not waited to see what the wizard wanted; instead he was levitating himself to confront the new arrival. He did not fly as easily or as well as Rudhira or Varrin or Desset had, but he was able to rise to the wizard's height, to face this intruder eye to eye rather than looking upward like a child facing a parent.

Then he spoke, his own voice booming out as unnaturally as the wizard's, interrupting the wizard's speech.

"I am the Lord of Warlocks," Faran said. "The Wizards' Guild has no authority over me!"

"Careful, Uncle . . ." Hanner said softly, staring up at the two men. He and Faran both knew that a wizard's dagger held immense magic, and that goblet was surely not just some obscure ceremonial token.

And to claim the title of Lord of Warlocks—who knew where that might lead?

"You are condemned for crimes committed before the Night of Madness transformed you, Lord Faran," the wizard said. "And thus, as commanded, I perform this spell." He raised the goblet in one hand, drew his dagger with the other . . .

And froze as Faran's magic reached out—Hanner could see it, with his warlock senses. Warlockry seemed sharp and crisp, as if the air around Faran were impossibly clear; it closed around the wizard.

But the wizard was surrounded by an aura of his own magic, especially around the tools he held, and where warlockry seemed preternaturally clear, Hanner perceived wizardry as a thick haze of distortion. Faran's warlockry cut through that haze enough to stop the wizard's hands for a moment, but the wizardry dissipated the warlockry, and Hanner could see that Faran's hold was weakening.

And then the wizard seemed to flicker—he vanished, and almost instantly reappeared a few inches to one side. Hanner had no idea what sort of spell had done this, but it was obviously some sort of prepared protection. Faran's magic swirled and shifted, reaching out again, but not fast enough.

The dagger plunged into the stuff in the goblet—Hanner could not see what it was, but there was something brownish in the crystal vessel.

"No!" Hanner cried, lashing out with his own magic, desperate to stop whatever spell the wizard had prepared.

He was unpracticed, untrained, and not much of a warlock to begin with. He tried to focus on movement, to halt whatever the wizard was doing, but he could not stop the wizard's hands, could not even touch the goblet or knife through the haze of wizardry that surrounded them.

Instead he reached into the wizard's chest and closed his magic around the wizard's heart. He squeezed, not to harm the man, but merely to *stop* him while Uncle Faran still lived.

The wizard gasped and convulsed in midair, flopping like a speared fish—but Hanner was no longer looking at him; he was instead staring up at his uncle.

Faran's skin had gone white the instant the tip of the dagger had touched the substance in the goblet; a second later his clothes, too, were white and stiff. His green cloak was bleached to bone-white in an instant, and as rigid as bone. The braided black queue of his hair was as white as any old man's, and frozen in midbounce.

And then it was done. Faran of Ethshar had been turned to stone.

And stone cannot fly. A statue cannot use warlockry to levitate. Faran's petrified remains fell to the floor as if a string had been cut.

And shattered. Shards of broken marble scattered in all directions, skittering and spinning across the magically hardened floor.

"*No!*" Hanner screamed, running forward, knocking stone fragments aside.

He heard the rustle of fabric and looked up to see the

hooded wizard falling as well. The corpse landed with a sodden thump.

Hanner stopped running. It was too late.

For a moment complete silence fell as the occupants of the room stared in shock. Then Nerra screamed and collapsed, sobbing.

Lord Clurim, recovering from his stunned astonishment, hurried to the fallen wizard.

"They killed each other," Kirsha said. She spoke quietly, but her voice carried in the stillness, and everyone present heard her.

Desset looked at the broken marble, at the fallen wizard, at the shattered window, and announced, "I'm going home." She turned, trembling, and walked quickly back out of the room.

"The guards!" another warlock called after her. "What about the guards?"

"What *about* them?" Desset called back. "They couldn't stop me on the way in, and they can't stop me now."

"She's right," someone else said. "We can go. They can't stop us."

"Why would they *want* to?"

There was a general mutter of agreement, and the entire group of warlocks began leaving.

Hanner watched them go, but felt no urge to join them. He stood where he was.

This was his home, after all. He was back in the Palace where he belonged, and no one here knew he was a warlock. Under the circumstances, he doubted the overlord would demand he leave again.

And he thought his sister Nerra would need someone to look after her, at least until the shock of Uncle Faran's death had passed.

He turned and hurried to Nerra's side. He put a comforting arm around her, but did not say anything.

Lord Clurim, kneeling beside the wizard's corpse, looked up to see the warlocks flee, glanced at Hanner and Nerra, then told no one in particular, "I don't know who this is—I never saw him before."

Hanner looked up. "He was from the Wizards' Guild, he said. He didn't give a name."

"I know," Clurim said. "But he's dead, and the Wizards' Guild doesn't like it when wizards die unexpectedly."

Hanner hesitated. He didn't like to lie outright, so he didn't want to say that Faran had killed the wizard and had already paid for it, but he certainly wasn't about to admit that *he* had stopped the wizard's heart.

"I'd better go tell Azrad," Clurim said, getting to his feet. He hurried out one of the small side doors.

And Hanner and Nerra were alone in the great audience chamber. Still holding his sister, Hanner looked around the vast space.

The doors were twisted into scrap, a dozen chairs broken. The statue that was all that was left of Lord Faran was shattered into a hundred pieces, the largest consisting only of the chest and one upper arm; the robed corpse lay across a few of the smaller fragments. The gaping hole in the central window was letting in warm, damp air that smelled of the sea.

So much, Hanner thought, for the benefits of open confrontation.

"Come on," Hanner said, getting to his feet and taking Nerra's arm. "Let's go upstairs, away from all this. I'll send someone for Alris later."

"He's really dead," Nerra said—the first intelligible words Hanner had heard from her in days.

"He's really dead," Hanner confirmed.

"Lord Clurim wanted me to tell him what Uncle Faran was planning," Nerra said as she stood up, still somewhat unsteady. "When I couldn't do that he wanted me to try to talk him into accepting exile. We were waiting here to meet Lord Azrad to discuss it."

"It wouldn't have worked," Hanner said.

"I know. I could never talk him into anything he didn't

want to do." She glanced at the dead wizard. "At least he took his killer with him."

"I wonder if anyone's ever done that before," Hanner murmured.

Of course, Faran hadn't really done it, but it would make a good story.

And the Guild had executed him not for warlockry, but for all his years of accumulating magical paraphernalia when he was Azrad's chief advisor. The wizard had said so.

That presumably meant that the Wizards' Guild still had not yet decided to wipe out the warlocks—at least, not officially. Otherwise, why bother explaining the reasoning in killing Uncle Faran?

Someone should talk to them, Hanner thought. Someone should convince them that warlocks meant no one any harm. At least, the surviving warlocks; obviously, Uncle Faran had been dangerous, but he was gone.

Someone *had* to talk to them.

It was the Guild, after all, that was the real threat to the warlocks; Lord Azrad and the city guard were not a serious problem. Faran had demonstrated that much before he died. So long as the warlocks worked together, ordinary people could not harm them—only magic.

But magic could probably slaughter them all. Not just wizardry; Hanner had no idea how warlocks would fare against a horde of demons, or the ancient Northern weapons the sorcerers used.

And it appeared that their own magic would defeat them, in time, as it had Rudhira and Varrin.

That, at least, was slow, and could be anticipated and countered. If a warlock took the nightmares as a sign to stop using his magic, Hanner thought that he might live out the rest of a normal life in relative peace. Hanner certainly intended to try.

Of course, that was assuming there were no more surprises in the nature of warlockry, and Hanner didn't know whether that was the case. *Nobody* did.

The Calling put a real limit on what a warlock could do. Lord Azrad had feared that a warlock might take over the city, declare himself ruler in the overlord's place—and in fact, Faran might have intended to do just that.

But doing that, Hanner saw, would be slow suicide. In order to hold power claimed by magic the warlock would need to use his magic regularly, to prove it was still potent, to fight off competing claimants—and if he did that, then the Calling would take him that much sooner.

If someone would just *explain* that to Azrad . . . and, more importantly, to the Wizards' Guild.

But it wasn't Hanner's problem. He had done enough. He had fought against the chaos on the Night of Madness, and been banned from his home for his efforts; he had helped the warlocks band together, and seen his uncle murdered in response. And talking to anyone wasn't his strong point; he always said the wrong thing.

He had done enough, and he had had enough.

"Come on," he told Nerra, turning away from the wreckage. "Let's go upstairs."

Chapter Thirty-seven

Manrin looked out a third-floor window at High Street. It had taken a quarter hour for the watchers to trickle back after Lord Faran had led his party off toward the Palace, but they had returned, and once again were flinging bricks and stones at the house.

None of these missiles ever struck the building; the warlocks remaining downstairs deflected them all. It seemed a rather pointless exercise, really, but that didn't stop the attackers.

No one would ever dare throw rocks at wizards that way,

Manrin thought. Wizards had *respect*. Warlocks, at least so far, clearly did not.

Lord Faran would have to change that.

Manrin considered that for a moment—what would it take to change it? What did wizards have that warlocks didn't?

Well, they had been around longer, of course. They often wore distinctive robes. And they had the Wizards' Guild, with its clear-cut rules. They were a familiar part of the World, while warlocks were still new and strange. Warlocks looked like ordinary people, but they weren't, and that scared people. They didn't know who the warlocks *were*.

That was something Lord Faran should fix, once he had taken over the city from Lord Azrad—as Manrin was sure he would do. He should give the warlocks some sort of uniform and devise a set of rules, Manrin thought, and then send someone out to explain the rules to everyone. Make them consistent and familiar, that's what would help them fit in.

And convince those people out front that no, the warlocks had *not* stolen their family and friends.

Lord Faran hadn't done any of that yet. He had gathered all the warlocks together, which was good, since there was strength in numbers, and he had given them some leadership and a little basic organization, sorting out who could do what, but he had left them a motley, ill-assorted bunch and kept them hidden away in this mansion, and he hadn't set out solid rules. He hadn't even *tried* to talk to the rock-throwers about their missing loved ones.

Manrin decided he would make some suggestions when he next saw Lord Faran.

Then he noticed, out in the street, that the watchers were looking east along High Street rather than at the house. He leaned forward and peered off to the left.

Running figures were approaching—and *flying* figures, as well. Warlocks, returning from the Palace! Manrin started to smile, thinking that this meant the conquest was already secured, but then he stopped.

Why were they *running*?

"Oh, no," he said.

He didn't see little Rudhira's distinctive green skirt and red hair, or Varrin's multicolored linen tunic, or Lord Faran's silks, and he wasn't sure what that meant, but he didn't think it was a good sign.

Then the vanguard of the returning warlocks neared the line of watchers, and the watchers were abruptly flung back, tumbling down the street as if swept by a gigantic hand, clearing the area in front of the house.

The returning warlocks would be in the house in seconds, and Manrin decided he wanted to be there, to hear what had happened. He turned and headed for the stairs.

A moment later he trudged panting down the steps—he was really too old for all this climbing and wished that people in Ethshar of the Spices didn't build such tall houses. In Ethshar of the Sands only a handful of structures had more than two floors—the Palace, the Great Lighthouse, Grandgate—because the ground wasn't stable enough to support anything higher without either magic or amazing luck. A four-story house was ostentatious even here; back home it would have been completely ridiculous.

By the time he was midway down the second flight the ground floor was swarming with frightened people, awash in a babble of voices.

One of them was Ulpen, who looked up the stairs and called, "Master!"

Manrin stopped.

Other warlocks heard Ulpen call out and looked up the stairs at Manrin. The old wizard could hear them muttering to one another.

". . . he's a wizard, he knows about magic . . ."

". . . can talk to the Guild . . ."

". . . used to running things . . ."

". . . has experience . . ."

"Master," Ulpen said loudly, "Lord Faran is dead. Will you lead us now?"

Manrin frowned. The lad was being ridiculous. And Lord Faran was *dead*?

Manrin had not expected that. He had not thought anything would stop Lord Faran, certainly nothing short of an all-out assault by the Wizards' Guild.

"What happened?" he asked. "How did he die?"

"A wizard turned him to stone," Kirsha called up to him.

"But he killed the wizard, too," someone added.

Then the Guild *had* intervened. That was bad. Manrin had hoped that the Guild might indeed come to the aid of their fellow magicians in the end.

"We need a leader, Master," Ulpen said.

Manrin snorted derisively. "I'm an old man, a wizard," he said. "I'm not a lord. I'm not even from this city."

"We need *someone*, Master. You were a Guildmaster, even if you weren't a lord, and isn't that more appropriate for a group of magicians?"

"It sounds to me as if *you're* taking charge, Ulpen!" Manrin tried to make plain in his tone and expression that he thought this was a *good* thing. If someone was going to face the Guild's wrath, Manrin would be happy to have it be someone other than himself. And the Guild might well take pity on a mere apprentice.

"Me?" Ulpen gasped, a hand on his chest. "I'm only sixteen!"

"And I'm a hundred and eleven, which is too old to be running around fighting soldiers."

"We'll fight *for* you!" Othisen shouted. There was a ragged chorus of agreement.

Manrin sighed. It was clear he wasn't going to get out of this easily—and really, if someone was going to have to negotiate with the Guild, he had to admit he was more qualified than anyone else in this mad assortment.

But he still didn't want the honor. "Is there no one else more suitable?" he said. "What about that other young lord, Lord Hanner?"

"He's not even a warlock," Ulpen said.

"And he didn't come back with us," Kirsha added. "He stayed in the Palace with his sister."

"He did?" This was from Lady Alris, on the fringe of the crowd. She had been sitting in the parlor when the others had returned from the Palace, and now she was standing in the doorway, listening.

Several voices replied, and the gathering dissolved into noisy chaos for a moment. Manrin, looking down from above, noticed young Shella, the former apprentice witch, standing in one corner, clearly trying to say something, but being ignored as the others all shouted at one another. She appeared to be on the verge of tears.

That was too much. He could never stand the sight of weeping children, and Shella reminded him of his granddaughter Planette.

"Silence!" he bellowed, hands raised, augmenting his voice with warlockry as Rudhira had taught him.

Silence fell. A dozen worried faces looked up at him.

"It would seem I *am* your new leader, whether I like it or not," Manrin said. "Well, if I am to lead you, I need to know who you all are, what you can do, and what has happened so far—as you may have noticed, I have spent much of my time upstairs, using what wizardry I still have to study our situation. I have missed details of events down here, even while I learned things the rest of you don't know. I do have some ideas—I had intended to speak to Lord Faran about them upon his return, but it appears that if he is indeed dead, I will have to act on them myself. First, though, I need to know just what has really happened, to Lord Faran and to the rest of you." He pointed at Ulpen. "I'll hear you one at a time, starting with my apprentice."

For the next two hours Manrin questioned the other warlocks. He learned about the Calling, and how it had taken Rudhira and Varrin; he learned about Lord Faran's ghastly death at the hands of the Wizards' Guild. He took a roll call, learning who was still in the group and who had fled, going home or hiding elsewhere, and he sorted the warlocks out by their level of power, as Faran had.

When that was done he thought he had a fairly good understanding of the situation—and he didn't like it much. Varrin had done serious damage to the Palace, and Faran had slain a high-ranking member of the Wizards' Guild—executions were never left to anyone of low rank. The party as a whole had further antagonized the entire city by their march through the streets.

But it might not be too late to make amends, Manrin thought. Lord Faran's death, while a tragic loss, was also an opportunity. Their dead leader could be made a convenient target for the city's anger and mistrust. The warlocks could blame Lord Faran for all the harm they had done, absolving the survivors of any responsibility.

But, Manrin was convinced, they had to present themselves as real magicians, a lawful part of the city, not a mysterious, lawless, alien force.

He started to explain this to his new followers, but had not gotten very far before Kirsha demanded, "How?"

Manrin stopped. "How what?" he asked.

"How can we present ourselves as normal magicians? We're not—we're from all over the city, from a dozen different backgrounds, not people who served a proper apprenticeship to learn a trade. Just look at us!"

"You have a point," Manrin said, "and I've thought about it. I think we need to do something to make ourselves look more like a coherent group. Perhaps if we all dyed our clothes to one color? Red might be nice. Is that man Bern around? He might be able to help . . ."

"He's in the kitchens somewhere," Shella called. "I'll go find him."

"We can't dye all our clothes red," Desset said. "You can't dye dark colors red; the old color will show through. We'd need to get all new clothes."

"We could dye everything black," Othisen suggested. "Black will cover anything."

"Then we'd look like demonologists," Alladia said.

"Is that bad?" Desset asked. "Everyone knows demon-

ologists are magicians, and they may not like them, but
nobody throws bricks at their windows."

"Exactly!" Manrin said. "Black it is, then—from now on,
warlocks wear black."

"But they'll think we're all demonologists!" Alladia protested.

"Better that than thinking we're warlocks, I'd say," Yorn
commented.

"Black," Manrin said. "You chose me to lead you, and
as your leader, I tell you to wear black—if Bern can get us
the dye."

Desset nodded. "Everyone looks good in black, too."

Manrin didn't think everyone present agreed with that,
but he wasn't about to let his followers argue about trivia.
"And we'll need to advertise," he said. "Ordinary magicians
are useful, they earn their living from their magic. Well, we
can all do things that people will pay for—we can heal
wounds as well as anyone, we can open locks, we can break
things or repair things. We need to let everyone know that.
Right now, thanks to those of us who did things we
shouldn't have on the Night of Madness, they think of us
as thieves and bullies, not honest citizens, and we need to
fix that. Some of us should volunteer to help rebuild the
shops and houses that got smashed on the Night of Madness. And people think we kidnapped all those people who
disappeared out of their beds—we need to convince them
we didn't."

"How do we do *that*?" Yorn called. "What are we going
to say?"

"We'll just tell them the truth," Manrin said. "Eventually
maybe it will sink in."

"But how can we advertise?" Kirsha asked. "We can't
just hang out a signboard!"

"Not here, no," Manrin agreed. "We'll need to rely on
word of mouth. Those of us who have friends and family
should let them know. The word will spread."

"Do you really think anyone will hire us?" Kirsha asked.
Before Manrin could reply, Zarek asked, "Can we still

stay here? If Lord Faran is dead, who owns this house?"

Manrin had been about to answer Kirsha, but now he stopped dead, mouth open.

"I don't know," he said at last. "Did Lord Faran have any children? Or perhaps Lord Hanner's parents?"

"Our parents are both dead," Lady Alris said from the parlor door. "If Uncle Faran ever acknowledged any children, I don't know about it. I think Hanner and Nerra and I were his closest kin."

"Thank you, Lady Alris," Manrin said. "Then unless there's a settlement we don't know about, Lord Hanner would now own the estate, with an obligation to provide for his sisters."

"Is Bern here?" Alris asked. "He should know."

"Here he is," Shella called, leading Bern by the hand through the crowd at the dining-hall door.

"Good!" Manrin said. "Bern, Lady Alris, if the three of us could speak somewhere . . ." When neither of them protested, Manrin smiled and said, "Good! All of you, we have seen that confrontation with the overlord and his guards is not going to get us anywhere. Lord Faran meant well, and he did a good thing gathering us here and teaching us what we are, but trying to conquer the city is not for us. What we need to do is make a place for ourselves, a place that the rest of the city will accept. While I speak with Lady Alris and Bern, I want the rest of you to think about what we can do to fit in, to make ourselves useful and welcome. For now, it appears we are still welcome here—Lord Hanner has not come and ordered us to leave—but we have to consider the possibility that we will need to leave and go elsewhere. If you have any suggestions or questions, find me later and we'll discuss them."

With that, he beckoned to Alris and Bern, then turned and headed back up the stairs.

The two followed him up to a study on the third floor, where they settled in for a long discussion of household affairs and Lord Faran's family history.

The news, Manrin thought, was mixed. It did indeed appear that Lord Faran had no family except his sister's children, and so far as anyone knew none of his many women could claim to carry his child or even to have married him. If Lord Hanner was Faran's heir that was good—an actual warlock would have been better, but Lord Hanner had certainly appeared sympathetic enough.

The bad news came from Bern. The household supplies were running low. He could get to market only when one of the more powerful warlocks got him safely past the thugs in the street. And worst of all, the household funds were exhausted—he was operating on credit. Lord Faran's credit had already become questionable, and when word got out that he was dead it would be cut off completely.

The warlocks needed to find another source of income immediately; that need was rather more urgent than Manrin had realized.

Of course, he had his own money, back in Ethshar of the Sands, and some of the other warlocks presumably had full purses, but even so, they really needed to start earning.

There were half a dozen bloodstones in one of the hundreds of drawers of wizard's supplies that Lord Faran had collected, and those could be enchanted with the Spell of Sustenance so that whoever carried them would need no food or drink, but even though many of the warlocks who had accompanied Lord Faran on the march to the Palace had not returned, there were far more than half a dozen people in the house. Besides, the bloodstone spell was not healthy if used for too long. A sixnight or two would be no problem, but if the days turned into months . . .

It was hard to believe how much his life had changed in just three days. He had been a respected and wealthy wizard, a Guildmaster, with friends and family, and now he was an outlaw, a warlock, worrying about paying for his next meal.

Manrin shook his head at the thought. He really was too old for this sort of thing.

After several minutes of conversation Bern insisted on leaving to prepare supper—he had been starting on that when Shella had fetched him from the kitchens. That left Manrin and Alris alone in the study. Manrin tried to question Alris about her uncle's plans and what her brother might do, but Alris was hardly brimming over with information or enthusiasm.

And after all, why should she be? She wasn't a warlock, just an ordinary girl, and her uncle had just died, which had to be a blow even though she hadn't appeared to like him much. She probably just wanted to go home to the Palace, to see her sibs and resume her former life.

All the same, Manrin kept her there talking until Shella came upstairs to call them to supper.

At the meal Alris sat in sullen silence while the warlocks talked about what they should do. She should be taken home to the Palace at the first opportunity, Manrin decided as he pretended to listen to Othisen's schemes for using warlockry on his father's farm.

And Othisen should go home, as well, he thought.

In fact, *all* the warlocks probably ought to return to their old homes, Manrin thought—at least, those who had homes. Surely, most people would accept them back. They could claim that Lord Faran had gone mad and led them astray.

But those who were still in the house did not seem ready to go, and Manrin saw no need to chase them out hastily.

Some, like Zarek, had no homes to return to.

And Manrin himself—what good would it do him to go home, to a wizard's house, when he could no longer function as a proper wizard? What good would it do Ulpen or Shella to go back to an apprenticeship he or she could never complete?

No, there were still reasons for some of them to stay.

The discussion of what they were to do dragged on long after the meal was over, with no signs of ending anytime soon, until finally Manrin yawned widely, picked up a candle, and announced he was going to bed.

At the top of the first flight of stairs he hesitated; he and Ulpen had shared a room, but he was now the leader in Lord Faran's place; shouldn't he take the master's bed? He walked down the passageway to the north end and through the double doors into the great bedchamber.

Yes, he thought, as he stood in the doorway and looked wryly at the sculpture and other furnishings, he really ought to spend at least one night here, just so he could someday tell his grandchildren about it. He set the candle on the nearer nightstand and prepared for bed.

Tired as he was, he had no trouble falling asleep despite the unfamiliar surroundings.

Chapter Thirty-eight

Manrin had no idea how long he had been asleep when the dream began. He knew at once it was a magical dream, and after all he had heard about the Calling that afternoon he was relieved to see that it was wizardly in nature, and not his first warlock's nightmare.

He found himself standing in a bare stone room he did not recognize, facing Ithinia of the Isle, senior Guildmaster of Ethshar of the Spices and rumored member of the Inner Circle of the Wizards' Guild. The clarity of details and Ithinia's awkward behavior convinced him that this was no ordinary nighttime fantasy, but a sending.

"The Spell of Invaded Dreams, eh?" he asked when Ithinia seemed to be in no hurry to speak. "The Lesser or the Greater? Can you hear me?"

"I can hear you," the dream Ithinia said. "This is the Greater Spell of Invaded Dreams, and we can speak freely."

That was reassuring. The Greater Spell took significantly more effort; if the Guild had simply wanted to send him a message they would have used the Lesser, which only communicated in one direction, from wizard to dreamer. The

Greater Spell, which allowed communication in both directions, indicated that they wanted to talk.

"I take it that the Guild has something to discuss with me?" Manrin said.

"Indeed," Ithinia agreed. "We are aware that you, and the apprentice Ulpen, are now warlocks, as are some fifty-six other wizards of varying experience and power throughout the Hegemony of the Three Ethshars."

Manrin's dream-self blinked in surprise. He had had no idea there were others besides Ulpen and himself. "Fifty-six others?" he said. "Where?"

"Scattered," Ithinia told him. "Fourteen are within the walls of Ethshar of the Spices."

"In this house?"

"No, in their own homes. That doesn't matter. Guildmaster Manrin, I am not here to discuss others; I am here to discuss *you*."

"Ah. And what is it you wish to discuss?"

"Guildmaster, you know the Guild's rules. Wizards are not to meddle in other forms of magic."

"I didn't meddle in anything," Manrin said. "I had it thrust upon me, just like all the others."

"Yes, we know. Nonetheless, you are now both a warlock and a wizard, and the Guild does not permit this. There are too many unknowns, too many risks. Warlockry and wizardry interfere with each other in too many ways."

"So what am I to do, then? I can't stop being a warlock, can I? Have you found a way to reverse whatever it is that did this to me?"

"No," Ithinia said. "You can't stop being a warlock. The change appears to be irreversible. However, the power you now wield does not derive from you, but from an outside source. It would be enough if you were cut off from that source. You would still be a warlock, but you would be completely powerless to use your warlockry."

"Can that be done?" Manrin asked, startled.

"Not while you remain in the World. However, the Guild

has access to places outside the World. If you choose, you can be exiled to such a place."

Manrin considered that, but only briefly. "I wouldn't accept exile from Lord Azrad," he said. "Why should I accept it from you?"

"You did not swear to obey Lord Azrad. You did swear an oath, when you were accepted as an apprentice, to obey the rules of the Wizards' Guild."

That was undeniably true, but Manrin was not ready to yield. "To leave the world . . . I assume that these places you describe are magical creations?"

"Yes."

"Small places, then? Not so much as a village?"

"Yes."

"I would be choosing to spend the rest of my life in prison."

"Yes."

"And you think I'll agree to this?"

"If you choose to remain a wizard, yes."

"Well, how could I not . . ."

He stopped, and even in the dream he could feel his face turn pale.

"Oh, no," he said.

"You can stop being a wizard," Ithinia said. She pointed at Manrin's belt.

In the dream his dagger, his athame, slid from its sheath and hovered before his eyes, seeming to fill his field of vision. The image of Ithinia seemed to recede into the distance, though he and she were both still in a small stone room.

"Without the athame you are no longer a wizard," Ithinia's voice said, though he could no longer see her speak. "Break it, and we will let you remain alive in the World."

"But part of my *soul* is in it!" Manrin protested. "I wouldn't be whole!"

"Nevertheless, you must choose," Ithinia insisted. "Warlock or wizard."

"If I had a choice, I'd rather be a wizard," Manrin said. "But I *don't* have a choice—I'm both!"

"The Guild cannot permit you to be both and go free," Ithinia said. "You must break your athame, accept magical exile, or die."

Manrin stared miserably at the floating knife. "I've lived in the World as a wizard, bound to this dagger, for ninety-eight years," he said.

"And you are forbidden to remain a wizard so bound, and living in the World. You swore obedience."

His dream-self reached up to touch the dagger; it vibrated as his fingers neared it.

"If I break it, you'll let me live and remain free?" he said. "Then the Guild has decided not to exterminate the warlocks?"

Ithinia hesitated. "If you break it, we will not kill you now," she said.

Manrin closed his eyes wearily. "But you might later," he said. "The Inner Circle has not yet decided on what to do about the warlocks, then?"

"We have not yet decided," Ithinia admitted.

He opened his eyes again, grabbed the athame, and thrust it back in its sheath on his belt.

"I won't do it," he said. "I ask you to reconsider."

"We *have* considered this," Ithinia said. "We have debated it for days, and while we have not yet decided about *all* warlocks, we have decided to enforce the existing rules. All nobles who have become warlocks must renounce their titles or die; all wizards must destroy their athames, or accept eternal exile from the World, or die. We leave the other magicians to their own people, but we know that warlocks cannot summon either gods or demons, so we have no fear of warlock theurgists or demonologists."

"I won't do it," Manrin said. "I won't throw away my freedom, nor a century's experience."

"Then we have no choice but to kill you."

"You can try," Manrin said, "but I am the leader of a band of warlocks, and I still retain many of my old protec-

tions—not least this athame you want me to destroy! I may
not be so easy a target as you think, and you may not be
pleased with the results if you antagonize the warlocks. We
aren't as weak as the witches or sorcerers. Remember that
Lord Faran took his executioner with him!"

"We remember," Ithinia said.

And then she was gone, and Manrin woke up in Faran's
gigantic bed, staring up into the darkness.

"Protections," he mumbled, pushing the bedclothes aside.
"I need protec . . ."

Then he felt the hands close around his throat—clawed,
inhuman hands. Faint light came from the windows and the
crack beneath the doors, but he could see nothing at all; his
attacker was invisible.

"Fendel's Assassin," he said. "Good choice. And of
course you wouldn't give me time to prepare; that would
be stupid. I should have known."

And then the grip tightened, and he could no longer
breathe, let alone speak.

Chapter Thirty-nine

Lord Hanner awoke on the morning of the eighth
day of Summerheat in his own familiar bed, in his own
familiar room in the Palace, and spent several minutes lying
there, simply enjoying the sensation.

Then he remembered how he had come here, and that
Uncle Faran was dead, and all his joy in being home evap-
orated.

It might not even *be* his home much longer. He lived in
this apartment because Uncle Faran had been chief advisor
to the overlord; now Faran had not merely quit, he had died.
Unless Hanner or one of his sisters found a position in the

overlord's service, the overlord would probably order them all out eventually.

Uncle Faran had died. Hanner had still not fully absorbed that fact. Faran had been turned to stone and shattered. Petrifaction might be reversible sometimes, depending which spell was used, but nobody could reassemble a broken statue and then restore it to life intact. Faran was gone.

There could be no funeral, no pyre to send Faran's soul heavenward in the rising smoke; Faran was just gone. His marble remains could be collected, but there was no point in it—whatever was going to become of his soul had already happened. His ghost might still be in the Palace somewhere, might even manage to haunt it; half a dozen other ghosts were already said to be harmlessly resident, though Hanner had never encountered any of them. Faran's soul might be trapped forever in the stone or might have freed itself somehow when the stone broke open—those were all possible, and Hanner had no idea which had happened.

He would probably *never* know. Necromancy was expensive and unreliable.

Hanner sat up in bed and sighed. No matter how much he desired it, his life could never again be what it had been before the Night of Madness. Uncle Faran was dead. He could no longer be his uncle's aide; he would need to make a new career.

Uncle Faran was dead.

Abruptly, Hanner broke down in tears.

He couldn't remember a time when Uncle Faran hadn't been there; even when both his parents were alive and present, Faran had always been around. After Hanner's father disappeared, Faran helped his sister, Hanner's mother, with her three children.

And when their mother died, Faran took them all in and looked after them. He had been all they had left.

Hanner had loved and respected his uncle. It wasn't the same sort of love he had felt for his mother or father; Faran hadn't been anywhere near that close, and he had often overridden their desires in pursuit of his own ideas of what was best. But still, he had always been there, had always made sure Hanner and Nerra and Alris were safe. He had been the center of the family, the core they all revolved around.

Now that center was gone, leaving Hanner the eldest of the family.

He sat in his bed crying for several minutes, but at last regained control of himself and wiped his eyes with the bedsheets. When he felt sufficiently recovered he slid out of the bed and got dressed.

Nerra was slumped on the window seat in the sitting room, looking eastward over the Old City, and Hanner was fairly sure she had been crying, too.

"I can't believe he's gone," she said.

"I know," Hanner said.

Faran was gone—and that meant Hanner, as the eldest, was the head of the family. That meant, he realized, that he was responsible for the care of his sisters.

Nerra was eighteen, old enough to care for herself, but Alris was not.

Alris was still at the house on High Street. At least, Hanner certainly hoped she was, since she wasn't here. He would have to fetch her back to the Palace. If the overlord was still forbidding people entrance . . .

Well, if he was, that was foolish. The warlocks had demonstrated beyond question that if they wanted in, Azrad couldn't keep them out. If those orders were still in effect Hanner would just have to sneak Alris in anyway. He thought he could use his own warlockry to do it, if necessary, as he had at the house.

He would need to be very, very careful from now on, though, so as not to let anyone know that he was a warlock. Lord Azrad had sentenced the warlocks to exile, and the Wizards' Guild might well intend to exterminate them; Hanner had no intention of submitting to either fate.

For one thing, he was head of the family. If he were exiled, how could he look after Alris? There was no reason *she* should be exiled.

He would definitely need to fetch her home, right after breakfast.

"Have you eaten?" he asked.

Nerra turned up a hand. "I'm not hungry."

"Nerra, I know you're grieving—so am I—but today may turn out to be extremely busy. It's not impossible that Lord Azrad will have us thrown out of these apartments. I really think you should eat something."

Nerra did not say anything in reply, but she got up from the window seat and trudged toward the door. Hanner followed.

In the kitchens Hanner watched to make sure Nerra actually was eating her portion of bread and salt pork, and wondered whether Uncle Faran had any bloodstones in those drawers on the third floor, and whether Manrin might be willing to enchant them. That would keep Nerra's strength up while she worked through her grief. In many ways, while Hanner had been the one who worked as Faran's assistant, it was Nerra who had been closest of the three of them to Uncle Faran.

Of course, any dealings with Manrin, a warlock, might be dangerous, Hanner thought; maybe they should go to the Wizards' Quarter to buy the Spell of Sustenance.

It would be far more efficient to have it when collecting Alris, though. Besides, High Street was so much closer.

And if the overlord did decide to throw them out of the Palace they would probably be living in the house on High Street for a while anyway.

For now, though, they would eat like anyone else. Hanner looked down at his hand and realized he had not yet eaten his own breakfast. He took a bite of pork and chewed dutifully.

People wandered in and out of the kitchens as they ate, all going about their business in so familiar a fashion that Hanner's heart ached to see it. Faran's death had not disrupted anything here, nor had the warlocks, nor the destruction in the great audience chamber. The only visible change was Hinda's absence—a sixnight ago she would have been all over the kitchens, running errands for the cooks.

No one spoke to Hanner and Nerra, though; they finished their meal in silence, brushed crumbs from their clothes, and made their way through the familiar stairways and corridors back to their apartments . . .

Where they found Bern, Alris, and two burly guardsmen waiting for them in the corridor.

"What's going on?" Hanner asked as he ambled along the passage toward them.

Alris glanced up at one of the guards who said, "Lady Alris brought this person into the Palace with her, and we didn't want to leave them unattended."

"He might be a warlock who put a spell on her," the other guard offered.

"Bern? Bern's not a warlock," Hanner said. "He's my uncle's housekeeper."

"I *told* them that!" Alris said angrily.

"Yes, you did, my lady, but we had to be careful, with all this trouble we've had the past few days."

The other guard started to speak, then hesitated. "What is it?" Hanner asked him.

"My lord," the soldier said awkwardly, "is it true your uncle is dead? That's what we heard, but you know how rumors are."

"I do know how it is," Hanner agreed, "but this one is true. Lord Faran is dead."

"The wizards killed him?"

"Yes."

"I'm very sorry, my lord." He sounded quite sincere.

Hanner could feel his throat tightening as he replied, "Thank you." He blinked, just to make sure no tears would escape, and said, "Might I ask you a question in return?"

"Of course, my lord."

"Just what is the situation here? A couple of days ago the overlord wasn't allowing *anyone* into the Palace, for fear warlocks would get in, but here you've let Al . . . Lady Alris and Bern in. Has the order been rescinded?"

"Yes, it has," the guard said. "Last night. After all, those warlocks made it pretty clear yesterday that if they wanted to get in we couldn't stop them, and if we're going to have workmen in to repair the damage, and magicians in to make sure it doesn't happen again, well, we can't keep *everyone* out. So we're back to the old rules—anyone with business in the Palace, or who knows the password, is allowed in."

Hanner nodded. "That makes sense," he said. He resisted the temptation to add that that made it all the more surprising Lord Azrad had agreed to it. "If you heard about my uncle's death, did you hear anything about who is to replace him as the overlord's chief advisor?"

The two soldiers glanced at each other. "There's talk that Lord Ildirin will be promoted," one said.

"Or Lord Karannin," the other added.

"Or even Lord Azrad the Younger," said the first.

"So he intends to keep it in the family, then?"

"I don't think he trusts anyone else anymore."

"Except us, of course, but we aren't courtiers."

Hanner grimaced. "Of course," he agreed. "And do you know what Lord Azrad intends to do about the warlocks?"

The soldiers looked at each other again.

"I don't think we can talk about that," one said. "After all, you were with those warlocks, and they might be listening in with their magic."

Hanner smiled. "Warlocks can't do that," he said. "Their magic doesn't work that way."

The guardsman turned up a palm. "I wouldn't know, my lord. I'm not sure *anyone* really knows what a warlock can and can't do, when they're so new."

"Better to be safe," the other added.

"Has anyone said anything about me?"

"Not that I've heard, my lord."

The other didn't answer with words, but raised an empty hand.

"Well, thank you," Hanner said. He could see Alris looking angrily impatient, and Bern looking worried. He pointed at Bern. "I can attest that this man is Lord Faran's housekeeper, and at least as of yesterday he wasn't a warlock. Unless someone turned him into one overnight, I assume he still isn't."

"Thank you, my lord." The guard glanced at his companion. "I suppose we'll be going, then."

"Good enough," Hanner said. "Thank you for escorting them here."

The two soldiers both essayed quick little bows, then turned and marched off while Hanner unlocked the door to the family's rooms.

"You heard about Uncle Faran?" Nerra asked.

"Yes," Alris said. "It sounds *horrible*! Poor Uncle Faran!"

"It was quick," Hanner said as he swung the door open and stood aside to let the others in.

When they were all inside, and the door closed, Hanner said, "I assume you're here, Alris, simply because you wanted to come home—but, Bern, why are *you* here? Are the warlocks throwing out everyone who isn't one of them?"

Alris and Bern exchanged glances. "No, my lord," Bern said. "I'm afraid we're here with bad news, and ... well, we need your advice."

Hanner's stomach began to hurt. "More bad news?" he said. "It isn't enough that Uncle Faran and Rudhira and Varrin are all gone?"

"It's about the wizard," Alris said as she settled onto a chair.

"Ithinia?"

"No, no," Bern said quickly. "Manrin the Mage."

"What about him?"

"We found him dead in his bed this morning," Bern said. "That apprentice wizard, Ulpen, says that he was killed by wizardry for refusing an order from the masters of the Wizards' Guild."

Hanner considered this for a moment, then asked, "And how does Ulpen know this?"

"The Guild sent him a dream," Alris said. "With the same order. Only he obeyed."

That more or less made sense; Hanner had heard the Spell of Invaded Dreams described, though he had never experienced it directly. "What was the order?"

"He won't say," Bern replied.

"But he says he's not a wizard anymore," Alris added. "Not even an apprentice. He's just a warlock."

Hanner's eyes widened. "I didn't know that was possible."

Alris turned up a palm. "That's what he *said*."

Hanner nodded. It made sense. The Wizards' Guild was enforcing its rules, as they had with Uncle Faran—no hereditary nobles could use magic, and no one could use more than one kind of magic.

Manrin and Ulpen hadn't *asked* for a second kind of magic, so the Guild had offered a choice—give up one, or die. And there was no way to give up warlockry.

Apparently there was a way to give up wizardry. That was interesting, if not particularly useful information.

And while news of Manrin's death was also interesting, and somewhat distressing, Hanner had hardly known the old man and did not quite see what it had to do with *him*. He was about to say so when there was a knock on the door.

"I'll get it," Alris said, bouncing up from her chair.

She opened the door, and Hanner heard a familiar voice say, "Alris? You're home?"

"Mavi!" Nerra said, rising from the window seat. "Come in!"

Alris ushered Mavi in, where Nerra embraced her. Hanner smiled at the sight of her, but did not touch her.

"Good morning, Mavi," he said.

"Hanner!" She smiled a broad, bright smile at him. "It's good to see you back where you belong. I heard they were letting people into the Palace again, so I came to see how Nerra was doing—I should have realized you'd be here, too!" Then she noticed the other man and looked questioningly at Hanner.

"Bern was about to explain why he came," Hanner said. He looked at the servant expectantly.

"Oh," Bern said. He glanced at Mavi, then said, "It's simple enough, my lord. With your uncle's death, you are now the owner of the house at the corner of High Street and Coronet, and therefore my employer. I came to discuss the nature and terms of my further employment there, if any, and your plans for the property."

"Lord Faran is *dead*?" Mavi asked, clapping her hands to her mouth in horror.

"He died yesterday," Hanner said. "The Wizards' Guild killed him for meddling in magic."

"But he killed the wizard they sent," Alris added. Hanner did not contradict her; the weight of that unknown wizard's death was on his own soul, and he thought he might well have to deal with it eventually, but for now it would do no one any good to reveal the truth.

"That's terrible!" Mavi said, falling onto a chair. Nerra patted her hand comfortingly.

"Please forgive the interruption, Bern," Hanner said when Mavi was settled. "You were saying?"

"I was saying, my lord, that you are the eldest surviving member of Lord Faran's family, and are therefore his heir— he named you as his heir in papers he left in my care, to remove any possible question."

It was Hanner's turn to feel unsteady on his feet, but he remained standing. He had not thought Uncle Faran had thought highly enough of him to have made out such papers.

"He did?"

"Yes, my lord. Where his ownership of that house had been kept secret, he wanted to be certain there would be no confusion on this point."

Hanner glanced at his sisters.

"Well," he said, "at least we'll have somewhere to live if Lord Azrad evicts us."

The legacy meant rather more than that, Hanner knew. While he was unsure how much money Uncle Faran had left, he had seen the furnishings of that house, in particular the magical materials and devices on the upper floors, and he knew that he could sell them off for enough to live on for a long, long time. His future, and the future of his sisters, was suddenly far less uncertain.

"That's assuming the warlocks let you in," Nerra said. "Haven't they taken over that place?"

"Uncle Faran invited them," Alris said. "We can uninvite them, if we choose. Besides, most of them have already left—they got scared by what happened yesterday, with Rudhira and Varrin being Called, and then Uncle Faran dying, and then Manrin."

"They have?" Hanner asked Bern.

"Yes, my lord," Bern said. "I believe only eleven warlocks remain in residence." He cleared his throat. "Which brings me to another reason I have come. We need to know your intentions toward those who remain and any others who may return."

"My intentions? Well, I don't see any reason to cast them out into the streets—they're our guests, and some of them have nowhere else to go but the Hundred-Foot Field."

"Don't be stupid, Hanner," Alris said. "Of course there's a reason. They're *warlocks*."

Hanner glared at her. "I don't see why that makes any difference."

"I'm afraid it does," Bern said. "Quite aside from the bricks and torches that continue to be flung at the house, and the risk of damage from experimentation by the warlocks themselves, there is the question of what the authorities will do."

"The authorities? You mean the overlord?"

"The city guard, yes. And the Wizards' Guild. My lord, if they do set out to exterminate the warlocks, it would be far simpler for them to destroy that house, and everyone in it, than to kill the eleven of them one by one."

"Destroy it how?" Hanner asked. "The overlord isn't about to simply burn down a mansion in the New City— what if the fire spreads?"

"I wasn't thinking of the overlord, my lord. I was thinking of the Wizards' Guild."

"Oh," Hanner said.

He could hardly argue with that. Nobody really knew just what the Wizards' Guild was capable of. They had a reputation for ruthlessness—though how well deserved it might be Hanner did not know. He could not think of any instance in his lifetime when the Wizards' Guild had destroyed an entire house in the middle of the city—but he certainly couldn't say they wouldn't do it. They very well might.

One spell would probably be cheaper than eleven, and wizards were always aware of the costs of what they did.

Some people might argue that destroying a mansion full of valuables was a high cost in itself, but Hanner knew better. That wasn't how the Guild thought. It wasn't *their* mansion, and its destruction would reinforce the Guild's reputation for fearsomeness.

The Guild wanted to be feared. Hanner had learned that long ago in talking to the magicians in the Wizards' Quarter. It was much easier to convince people to obey your orders if they were terrified of you. Smashing an entire mansion to pebbles and kindling, or burning it to the ground, or simply causing it to vanish, would provide exactly the sort of example that the Guild wanted—a demonstration that no one, no matter how wealthy or powerful, could defy them.

Uncle Faran had always believed that the Guild wanted power for its own sake, that they were building up their authority little by little with the goal of eventually ruling the World, and he had resented that. He had told Hanner that the Guild was virtually ruling the World *now*, and that soon, when they were sure no one could oppose them effectively, they would do so openly. He had constantly sought ways to convince everyone of this, and ways to oppose the Guild's plans.

Hanner had never believed a word of it, and he had tried for years to convince his uncle otherwise. It was plain to Hanner that Faran's beliefs made no sense. After all, if the Wizards' Guild wanted to rule the World openly, they could do it at any time. For all Uncle Faran's theories and studies and bluster, he had never found anyone who could stand up to the Guild.

The closest he had ever come was the warlocks he led to the Palace, and all that had done was get him killed.

No, Hanner thought he knew what the Wizards' Guild wanted. He had talked to dozens of wizards over the past few years, from the newest apprentices up to Guildmaster Ithinia, and they had told him what the Guild wanted, and he believed them.

What the Guild wanted was to avoid trouble.

The Guild had been created by the wizards near the end of the Great War, a little more than two centuries earlier, not to rule the World, but to *protect* it—from wizards. They had foreseen the possibility that the great wizards of Ethshar, once the war was over and their common foe was finally destroyed, might fight among themselves. They had all seen, in the course of the fighting, what magic could do when used without restraint—the eastern portion of Old Ethshar was said to still be a lifeless desert, two hundred years after the war, and the devastation of the Northern Empire's heartland was rumored to have been even more complete, though so far as Hanner knew no one had ever gone there to check.

So the wizards had made a pact—any magician who might cause trouble, any magician who became involved in government or who tried to combine too many skills, would be killed out of hand, before he could cause real trouble.

That was the Guild's whole reason for existence, according to the wizards. Hanner believed it; Faran never had.

The Guild's entire philosophy was to smash potential trouble before it became more than mere potential—take a little trouble now to prevent far more later.

Flattening a house full of warlocks would fit right in with that philosophy.

But the warlocks were Hanner's guests. He had brought them there. No matter how dangerous their presence might be, he would not simply throw them out into the street.

But he might want to ask them to find another place.

"Who's in charge there?" he asked. "Who's leading the warlocks now that Uncle Faran is dead?"

Bern and Alris exchanged glances.

"*You* are," Alris said. "At least, that's what they want."

"That's another reason I'm here," Bern said quickly before Hanner could respond. "After Lord Faran died they chose Manrin as their new leader, but then *he* died, as well. Some wanted Ulpen next, but he's still so young, just an apprentice, that the others objected, and he refused. So now they invite *you* to come lead them. Zarek in particular spoke strongly in favor of the idea—he says it was *you*, not Lord Faran, who first gathered them together on the Night of Madness."

"I was hoping no one would remember that," Hanner said.

"But *Hanner* can't lead them!" Mavi protested. "He's not even a warlock."

Hanner looked at her.

He could refuse. He could agree with Mavi that it was absurd for a nonwarlock to lead a band of warlocks. He could evict them from his house and go live there in peace, a young man of good birth and inherited wealth; he could court Mavi and maybe marry her, and they could live there together. He could let the warlocks fend for themselves, let them be scattered, perhaps forced into exile or killed off by the city guard or the Wizards' Guild.

It really wasn't his problem. He hadn't asked for any of this. He hadn't done anything wrong.

But neither had any of the other warlocks.

Someone had to lead them. Someone had to show them what they could do and represent them to the World. Hanner had gathered them, then abdicated his position to Uncle Faran.

But Faran had gotten himself killed. As had Manrin, less than a day later. And the warlocks had now chosen Hanner to lead them, even though none but Shella knew he was one of them.

The job certainly wasn't safe, but Hanner felt he could avoid it no longer. It was time to stop delaying, stop his pretenses that he could ever return to his old life.

"I'll go," he said. "Mavi—I *am* a warlock."

Chapter Forty

For a long moment the room was silent as the others stared at him in shock. Then Alris laughed.

"Ha!" she said. "I should have known. You acted so strange sometimes! And that girl, Shella—she knew, didn't she?"

"Yes," Hanner admitted. "She knows."

"You didn't tell me," Mavi said, and Hanner could hear the hurt in her voice. "You never said a word!"

"Mavi, I didn't know at first," Hanner said hastily. "And you said . . ." Then he stopped, realizing he was once again about to say the wrong thing.

But he wouldn't. He would say the *right* thing this time.

He took a deep breath and continued, "Well, it doesn't matter what you said. You're right. I'm sorry." He hesitated. He knew better than to approach her; she would bolt, he was sure. "You stay here and talk to Nerra," he said. "I'll go back with Bern. I hope I'll see you again." He bowed and headed for the door, beckoning to Bern.

Mavi watched him go, saying nothing.

Bern was frozen at first, then realized what was happening and hurried after Hanner.

When they were both in the corridor, Hanner closed the door of the apartments and said, "On the way you can tell me more of what's happened since Uncle Faran's death."

"Of course," Bern said.

By the time they were out of the Palace Bern had described the disorganized remnants of Lord Faran's little army returning in panicky disarray to the house, and explained how Ulpen and the others had talked Manrin into assuming leadership of the group.

By the time they reached High Street, Bern had explained Manrin's plan to establish warlocks as just another sort of magician, with standard attire, apprenticeships, fees for service, and so on.

"That's sound thinking," Hanner said as they turned the corner. That would suit the Wizards' Guild, he thought. If warlocks were a known quantity, bound by accepted rules, they would be less likely to stir up trouble.

Of course, it would also remove one of the warlocks' current strengths—no one knew who they were, or how many of them might be out there.

On the other hand, that strength was one reason they were seen as a danger. If the warlocks operated from shops, in distinctive costumes, like other magicians, they wouldn't seem anywhere near as threatening.

And nobody said that *all* warlocks had to wear black and hang out signs, or that a warlock couldn't change his clothes when the occasion arose.

But if the general population *thought* they knew who all the warlocks were, that might be enough. The wizards had created the Guild to protect the World from wizards. Perhaps if warlocks were to create their own guild . . .

But they wouldn't want to call it a guild; imitating the wizards too obviously might seem audacious, even presumptuous. A brotherhood or sisterhood, like the witches, might seem sinister—and besides, Hanner saw no reason to form two organizations rather than one. Something that would suggest peaceful discussion and openness, rather than secrecy or authority, would be good.

A council, perhaps.

That sounded right. The Council of Warlocks. Like Sardiron's Council of Barons.

Just giving them a name and public identity wouldn't be enough, of course. Those people in the street had not just been upset because a bunch of strangers had acquired mysterious new magic; they were frightened and angry because friends and neighbors and relatives had disappeared on the Night of Madness, and they thought the warlocks were responsible.

Somehow, the warlocks—the *Council* of Warlocks—would have to convince them otherwise.

And beyond that, even people who didn't think that the warlocks were responsible for the disappearances, who didn't think there was some vast conspiracy behind it all thought warlocks were dangerous. Warlocks *were* dangerous, as they had demonstrated under Faran's leadership. The Council, once it existed, would have to convince everyone that danger was under firm control.

At this point, no one would believe anything warlocks told them. Hanner would need to find someone they *would* believe, and convince that someone to speak up on the warlocks' behalf.

The obvious possibilities were the established powers of the Hegemony—the overlords, the city guard, the Wizards' Guild, the Sisterhood of Witches, the Brotherhood of Witches, and so on. The overlord and the Guild in particular would be convincing, since both had acted openly against the warlocks. If Hanner could just convince Lord Azrad . . .

He stumbled over his own feet at the thought and realized that Bern had continued to talk, explaining how the warlocks had reacted to Manrin's proposals, while he had been lost in his planning.

He listened for a few seconds, decided that what Bern was saying wasn't important and he could always ask Bern to repeat it later, and resumed his chain of thought.

If Uncle Faran hadn't been able to talk sense to Lord Azrad, Hanner certainly couldn't hope to. The Wizards' Guild, though—the Guild wanted to minimize trouble. If they thought wiping out the warlocks was the way to do that, then Hanner and the others were as good as dead—though they'd take several wizards with them, he was sure.

But if they were convinced wiping out the warlocks

would be more trouble than accommodating them, then the Guild would be the warlocks' natural ally. Faran had talked about appealing to them as fellow magicians, but hadn't really carried through. Hanner knew better than to try to appeal to their better nature or fellow feeling, but if he could present them with solid reasons that accommodation with the warlocks would be in their own best interests . . .

He thought he could.

"I need to talk to Ithinia," he said, interrupting Bern's description of how they had dealt with Desset's nightmares.

"Now?" Bern asked, startled.

Hanner looked around, suddenly aware that they were nearing Warlock House, and the normal morning crowds that had surrounded them since leaving the Palace were no longer present.

The people in the street had been pushed back away from them; they were walking down a cleared path leading directly to the open iron gate. Desset stood in the dooryard, watching them—clearly, the path was her doing.

"But she's already having nightmares!" Hanner said, breaking into a run.

Caught off guard, Bern took a moment to follow.

Hanner did not say anything, but inwardly he was seething. Didn't these people realize how the Calling worked? Hadn't they seen what happened to Rudhira and Varrin? The more magic a warlock used, the more powerful she became. The more powerful a warlock became, the more powerful the Calling was, until at last it became irresistible. The nightmares were a warning. Of the little group Bern had listed as still at the house Desset was the most powerful warlock remaining who had not been Called, with only Kirsha and maybe Ulpen coming anywhere close to matching her. That made her the obvious choice for big jobs like clearing a street so Hanner and Bern could get inside safely—but it also made her the *worst* choice, because at any moment the Calling might get the better of her and sweep her away.

"Get in here!" Hanner called as he pushed past her into the open doorway.

Startled, Desset and Bern hurried after him. He slammed the door behind them and turned to Desset.

"What is it?" she said breathlessly. "What's the matter?"

"*You* don't use magic anymore," he told her, shaking a finger in her face. "Not unless you absolutely must!"

"But Bern and Alris needed to get out, and you and Bern needed to get in," Desset protested.

"I don't care," Hanner said. "It's not your job! Get one of the others—or if one can't handle the job, get two or three or four. But not *you*. You've had the nightmares."

Desset's mouth opened, then closed.

"You'll hear the Calling!" Hanner said. "Like Rudhira and Varrin. Unless you *want* to go flying off northward in the middle of whatever you're doing, and never come back!"

"Oh," Desset squeaked.

"Oh," Bern said. "I didn't think . . ."

"Obviously," Hanner said, turning to Bern—and realizing that they had an audience. The other warlocks were watching them.

Zarek had stayed, of course—he wouldn't be in any hurry to go back to the Hundred-Foot Field. Kirsha—Hanner didn't know much of anything about her background, but apparently she still preferred the mansion to her home. Her cousin Ilvin had stayed, as well. Hinda wasn't allowed back in the Palace. Alladia, Shella, Ulpen—their former lives as other sorts of magicians were gone. Yorn, outcast from the city guard, remained, as well as Mavi's friend Pancha, and one other whose name Hanner didn't remember at first.

Artalda, that was it. Artalda the Fair.

Most of them were wearing black now, he noticed—not their own clothes dyed, as Manrin had suggested, but assorted mismatched garments apparently pilfered from Uncle Faran's wardrobes, most of them ill-fitting, since only Yorn matched the late Lord Faran's height.

They were not an impressive bunch, but they were what

he, and all the warlocks of the World, had to start with.

And the time had come to start. If he was going to be their leader, he knew he had to establish his authority at once.

"Good morning, all of you," Hanner said. "Just to reassure you, you are all still welcome in this house. As you see, I've chosen to accept your invitation to return and lead you."

Saying it openly felt oddly pleasant. It felt *right*. All his life he had carefully stayed in the background, in his uncle's shadow, doing as he was told no matter what he thought of it. He had always refused to take on any real authority because he had always thought there was someone better, someone more qualified.

Now, here, at last, he did not think there was. The time had come to assert himself.

"My lord," Yorn said, bowing. The others followed suit with varying degrees of awkwardness.

"Don't call me 'lord,' " Hanner said. The term reminded him of his old life, where it had been almost a mockery— he had never been lord of anything, despite the title. "If I'm leading you, instead of serving the overlord, then I can no longer bear that title."

Yorn straightened up. "Then how should we address you, uh . . . sir?"

" 'Sir' is perfectly acceptable," Hanner said. "I believe my actual title ought to be Chairman, though."

"Chairman?" Kirsha asked.

"Chairman of the Council of Warlocks," Hanner said.

"There's a Council of Warlocks?" Zarek asked.

"There is now."

"Where?" Shella asked.

"Here," Hanner said. "The twelve of us." He glanced at Bern. "I'm afraid you don't qualify for membership, Bern, unless there's something you haven't told us."

"No, I do not, my l . . . sir," Bern said, stepping back toward the dining hall.

"We could do something about that, if you like," Hanner

said. "Shella, here, taught us. We could take you on as an apprentice."

"No, sir."

"You said earlier that you wanted to discuss the terms of your employment," Hanner said. "We never really did. I think I should make it clear that this house is now the headquarters of the Council of Warlocks, and if you stay on—which you're quite welcome to do—it will be as an employee of the Council rather than working for any individual."

"I . . . I can accept that, sir, but I do not wish to *be* a warlock."

"I don't blame you," Hanner said. "We have formidable enemies, several weaknesses . . . it's hardly a life you'd choose, eh?"

"Exactly, sir," Bern said, visibly relieved.

"Well, I hope to improve that," Hanner said. "And when I have, perhaps you'll reconsider."

"Or perhaps not. Please, sir . . ."

"We'll leave it for now, Bern. Thank you for staying on." Hanner turned back to the others. "Now, as I've just said, we are the Council of Warlocks. We are going to be the organization that warlocks answer to, as wizards answer to their Guild. We are going to make rules and enforce them, and establish just who and what a proper warlock is. If this isn't what you want, then leave now."

The warlocks glanced at one another. Then Ilvin said, "Excuse me, sir—perhaps I've misunderstood something, but if Bern doesn't qualify for membership, how can *you* appoint yourself as Chairman?"

Hanner smiled. He had expected that question. He pointed, and a lamp lifted from a table.

"I'm qualified," he said. "I didn't mention it before because my uncle was running things, but now that he's gone the time to hide is past."

"*I* knew he was a warlock!" Shella said proudly.

"Yes, you did," Hanner agreed. "Now, we will begin with rules on attire and deportment, then discuss the nature of the nightmares and the Calling, and how this affects us. I want to get through this quickly."

"Why?" Shella asked.

"Because we have several things to do, and we don't know how much time we have to do them. The guard could make another assault, or the Wizards' Guild might reach a decision and attempt to act on it," Hanner said. "I want to get a few basics established and learn exactly what the situation is here—for example, what's been done with Manrin's body?"

"It's still upstairs," Bern said.

"Well, it must be dealt with eventually. At any rate, once the essentials here are settled, I'll go talk to the Wizards' Guild."

"About Manrin?" Ulpen asked.

Hanner smiled.

"Among other things," he said. "There are also a few things I need to explain to them about warlocks."

Chapter Forty-one

Demonologists usually wore black robes as their formal garb and trimmed them with red. Therefore, to prevent confusion, warlocks would never wear robes—they would wear black tunics, but not full robes—and they would avoid red trim. Gold or white trim would be acceptable, to make their appearance less forbidding.

Warlocks would be polite but aloof in public, as befitted respected magicians.

The most powerful warlocks were most susceptible to the Calling. Therefore, they would use their magic as sparingly as possible. For any specific task, the weakest warlock who could handle it safely would be given that duty.

Warlocks would obey the law, so that the overlord would have no valid grounds for exiling or killing them. Any Council warlock who found another warlock breaking the law must stop him immediately, by any means necessary, up to and including stopping his heart. If the criminal was more powerful than the Council member, then aid should be called in at once—Hanner's group had demonstrated, on the Night of Madness, that warlocks working together could overcome a single warlock more powerful than any of them.

If any of them came across damage done by a warlock, they would offer to help repair it, but they would not force their aid on anyone who did not want it.

Those were the rules Hanner set forth. He had gathered the entire group in the dining hall; though Ulpen was posted at a front window, ready to ward off anything thrown at the house, the rest were seated around the table.

Hanner also explained everything he knew about the Calling, including his theory that it was responsible for the disappearances on the Night of Madness.

And when that was done, he said, "Now I need to talk to the wizards. Ulpen, how can I contact the Guild?"

"Uh . . ." Ulpen had not been expecting the question; he stared stupidly across the dining table at Hanner for a moment before collecting his wits.

"I don't know," he said at last.

Hanner frowned. "You don't have any idea?"

"I'm afraid not."

"Then we'll have to improvise." Hanner thought for a minute, then looked around at the others.

Desset was there, looking oddly distracted; she glanced northward. Hanner was not about to ask her to do *anything*. He wondered if sending her farther south, farther from whatever was calling her, might help. The peninsula that separated the Gulf of the East from the Ocean only extended for a few leagues south of the city, though. Perhaps if she went to the Small Kingdoms . . .

But it wasn't urgent yet, and speaking to the wizards before they made their decision was vital.

Ilvin and Yorn weren't powerful enough to be any use; he wasn't sure about some of the others. Ulpen was a possibility, but really, the best choice was obvious.

"Kirsha," he said, "can you fly me up above the city?"

She blinked at him. "I think so," she said. "Where to? How far?"

"I don't know yet." He frowned slightly and asked, "Have you had any nightmares since that first night?"

She hesitated, then said, "No."

He was not happy about the hesitation, but he was not going to choose someone else now; he didn't want Kirsha to think he didn't trust her. She would probably think it was because of her crimes on the Night of Madness.

"Good," he said. He glanced at a window; the sunlight was slanting from the west, the afternoon well advanced. They had spent most of the day establishing and explaining the Council rules.

He didn't want to waste any more time. He pushed back his chair and got to his feet.

"Come on," he said. "The rest of you stay here. You might want to consider how the succession for the chairmanship will work."

The moment the words left his mouth he knew he had reverted to his old ways and said the wrong thing, reminded them all that he was about to attempt something dangerous, possibly fatal—but it was too late to take the words back, and he had business to attend to.

He hoped that he wouldn't have any such lapses while speaking to the wizards.

Together, he and Kirsha made their way out through the back of the house into the walled garden. There Hanner pointed upward.

"Fly," he said. "And take me with you."

Together they rose upward. When they cleared the rooftop of the mansion Kirsha paused. "Where to?" she asked.

"Up higher," Hanner said. "Until we can see the entire city."

She looked uncertain, but turned up a palm. "All right," she said, and they began rising again.

Hanner looked down and watched the World drop away beneath his feet. The surrounding buildings turned until only the roofs were visible, and then shrank down to the size of floor tiles. The people in the streets dwindled to insects. The sunlight grew brighter, uncomfortably so— Hanner could not look to the southwest.

The air grew cooler, despite the summer sun, and the breeze began to tear at him, flapping his sleeves. He felt a sudden rush of panic.

"Here," he said. "This is high enough." He looked north and saw the Gulf; to the west he could see the towers of Westgate and the shipyard light. The city still reached the horizon to the southeast, but this was enough.

Their ascent stopped abruptly, and Kirsha shivered. "What are we doing up here?" she said.

"Calling the Wizards' Guild," Hanner said. He cleared his throat and reached out with his magic to feel the air around him. Then he shouted, "Hear me!"

He could feel the sound moving outward through the air, and he stretched out his warlock's power to strengthen it.

"Should I help?" Kirsha asked.

"You just keep us up here," Hanner said, speaking normally. Then he called out again, putting his magic behind it more strongly.

"Hear me, wizards of Ethshar! I must speak to your leaders at once!"

The city below showed no sign that anyone had heard him.

"Take us that way," he said, pointing southeast, toward the Wizards' Quarter. "And down a little."

"Yes, sir," Kirsha said.

They descended gently, moving across the city; sunlight blazed from the surfaces below. As they moved, Hanner took a deep breath and shouted again, "Hear me, wizards of Ethshar! I must speak with you!"

They drifted on; at Hanner's direction Kirsha leveled off,

still at least a hundred feet up. He repeated his call.

The sun made its way down the western sky; an hour passed, and still they drifted, Hanner calling occasionally.

"You aren't getting tired, are you?" he asked Kirsha at one point.

"No," she said. "If anything, I feel stronger than ever."

"That could be bad," Hanner said.

"Should I go back, then?"

"No. We need to give them time to arrange matters. You should be all right."

They passed over the Arena, and Hanner called again.

And then Kirsha called, "Look!" She pointed to the south. Something was rising toward them, something brightly colored and larger than a man.

"Stop here," Hanner said, and Kirsha halted their southward drift.

The rising shape became clear, and Hanner realized it was a man sitting cross-legged on a carpet—a flying carpet, perhaps eight feet by twelve. The man wore red and gold robes, and the carpet was dark blue patterned in gold.

The carpet was coming toward them, swooping gracefully through an upward spiral. Hanner waited.

A moment later the carpet reached their own level and stopped a dozen feet away. The seated man—the wizard, certainly—was no one Hanner had ever seen before; he was short, stocky, and going gray. Hanner sensed an odd wrongness about him, but could not say what it was. He frowned. He hoped that this really was a wizard and not some sort of illusion.

"*Hai!*" the seated man said. "What do you want with us, warlock?"

Hanner ignored the feeling of wrongness and replied, "I need to speak to whomever it is that's going to decide what the Wizards' Guild does about warlocks."

"If the Guild wishes to hear from you, they'll summon you," the red-robed man said.

"My uncle Faran waited to be summoned," Hanner said. "That didn't work out well. The Guild would summon me if they knew what was best for us all, themselves included. They don't know that yet, because they haven't heard what I have to say. Surely, you don't maintain that even the Guild knows *everything*. Ithinia never thought it necessary to speak to Lord Faran, and see how *that* turned out."

"Don't threaten me, warlock," the wizard said warningly. "I think you'll find me harder to kill than Lord Faran's executioner."

"I was not making threats," Hanner said. "I merely speak the truth."

The mention of Faran's executioner, however, gave him the clue he needed to recognize the nature of the wrongness he had felt.

The wizard had no heartbeat. In fact, he had no heart in his chest. Hanner could feel only a magical darkness where a heart should be. Stopping his heart, as Hanner had done to Faran's slayer, would not be possible.

Hanner had heard of wizards doing this, hiding their hearts before undertaking some particularly perilous task; they could still be hurt, but the heart would keep beating, wherever it was stored, and the wizard would not die of injuries that would ordinarily be instantly fatal. He *would* be harder to kill, Hanner thought—but probably not impossible.

If the wizard had taken such a precaution before coming to speak to him—well, it would seem that the Wizards' Guild did accept that warlocks could pose a real threat.

That was promising, in a way.

And that they had prepared this messenger to speak to him, rather than sending some magical assassin after him, was even more promising.

While Hanner considered this, the wizard had considered Hanner's words. Now he responded.

"Very well," he said. "I'll bring you to them."

Hanner turned to Kirsha. "Put me down on the carpet," he said.

"Sir, are you sure—"

"I'm sure," Hanner said, cutting her off. "I've dealt with

wizards for years. Put me on the carpet, then go back to the house and wait for me. And don't use any more magic until tomorrow. If you have nightmares tonight, don't *ever* use any more."

"As you say." Hanner felt himself pushed forward, and a moment later his feet touched the thick pile of the carpet. He stepped forward cautiously.

It was like walking across a featherbed; he sat down quickly, and the wizard moved aside to make room.

Hanner turned to see Kirsha still hanging unsupported in midair, staring at him.

"Go on," he said, waving to her. "I'll be fine. We all will."

She waved back, then turned and flew away.

Then Hanner turned to the wizard. "I am Hanner the Warlock, Chairman of the Council of Warlocks," he said.

The wizard looked at him silently for a moment, then said, "I'm a wizard. You don't need my name."

Names had power, Hanner remembered—some spells required the name of the person the spell would affect. The wizard was not simply being rude.

"Please yourself," Hanner started to say, but the final syllable stretched out and vanished as the carpet abruptly turned and swooped downward. Wind rushed past him, yanking his words away. He closed his eyes against the drying wind, and when he opened them again the carpet was sailing into a great dark opening in an upper floor of a building he did not recognize.

Once inside, the carpet settled to the floor, and abruptly became as flat and lifeless as any ordinary rug.

Hanner looked around at a large rough chamber where most of one wall was open to the outside. There were no furnishings, no windows other than the open wall; overhead were the bare rafters of a peaked roof.

The wizard got to his feet, then turned and watched, not offering his hand, as Hanner rose. "This way," he said, pointing to a small, perfectly ordinary wooden door.

Hanner followed the wizard through the door into a small,

bare, wooden room, where assorted cloaks and hoods hung on a row of pegs on one wall. The wizard selected a blue velvet hood, one with no eyeholes, and handed it to Hanner.

"Face that door," he said, pointing at another ordinary wooden door. "Then put this on."

Hanner obeyed and found himself blinded—but he was a warlock; he could sense his surroundings with his magic, even through the opaque hood. The wizard stepped forward and opened the door, then stepped aside.

"Walk forward," the wizard said.

Hanner started forward, then hesitated a step from the open door. He could sense nothing beyond it—not empty space, but nothing at all. Something there blocked his warlock sight completely.

Some sort of wizardry, presumably—warlockry and wizardry did not work well together, he remembered.

"Go on," the wizard urged him. "Straight ahead, another step or two."

The Wizards' Guild would hardly have gone to this much trouble to kill him, but Hanner still hesitated—something deep inside him did not *like* that blank emptiness. He reached out to touch it . . .

And suddenly he was genuinely, completely blind; his warlock sight had vanished as completely as the light from a snuffed candle. Panicked, he reached up and snatched off the hood.

He wasn't in the little wooden room anymore. There was no open door before him, no wall, no sunlight spilling in through the open side of the room behind him where the carpet had landed. Instead he stood on rough slate pavement in a vast, torchlit hall. Ahead of him stretched two parallel rows of gray stone pillars, each pillar as big around as a century-old oak, with twenty feet between the rows and each pillar eight or nine feet from the next. For the nearest part of each row, each pillar bore a pair of torches set in black iron brackets slightly above the level of a tall man's head.

He could not see the end of the hall; the torches stopped

some dozen pillars, perhaps thirty yards, before him, but the pillars continued on into the darkness beyond. He could not see the side walls clearly, but they were perhaps twenty feet beyond the pillars on either side.

In the torchlit stretch before him stood a great dark wooden table, strewn with papers and objects. He could see cups and bowls and staves and jewels and books and a hundred other things, mixed together seemingly at random.

And around this table stood a score of wizards, male and female, all apparent ages, in robes that ranged from unadorned gray to the most elaborate embroidered polychrome fancywork he had ever seen.

"Hanner, Chairman of the Council of Warlocks," a woman said, and Hanner recognized her as Ithinia of the Isle, senior Guildmaster of Ethshar of the Spices. "No longer Lord Hanner of Ethshar. You wished to speak to the masters of the Wizards' Guild." She waved an arm at her companions.

"Speak," she said.

Chapter Forty-two

Where are we?" Hanner asked as he struggled to regain his composure.

"I quite literally cannot answer that completely, even if I wanted to," Ithinia said. "You are in a meeting place that is accessible only to the Wizards' Guild; that's all you need to know."

Hanner tried to reach out with his magic, and felt nothing at all. He was as powerless as if the Night of Madness had never happened.

"You've removed my warlockry," he said. "I didn't know that was possible."

That changed everything. If warlocks could be turned back to ordinary people, then the Calling could be averted, and Lord Azrad's fears assuaged, and order restored . . .

Ithinia's next words dashed that hope. "It *isn't* possible, so far as we know," she said. "Warlockry doesn't work here, but when you return to the World it will return, and you will be a warlock once again, at the same level as before."

"Oh."

That was different, and less encouraging—but still interesting. Perhaps the wizards could provide a refuge for warlocks who had reached the nightmare threshold and begun to hear the Calling.

"Have you *tried* to turn warlocks back?" Hanner asked.

"Of course we have," Ithinia said, visibly annoyed. "We've been doing intensive research on that question since the Night of Madness itself. We tried the Spell of Reversal, Javan's Restorative, the Ethereal Entrapment, healing spells, hypnotic spells, cleansings, holdings, rectifications, instrumentals, extractives, transformations, and regressions—multiple trials of each, some of them in slowed or stopped time. We've consulted with other magicians; herbalists and theurgists and sorcerers and demonologists couldn't even do as well as we did. Witches seem to have come nearest to success, and the Brotherhood's experiments are still continuing, but so far, it appears that once someone becomes a warlock, nothing will change him back. A large part of the difficulty lies in the way warlockry interferes with other magic. We thought we had the answer when we discovered that if a warlock is transformed into something else, such as an ape or cat, he is no longer a warlock—but we discovered that when returned to human form he is as powerful a magician as ever; we can't transform him into a human who is *not* a warlock by any method we've tried. Reversible petrifaction did no better. We thought of using Fendel's Lesser Transformation to turn a warlock into a human being who is identical save for not being a warlock, but we discovered that the spell did not affect the one portion that mattered—the core of warlockry in the subject's brain.

Wizardry simply can't affect it—not to transform it, nor remove it, nor alter it in any way. The only reason a transformed warlock can't use his magic is that whatever causes it only operates in human beings; the core always remains present, dormant but as untouchable as ever, in the subject of a transformation. In short, if you've come here hoping we can return you and your fellow warlocks to your former state, you've wasted your time and ours."

Hanner waved that idea away. "No, that wasn't my intent," he said. He had, as usual, said the wrong thing.

He couldn't afford to do that again. The time had come to say the *right* thing. His life, and the lives of all the other warlocks, might well depend upon it.

"I was distracted by the loss of my magic, that's all," he said. "I came for two reasons. Firstly, to ask what arrangements, if any, the Guild would like made regarding the remains of Manrin the Mage, and secondly, far more importantly, to offer information that I hope will help you decide the Guild's attitude toward warlocks." He looked over the assembled wizards, awaiting some comment.

A red-robed wizard at the far end of the table said, "We will see that Manrin's remains are transported to his family in Ethshar of the Sands for a proper funeral. You need not worry about that further."

That was a small relief. "And the information about warlocks?" he said.

None of them moved or spoke but Ithinia. "What information might that be?" she asked.

"I don't know how much you have already learned," he said. "Forgive me if I repeat what you already knew."

"Go on."

"Do you know about the Calling?"

"The summons to the source-point of warlockry, in southeastern Aldagmor? We are aware of it. We saw Varrin the Weaver and Rudhira of Camptown drawn away, and have observed dozens of others departing, though usually under less dramatic circumstances."

"Southeastern Aldagmor?"

Ithinia sighed. "It would seem that *we* are the ones providing information, not you!"

"An exchange is certainly welcome," Hanner said, smiling—he desperately needed to keep this discussion on friendly terms. "We only knew that they were going north; we didn't know their destination."

"Aldagmor. The phenomenon that began on the Night of Madness is centered there, and the closer one goes to that point, the more powerful it is, even now. Most of the Barony of Aldagmor has been depopulated, in fact—the *majority* of the population there vanished on the Night of Madness, and another large percentage has become warlocks, many of whom have since been summoned. That land is in chaos, and the only comfort we find in the situation there is that it was thinly populated to begin with. We do not wish to see anywhere else similarly transformed."

Hanner shuddered. "Neither do we," he said. "We have created a Council of Warlocks, and one purpose of our Council is to control the spread of warlockry and to stave off any further Callings." He hesitated, then asked, "Do you know where these warlocks are going? I mean, what's in Aldagmor that's attracting them?"

"No, we don't know," Ithinia said. "The Aldagmor source is like the core in a warlock's brain—wizardry cannot affect it, cannot see into it. Anyone who ventures too close—anyone, wizard, warlock, or otherwise—is drawn into it, and does not emerge."

Hanner nodded. He had pessimistically assumed as much. This confirmation was no surprise.

"You presumably came here to convince us not to destroy you all," Ithinia said. "I think you might do well to stop asking questions and start making your case."

"Yes, I know." Hanner took a deep breath, then said, "You're concerned with warlocks because you fear we're going to cause trouble. You think we might disrupt everything. The Guild exists to prevent magic from spreading chaos—you created it to keep yourselves from doing that." He suddenly realized that since wizardry could extend life or restore youth, that "you" might be more literal than he had thought—the very wizards who had created the Guild two hundred years before might well still be alive and seated before him. The idea staggered him for a moment, and he paused in his speech.

"Go on," Ithinia said.

"You had to put an artificial limit on your own power," Hanner said, "because there is no natural limit—wizards can live forever, learning more and more magic. If two of your mightiest members went to war, you could probably lay waste to the entire World."

"As the demons did to the eastern provinces, and the gods did to the Northern Empire's heartland," a gray-robed man said, startling Hanner. "They, too, have bound themselves now."

"Yes," Hanner said. "Yes, exactly. So you want warlocks removed, lest we become equally dangerous. But we *can't*. We *do* have a natural limit."

"The Calling, as you've named it," Ithinia said.

"Yes," Hanner said. "Exactly."

A white-haired man stirred in his seat and said, "We do not bother ourselves about witches, whose magic is limited to the energy of their own bodies, nor with sorcerers, whose talismans are not sufficiently powerful or long-lasting to seriously concern us. You warlocks, though, can reach a frightening level of power before the Calling takes you. Your Rudhira demonstrated that."

"Frightening, yes," Hanner admitted. "But still limited, and your own people can wreak considerable havoc before drawing the Guild's attention. I don't know whether the legendary Tower of Flame in the Small Kingdoms is real—"

"It is," the white-haired man interrupted. "It still burns."

"You see? The World is full of dangerous magic, yet it survives. And a powerful warlock who goes rogue can easily be handled."

Some of the wizards exchanged glances.

"Not so easily," Ithinia said. "Warlocks resist wizardry. It's as if you all bear powerful protective spells at all times.

We have had some unfortunate incidents already. You know of one of them; the spell we used on your uncle, Lord Faran, was the strongest petrifaction spell we know, and should be utterly instantaneous, yet it took a second or two to work, and he had time to retaliate. And Lord Faran was not a terribly powerful warlock, nowhere near Rudhira's level."

"It was not Faran who stopped his killer's heart," Hanner said. "I was able to see that, using a warlock's added senses. I hope you'll understand if I don't tell you who did perform the deed."

That created a stir, but before anyone could speak Hanner continued, "But that wasn't what I meant, in any case. Yes, you could destroy powerful warlocks with your spells, at some risk to yourself—but you could also slit their throats while they sleep. *Manrin* knew you far better than my uncle did, yet he didn't manage to take anyone with him."

Hanner paused for breath and heard someone mutter, "Elken, too."

He ignored that, and continued. "Even that isn't what I meant, though. Don't you see? You can use the Calling to do your work for you!"

Again, his words triggered unrest; the wizards shifted in their seats and looked at one another.

"If you keep throwing things at a dangerous warlock, it doesn't matter whether any of your attacks succeed," Hanner said. "He'll use his magic to defend himself. The more magic he uses, the more powerful he becomes. And the more powerful he becomes, the stronger the Calling becomes. Rudhira destroyed herself by lifting those ships—after she did that, the Calling was always there for her, growing steadily stronger."

For a moment the place was silent; then Ithinia said, "An interesting point."

Hanner knew he had said the right thing, finally. He was swaying them.

"That's one side," he continued. "Warlocks cannot cause the same level of destruction you fear, so there's no real need to destroy us. But there's another side. We *can* make any attempt to destroy us very costly."

"Go on," Ithinia said.

Hanner knew he had to phrase this carefully. He did not want to anger these people by seeming disrespectful or by threatening them openly. "You know we can kill you without touching you. You've seen us be obvious, smashing doors and so on, but we can be subtle. We can hide. We don't need to look like anything but ordinary people—did you know *I* was a warlock before this morning?"

"No," Ithinia said, "but we do have ways of finding out."

"And if a wizard's heart suddenly stops in the street one day, can you find out which of the dozens of people in the area is responsible?"

Ithinia frowned and glanced around at the others. "Go on," she said.

Hanner thought he heard someone whisper something faintly. He ignored that, as he had the earlier muttering, and went on. "You may think that there are only so many warlocks, and that once you've disposed of us all you're rid of the problem—but we can make others into warlocks. It's very easy, very subtle—the person altered wouldn't necessarily even know it at first."

"Wait a minute," the white-haired wizard said. He drew a dagger and placed it on the table, then fumbled with a pouch on his belt.

"What are you doing?" Ithinia asked.

"The Spell of Truth," the other replied. He mumbled something, gestured with the dagger, and did something Hanner couldn't see with his other hand. Then he pointed the knife at Hanner and said, "Repeat what you just told us."

"I said that we can make more warlocks. We can make *anyone* a warlock, easily, with or without their permission or knowledge."

"Are you *sure* of that?" the white-haired man demanded.

Hanner hesitated. He wanted to say yes, but he couldn't honestly. He admitted, "No, I'm not sure. We believe so, but there might be people we can't change. We can certainly change most people."

The wizard nodded. "Good enough," he said. "Then why *haven't* you? Why not turn all the World to warlocks?"

"I'm not eager to do something irreversible when we don't know what the results will be," Hanner said. "Besides, it's not as if most of us have found warlockry an unmixed blessing."

"But if you turned your enemies to warlocks—"

"They might still be our enemies—and they might be more powerful than us."

"But you have more experience."

"And we're closer to the Calling. We aren't in any hurry to go see what's in Aldagmor. If we *did* turn everyone to warlocks, and the Calling took us all, we might destroy the entire World. We don't want that any more than you do."

"Go on," Ithinia said.

Hanner sighed.

"That's most of it," he said. "If you do declare war upon us, we will fight, and we will fight with any means at our disposal. Wizards will die of heart failure, die in their sleep, die as they walk down the street. Wizards will find themselves transformed into warlocks, their familiar magic suddenly unreliable. Warlocks will appear throughout the city, throughout the *World*, anywhere we can get within a few yards of some unsuspecting innocent for a moment. You might win in the end, you might exterminate us or drive us all to the Calling, but would it be worth the cost?"

"What alternative do you offer?" the white-haired wizard asked.

"The Council of Warlocks," Hanner said eagerly. "We propose to organize all the warlocks, as they're discovered, and bind them by our rules. The warlocks who accept the Council's authority will obey the laws of whatever land they live in—here in Ethshar—"

"You aren't in Ethshar here," a beautiful woman who had not previously spoken interrupted. "In fact, you aren't even in the World."

"I'm sorry," Hanner said. "In Ethshar, then, they will obey the laws of the Hegemony and the commands of the three overlords. In the Small Kingdoms they will obey the laws of the various kings and queens. In Sardiron they will obey the barons. Whatever the law is, warlocks will be bound by it, and other warlocks will cooperate, free of charge, in bringing to trial any warlock who does not. Council warlocks will operate openly, not in secret—we will distinguish ourselves by wearing black tunics, as you wizards wear your traditional robes. We will transform others to warlocks only as properly sworn apprentices, as other magicians do. We will regulate our members, like any guild— and two or more warlocks working together can overcome a single more powerful warlock, where other magic might encounter that interference you've noticed. We will require that no warlock use any other magic."

"And what do you expect in return?" the white-haired wizard asked.

"Very little," Hanner asked. "We ask that we be treated as magicians, not monsters. We ask that the Wizards' Guild not kill us, nor drive us into exile, nor aid others in doing so. And one more thing." He had almost forgotten it and shuddered at the possibility. Convincing the Wizards' Guild to leave warlocks alone was important, but it would hardly solve *all* their problems while warlocks were blamed for other crimes.

The wizards were waiting in expectant silence. He swallowed, then continued.

"All those people who vanished on the Night of Madness," Hanner said. "They were warlocks who heard the Calling, we're sure of it."

"So are we," the white-haired wizard said.

That statement was a pleasant surprise, and Hanner struggled not to react to it.

"But most people think *we* made them disappear," he said. "If the Wizards' Guild, and perhaps the other magicians, could tell everyone that we aren't responsible, that Uncle Kelder or Aunt Sarai was not kidnapped or eaten by warlocks, but *was* a warlock—that would be what we need to fit in peacefully, which is all we want."

"Warlocks *did* loot and burn and kill on the Night of Madness," Ithinia pointed out.

"Yes, they did," Hanner admitted. "And we're very sorry about that and will be glad to turn over for trial any *individual* who can be shown to have committed any such crimes. We've already done that, where we could—I personally delivered four warlocks to the Lord Magistrate of the Old Merchants' Quarter, who had them flogged."

"He speaks the truth," the white-haired wizard said. "The spell is still in effect."

"We can see that," the woman who had corrected Hanner's reference to Ethshar snapped.

"Is that it?" Ithinia asked. "Have you finished your speech?"

"Almost," Hanner said. "Just one more thing."

"Didn't he say that before?" a wizard muttered. Hanner ignored it.

"I've told you what we want of the Guild," he said. "To be left in peace and to have the truth about the disappearances told. I've told you what we offer in exchange—warlocks will be kept in order by the Council of Warlocks. I've explained why warlocks are not the threat some initially believed, in that the Calling limits us, and I've explained that neither are we harmless and easily obliterated, so that the peace we offer is reasonable. There's just one more thing to add. It's not a fact, but only a possibility, a consequence that *might* happen if you do refuse my offer and try to stamp us out."

"What is it?" Ithinia asked.

"You know that hundreds, maybe thousands of people flew off to Aldagmor on the Night of Madness. You know the most powerful warlocks have followed them. But there are things we *don't* know about warlockry. We don't know what causes it, how long it will last, or any of dozens of other things. So ask yourselves, when you consider declaring warlocks to be a menace to be stopped—what happens if the Calling *stops*?" He looked at the wizards and spread his arms dramatically.

"What happens if all those warlocks come back from Aldagmor and find out you've slaughtered their fellows?" he asked.

He knew that was something they hadn't considered; he knew he'd said the right thing. He looked at them, trying not to grin.

The wizards stared at him in silence.

Chapter Forty-three

The sound of a chair's legs grating on stone broke the silence. "I think I'll send you home now," Ithinia said as she rose.

Hanner bowed. "As you please," he said. "I've said what I came to say."

"And we'll consider it all carefully," Ithinia replied as she walked up and took his arm. She stooped and picked up the velvet hood Hanner had dropped. "Put this on," she said, holding it out.

Reluctantly Hanner obeyed, plunging himself into darkness.

Someone—probably Ithinia, though he had no way to be certain—took hold of his arm, turned him to the left, and led him away. He walked for what seemed a goodly distance, perhaps thirty or forty yards, with the grip on his arm guiding him.

Then his guide stopped.

"Put out your hand," she said—Ithinia's voice, as he had expected. He obediently raised one arm and held it out before him.

"Now step forward," she said, releasing her hold.

He stepped forward—and sensation flooded over him.

Light was seeping up beneath the mask; he was somewhere brighter than that gloomy pillared hall. He could hear the distant buzz of a city. And his warlockry had returned; he could sense his surroundings, feel the structure and patterns of the air and space around him.

He snatched off the hood again.

He was standing in a pleasant little room, one he didn't recognize—definitely *not* the bare little chamber the carpet had delivered him to. This room had broad windows on two sides, hung with lace curtains; steeply slanting sunlight was pouring in. The walls were plastered and painted white, brightening the room even more. A wicker divan stood to one side, and half a dozen little tables were scattered about. There were two doors—one in a windowed wall, presumably leading outside, and one in a solid wall, presumably leading to another room.

Hanner stepped over to a window and looked out, and saw a lush garden. Chrysanthemums lined a brick walk that wound between flowerbeds and neatly trimmed hedges.

He didn't recognize it.

He could be almost anywhere, he thought. This might be in Ethshar, or at some wizard's country estate, or a castle garden in the Small Kingdoms. He wasn't sure what was expected of him, or why he had been sent here—hadn't Ithinia said she was sending him home?

This wasn't any room he recognized in Uncle Faran's house, nor did the visible portion of the garden look familiar, but wizardry was capable of infinite surprises. He tried the interior door and found it locked.

He could have opened it—he was a warlock again, after all—but he decided to try the other door first.

The door to the garden opened readily, and he stepped outside, blinking in the bright sun. It was low in the west, just barely clearing walls and rooftops to his right.

He heard a creak and looked up to see a gargoyle looking down at him.

"Who are you?" the gargoyle demanded in a voice like

stones grating together—which was probably produced, Hanner realized, by stones grating together.

Hanner glanced along the stone facade of the house from which he had just emerged and saw half a dozen other gargoyles, most of which appeared to be animate.

"I'm Hanner the Warlock," Hanner said. "Where am I?"

"You're in the garden of Ithinia of the Isle," the gargoyle replied. It had trouble pronouncing the name, saying something resembling "Ishinia."

Suddenly his presence here made sense to Hanner; naturally, Ithinia would have some means of getting home quickly from that mysterious place where he had spoken to her. It was most likely a Transporting Tapestry, he guessed, which would always deliver a person to the exact same location, no matter who it was or where he started. She had directed it to the little room on the back of her house.

"The house on Lower Street, in Ethshar of the Spices?" he asked the gargoyle.

"Yes," it said.

"Ah! Your mistress said she would send me home, and she almost has—I live quite near here. Could you direct me to the street?"

"To your right," the gargoyle said—it had no hands to point with, just claws and wings unsuited to the task. "There's a path to the front of the house. Latch the gate behind you."

"Thank you," Hanner said. He started to bow, then stopped, feeling foolish; bowing to a chunk of magically animated stone seemed silly. To cover his confusion he turned as directed and hurried away.

A moment later he was on Lower Street. Twenty minutes later he was at the front door of Warlock House, on High Street; Kirsha had been waiting at a window and had provided him with magical protection from the watchers in the street so that he could enter safely.

"What happened?" she said as he stepped inside. "What did the wizards say?"

"That's a little hard to explain," Hanner said as half a

dozen of the others appeared to hear what he had to report. "They haven't made a final decision yet, but I'm optimistic that they'll see our point of view and decide to let us remain."

"Is there anything we should do to help?" Yorn asked from the parlor doorway.

"Yes," Hanner said. "I said that the Council of Warlocks would take responsibility for *all* the warlocks in Ethshar. That means we need to find them all and convince them to accept our authority. I want all of you who feel able to go out and find warlocks. We know who some of them are, since they were here before, but there must be others. Find them and tell them that the Council of Warlocks requires them to agree to abide by our rules."

"Could it wait until after supper?" Bern asked from the door of the dining room.

Hanner suddenly realized he was indeed hungry.

"I think so," he said.

In fact, it waited until morning. The evening was spent reviewing just what Hanner had committed his Council to and planning out who would go where. Hanner had hoped that word would come quickly of the Guild's decision, but that didn't happen.

However, there was a sudden disturbance upstairs midway through the evening; Hanner hurried to see what was responsible for the thumping and rushing he heard.

The sound came from the master bedroom; Hanner flung the door wide.

The windows overlooking the garden were open, and a warm wind was rustling the bed curtains. Manrin's body, along with the bedclothes that had been wrapped around it, was gone.

That was one less thing to worry about—and it meant that the Guild was acting on one part of Hanner's requests, at any rate. Hanner closed the windows carefully, then went back downstairs to continue the planning session.

Hanner did not sleep in Faran's bed that night; the memory of Manrin's corpse was too fresh. Instead he slept in one of the other rooms, where his sleep was interrupted twice by Desset's nightmares.

After the second, as they stood in the hallway outside her room, he told her sternly, "No more magic! Not even little things. You're very close to being Called."

"I know," Desset said, and even as she did she idly sent a candlestick drifting through the air. Hanner snatched it away from her.

"Maybe you should go farther south," he said. "The Calling should be weaker if you're farther from Aldagmor."

"But we're all *here*," Desset protested.

A thought struck Hanner. "You know," he said, "there's a place where warlockry wouldn't reach you at all, and the Calling would never bother you. But I don't think you'd want to live there."

"Where?" Desset asked, astonished.

Hanner realized he couldn't answer that. "You can't get there anyway," he said. "Only wizards go there." But he thought that the possibility of a wizardly refuge from the Calling was one that might be worth pursuing further.

After that incident they returned to their beds, and the remainder of the night passed without further disturbance.

In the morning half of the dozen warlocks ventured out into the city, seeking out more of their kind. Amost immediately they met with modest success, which they reported back to Hanner before heading out again. A warlock's special perceptions, as Shella taught them, could be used to spot other warlocks.

When they found these others their official presentation was simple enough. "We represent the Council of Warlocks. We've been negotiating terms with the Wizards' Guild, and we need the support of every warlock we can find." Beyond that they answered whatever questions they could and generally exhorted the other warlocks on the virtues of solidarity.

Every warlock they spoke to had encountered hostility. The ones who had previously stayed at Warlock House but had gone home after Lord Faran's death, or Manrin's, had not found themselves made welcome in those homes. Several had left again and gone into hiding in various places; one group had gathered in the Hundred-Foot Field, where Zarek found them.

All of them listened to the news of the Council's formation with interest. Some agreed to join; others preferred to wait and see what developed.

Only a handful actually wanted to return to Warlock House, but that suited Hanner well enough; he didn't see any reason to give Lord Azrad any more convenient a target than necessary, should the overlord decide to continue his attempts to exile the warlocks.

He didn't really think Azrad would bother, though.

It was slightly after midday when he discovered he was wrong.

Chapter Forty-four

Hanner was on the third floor, going through the drawers of magical paraphernalia Faran had accumulated, trying to decide whether he should try to sell the entire collection as a lot or piecemeal, when he heard shouting.

He hurried to a front window and looked out at the street.

"Blast," he said.

Soldiers were marching up High Street toward the house, for the third time since the Night of Madness.

"Doesn't he *learn*?" Hanner muttered. Then he turned and headed for the stairs.

When he reached the parlor he found Shella, Ulpen, Hinda, and Desset crowded at the front windows, watching the guards' advance. "What's happening?" he asked. "Are you pushing them back?"

"No," Ulpen said. "How can we? There are *hundreds* of them!"

"*I* could," Desset said uncertainly.

"*No,*" Hanner immediately replied. He looked at the others.

Ulpen was the most powerful of them, Shella next, then himself, and finally poor little Hinda—and none of them were especially powerful; of the five warlocks in the room only Ulpen and Desset could fly reliably, and letting Desset fly might mean watching her fly off northward, toward Aldagmor. Hanner and Shella could get themselves off the ground, rather unsteadily; Hinda couldn't even manage that.

"Who else is in the house?" Hanner asked.

"Bern," Shella said.

"That's *all*?"

"The others are out recruiting," Ulpen said. "You told them to go."

Hanner could not deny that. He realized that he might have made a fatal error in allowing the group's little remaining strength to be so spread out.

But he hadn't thought Azrad would try again! Hadn't he had *enough*, having his doors smashed in?

And as he thought that, he looked out the window and saw the battering ram being brought into position.

"This is stupid," he said. "There's no point in letting them wreck the house!" He hurried back into the hallway and opened the front door.

"*Hai!*" he called, using his magic to amplify his voice. "What do you think you're doing?"

The soldiers stopped what they were doing and turned to look at him.

"Who's in charge here?" Hanner bellowed.

Captain Naral stepped forward, up to the iron gate; Hanner waved a hand, and the gate swung open.

Naral watched this display of magical power expressionlessly, then stepped into the gateway and said, "I am in command of this party, Lord Hanner."

"I'm not *Lord* Hanner," Hanner replied, exasperated. "I

am Hanner, Chairman of the Council of Warlocks."

"The overlord does not recognize any such title," Naral replied. "In fact, he now rejects the very word 'warlock.' He has ordered that all the madmen wielding power given them by the spell that struck the World on the Night of Madness be removed from the city immediately, and from the Hegemony of Ethshar as soon as practical. Any who resist this order will be summarily executed."

"If anyone's gone mad around here, it's Lord Azrad," Hanner replied. "I knew he could be reluctant to face reality, but this is absurd!"

Naral's rigid expression softened slightly.

"I think your uncle's betrayal and death struck him hard, my lord."

"I am *not* your lord!" Hanner said. "I know you mean well, Captain, but I cannot allow you to call me by that title. The Wizards' Guild does not allow magicians to hold high office, and that includes warlocks."

"The Wizards' Guild has been notably silent on the subject of warlocks," Naral replied. "The overlord has been trying to communicate with the Guild since the Night of Madness, and has received nothing but silence and vague promises of a later agreement. It hasn't helped his temper, my . . . sir."

"It hasn't helped *mine*, either," Hanner said. "I am trying to control it, Captain, but this is the third time Lord Azrad has sent troops to remove loyal citizens of Ethshar from this house. I would think he would have learned better by now."

"Lor . . . um, Hanner . . ."

"Address me as Chairman, if you need a title," Hanner said. He had not been using a title, but clearly Captain Naral would be happier with one.

"Chairman, then," Naral said. "Lord Azrad is not the fool you seem to think him. We know that Lord Faran is dead, and that your most powerful magicians have flown off northward—though we don't know why. We know that most of the others have scattered through the city, trying to recruit more people into your outlaw band."

"Outlaw?"

Naral refused to be interrupted; he continued, "You have only a handful of people here at present. I have three hundred men and a dozen assorted magicians with me. I believe that we can take you by force, if necessary. My orders are to destroy this center of insurrection once and for all, burn the house and smash the walls—the overlord sees it as a center of rebellion and demands that it be removed."

"Rebellion?" Hanner said. "You clearly have people watching us—magicians, presumably. You know we've been recruiting warlocks to join us. Has anyone told you what terms we've been offering those recruits?"

He waited a second or two, but Naral plainly did not intend to answer.

"We're requiring them to swear to obey the overlord's laws, Captain! What sort of rebellion is that?"

"I have my orders, Chairman Hanner," Naral said. "I am to remove you if possible, kill you if not, and then destroy this house."

Hanner's temper got the better of him; he reached for the captain's throat, not with his hands, but with warlockry, and squeezed gently.

Naral's breath stopped, and his eyes widened. His hands flew to his throat. Behind him, a dozen soldiers raised their weapons.

"I could kill you before you could touch me, Captain," Hanner said. Then he released his hold.

Naral gasped, swallowed, then said, "And this is how you obey the law, Chairman?"

Hanner started to respond, then stopped.

Naral was right. Hanner had said that warlocks would obey the city's laws, and the overlord made those laws. The whole point of his Council of Warlocks was to convince everyone that warlocks would be law-abiding citizens.

But if they were to be exiled anyway, what was the use of it all?

Still, he saw no ethical way out. He had said they would obey the law, and obey it they would.

Perhaps, if they were obedient enough, even Azrad would be ashamed and revoke his sentence of exile.

"Captain," Hanner said, "you're right. We will accept the overlord's judgment. However, I want to make a few things clear first." He raised his voice, putting his magic behind it.

"If we chose to fight," Hanner said, "you might defeat us, but many of you would die in the process. We have the same right to defend ourselves and our home as any other citizens of Ethshar. Be grateful that we do *not* choose to fight—and tell the overlord so. We have sworn to behave as peaceful citizens, and we will abide by that oath—tell the overlord *that*, as well. We will accept the overlord's commands—but we ask him to reconsider. And we ask for a few moments to gather our belongings from our home before you destroy it. I would point out that my uncle spent much of his fortune in furnishing this house, and the overlord now proposes to simply throw away this wealth in his foolish fear of warlocks. Furthermore, he is acting against his own best interests—with the Council driven from the city, the warlocks who remain in hiding will be free to kill and steal, unhindered by any oaths or the oversight of their fellow warlocks. May he enjoy this unjust and wholly avoidable disaster he has brought on himself!"

Captain Naral hesitated. Then he said, "You'll come peacefully?"

"We will," Hanner said—though he could feel a mental pressure that he knew was the other warlocks, watching him and disagreeing. "May we fetch our belongings?"

"You have a quarter of an hour," Naral said.

"Thank you." Hanner bowed slightly, then turned and marched back into the house.

The others met him in the hallway.

"Hanner, have you gone mad?" Desset demanded.

"We swore to obey the law," Hanner said. "This is the ultimate test of that oath. If we fail the test, then they'll *never* trust us. If we yield, Lord Azrad may reconsider—or some warlock who never agreed to the Council's terms in the first place may stop his heart one night, and his son may think better of driving us away."

"I could send them all running back to the Palace!" Desset said.

"And you'd be flying northward to Aldagmor ten minutes later," Hanner retorted. "Now, we need to grab whatever we want to take with us. Someone tell Bern to bring the household funds, if there are any left. Everyone get your own belongings ready by the door, then come upstairs—we're warlocks, so we should be able to carry a goodly portion of Uncle Faran's collection of magic, and I expect we'll be able to sell that anywhere."

"I don't like this," Hinda said.

"None of us do," Hanner told her. "Now, go on—we only have a few minutes!"

They were hauling their bundles out into the dooryard, ignoring the taunts of the watching civilians, when Hinda burst into tears. Shella hurried to comfort her.

"I've never been out of the city!" Hinda wailed. "I don't want to go!"

"None of us do," Shella told her as she wrapped her arms around the younger girl. Ulpen and Desset watched the two girls silently. The scene reminded Hanner of something; he turned to Captain Naral.

"I still have family in the Palace," he said. "My two sisters are there. Could someone take them word of what's happened?"

"I think . . ." Naral began.

He didn't finish the sentence; as he spoke the earth suddenly shook, and a tremendous roaring filled the air. Soldiers tumbled to the ground. Hanner watched in astonishment as the surface of the street rose up into a mound, sending guardsmen rolling away to every side.

The disturbance was contained in a small area, though—Hanner could see that while Warlock House and its immediate neighbor to the east were shaking, as was the house directly across High Street, the buildings on the far side of

Coronet Street or farther along High Street were still and solid.

This was not, then, a natural earthquake.

The mound rose higher and grew wider until it stood perhaps eight feet high and twenty feet across, filling the street from the iron fence in front of the dooryard of Warlock House almost to the front of the house across the street; then it split open. A fissure began near the top on the side facing Hanner, quickly stretched vertically, and then widened. The two halves of the mound fell away, crumbling to dust and sinking back into the street.

And where the mound had been stood half a dozen wizards, in their finest robes, each with a gleaming dagger in his or her right hand, and a six-foot staff in the left.

The rumbling stopped and the dust settled, leaving the wizards standing silently in a cleared circle of street, scattered guardsmen lying strewn about them.

Hanner recognized all the wizards' faces from the meeting in that mysterious columned hall. He smiled wryly. He still didn't know why the wizards had appeared, here and now, but he was impressed.

"They certainly know how to make an entrance," he said, to no one in particular.

Captain Naral had caught himself against the gatepost and stayed on his feet; now he turned to face the wizards and demanded, "What are you people doing here?"

Hanner couldn't fault the captain's courage; not many men would shout like that at a group of wizards who had just manifested themselves so spectacularly.

"We have come to prevent Lord Azrad from making a mistake," Ithinia of the Isle announced, raising her staff. "The Wizards' Guild recognizes the Council of Warlocks as our equal in rights and privileges under the ancient laws of Ethshar, and as the rightful governing body of all warlocks. The overlord has no more authority to exile the Council from this city, nor to destroy its headquarters, than to exile *us*, or destroy our homes."

Captain Naral looked quickly at Hanner, then back at the wizards.

"Oh," he said.

Hanner cleared his throat. "In light of this new development, Captain," he said, "perhaps you might take it upon yourself to return to the Palace and ask Lord Azrad to reconsider your orders."

"I think that's an excellent suggestion, my lord," Naral replied.

Hanner didn't bother correcting him this time.

As Naral turned to go an old man shouted at the wizards, "Are you all mad? The warlocks stole my son!"

One of the wizards raised her staff and gestured, then spoke.

"Kennan of the Crooked Smile," she said, "your son Aken was not taken by warlocks. Aken was a warlock himself, and was drawn to his doom in Aldagmor by the same power that draws all warlocks. Go home and tend to your son's family, not to some misdirected vengeance."

Kennan's jaw dropped, then snapped shut. He blinked, backed away a step, then turned without another word and began marching away.

Hanner watched him go and saw that the other watchers who had haunted High Street were starting to scatter as well.

"Thank you," he said to the party of wizards. "As one magician to another, from the bottom of my heart, I thank you."

Chapter Forty-five

Negotiations with wizards were always a challenge, but in the end Hanner thought he got a fair price for the fortune in wizardly supplies and artifacts that Uncle Faran had stored away. That turned out to be the easy part.

Finding sorcerers who would pay decently for the talismans on the fourth floor took a few sixnights. The various shrines, altars, and pentacles turned out to have no inherent magic at all—Alladia explained to Hanner that shrines *never* did, that wasn't how the gods worked, and demons presumably operated on similar principles—so they brought relatively little, and as many of them wound up going to wealthy neighbors to decorate their homes as went to theurgists or demonologists for serious use.

Hanner didn't get so much as a brass bit for the stores of herbs; the herbalists he talked to weren't interested, since many of the plants hadn't been stored properly or were simply too old to be trusted. One old woman finally agreed to clean out the entire store in exchange for whatever she found useful.

And then there were the things that Hanner couldn't identify—dozens of assorted statues, a collection of notched sticks, several ordinary bricks marked with numbers written in black wax, unlabeled jars of brown goo, stones carved into unrecognizable shapes, lumps of dried fungus, various machines built of gears and springs that didn't appear to do anything, and so on. Faran had labeled and organized most of his collection, but several items had remained completely anonymous, and some of the labels on others were hopelessly cryptic; Hanner had no idea, for example, why Faran had tagged a chunk of rock "Under G. 4996," or written "Red Glow" on a jar of seawater. A glance through his uncle's notebooks convinced Hanner that Faran had been trying to find a unifying theory for *all* schools of magic and had collected objects he thought might have magical properties not yet recognized by any of the existing schools, but how he had made some of his selections remained a mystery.

In the end Hanner gave up the idea of being able to use the entire house and shoved all this unsold detritus into four rooms at the back of the top floor. He hoped that someday some scholar more gifted than himself might want to sort through it all and continue Faran's research.

That left three and a half floors for the use of the Council of Warlocks, and for Hanner's own home.

The proceeds from selling the collection were enough to furnish the upper stories and to commission a generous supply of black clothing from the weavers in the Old Merchants' Quarter, with a goodly sum left over. Hanner offered this surplus as loans to warlocks who wanted to set up shop—preferably in the Wizards' Quarter, with the other magicians. There were a few shops available for sale and rent—some of them shops vacated by magicians or other tradesmen who had vanished on the Night of Madness.

Hanner accompanied Ulpen and Shella in negotiating the purchase of one such shop, to provide an adult presence, and was pleased to see how cooperative the sellers were. He knew that a sixnight earlier they would never have been willing to sell to warlocks, but the Wizards' Guild had been effective—and surprisingly enthusiastic—in spreading the word that the hundreds who vanished had been warlocks, not the victims of warlocks.

The existence of the Council of Warlocks, and its assurance that its member warlocks were bound by the same laws as everyone else, also helped. That the Council had sent warlocks to help in rebuilding homes and shops wrecked on the Night of Madness helped even more.

This activity made the Council visible, and new warlocks appeared steadily in response, eager to sign up, transforming Hanner's creation from theory to reality. Three rooms on the ground floor of Warlock House had been converted into a school and office where these newly arrived warlocks were taught the Council's rules and questioned about any crimes they might have committed. Those who were deemed acceptable then swore the Council's oath and were given a black tunic and a document recording their admission to the Council.

Those who were not found acceptable were turned over to the city magistrates or ordered into exile—and in some cases forcibly flown over the city wall.

As yet, the Council had not had to kill anyone. Hanner suspected that couldn't last forever, especially since the triumvirate had agreed that the single Council of Warlocks would, when it was able, have authority over the entire Hegemony of the Three Ethshars, and not merely Ethshar of the Spices. He had already approved subchairmen to organize the Council's offices in Ethshar of the Rocks and Ethshar of the Sands.

He found it odd to realize that he, useless Hanner, the lordling who had never found a proper place for himself in the overlord's service, was on his way to becoming master of perhaps the third most powerful organization in the World, after the Wizards' Guild and the Hegemony itself.

All in all, by the end of the month of Summerheat matters seemed to have settled down and turned out about as well as he could have expected.

Hanner's confidence had not yet grown to the point, however, that the summons to the Palace failed to worry him.

He looked at the message thoughtfully. It was politely written, but very definite—the presence of Hanner, Chairman of the Council of Warlocks, was requested in the Great Hall of Audience in the Palace of the Overlord of Ethshar of the Spices at four hours after noon on the first day of Summersend, in the Five Thousand Two Hundred and Second Year of Human Speech.

Hanner knew well that the overlord would never have sent Ithinia such a message, naming an exact time and date; he would have requested her to arrange for an audience at her earliest convenience. To accept this directive without quibble would mean acknowledging that he was not Ithinia's equal in rank, and she was merely the senior wizard in the city, while he was theoretically the senior warlock *anywhere*.

But realistically, arguing with it would be stupid and arrogant.

"Tell the messenger to tell Lord Azrad I will be there," he said, dropping the message on his writing table.

"Yes, sir," Ilvin said, raising a spread-fingered hand to his chest in the odd salute some of the warlocks seemed to have picked up as a mark of respect. He turned and hurried out of the room.

Hanner stared after him. Ilvin was still not at all a powerful warlock, but he had proven to have a talent for getting things done around the Council's headquarters; Bern was still in charge of the kitchens, but Ilvin had taken over most of the other household administration. He was very useful indeed.

Desset, meanwhile, who remained the most powerful warlock in the city, was virtually useless—she struggled constantly to not use her magic, and even so frequently had various small objects floating around her. Her nightmares grew steadily worse, and she had begun to spend long stretches of the day sitting in the garden staring northward.

Hanner had hoped that inaction might cause warlockry to atrophy and the danger of the Calling to recede, but apparently it didn't work that way. He repeatedly advised Desset to pack up a few things and move south, out of the city and farther from Aldagmor, but she was unable to bring herself to do so. He even spoke to Ithinia about the possibility of providing some sort of magical refuge, like that meeting hall, but while Ithinia promised to mention it to the Inner Circle, she also told him he would have a better chance of convincing them to spend the next hundred years standing on their heads. The Guild did not do favors for anyone, not even wizards, without an ulterior motive.

"Could we *buy* a refuge, then?" Hanner asked her.

"That might be possible," she admitted. "You wouldn't need to trouble the Guild about that; just find a wizard who knows the appropriate spells and hire him to do the job. You can expect to pay an obscene amount for it, though."

"I see," Hanner said, and he pushed it to the back of his head, to be attended to when other matters were under better control. The Council had money, but not an obscene amount of it as yet.

He might mention to Lord Azrad the idea that it would be worthwhile for the city to finance such a purchase, so as to have a reserve of powerful warlocks in the triumvirate's debt who could be called upon in an emergency.

That assumed, of course, that Lord Azrad had any interest in Hanner's desires, and didn't intend to order the Council out of the city. For the past three sixnights Hanner and his representatives had been dealing peacefully with the city government, but always through intermediaries—usually Azrad's brothers, Clurim, Karannin, and Ildirin—and never directly with the overlord. This audience—if it *was* really an audience with Lord Azrad, as Hanner noticed that the message did not actually say Azrad would be in the audience chamber—might indicate that the overlord had changed his mind again.

Hanner certainly hoped not, and did not intend to do anything to antagonize Lord Azrad.

Accordingly he arrived in the entrance hall of the Palace exactly at the appointed hour and was greeted and escorted through the great velvet curtains that were serving as a temporary replacement for the not-yet-repaired golden doors.

The room was more populated than it had been on that dreadful occasion when Faran had led in a horde of angry warlocks, but still far from crowded; perhaps a hundred guards, servants, and courtiers were arranged here and there, standing, seated, or going about various errands. Hanner noticed his sisters standing in a knot of nobles near the east wall.

He had not heard from them in a twelvenight, and he had been too busy with Council business to worry about that silence; he hoped they were well.

He hadn't heard from Mavi, either, but he firmly pushed that thought out of his mind and concentrated on his surroundings.

As expected, Azrad was indeed present, sprawled heavily on the throne, sitting motionless as Hanner was led in and presented.

"Hanner the Warlock, Chairman of the Council of Warlocks!" the herald announced, and Hanner bowed deeply.

"It's good to see you again, Hanner," Azrad said when Hanner straightened up.

"And of course, it is always a pleasure to see you, my lord," Hanner replied.

That said, the two men stared silently at each other for a moment. Then Azrad said, "You're here because I wanted to see you in person, rather than doing everything through my brothers. I wanted to see how you'd changed."

Hanner bowed again, this time with arms spread. "I am as you see me, my lord," he said.

"You're wearing black."

"I'm a warlock, my lord."

"You look well. Have you lost a little weight?"

"I might have, my lord; I'm not sure. I've kept very busy of late."

"You've been eating well?"

"Oh, yes. My housekeeper sees to that."

Azrad nodded. "That's good. We should have met somewhere less formal, perhaps—the private audience chamber or my apartments—but I wasn't sure of the protocol, given your new status."

Hanner smiled. "I'm still me, Lord Azrad. I would be pleased to meet with you wherever you might choose. As Chairman of the Council, I am still subject to the laws of Ethshar—treat me as you would any other magician."

"Yes, well—you shouldn't be a magician." Azrad frowned. "You never served an apprenticeship. I don't approve of this mysterious *thing* that happened, not at all—but I do accept that it happened, now, and I'll live with it. I can't fight you *and* the wizards."

"We have no desire to fight anyone, my lord. We just want to live in peace. The madness of the Night of Madness ended long ago."

"Yes, I accept that," Azrad said irritably. "I said so. And that's why you're here. If you warlocks are going to be magicians like all the others, then you're responsible for any damage you do with your magic." He gestured at the far end of the room. "Are you going to pay for those doors? And the chairs? The artisans are asking *three hundred rounds of gold* to repair just the doors!"

Hanner blinked, then turned to look thoughtfully at the velvet curtains.

"We can't afford that much at present, my lord," he said, turning back, "but I believe we can repair the doors ourselves. Warlockry can repair as well as destroy. Surely you've heard that we have been aiding in repairs elsewhere."

It was Azrad's turn to be surprised. "Yes, but . . . those doors are huge!"

"I believe we can handle them." In fact, he *knew* his warlocks could handle the job; this was exactly the sort of thing warlockry did well.

"Can you really? Excellent!"

Hanner could not resist a small jab. "We have not done so previously, my lord, because you have maintained strong restrictions on admitting warlocks to the Palace."

"Well . . . yes. Fine. The restrictions won't be applied to anyone who comes to make repairs."

"Then I'll send some warlocks as soon as I get home," Hanner said.

"Good!" Azrad smiled. "I hate those curtains. It's drafty in here, even with the window repaired."

"We could have done that as well, had you asked," Hanner said.

"Don't worry about it," Azrad said, waving away the subject—which Hanner assumed meant it had been done by the palace staff, or by workmen who charged far less than goldsmiths. "But the chairs . . ."

"I'm not sure about those," Hanner said. "My warlocks will look at them and let you know."

"Good, good." The smile faded. "That brings us to personal matters, the other reasons I insisted that *you* come, rather than one of your underlings."

"Yes, my lord?"

"We still have your uncle's remains," Azrad explained.

"I'm really not sure what to do with them—an intact statue would join the others, and an ordinary corpse would be properly burned or otherwise dealt with, but a shattered statue . . ." He turned up a palm. "Perhaps you could reassemble the pieces somehow, maybe even bring him back to life."

Hanner considered that for a moment. He was fairly certain that warlockry could indeed reassemble the pieces and fuse them back together, but restore Faran to life? Warlockry couldn't do that; only wizardry could, if it was possible at all.

And since Faran had been killed by the Wizards' Guild, Hanner doubted any wizard would dare attempt a revival.

But it would be a proper and respectful thing to reassemble the pieces and set the statue somewhere.

"Thank you, my lord," he said. "I would be pleased to take Lord Faran's remains."

"Good," Azrad said, clearly relieved. He looked up and beckoned. "Clurim, it's your turn!"

Startled, Hanner turned to see Lord Clurim emerge from the little cluster of nobles to the east.

"We understand that you're now the head of your family," Azrad said. "As such, Lord Clurim has a request to make."

Anything that called for the head of his family must involve his sisters, Hanner realized. Nerra was of marriageable age, but Clurim already had a wife . . .

It was Alris who was following Clurim out of the crowd.

"It's about your sister," Lord Clurim said. "Alris has asked to become my apprentice. Ordinarily . . . well, she's a month past thirteen, which is a year older than she should be, and you've foresworn your title, and . . ."

Hanner held up a hand. "My lord," he said, "I have no objection if my sister wants to be your apprentice; in fact, it would remove one of my worries." He smiled at Alris.

"Well, that's good," Clurim said. He turned to Alris. "Come on, then." He marched toward one of the side doors.

Alris waved quickly to Hanner, then hurried after her master. Hanner watched them go.

That really *was* a relief—he had wondered what would become of his sisters. Neither was interested in becoming a warlock; Nerra had been repulsed by the very idea. Alris, who a few months before had been desperate to learn some sort of magic, had given it some serious consideration before rejecting the offer.

"I've seen quite enough of warlocks already," she said. "You aren't what I want to be."

He would have thought she had seen enough of the Palace, as well, but apparently not. As apprentice to the Lord of the Household she would see every bit of it, and could expect to someday become Lady of the Household, responsible for running the place.

"That's all, then," Lord Azrad said, startling Hanner anew. He quickly turned back to face the overlord, but Azrad was waving a dismissal.

"It was good to see you, Hanner," he said. "I'll have my people bring out your uncle's remains, and don't forget to send those warlocks to fix the doors."

Hanner bowed an acknowledgement and stepped backward, away from the throne. He found a servant ready to lead him out of the audience chamber through one of the small side doors; a delegation of merchants was waiting at the drapes for their turn to speak to the overlord.

Hanner let himself be led and found Nerra following him. A moment later the two of them were in a stone corridor, walking side by side in silence.

Hanner broke that silence by remarking, "So Alris found herself an apprenticeship after all."

"And about time she did," Nerra said. "She spent most of the last year sitting around complaining how bored she is."

"I wonder why Uncle Faran didn't make it a point to look for an apprenticeship for her, then. I mean, I know she wanted to be a magician, and of course he wouldn't allow that, but surely he could have asked the other lords or found her a respectable trade somewhere."

Nerra looked up at him, startled. "You really don't know why she wouldn't take an apprenticeship in the Palace?"

Hanner's puzzlement was obvious. "Should I?"

"Yes, you should. Sometimes, Hanner, you can be blind. She didn't want to stay that close to Uncle Faran for the rest of her life, where he would try to run everything she did."

"Oh," Hanner said. "But then, couldn't he have found her a respectable apprenticeship somewhere else?"

"Uncle Faran didn't want the distraction," Nerra said. "And he wanted to keep her around so he could marry her off to Lord Ederd's son, so she'd wind up the mother of an overlord."

"I heard him suggest that," Hanner admitted. "In fact, I knew he wanted to arrange good marriages for both of you, but I didn't realize he was that determined—or that you didn't like the idea." He frowned. "Ederd the Younger is only a year younger than I am." He glanced at Nerra. "Why didn't he try to marry *you* off to him?"

"He did," Nerra said. "Remember when we sailed to Ethshar of the Sands last year? But so far we weren't cooperating, Ederd and I, so he wanted Alris as his last resort."

"Then what did he plan for you, if Alris married Ederd?"

"I was to marry a high-ranking wizard, so I could be his spy in the Guild." She grimaced. "I hate wizards."

That sounded very like Uncle Faran.

"So what do you plan to do now?" Hanner asked. "Alris found an apprenticeship, but you're already eighteen—*you* can't do that."

"Oh, I expect I'll marry someone," she replied. "I don't have anyone in mind yet, but I have someone playing matchmaker." They had reached the end of the corridor; Nerra opened the door at the end, and they stepped through it, out into the central hallway.

"Who's your matchmaker?" Hanner asked. "Perhaps I could help . . ."

"She is," Nerra said, pointing.

Hanner turned and saw Mavi standing near the entryway, silhouetted in the light.

She was more beautiful than he remembered. He instantly forgot about Nerra and hurried toward her, leaving his sister laughing at his back.

Mavi heard his approaching footsteps and turned; she recognized Hanner, and her face lit in a shy smile.

Hanner was overwhelmed by the sight of that smile; he had feared she would frown or turn away.

"Hello," she said.

"Hello," Hanner replied, stopping a respectful distance away, unsure of his reception. She seemed happy to see him, but he still remembered the look on her face when he admitted that he was a warlock.

Mavi's next words dispelled some of his remaining concern. "I missed you," she said.

Hanner made a happy, wordless noise of agreement.

Mavi stepped toward him. "You know, Hanner, I think I'm getting over my aversion to warlocks," she said. "You and your Council have really done an amazing job of making them respectable."

Hanner smiled broadly and took her hand; she did not pull away.

"We could make *you* a warlock," he said.

She laughed. "I'm not *that* fond of warlocks!"

Then she stepped into his arms and added, "Yet."

Epilogue

It was later established, by a commission of scholars appointed jointly by the overlords of the Hegemony of the Three Ethshars, that the creation of the warlocks began four hours and eighteen minutes after sunset on the fourth day of Summerheat in the Year of Human Speech 5202.

This seemed to hold true throughout the inhabited World; the nightmares did not arrive any sooner in Aldagmor than in the farthest corners of the Small Kingdoms, nor did those who later became powerful warlocks receive them a moment earlier or later than those who never again showed any sensitivity to this new sort of magic. Everywhere, and for everyone, the dreams and the magic came at the same instant.

In Ethshar of the Spices the final count of persons reported missing on or immediately after the Night of Madness was 1,108. Forty-one people died in the confusion; how many of the 41 were warlocks or other magicians was never reliably determined.

In Ethshar of the Sands there were 983 missing, 38 dead.

In Ethshar of the Rocks there were only 622 missing, but due largely to the actions of one particularly dangerous warlock, Shemder Parl's son, who was eventually removed by the Wizards' Guild, the death toll still reached 42.

No adequate counts were ever made for the rest of the Hegemony, or for any of the lands outside the Hegemony. The number of disappearances for the Baronies of Sardiron unquestionably ran well into the thousands, and the deaths and acts of destruction were numerous and widespread there, while the more southerly Small Kingdoms were barely affected—for Sardiron the Night of Madness was a major crisis, yet in Semma and Ophkar it went completely unnoticed. Reactions by those governments were in proportion; however, the decree of a death sentence for performing warlockry in the Baronies of Sardiron was rescinded in the month of Leafcolor after several unpleasant incidents involving Called warlocks on their way to Aldagmor.

By the Festival of the Year of Human Speech 5203 the Council of Warlocks under the direction of Chairman Hanner reported a total membership of 7,976 acknowledged warlocks, counting apprentices.

The ruling triumvirate of the Hegemony found this entirely acceptable.